VAN BUREN DIS̶̶̶̶ P9-DDZ-776
DECATUR, MICHIGAN 49045

Got the Look

Got the Look

James Grippando

HarperCollins*Publishers*

Gri

This is a work of fiction. The characters, incidents, and dialogues are products of the author's imagination and are not to be construed as real. Any resemblance to actual persons, living or dead, is entirely coincidental.

GOT THE LOOK. Copyright © 2006 by James Grippando. All rights reserved. Printed in the United States of America. No part of this book may be used or reproduced in any manner whatsoever without written permission except in the case of brief quotations embodied in critical articles and reviews. For information, address HarperCollins Publishers, 10 East 53rd Street, New York, NY 10022.

HarperCollins books may be purchased for educational, business, or sales promotional use. For information, please write: Special Markets Department, HarperCollins Publishers, 10 East 53rd Street, New York, NY 10022.

FIRST EDITION

Designed by Nancy B. Field

Printed on acid-free paper

Library of Congress Cataloging-in-Publication Data
Grippando, James.
    Got the look / James Grippando.—1st ed.
        p.   cm.
    ISBN-10: 0-06-056458-X
    ISBN-13: 978-0-06-056458-2
    1. Swyteck, Jack (Fictitious character)—Fiction. 2. Attorney and client—Fiction. 3. Miami (Fla.)—Fiction. I. Title.

PS3557.R534G68   2006
813'.54—dc22   2005046006

06 07 08 09 10 WBC/RRD 10 9 8 7 6 5 4 3 2 1

For Tiffany.

And then there were five.

Got the Look

1

.

The sun never shines beneath the Devil's Ear.

FBI Special Agent Andie Henning must have heard that warning a dozen times on her way to Ginnie Springs, Florida. The Devil's Ear was one of the more spectacular openings to the watery underworld of the north Florida aquifer, a dark and dangerous lime-stone labyrinth of interconnecting caves and caverns that discharged 7.7 billion gallons of crystal clear drinking water every day.

"How much farther?" Andie shouted over the roar of the single out-board engine. The boat was at full throttle, throwing a V-shaped wake against the inky black riverbanks. The Santa Fe was a relatively shallow river, better suited to canoes and kayaks than to large motorboats. Only an experienced driver could head downstream at this speed, especially in the dead of night. Somewhere in the darkness were egrets and alliga-tors, but at midnight the forest slept. The tall cypress trees were mere silhouettes, their moss-clad limbs barely visible against the starlit sky. A thin blanket of fog stretched across the river, waist deep to those on-board. The speedboat cut through it like a laser on cotton candy. Andie zipped up her FBI jacket, staving off the wind chill.

"About two more minutes," shouted the boat driver.

Andie checked her watch. She hoped they had two minutes.

The kidnapper's late-night call had confirmed the family's payment of a ransom, contrary to FBI advice. One million dollars in cash seemed like a lot of money to the average person, but it was hardly a hit to Drew Thornton, one of Ocala's richest horse breeders. The clipped phone message advised that Mrs. Thornton could be found beneath the Devil's Ear. It took only a minute to decipher what that meant. The sheriff's office deployed emergency/rescue divers immediately. Andie and two agents from the Jacksonville field office went with them. They were part of the FBI team assigned to the Thornton case, and Andie was the only negotiator staying on-site in Ocala throughout the three-week ordeal.

The engine went quiet, the anchor dropped overboard, and the boat came to a stop. Immediately, the team moved into position.

"Bottoms up!" shouted the rescue team leader.

Three scuba divers splashed into the river. With the flip of a switch, handheld dive lights turned the black water into a clear, glistening pool. The driver of the boat was Sheriff Buddy McClean, a bulky man in his fifties. He and a deputy remained onboard with Andie and the two FBI tech agents. The deputy controlled the lifeline, a long synthetic rope that tethered each diver to the boat. It was their road map back from the cave network. One of the techies helped feed a transmission wire as the divers descended with an underwater video camera. The other agent fiddled with the monitor, trying to bring up an image.

Hundreds of air bubbles boiled to the surface. The lights grew dim beneath the boat, and suddenly the river returned to black. It was as if someone had pulled the geologic plug, but the monitor screen glowing brightly in the darkness told a different story.

"There it is," said Sheriff McClean. "Devil's Ear."

Andie checked the monitor. The lights and underwater camera allowed her to see exactly what the divers saw. The team was inside the cavern, somewhere below the riverbed. Andie asked, "How well do your divers know these caves, Sheriff?"

"All too well," said McClean. "Since I first swam here as a teenager, there's been over three hundred scuba divers gone down in Florida's caves and never come up. Devil's Ear has claimed its fair share of unwilling souls. Pulled two out myself in my younger days."

"What's the chances Mrs. Thornton's actually alive?" asked the deputy.

Andie didn't answer right away. "We've had cases where kidnap victims were buried alive and came out okay."

"Yeah, but under*water?*"

"Can't say that I've heard of it," she said. "But there's a first time for everything."

There was silence onboard, as if they all feared that this was more likely to be the recovery of a body than the rescue of a victim. But that didn't mean they'd given up hope.

What if she is alive? thought Andie. Did that poor woman have any idea where she was? Somewhere beneath this black riverbed, beneath God only knew how many feet of sand and solid limestone, lay a living, breathing wife and mother. Perhaps she was trapped in some pressurized tank or capsule, a dark and silent cocoon, enough air for an hour or two. Or worse, maybe her kidnapper had turned her loose down there with nothing but a mask, tank, and regulator. Either way, she'd be in total darkness, unable to find—no, *feel*—her way out of this aquatic honeycomb. Perhaps she could hear or possibly even feel the strong currents rushing past her, cool springwater flowing as fast as a hundred cubic feet per second. She might decide to go with the flow, or try to fight it, no way of knowing which way was up. Jagged rocks could cut like knives. A sudden change in ceiling height could damage her breathing equipment or knock her unconscious. But not even in her most harrowing moment of panic could she even begin to imagine that some of these cave systems stretched as long as seventeen miles, that she could be carried hundreds or thousands of feet below the surface, that the average liter of drinking water drawn from Florida's aquifer percolated and circulated around and around for twenty years before reaching the surface.

Unconscious, thought Andie. Alive but unconscious. That was by far the best-case scenario.

"Where are they now?" asked Andie.

Sheriff McClean took a closer look at the screen. The divers had long since passed the point where it mattered if it was night or day. "I'd say about two hundred feet into the cave."

"How can you tell?"

"See that rock formation there, just ahead of them?" he said as he pointed to the monitor. "That thing that looks like a big, open whale's mouth is called the lips restriction. It's the first real narrowing you reach in the Devil System."

"They're going through that?" asked the tech agent.

"Sure. Right now they're in the gallery, which is basically a big passageway that takes you from the entrance to the first breakdown. There's plenty to explore beyond those lips."

"How deep are they?" asked Andie.

"Maybe fifty feet. Doesn't get much deeper than that in this part of the system. Which gives me a little hope that, you know . . ."

That Mrs. Thornton could be alive. He didn't have to say it.

On-screen, the lead diver passed through the lips, like Jonah swallowed by the whale. The videographer followed behind, his camera jerking back and forth as he made his way through the opening. The image steadied as the crew regrouped on the other side of the lips. Here, the camera didn't have to move up and down from top to bottom. One frame could cover the entire cave, sandy floor to limestone ceiling. The divers shifted their adjustable tanks from the usual position on their backs and brought them under their bellies so that the equipment wouldn't hit the rugged limestone formations overhead.

Slowly, the camera swept the cave, aided by the powerful dive lights. It reminded Andie of an ancient tomb, a flooded version of the Roman catacombs, though she tried not to dwell on that characterization. Not with a woman's life hanging in the balance.

"What's that?" she asked.

The camera focused on a long, smooth shaft protruding from the wall.

"Looks like a bone," said the tech agent.

"You think it could be—"

"No way," said the sheriff. "That's been there for centuries, probably from a whale or maybe even a mastodon. All kinds of prehistoric relics down there. Used to be more, till all the jackass tourists came along and started hauling stuff away to make paperweights."

The camera shifted away and focused on the third diver. All lights were upon him. He was holding a glass vial in his gloved hand. He broke the vial, and a thin blue streak stretched across the screen.

"That's a dye," said the sheriff. "They're testing the current. It's not always easy to tell which way the water is circulating down there. Generally it flows up, like a chimney, but a lot depends on the amount of rainfall we've had lately, whether there's been any new cave-ins or sinkholes in the system. I've seen ponds drained so quickly that trees get yanked right off the banks, like the baby going out with the bathwater. It's tricky stuff down there. Even an experienced diver can get disoriented pretty easily."

"Are you saying they're lost?" asked Andie.

"Not hardly," said the sheriff. "With all those passageways, they're just trying to figure out where Mrs. Thornton might end up."

"You mean if she's dead or if she's alive?"

"I mean if she's down there," he said, making no predictions.

On-screen, the wisp of blue dye faded away. The lead diver made a gesture, and the team did an about-face.

"Are they going back?" asked Andie.

"Yeah, but not exactly the same way they came in. Looks like they're taking the lips bypass, which also connects to the gallery."

The divers followed a narrow corridor to a broader opening. Perhaps an expert could appreciate the different shades of Oligocene limestone, the mosaic of fossilized scallops and sea biscuits against the pale pitted stone, the variety of formations and surface textures that had developed over thirty million to sixty million years. But to Andie, watching a monitor, it was all starting to look the same. No wonder so many divers had taken their last breath while swimming around in circles, some never realizing that safety lay just a few feet around the next turn.

"They're headed toward the grate," said the sheriff.

"What's that?" asked Andie.

"There's a passage to the main tunnel that's blocked off by a steel grate. After losing a good two dozen divers down there, it seemed wise to bar it off and keep any more from going in."

"So the dye is leading your dive team to the main tunnel, where all those people died?"

Before the sheriff could answer, the on-screen image grabbed their attention. At first, it was little more than a blotch of color against the brownish green limestone. The form was too irregular, too twisted, to be human. Slowly, however, the camera zoomed in, and the parts became a whole.

"Oh my God," said Andie, her words coming like a reflex.

It was a disturbing yet surreal sight. In these flowing crystal waters, the shoulder-length hair seemed to float so peacefully, like a sleeping mermaid's locks. The woman was unconscious, if alive, her twisted torso pressed against the steel grate by the sheer force of the aquifer's current. The right leg was caught in the bars that blocked off the entrance to the main tunnel, obviously broken, as it was bending at a severe angle below the knee. She was clothed, but the pants and shirt were torn, and the skin showed numerous scrapes and cuts. It reminded Andie of a drowning victim she'd seen pulled from the Columbia River in her native Washington State, the body having taken a beating as it flowed downstream.

"That's Ashley Thornton," said McClean.

"You sure?" asked the tech agent.

"Who else would it be?" said Andie.

Below, the divers moved in quickly. The videographer continued to film while the others moved into rescue mode. The lead diver immediately began working on her leg, trying to free it from the bars, shooing away the little mustard-colored eels that swarmed around the body like underwater buzzards. The other diver removed his glove to check her pulse, then immediately applied an Air Buddy system to her mouth.

Andie said, "That Air Buddy won't do much good if her lungs are full of water."

"Gotta try," said McClean. "Survival time can be greater in water this clear and cold."

"It's still a matter of minutes," said Andie. "Freshwater goes straight to the bloodstream. Her red blood cells are bursting as we speak. We're looking at hypoxia or heart attack, if we aren't already there."

More little eels arrived with each passing second, nipping at the divers now, as if testing to see if they, too, were for the taking. The second diver checked the woman's pulse once more. He looked straight at the camera and shook his head, which did not bode well. Her only hope was CPR, which meant bringing her to the surface immediately, though the divers themselves had to avoid the bends. The diver made a frantic gesture toward the lead diver, who was working feverishly to free the woman's leg from the bars. The videographer laid the camera on the cave floor and swam over to help.

The divers were off camera, but the stream of video continued. The crew onboard could see only the sandy floor and the victim's arm.

"What is that?" asked Andie as she pointed to the screen.

The others looked more closely. Something was wrapped around the victim's wrist. It was a bracelet, though not a piece of jewelry that a woman would wear. It looked more like the plastic identification bracelets worn by hospital patients.

"Was Mrs. Thornton in the hospital before she was kidnapped?" asked Andie.

"Not that I know of," said the sheriff.

"I think I see some lettering on it," said Andie.

The tech agent adjusted the contrast so that the bracelet was easier to examine. The writing came into focus.

"Can you read that?" said the sheriff.

"Freeze it," said Andie.

The tech agent stilled the frame. "Looks like two words," he said. "I can probably make them a little bigger and clearer." He worked with it, and the first letter came into focus.

"W-r . . . something," he said. "Last letter also looks like an *r*."

"Can you bring up the rest?" said Andie.

He made one more adjustment. Two words appeared. They weren't perfect, but they were clearly legible.

"Wrong number," Andie read aloud.

The sheriff grumbled. "Wrong number? That son of a bitch. Does he think he's funny or something?"

"It's not a joke," said Andie, her eyes never leaving the screen. "It's a message. And I think I know *exactly* what he's telling us."

2

Yale Law School. Four years of defending Florida's death-row inmates. A respectable stint as a federal prosecutor, and then back to private practice, where he handled Miami's most captivating murder trial in years. After all those accomplishments, the colorful career of Jack Swyteck—the son of Florida's former governor—had taken a curious turn.

"It's a battle between neighbors," Jack told his best friend, Theo Knight.

"It's a fight over a penis," said Theo.

Jack winced. "I prefer to call it artistic differences."

"Over a penis."

"Well, yeah, if you want to be crude about it."

"No, if I wanted to be crude, we'd be talking about a rock-hard, fourteen-inch—"

"Okay, okay. Will you help me or not?"

Theo smiled. "Course I'll help ya, buddy. I'm always there to help."

It was odd, but Theo had a way of making it seem almost normal to be discussing a rock-hard penis in the context of Jack's newest case. Theo was Jack's "investigator," for lack of a better term. Whatever Jack needed, Theo went and got it, whether it was the last prop plane out of Africa, a full confession from the loser who torched Jack's convertible, or an explanation for a naked corpse found in Jack's bathtub. Jack never stopped wondering how Theo came up with these things. Sometimes he asked; more often, he simply didn't want to know. Theirs was not exactly a textbook friendship: The Ivy League son of a governor meets the black high school dropout from Liberty City. But they got on just fine for two guys who'd met on death row, Jack the lawyer and Theo the inmate. Jack's persistence had delayed Theo's date with the electric chair long enough for DNA evidence to come into vogue and prove him innocent. It wasn't the original plan, but Jack ended up a part of Theo's new life, sometimes going along for the ride, other times just watching with amazement as Theo made up for precious lost time.

At four o'clock Friday afternoon they were inside the public-hearing chamber at Coral Gables City Hall. It was Jack's job to present an argument to the all-powerful board of architects, a group of mostly well-meaning volunteers who held the final say on whether any proposed structure was in keeping with the city's strict aesthetic standards and, more important, with the personal whim of the board's most arrogant members. Jack's client had placed a seventeen-foot statue in his backyard in Gables Estates, an exact duplicate of the *David* in Florence, Italy. Well, not quite an *exact* duplicate. Experts have long noted that, perhaps because the artist realized that his statue would stand high on a pedestal and be viewed from below, Michelangelo intentionally made the right hand much larger than the left so that, to the viewer's eye, it would appear anatomically proportionate. For reasons that could hardly qualify as artistic, Jack's client took this "big hand" anomaly to its inevitable twenty-first-century, Viagra-crazy, size-*does*-matter cultural extension. (What did women always say about guys with big hands?) The end result was a *David* that, if reduced proportionately to a man of average height, would sport a fourteen-inch penis.

The neighbor complained.

Jack was on the case.

Theo, naturally, was loving it.

Of course, Jack could readily appreciate the opposition. He had no interest in owning a *David* with a Goliath-sized penis, and he probably wouldn't want it in his neighbor's yard, either. But his client had dug in his heels, and it was Jack's job to convince the board of architects that it was a homeowner's God-given right to erect whatever he wanted, no pun intended. He also knew that he didn't have a chance in hell of winning. So he might as well have fun.

"Ladies and gentlemen," he said, addressing the twelve staid board members, "thank you for your time on this matter. If you'll indulge me for a moment, I thought we'd begin our presentation with a song. Not just any song, but the official state song of Florida, 'Old Folks at Home,' or perhaps better known simply as 'Suwannee River.' It will be sung a cappella by my distinguished and surprisingly musical assistant, Mr. Theo Knight. Theo, if you please."

The chairman leaned toward his gooseneck microphone and said, "Mr. Swyteck, this is highly irregular."

"We'll be quick, I promise. Theo, from the top."

Theo took a moment, as if getting into role. He was an imposing man with the brawn of a linebacker and the height of an NBA star, sort of a cross between the Rock and a young Samuel L. Jackson on steroids. His prison time came as no surprise to anyone, but that bad-boy image served him well. He could flash a friendly smile or a menacing glare, and either way you got the message that he took crap from no one.

For this little number, Theo rounded his shoulders, head down, as if he'd been out in the field picking cotton since sunrise. Then he sang in a baritone voice that filled the old stone chamber, using the exact plantation dialect that Stephen Foster had penned:

> *Way down upon de Suwannee Ribber,*
> *Far, far away,*
> *Dere's wha my heart is turning ebber,*
> *Dere's wha de old folks stay.*

"Mr. Swyteck, please," said the chairman, groaning.

"Keep singing, Theo. Go straight to the chorus."

Theo took it up a notch, his voice louder and fuller.

"All de world am sad and dreary,
Eb-rywhere I roam;
Oh, darkeys, how my heart grows weary—"

"Stop right there," said Jack. "Did I hear you right? Give me that last line one more time, please."

"Oh, darkeys, how my heart grows weary,
Far from de old folks at—"

"Okay, stop." Jack canvassed the board but said nothing more. He simply let those lyrics lie exactly where Theo had dropped them, right on their inflated heads, draped over this distinguished deliberative body like an itchy blanket. Everyone felt the discomfort, but they were drowning in the seas of political correctness, not sure how to handle this one.

Finally, Jack voiced his incredulity. "'Oh, darkeys'? 'Oh, *darkeys*'? Now, there's a state song fer ya. Don't you think?"

A volley of awkward glances bounced across the dais. Finally, the chairman crawled out from under that figurative blanket, stroking his gray handlebar mustache as he spoke. "Mr. Swyteck, what exactly is your point?"

"Glad you asked, Mr. Chairman. We're here today arguing whether a homeowner can place a statue on his own property, the original of which is an undisputed masterpiece that stands in a museum and is seen by millions of people every year. And the reason for this feud is that one extremely wealthy neighbor might someday look out the back window of her ten-million-dollar waterfront estate and be offended. At the same time, we have an official state song about darkeys, and nobody says a word. Do you think maybe—just maybe—this might be a classic case of money talks and much ado about nothing?"

Jack continued for several more minutes, and they seemed mildly intrigued by his creativity. In the end, however, Michelangelo himself couldn't have reshaped their sense of good taste and decency with a hammer and chisel. The statue was voted down twelve to zero. At least for the time being, Coral Gables would remain "the City Beautiful."

Twenty minutes later, Jack and Theo were at the other end of Miracle Mile, laughing over a couple of beers at Houston's. The happy-hour crowd was just beginning to arrive, so there were still a few open stools at the bar. They drained the first round quickly, and then Theo ordered two more drafts.

"Sorry you lost the case," said Theo. "Still think my straw hat and a little 'Zippity Do Dah' could have made the difference."

"Not that important, anyway."

"Right. Sort of a pissant case for a hotshot lawyer like yourself, isn't it?"

Jack selected a tortilla chip and gathered up some fresh salsa. "William Bailey asked me to take it as a favor for one of his clients."

Theo made a face, clearly disapproving. William Bailey was the managing partner of Bailey, Benning, and Langer, Miami's oldest, largest, and most self-important law firm. It was no secret in the legal community that BB&L was looking for a real trial lawyer to head its litigation department.

"They're getting their hooks in you, Jack buddy. Take a few cases, get to know their clients. Next thing you know, you got a nice corner office, two dozen young lawyers think Mr. Swyteck's shit don't stink, and your FYN is off the charts."

"My FYN?"

"Your fuck-you number. The amount of money you need to have stashed away in order to walk up to the stuffed prick who signs your pay-check and say, 'Fuck you, buddy, I'm outta here.' Miami's highest FYN gots to be a partner at Bailey, Benning, and Langer."

"I'm not selling out."

"I hears you saying it, man. But you dance long enough with any-body, you end up begging for the pooty."

Theo was about to say more, then stopped, his gaze suddenly fixed toward the entrance. Jack turned to see a striking brunette walk toward the hostess. She wasn't dripping with sexuality like so many of south

Florida's walking billboards for plastic surgery. She was captivating on a more intriguing level, dressed in a black Chanel suit with an open collar, only a hint of cleavage, the jacket cut just sharply enough to suggest that a pretty amazing body went along with that classic face.

"Good," said Jack, "she's here. That's the woman I wanted you to meet."

"*That's* Mia? You're dating *her?*"

"Yeah. Better than eight weeks now."

For the first time in ten years, Theo was speechless.

"What's wrong?" said Jack.

"You didn't tell me she was gorgeous."

"Maybe I didn't think it was all that important."

"Yeah, right. And maybe I'll be elected governor of Utah. How do you go two months seeing a woman like that and not give me an eyeful?"

"You always made excuses. I figured you had no interest in meeting her."

"I just didn't want to have to pretend I liked some loser who'd probably end up dumping you anyway. But damn, Jack. Didn't know you had it in you."

"Is it my imagination, or did you somehow manage to insult me thirty-six different ways in just three sentences?"

"No, man, it's a compliment. How old is she? Twenty-five?"

"Older than she looks. So don't look at me like I'm robbing the cradle."

"Rob away. Got no problem with that. Except . . ."

"Except what?"

"I was just thinking. She looks the type who'd go for a rich lawyer."

"What are you saying now? The regular Jack Swyteck isn't good enough for her?"

"I would never say that." He gave Jack an assessing look, then asked, "Would you?"

Jack's mouth opened, but the words took a little longer. "Do you honestly think I'm courting a white-shoe law firm because I'm trying to impress a woman?"

"All I know is that the old Jack Swyteck wouldn't go near a place like Bailey, Benning, and Langer. Now you're doing William Bailey personal favors, representing his client in a dumb-ass dispute before the hoity-toity Coral Gables Board of Architects. And surprise, surprise. That sudden change of heart coincides with the arrival of a bombshell named Mia."

Jack exaggerated his indignation, just being funny. "I'll have you know that she happens to like this average Joe for who he is."

"How do you know that?"

"Because it was her suggestion that I defend my client's statue of David on the grounds that a fourteen-inch penis is not large."

Theo's beer nearly came through his nostrils. "Right. You two had sex yet?"

That was a far more complicated question than Theo could possibly have imagined. "I'm not one to kiss and tell," said Jack.

Theo nodded. "Obviously it was with the lights off. Things always seem enormous when you can't see them, like when your tongue's going crazy trying to work out what feels like a fucking Cadillac stuck between your molars, but in reality it's just this teensy-weensy shred of—"

"Yeah, yeah. Got your point. Thanks, pal."

"Don't mention it."

Jack caught Mia's eye across the bar. She gave Jack a little wave and a smile, then started toward him. As she approached, Jack couldn't help but notice that each time they got together, he felt happier to see her. His mind started to compute what that might mean, but he quickly shook it off, trying instead to enjoy the moment. Because it was indeed special.

Twice in the span of ten minutes, Theo Knight had been stunned into silence.

3

.

J ack was lighting candles. Four on the coffee table, six on the mantel, a dozen more placed strategically around the room. He stepped back to admire the warm glow.

Candles, he thought. *I'm actually lighting candles.* The last time he'd done that, a hurricane was barreling down on Miami, and his Cuban grandmother was on her knees praying aloud to Santa Barbara and San Lázaro. This evening, however, Abuela was nowhere to be found. There was no power outage. Nor was it anyone's happy birthday.

This was all about Mia.

She was truly gorgeous, as Theo had so enthusiastically pointed out, but attracting beautiful women had never really been Jack's problem. Finding one with her head screwed on straight, however, was another matter. He was over six feet tall with dark eyes that hinted at his half-Latin heritage. His ex-wife used to say that he had the rugged good looks to be an instant heartthrob as a country singer, except that he couldn't sing worth a damn, he looked ridiculous in hats, and he was only slightly less country than Art Buchwald. Now that she was out of his life, he relied exclusively on Theo for backhanded compliments that cut him to shreds.

He inhaled, drawing in the aroma. Fresh, spicy cinnamon. Those candles were working their magic. Barely a hint remained of his paella à la napalm. Oh, yes, burned to a crisp. Who knew that one hour at 325 degrees didn't translate to half an hour at 500 degrees? Not that the meal would have been edible anyway. It was beyond Jack's comprehension that a so-called celebrity chef could have his own TV show when his best-selling cookbook didn't even tell you to *boil* the rice before putting it in the freakin' oven.

"Jack, what's that smell?"

He turned to see Mia standing in the hallway. She was wearing one of his dress shirts, which was now the odds-on choice to be his favorite article of clothing.

"Cimamanonon," he said, then untied his tongue. "Cinn-a-mon. There. See, I can talk."

She'd been napping while he cooked, and there was still some sleepiness in her expression. She smiled as she came to him, then draped her arms atop his shoulders, looking him in the eye. "Are you cooking?"

"Trying."

"What is it?"

"I call it paella DOA."

"Paella what?"

"Nothing. Let's make it a fun Saturday night. I'll take you out to dinner."

Her expression fell. "*Dinner?* I thought you were making lunch. What the heck time is it?"

"Almost six."

"Oh my God! You mean I've been asleep all afternoon?"

Jack grinned like a proud nineteen-year-old. They'd seen the sun rise, slept for a couple of hours, then done a morning encore. "Nothing like starting your day with six or seven orgasms."

"Don't flatter yourself, bucko."

"Three or four?"

"Mmm . . . no."

"A mild tingling sensation that beats the hell out of pressing your privates against a washing machine on spin cycle?"

She laughed through her teeth, but her smile slowly flattened into a tight line of disappointment. "I can't do dinner with you tonight. I have to go."

"Go where?"

"Home."

"Why?"

"I have . . . plans."

He took a half step back, leaning against the counter. "Oh. Would that be something like I-gotta-wash-my-hair plans, or some other kind of plans?"

"It's not a date, if that's what you're asking. I told you I'm not interested in seeing anyone else."

"Then why do you have to go?"

"It's my friend Emilia. She got divorced a month ago. I've been promising to do something with her for three weeks now, and so we agreed on tonight."

"Can't you cancel?"

"Jack, come on. You're divorced. You know I can't do that to her."

Yup. He definitely knew. "Okay, you're right. I really should stay home and start chiseling that paella out of my baking pan anyway."

"I knew you'd understand." She took his hand, then kissed him on the corner of the mouth.

He started to kiss her back but pulled away. "You should get going. Let's not start something we can't finish."

"I can stretch it out another half hour, for sure. That's plenty of time for me to teach you a thing or two."

"Oh really? And what exactly do you think you can teach me?"

"Lots of things."

"For example?"

"Well," she said, "do you know what kisses have in common with real estate?"

He thought for a second, though the atmosphere was becoming less and less conducive to coherent thinking. "No, can't say that I do."

She pressed against him, lightly kissing his mouth, his chin, his neck as she spoke. "Location . . . location . . . location."

"Yeah, uh. That's, um, definitely, you know—"

"Jack?" She was suddenly up on her toes, meeting him eye to eye. "Yeah?"

"We're down to twenty-nine minutes, and we've got a lot of zip codes to cover."

"Tough job," he said as he led her toward the bedroom, "but somebody's gotta do it."

Mia left before seven o'clock, and by 8 p.m. Jack was on his way to the Ritz-Carlton. Jack had made the mistake of answering the phone after Mia left, hoping that she'd changed her mind and was on her way back. Much to his disappointment, it was William Bailey of Bailey, Benning, and Langer. One of his partners had canceled out on a big fund-raising event over at the Ritz. The firm had an extra invitation. William thought of Jack.

"Sorry, I don't have a date," said Jack.

"Just come for cocktails. Stag's fine."

"Thanks, but—"

"Jack, the CEO of Rubillo and Porter is one of my guests, and his accounting firm happens to be the seventh largest in the country. Between you and me, his head's probably about to roll in another one of those funny-number Wall Street accounting scams. Odds are he'll need a damn good criminal defense lawyer."

Jack considered it. William had promised that if Jack did him the favor of taking the statue of David case, better things would come his way. Of course, he could hear Theo's voice in the back of his mind, accusing him of selling out. But he could also hear his landlord calling for last month's rent, which the Law Offices of Jack Swyteck, PA, still hadn't paid.

"All right. I'll do cocktails."

The Ritz in Coconut Grove was a twenty-minute drive from his house on Key Biscayne, but that was plenty of time for second thoughts. He'd never worked at a big firm, except in law school as a summer associate. But he knew how the invitations to these high-priced social events were distributed. The marketing director made it sound like the most sought-after ticket since the World Series, but there were rarely any takers until the final threatening e-mail from the managing partner. "Come on, people, this is utterly embarrassing! If I don't have twelve bodies to fill the firm's table by noon today, then I swear the annual partners' retreat will be catered by the same slophouse we use for the staff holiday party. No, I am NOT kidding!"

Jack's cell phone rang just as he valeted his car. It was Theo.

"You have radar or something?" said Jack. "Or is it already plastered all over the Internet that I'm being fitted for golden handcuffs?"

"Does that mean you're seeing Mia again?"

"No. She has plans tonight."

"Sorry, dude. You need a Xanax or something?"

"No, I don't need a Xanax."

"Stripper?"

"No."

"Hooker?"

"Hardly."

"Then what, Jack?"

"What do you mean 'then what'? You called *me*, remember?"

"Oh, right. Just checking up on my old friend, that's all. I hardly hear from him no more, now that he's *in love*." He said "in love" like one of those smarmy DJs who played old Barry White tunes at 3 a.m.

Jack was about to deny it, then stopped himself. The first George Bush was president the last time Jack had carried a personal relationship this far. Although he and Mia had yet to exchange I-love-yous, even a guy on romantic life support could see that the only remaining question was who would be the first to utter those three little words. That was where he stood, at least. He hoped she felt the same.

"Things are going really well with Mia. You should be happy for me."

"I am. Let's go out and celebrate."

"Can't. I got this thing."

"Thing?"

Jack saw no easy way to spill it. "It's something William Bailey invited me to, all right? Purely a networking opportunity."

There was silence on the line. Finally, Theo spoke, his voice dripping with disapproval. "Man, you got it bad." He hung up before Jack could answer.

Jack started to dial him back, but he didn't see the point. Better to let his friend have a few drinks and cool down while pondering one of the essential mysteries in the life of Theo Knight, such as, If a tree falls in the woods, will its in-box suddenly be flooded with Viagra e-mails? Jack tucked his phone away and entered the Ritz.

The cocktail reception was in the Grand Ballroom. Jack took the escalator up two flights and got off at the terrace level, where the party was in full swing. Lots of designer dresses and carats on loan from Van Cleef & Arpels. The murmur of countless conversations buzzed all around him, but it couldn't drown out Theo's voice in his head. *Do I really have it bad?* Jack wondered. And what was *it*, anyway? Like Mia said, there was nothing wrong with wanting to be paid what you're worth. Jack had done plenty of public-service work, jobs that didn't even earn him enough money to pay off his student loans. He'd walked away with virtually nothing from his divorce except a car that was later torched. He wasn't about to jump into William Bailey's lap. But if he was going to continue to be his own boss, he needed to earn the trust of someone like Bailey, a consummate rainmaker who had no stomach for a criminal courtroom, and whose clients would gladly hand over both Park Place and Boardwalk to any lawyer who made sure they did not go directly to jail.

"Jack, glad to see you made it," said William Bailey with a smile.

"Guess I'm just a sucker for an open bar."

"Actually, drink tickets are ten bucks each."

A thousand dollars per person and still a cash bar. All for a good cause, however, like a new Mercedes for the CFO of some "not-for-profit" health plan.

Bailey pulled a roll of tickets from his pocket, ripped off about a half dozen for Jack. "My treat. But first, let me introduce you to some friends of mine."

Jack felt his elbow being pulled away from the bar, and his body reluctantly followed. Over the next twenty minutes, he met several dozen people who assumed that, because his last name was Swyteck, Jack yearned for war stories about his famous father. So he pretended to be amused as they carried on about the time they'd golfed, drunk, fished, or campaigned with former governor Swyteck, though he wasn't at all in the mood for a bunch of name-droppers who knew the real Harry Swyteck about as well as they'd known the real Elvis Presley.

In the midst of the mind-numbing drivel, Jack's gaze was drawn toward the vision across the room. She was standing with her back to him, wearing a spaghetti-strapped black cocktail dress. Her hair was up in a braided twist, and the sparkle of diamond earrings played nicely against the olive skin and the gentle curve of her neck. He didn't mean to stare, but for some reason he couldn't take his eyes off her.

The sound of William Bailey's voice brought him back to reality. "Jack, I'd like you to meet Ernesto Salazar. One of my best and oldest clients."

Jack smiled and shook hands as the other men kidded each other about *Who you calling old?* Jack only half listened. He was shooting subtle glances across the room, checking out that same spot near the bar, searching for the captivating woman in the black dress.

Bailey said, "Ernesto just got back from Argentina this afternoon. He's been in Buenos Aires for the past nine weeks putting together a huge wireless cell-phone deal."

"Ten weeks," said Ernesto.

Jack said something to keep up his end of the conversation, but his focus was on catching a break in the crowd and gaining a clear line of sight toward the bar. He wasn't sure why, but something—no, *everything*—inside him was telling him to find that woman in the black dress. Finally, he spotted the sparkle of her diamond earrings, and for a split second he caught just a glimpse of her profile. But the crowd shifted, and a server stepped up to offer him a glass of champagne. By the time he found another opening, the black dress was gone.

"There she is," said Ernesto.

"Who?" said Jack. He suddenly felt like a middle-schooler caught with a stolen *Playboy* magazine.

"Ernesto's wife, of course," said Bailey.

"Let me introduce you," said Ernesto. It would have been futile to call out to her with all the noise, so he hand signaled, trying to catch his wife's attention. Either she didn't notice or she was ignoring him, showing him only the slender curve of her back. Ernesto excused himself and strategically maneuvered his way around several circles of conversation.

Bailey laid a hand on Jack's shoulder, his voice low but showing some irritation. "You seem distracted, Jack. Something wrong?"

"I'm fine," said Jack as he watched Ernesto approach the woman in the black dress and take her by the hand. She turned, but the crowd around Jack had swollen, and not until Ernesto and his much-younger wife meandered back through the maze of laughing and chatting guests did Jack get his first look at her face.

His instincts had been dead-on.

"Jack Swyteck, please meet my wife, Mia."

Jack couldn't move. The words seemed to echo in his brain . . . *my wife, Mia . . . my wife, Mia.* It was as if someone had switched on a giant vacuum beneath his feet and was trying to suck his very soul down through the floor. He just looked at her, and she at him, her eyes pleading: *Don't say a word.*

Bailey nudged him and said, "Now you know why Ernesto is so glad to be home after ten weeks in South America."

No words would come, but finally Jack found his voice. "Yeah. Now I know."

Mia offered her hand, the consummate actress. "Very nice to meet you, Mr. Swyteck."

It tapped every ounce of strength to take her hand, and it felt strangely cold as their skin touched. "Yeah," said Jack in a hollow voice. "Lovely."

4

V ery nice to meet you, Mr. *Swyteck*. Yes, indeed. And it was very nice seeing you naked, making you scream, and hearing you say that you weren't interested in seeing anyone else but me, all while the husband you conveniently forgot to tell me about was two thousand miles away on business in South America.

Very nice to meet you, too. Mrs. *Salazar.*

It was Monday night—a full forty-eight hours after the disaster—and Jack's anger was still roiling. Mia had gone to great lengths to make her scheme work. The Palm Beach lifestyle, her circle of friends, and the waterfront mansion were all left behind, ninety miles north of Miami. Her husband owned property all over the world, so she moved into their condo on South Beach, living the ten-week life of sex and the single girl. She put the wedding band in the jewel box. She told her friends she was "traveling." She told Jack she was studying for her licensing exam and looking for the right job as a real estate agent—hence her little joke about kissing and real estate . . . location, location, location. Jack had bought it completely, the entire amazing, beautiful, lying package.

"I knew there was something I didn't like about her," said Theo. He was on Jack's couch, remote control in hand, eyes glued to the TV screen.

"Right," said Jack. "The only thing you didn't like was that she's not into group sex."

"Actually, I think she might have come around on that."

Jack could only wonder if there was anything else Theo might like to say in his undying effort to make matters worse. He went to the kitchen to grab a cold beer.

In hindsight, the warning signs had been there. When their talks became personal—when Jack opened up about mistakes he'd made, his failed marriage and relationships—she wasn't as specific about her own past as she might have been. He never actually met any of her friends. She would sometimes veto his restaurant choices for no apparent reason. Typical guy that he was, he didn't mind in the least that she seemed more interested in talking about him. Of course, it wasn't that she was so totally taken. She was just hiding herself.

"Fool, fool, fool," he said into the open refrigerator.

"You left off a 'fool,'" Theo shouted from the couch.

Jack twisted the cap off his beer bottle and returned to the living room. "Of all the guys in the world, why do you think she had to pick me?"

"Tom Cruise is too savvy?"

"Seriously. What did I ever do to her?"

"Nothing. Sometimes the world is a random place."

"I don't believe that."

"Eighty-four percent of the world disagrees with you."

"How do you know that?"

"It's a statistical fact. Then again, sixty-one-point-seven percent of all statistics are made up on the spot, so you never really know."

It was impossible to have a serious conversation when Theo had a remote control, two basketball games, and a picture-in-picture television set. Jack went back to the kitchen and stared out the window. Some explanation would have been nice, and he was starting to wish he'd made more of the conversation Mia had forced on him earlier in the day. The psycho-calling had actually started around midnight

Saturday and didn't stop until late Sunday night. Jack ignored all her pleading messages. She waited until Monday morning to show up, unannounced, outside his law office. Part of him had wanted to keep on walking and tell her to get lost. But something—and it was more than just curiosity—had made him stop and listen to what she wanted to say.

"I'm sorry, Jack. Truly sorry."

"That doesn't really help," he said.

They were standing beside one of those pathetic little olive trees that sprouted from a square hole in the sidewalk in the name of city-sponsored landscaping. The morning traffic was streaming past them. Mia had a tired, sorrowful look on her face, as if she hadn't slept since Saturday. She glanced across the street, toward an old man who pretended not to notice as his collie fertilized one of the sickly olive trees.

"The other night," she said, "when I was at your house before the cocktail party. I want you to know that I meant what I told you before I left. I have no interest in seeing anyone else."

"You mean besides your husband?"

"I don't have what you'd call a happy marriage. I never have. Ernesto has done this to me for years. Cheating, I mean."

"Really? How long have you been doing it to him?"

Her eyes were like lasers, and they were aimed straight at Jack. "I'm not like that. This whole thing is new to me. It started and ended with you."

"I see. One dumb lawyer evens the score for Ernesto's string of bimbos—is that it?"

"Stop it," she said, her voice breaking. "This wasn't about getting even. Our marriage was over before he left on his business trip."

"It sure didn't look that way at the cocktail party."

"Ernesto Salazar doesn't easily let go of the things he wants."

"You're not a thing."

"You're not Ernesto."

"Did you tell him you wanted a divorce?"

"I did, a few months ago. He asked me—no, he *warned* me to think long and hard before I take that step. It was like a threat. Scared me enough to drop it for a while. Then I met you, and I realized that I had to get out."

"So it's my fault, is that it?"

"No. You were anything but to blame. You were . . ."

"What?"

"Nothing. Just forget it."

"No, tell me, please. I'd really like to know exactly *what* the hell I was."

She looked away, then back. "You were the first man I've made love to in almost two years."

It wasn't the answer he'd expected. "So, you and Ernesto . . ."

"I told you: The marriage was over long before I met you."

Jack certainly knew what a failing marriage could do to one's sex life, no matter how great the glory days had been. But two years was a long time, especially for two people who were still living together in the same house. "Mia, you really don't have to explain."

"I feel like I owe you this much."

"Trust me, it's not going to make things any different between us. You lied to me in the worst way. End of story."

"I don't blame you if you hate me. But it killed me that I wasn't—that I *couldn't be*—honest with you. It still tears me up. I want to tell you the way it really is."

"I don't need to hear it now."

"Do you mean that?"

Of course he didn't. He wanted to hear it, absorb it, analyze it, the way any good lawyer would. Then he wanted to play it over and over again in his mind until his head exploded and his heart resembled a pincushion, like any other wounded lover. But his Y chromosome was slapping him upside the head, pointing out rather convincingly that any self-respecting man would deny her the privilege of easing her conscience with a lame psychoanalytical excuse that would undoubtedly sound like television talk show drivel.

"I'm sorry. I have work to do. Good-bye, Mia." He ducked into his office before she could say another word. He was alone in the vestibule, lights off, leaning against the inside of the smoked-glass door, hoping that she wouldn't knock, hoping that she would. Should he have let her keep talking? Could she possibly have had a good reason for lying, something that made perfect sense and that would restore the broken trust?

Or is she just jerking my chain all over again?

An uneasy silence seemed to lurk outside the office door. Finally, he heard footfalls on the sidewalk. Two tentative steps—stop. Two more steps—stop. A click of her heel followed, then another and another, until their entire relationship faded into nothing.

Mia was gone.

5

F BI Special Agent Andie Henning watched through the calm eyes of a trained professional as the assistant medical examiner dissected Ashley Thornton's right lung.

Torrents of icy air gushed from the air-conditioning vents in the ceiling, making the autopsy room so cold that Andie almost had to remind herself that she was still in Florida. It felt more like winter in her native Seattle, where her remarkable performance in an undercover assignment caught the eye of the FBI Critical Incident Response Group. With a degree in psychology, she was quickly singled out as crisis-negotiator material. Seattle had no openings for field negotiators, so after intense training with the Crisis Negotiation Unit at the academy, she transferred to Miami, a city with enough real-life hostage-barricade incidents to keep a negotiator's skills sharp for life. Miami held the added attraction of being two thousand miles away from her ex-fiancé. But that was another story.

Bright lights glistened off the white sterile walls and buff tile floors. The unclothed, grayish purple cadavar lay faceup on the stainless steel table in the center of the room. Two deep incisions ran laterally from shoulder to shoulder, across the breasts at a downward angle meeting at the sternum. A long, deeper cut ran from the breastbone to the groin, forming the stem in the coroner's classic Y incision. The liver, spleen, kidneys, and intestines were laid out neatly beside a slab of ribs on the large dissection table. The cadaver was literally a shell of a human being, strangely reminiscent of the hollowed-out half of a watermelon on a table of hors d'oeuvres.

Andie smeared another dab of Vicks VapoRub beneath her nostrils to cut the odor. A trip to the medical examiner's office wasn't exactly a daily occurrence for an FBI agent. The vast majority of homicides were strictly state and local matters. Kidnapping, however, was a federal offense, and unfortunately Andie's increasing specialization in negotiation had earned her more trips to the medical examiner's office than desired.

"Very interesting," said Dr. Feinstein.

The doctor was still examining the right lung, working at a small and brightly lit dissection table on the other side of the cadaver. His powers of concentration were such that his bushy gray eyebrows had pinched together and formed one continuous caterpillar that stretched across his brow. He laid his scalpel aside and snapped a digital photograph, which gave Andie a moment of uneasiness. Not that it was the examiner's fault, but it seemed that humiliation of the victim continued even in death.

"What do you see?" asked Andie.

The doctor took a step back and almost smiled. Andie felt a digression coming on.

"The first thing you have to understand," said Feinstein, "is that drowning cannot be proven by autopsy. It is a diagnosis of exclusion, based on the circumstances of death."

"Ashley Thornton's case presents some rather grim circumstances."

"Yes, it does. But a dead body underwater does not always mean a drowning. I've seen victims strangled and then thrown into swimming pools. I've seen victims hit over the head with a hammer and then tossed into the lake."

"Are you suggesting that's what happened here?"

"Quite to the contrary. Yes, she has some scrapes, and a simple fracture where her tibia locked up with that steel grate inside the cave. The aquifer is moving water, so you can't expect to recover a body in perfect condition. The significant point is that I see no signs of life-threatening trauma."

"So, in your process of diagnosis by exclusion, what does that tell you, Doctor?"

"Not as much as *this*," he said, returning to the dissection tray. He grabbed a penlight and motioned Andie toward him. The focused beam of light was shining through the dissected wall of the right lung.

"Do you see that?" asked Feinstein.

"Looks like dirt."

"Sand. In a drowning case, that, my friend, is about as close to a home run as you can get."

"She has sand in her lungs?" asked Andie.

"Yes. Now, that's a critically important fact if you think about what happens when you drown. Your normal reaction when the head goes underwater is to hold your breath. Eventually, you can't do it any longer, and your body is forced to gasp for air. That presents a major problem if you can't reach the surface."

"Or if you're trapped inside an underwater cave."

"Exactly. So the victim starts gulping water into the mouth and throat, literally inhaling water into the lungs. This, of course, sends the victim into an even more frenzied panic, and the struggle becomes more desperate. If she doesn't break the surface, her lungs continue to fill, and she struggles and gasps in a vicious cycle that can last several minutes, until breathing stops."

"And the victim takes in sand with the water?"

"Not always. Sand can end up in the mouth and throat when the current pushes a lifeless body along the bottom. But here the body was essentially fastened to this steel grate, and sand ended up not only in the mouth and throat, but also in the lungs. And think about where this victim was struggling."

"In an underwater cave."

"A cave with a sand bottom. Drowning is a slow, agonizing death. The final minutes of life are sheer terror and panic. This woman was trapped in a cave with a low ceiling. The more she flailed around in the dark, trying to find air, the more sand she kicked up. Within the tight confines of this cave, the sand had nowhere to go except into her lungs."

Andie glanced at the dissected lung and said, "So, you're confident that this is a case of death by drowning?"

"As confident as I can be."

Andie thought for a moment, saying nothing.

Dr. Feinstein said, "Are you okay?"

"Yeah," said Andie. "It must be the odor that just got to me."

What she wanted to say was that she was embarrassed for a moment, put off by the way her own job almost forced her to stand beside a corpse and feel nothing but clever about slapping on a label like "death by drowning." It was never that impersonal for her.

"I guess what you're saying, Doctor, is that some sick bastard brought Ashley Thornton down into this cave, tied her to a steel bar, and then swam away and left her in the dark with no air tank. He left her there *alive*."

He glanced at Ashley's face. "I'm afraid so."

"Thanks, Doctor," she said, the words "slow, agonizing death" continuing to resonate in her mind as she left the autopsy room.

6

·

With all the personal distractions, Jack was glad to be in trial. A lawyer in trial was like a woman in labor. People generally didn't expect you to drop everything and run to the phone in the middle of it all.

Hello, this is God speaking. Is Mr. Swyteck available?

Sorry, sir, he's in trial.

Oh, don't bother him then. Just this little matter of his mortality we need to address. Ask him to call Me when he's finished, please.

People often said that William Bailey had more money than God. Apparently he had a greater sense of urgency as well. Jack was outside the courtroom, sipping water from the drinking fountain, when one of Bailey's personal assistants tracked him down.

"Mr. Swyteck, Mr. Bailey must speak with you immediately."

Jack straightened up and wiped a drop of water from his chin. His secretary had undoubtedly given Bailey the standard "He's in trial" response by telephone, and one of Bailey's fetch boys was promptly dispatched to the courthouse on a mission.

"Tell Mr. Bailey that I'm in trial, and that I'm working over the lunch hour."

"My apologies, sir. But Mr. Bailey told me not to take no for an answer. He and Mr. Salazar are expecting you. It has to do with Mrs. Salazar."

Mrs. Salazar. Strangely enough, somewhere in the cavernous hall-ways of the old courthouse, Jack could have sworn that a fat lady was singing. "All right," Jack said with resignation. "As long as I'm back by one p.m."

Alive.

At ten minutes past noon Jack was fifty-one stories above down-town Miami, though he hardly noticed the amazing view of cruise ships and the Port of Miami from the corner office of BB&L's managing part-ner. William Bailey was standing behind his desk, his arm resting atop a globe so old that Prussia was still a country. His most important client was seated at the far end of the leather couch, opposite Jack, who was in the winged armchair. Ernesto Salazar was a distinguished Latino with jet-black hair (dyed, of course) and the dark, piercing eyes of a shrewd negotiator. He was wearing an Armani suit, Gucci shoes, a Rolex wristwatch, and a deep scowl that Jack assumed was intended exclusively for him.

"My wife's gone missing," said Salazar in a somber voice.

Jack looked at Bailey, then back at Salazar. Nearly ten days had passed since Jack had met Mia's husband, and it was not yet clear that they knew about him and Mia. Before the conversation inevitably moved in that direction, however, Jack wanted some details. "How do you mean, missing?"

Bailey said, "She's been kidnapped."

The word hit him with surprising impact. Under Cupid's Rules of Love and War (Idiot's Edition), he technically shouldn't have given a damn. But he did. "Kidnapped? By whom?"

"We have no idea," said Bailey.

"Have you called the police?"

"No," said Salazar. "Like many wealthy South American families, the Salazars are no strangers to the threat of kidnappers. Rarely does it make sense to turn to the police in these situations."

"I can understand your view. But often there are good reasons to call the police."

"That's one of the reasons we called you," said Salazar. "Your advice."

"I'll help in any way I can." Jack paused to measure his words, as this seemed like the appropriate time to clear the air on his unwitting adultery. "Mr. Salazar, there's something I should probably—"

"Hold that thought," said Bailey. "I know you have to be back in trial by one o'clock, so please just let Mr. Salazar lay out the pertinent facts. We need your criminal-law expertise on one very specific point. Is that all right with you?"

"Sure," said Jack.

"Thank you," said Salazar. "Basically, I don't have a lot of information at this point. My wife went out last night with one of her girl-friends. I was dead tired. At around ten thirty, I went to sleep. When I woke up this morning, she'd already gone out for her run."

"What time was that?" asked Jack.

"About seven."

"What did you do?"

"Nothing, just then. But three hours later, she still wasn't home. I dialed her cell phone—she always carries it with her when she runs—and got no answer. Then I called her friend Emilia, but she didn't know anything. That's when I started to get worried."

Jack couldn't help noting the absence of any emotion in Salazar's voice. Some people reacted that way to a crisis, but Jack wasn't sure about Salazar. "Then what did you do?"

"I searched the house, the yard, the garage. Didn't see anything. That's when I decided to check my computer."

"Your computer?"

"Yes. My e-mail. I had a bad feeling about this. I had a sense that someone might have a note for me."

"You mean a ransom note?"

"Of course. Like I said, my family has been touched by kidnapping before. My uncle, when he was on business in Brazil, to be precise."

"I'm sorry to hear that," said Jack. "Did you find anything on the computer?"

"This," said Bailey as he stepped forward and handed Jack a printed e-mail. "We already checked out the source. It was a text message sent with a stolen wireless service. No way to trace it back to any specific person."

Jack would have expected no less. He read to himself, quickly but carefully. The message was short and to the point:

PAY ME WHAT SHE'S WORTH.
Further instructions to follow.

"That's it?" said Jack.

"That's the entire message," said Salazar. "Ever seen anything like it?"

Jack laid the paper flat on the coffee table in front of him. He read it again and said, "Can't say that I have. Then again, I prosecuted only two ransom cases at the U.S. attorney's office, and the kidnappers I defended on death row were never after money."

"Ever *heard* of anything like it?"

"No. Often it takes kidnappers time to formulate a demand, particularly if they're politically motivated. But when the objective is purely monetary, the number is usually pretty specific. Sometimes unrealistic, but specific."

"Sounds like a hoax to me," said Bailey.

"Could be," said Jack. "But until you can find out one way or the other, you need to make some threshold decisions. Number one, are you going to call the police?"

"No police."

"Then you'll have to decide who your point person will be. The note says that instructions will follow. Presumably someone will have to communicate with the kidnapper on your behalf."

"I think William should do that," said Salazar.

"Your lawyer is a good choice, if he's willing."

"I chose him as a friend, not as a lawyer," said Salazar, his tone taking on something of an edge.

"Even better," said Jack. "The other thing to consider is the ransom. The demand is open-ended, so you should start thinking about how much you're willing to pay."

"That's easy," said Salazar. "It says pay what she's worth. I pay nothing."

"I think what you're trying to say is that you've made a decision not to pay a ransom. Families do that. But just to be clear, that doesn't mean your wife is worth nothing. It means that—"

"No, I said precisely what I meant."

Jack did a double take. "You're saying that your wife is worth nothing?"

"Is there something wrong with your hearing, Mr. Swyteck?"

"No."

"Then why is this so hard for you to grasp? I pay what she's worth." Salazar moved to the edge of the couch, leaning toward Jack as he spoke in a coarse voice that was just above a whisper. "Mia was cheating on me. She's worth nothing."

His dark eyes were like burning embers. The anger was just as evident on his lawyer's face. At that moment, all doubt in Jack's mind evaporated: They knew everything.

Bailey shook his head, disgusted. "How could you, Jack?"

"I swear, I had no idea that—"

"Save it," said Salazar. "You've insulted me enough."

Jack wanted to explain, but who would believe it? His own culpability was secondary, anyway. It seemed bizarre that it should be him, but *someone* had to stand up for Mia. "I realize that I'm in no position to ask any favors, but hear me out. You have to act under the assumption that the kidnapper is willing to kill her unless you meet his demands. If you're not going to pay a ransom, that's fine. But you at least have to call the police."

"Why?" said Salazar. "Is there some law that requires a husband to notify them if his wife has been kidnapped?"

Jack didn't answer right away, not because he didn't know, but because he didn't like the way they'd set this whole thing up, toying with him. "Is this the so-called expert advice you need from me?"

"I would just like an answer to the question, Mr. Swyteck. As the husband, am I required by law to notify the police?"

"No, but if you're not willing to do what it takes to bring her back safely, you should call the police. It's the moral—"

"Moral?" he said, his voice rising. "You of all people presume to tell me what's *moral?*"

Jack didn't want to get into it with Salazar. He looked to the lawyer and said, "William, you know I'm right."

"I think you'd better go."

The discussion hardly seemed finished, but until Salazar cooled off, things could only spiral downward. "William, I'll give you a call when my trial adjourns for the day."

"Don't bother," said Bailey.

"We have it under control," said Salazar.

Jack wanted to slap both of them, tell them that they were playing with a woman's life. But it seemed pointless. He rose and started toward the door.

"Señor, aren't you forgetting something?" said Salazar.

Jack stopped to see him pointing toward the printed e-mail on the coffee table.

"I want to know," said Salazar.

"Know what?"

A trace of a smile seeming to crease his lips as he handed Jack the note and he said, "What's Mia worth to *you?*"

Jack locked eyes with him but said nothing. He tucked the note inside his jacket, then turned and left the office.

I t's a total chick magnet," said Theo.

They were cruising past the marina in Coconut Grove, Jack behind the wheel and Theo riding shotgun. For several months, Jack had been trying to find a suitable replacement for a charbroiled hunk of melted metal that had once been a classic Mustang convertible. Theo's sights were set on a 1966 Rambler Marlin, if only because its current sports-minded owner had quite naturally repainted the body in the official turquoise color of the Florida Marlins.

"Chick magnet, huh?" said Jack.

"Absolutely. And did I mention that, if driven regularly, it prevents heart disease and can even reverse the aging process in humans? All for just forty-four hundred bucks."

"Not *my* forty-four hundred bucks."

They stopped for a frozen lemonade at Kennedy Park, a tree-filled stretch of green space along Biscayne Bay that was popular with everyone from triathletes to tricyclers. The parking lot was adjacent to the heart trail, so a seat on the hood of the old Rambler with their feet resting on the chrome bumper offered Jack and Theo prime jogger viewing. Unfortunately, it appeared to be geriatric Tuesday, nothing but a steady stream of power-walking blobs of jelly that had somehow taken on human form through the miracle of spandex.

Their deal was that Jack would test-drive the laugh-out-loud-mobile if Theo would offer his street-smart, psychoanalytical take on Ernesto Salazar. For whatever reason, Theo had a knack for thinking like a dirtbag.

"It's obvious," said Theo.

"Tell me," said Jack.

"Simple. Mr. Salivar doesn't believe his wife is really kidnapped."

"Salazar, not *Salivar*. You make him sound like a Saint Bernard in a sausage factory."

"You want my opinion, then shut up and listen." Theo set his frozen lemonade atop the turquoise hood and ripped open a bag of chips. "Here's the thing. You got a gorgeous younger woman married to a fifty-something-year-old multimillionaire. Let's assume it was no lie when Mia said she and her husband stopped having sex. Imagine how totally ripped this dude is when he finds out she's bopping a hotshot lawyer. Hubby says, Beat it, bitch, you're outta here. She's gotta be looking at the short end of a prenup if he divorces her. So she fakes her own kidnapping to con him out of some ransom money."

"You honestly think that's what happened?"

"Doesn't matter. I'm telling you what must be going through Salad Bar's mind."

"Salazar, moron."

"Yeah, what you said. Anyways, he was acting way too cool at your meeting to be thinking she's really kidnapped. Nobody's got that much ice water in his veins."

"But what if Salazar does? What if he's so ticked off at his wife for cheating on him that he actually hopes the kidnapper slits her throat?"

"Ah, the Journey conundrum," said Theo.

"What journey?"

"Journey. Depending on who you talk to, one of the best or worst rock bands of the 1980s. One man's Sting is another man's Air Supply. Know what I mean?" He started singing "All Out of Love."

Jack blinked hard, incredulous. "What the hell does that have to do with anything?"

"You and Salazar are both looking at the exact same situation—a married woman goes missing after cheating on her husband. You see a kidnap victim in peril. He sees a conniving bitch with a plan. The Journey conundrum."

"Sounds like a bad title for a Ludlum novel. But focus for a minute, would you please? Aren't we overlooking an obvious third possibility?"

Theo nodded. "When Alcazar found out that you and his wife be doing the nasty, he killed her, and now he's trying to make it look like she got kidnapped."

"By Alcazar I assume you mean Salazar."

"Alcazar, Salazar, whoever. A man by any other name would still think with his dick."

That was Jack's thought entirely, but hearing Theo put it to Shakespeare only drove home the point. "Pretty logical way to look at it. Like you say, nobody's got that much ice water in his veins."

"Unless he's trying to cover his own ass."

"I guess that's what bugs me about Salazar's reaction to the kidnapping. When people choose not to call the cops it's usually because the kidnapper told them not to or because they're afraid that law enforcement might try to talk them out of paying a ransom. Here, Salazar is thumbing his nose at the kidnappers, and he *still* decided not to dial nine-one-one. That's a really dangerous situation if you're a kidnap victim."

"On the other hand, it's a nifty little tap dance if you killed your wife and want it to look like a kidnapping."

Jack spooned out the last of his frozen lemonade. "So, if you were me, you'd go to the police? Is that what you're saying?"

"Depends. If you think maybe Salazar killed his wife, then yeah, go to the police."

"What if I don't think he killed her? What if she really is kidnapped and Salazar is just being a hard-ass to spite her or teach her a lesson?"

"You want to know what I would do?" said Theo.

"Yeah, if you were me."

"I'd stick my head out the window and yell, 'Yo, bitch! Didn't your mamma ever teach you what goes around comes around?' Every day she was all kissy-faced, acting like you were her one and only. Every night she was probably on the phone telling Ernesto to please wire some more money from Buenos Noches."

"Buenes Aires."

"Whatever. My point is, why should Jack Swyteck be the white knight who mounts up and rushes in to save her?"

"Telling the police that she was kidnapped and giving them a copy of the ransom note is hardly rushing in to save her."

"Why do you care enough to even do that?"

"I don't know. Why did I spend the first four years of my career worrying that murdering scumbags who made you look like a choirboy might die in the electric chair? I have this sick humane streak that keeps me from wishing death on anyone. Even lying ex-girlfriends."

"That is sick."

"You think?"

"Absolutely. But it's one of the many reasons I love you, Jack baby," he said as he planted a big kiss on his friend's cheek.

Jack wiped it off, then drifted into silence, his thoughts interrupted by the crunching sound of Theo stuffing his mouth with snack food.

"Bistro chip?" said Theo, offering the bag.

Jack shook his head. Bistro chip. What a joke, the way marketing geniuses always attached a name like "bistro" to foods in need of a little spin. Salty carbs were bistro chips. A sack lunch on a commercial airline was a bistro bag. Goofy, yes, but it had to be one of the oldest games around. *Here you go, Socrates, try some of this bistro hemlock.*

"No thanks," said Jack.

Theo sucked the salt from his fingertips one digit at a time. "So, getting back to what I was saying before. You buying it or ain't you?"

"You mean your theory that Mia faked her own kidnapping?"

"No, no. This car, my man. The Marlin mobile."

Jack grasped the tacky hood ornament—an official Major League Baseball "Billy the Marlin" bobble head. "Think I'll pass. I mean, really: Who needs a chick magnet when I got you?"

Theo crumpled up the empty bag of chips, then unleashed a belch that nearly rattled the headlights. "Ain't dat the troot."

8
·

J ack didn't call the police. He didn't have to.

The FBI was looking for *him*.

The phone call came two days after the meeting in William Bailey's office. The agent told him only that she wanted to discuss the possible kidnapping of Mia Salazar. Forty-five minutes later, Jack was in a small conference room at the FBI's Miami field office. Special Agent Andie Henning was seated across the table from him.

"Thanks for coming in so quickly, Mr. Swyteck."

"It sounded important," said Jack.

During the drive up Jack had made a phone call to Gerry Chafetz, his old boss at the U.S. attorney's office, to get the skinny on Agent Henning. Typical of Gerry, the first thing out of his mouth was that Andie Henning was a looker. More to the point, however, Henning was new to Miami, a rising star from Seattle. A Junior Olympic mogul skier until her knee gave out, and a certified scuba diver by the time she was sixteen. Went straight to the FBI out of law school, never practiced. Only the twentieth woman in bureau history to make the "Possible Club," a 98-percent-male honorary fraternity for agents who shoot perfect scores on one of the toughest firearms courses in law enforcement. The kudos went on and on.

"And," Jack could almost hear his old boss saying for the third time, "did I mention she's a knockout?"

Not that such things mattered. Unless you were straight, male, and over the age of thirteen.

"As you know," Henning said in a businesslike tone, "Mia Salazar was kidnapped three days ago."

"Before we get started, I'm curious: How is it that I ended up on the FBI's interview list?"

"Mr. Salazar gave us your name."

He wondered how many colorful adverbs Salazar had squeezed between "Jack" and "Swyteck." *Jack backstabbing, wife-stealing, mother-bleeping Swyteck.* "It's interesting that Mr. Salazar called you. Last time we spoke, he said he had no intention of involving the police."

"He didn't call us," said Henning. "The kidnapper sent a copy of the ransom note to the FBI. When we called Mr. Salazar to discuss our plan with him, he told us to call his attorney, Jack Swyteck."

"But I'm not his attorney."

"Mr. Salazar says you are."

Jack could have set her completely straight, but his instincts as a criminal defense lawyer told him not to volunteer too much information until he had a better understanding of where Agent Henning's investigation was headed. "Mr. Salazar and I obviously have a few things to clarify," said Jack. "In the interest of keeping this conversation moving forward, what exactly did he tell you I was empowered to do as his attorney?"

"Deliver the ransom."

"Now I'm thoroughly confused. Again, when I last spoke to Mr. Salazar, it was my understanding that there wasn't going to be a ransom payment."

"There isn't. Not from him, anyway. It's our money."

"The FBI's?"

Agent Henning leaned forward, her hands folded atop the table. "Mr. Swyteck, I want to be as frank with you as possible about our strategy. Since you're a former prosecutor, I hope I have your assurance that this conversation isn't going to find its way into the newspapers."

"Of course."

"The kidnapping of Mrs. Salazar isn't the first of its kind. The ransom note, which you've seen, is a signature of sorts for a serial kidnapper. For lack of a better label, we call him the "Wrong Number Kidnapper."

"You mean like dialing the wrong phone number?"

"No. Nothing to do with that. His ransom notes put the onus on the family to place a value on their loved ones. Rather than demand a specific sum of money, he consistently uses the language 'Pay what she's worth.'"

"I saw that in the Salazar e-mail."

"What you haven't seen is the consequence of paying too little. In other words, of choosing the 'wrong number.'"

"Are you saying he's killed before?"

She nodded. "Ashley Thornton. Married to Drew Thornton in Ocala."

"The woman who died in the aquifer?"

"Yes."

"I read about that. Horrible. But I didn't know it was the same kidnapper."

"Not many people do. We've tried very hard to keep the 'pay what she's worth' ransom demand out of the media. It's the only way to be sure we aren't dealing with copycats or crackpots."

"Did Mr. Thornton refuse to pay a ransom?"

"Hardly. He paid a million dollars. Wasn't enough. Less than twenty-four hours after the cash was delivered, we found Mrs. Thornton's body in a cave beneath the Santa Fe River. A plastic bracelet around her wrist said, 'Wrong number.'"

"What would have been the right number?"

"That's the big question. A million dollars is a big ransom."

"So this guy doesn't care how much you pay. It's never enough."

"That's what we thought at first. But we pieced something interesting together through VICAP. It turns out that eight months ago, in north Georgia, the wife of a twenty-five-year-old auto mechanic was kidnapped. He got the same note: Pay what she's worth. The guy sold his truck, hocked everything he owned to scrape together nineteen thousand dollars. His wife was returned a day later, completely unharmed."

"Whoa," said Jack.

"Yeah, no kidding. By that standard, Mr. Salazar would have to come up with about forty million dollars."

"Now I understand why he refuses to pay."

"Really?" she said, her interest seeming to rise. "There have been verified ransom payments as high as sixty-five million dollars."

"I'm sure there have been."

"So, are you suggesting that forty million is way too much ransom money, period? Or do you know something about Mia that compromises her worth, to use the kidnapper's term?"

"I'm not sure what I meant, to be honest with you."

She paused, as if expecting him to say more. "You sure?"

He considered it, then said as much as he thought was appropriate. "You should probably ask Mr. Salazar that question."

"I will," she said as she penciled a little notation on her yellow pad.

Part of Jack wanted to speak up, but the words caught in his throat. That he hadn't known Mia was married lessened his sense of shame, but it only added to the embarrassment of being duped for so long. Agent Henning moved on before he could say more.

"Anyway, in light of all this, we're taking a new strategy with Mrs. Salazar's kidnapping. That's the reason you're here."

"What can I do?" asked Jack.

"We want someone to deliver a much smaller amount of cash. Say, ten thousand dollars. It's not ransom money. It will be characterized as a down payment for some proof that Mia Salazar is still alive."

"Proof-of-life money?"

"Yes, except that our objectives are much broader than that. One, we want to prolong negotiations, keep Mrs. Salazar alive as long as possible. Two, we want to negotiate a drop-off on our own terms, where we can hopefully learn more about our kidnapper. And three, in hopes of hitting the home run, the bills will be marked. Maybe he'll take the dough and sprinkle a few bread crumbs around town that will enable us to track him down."

"You want me to be a bagman?"

"Not a very flattering term, but basically yes."

"Why me?"

"Like I said, Mr. Salazar recommended you."

"As his attorney," said Jack. It was as if the proverbial lightbulb had suddenly switched on.

"Yes. As his attorney." The way she said it, she seemed to sense that this attorney-client relationship had something more to it. But Jack was not yet inclined to elaborate.

"Let me talk to Mr. Salazar and get back to you," said Jack.

"I hate to rush you, but we do need an answer soon. Naturally, time is of the essence."

"I understand."

"We're not trying to make a cop out of you. On the contrary, we want the delivery to be made by someone who has no discernible connection to law enforcement. Mr. Salazar has chosen not to do it personally. His attorney is a credible substitute."

"Was it his idea or yours to bring me into this?"

"His. But I did assure Mr. Salazar that we'll do everything in our power to protect you."

He can only hope it's not enough, thought Jack, the figurative lightbulb glowing ever brighter. "Thanks. I'll let you know as soon as I can."

They exchanged pleasantries as they rose and left the conference room. Agent Henning escorted him toward the end of the hall, where the receptionist was seated in an encased booth of bulletproof glass. Another set of glass doors separated the secured area from the waiting room, offering Jack a clear view of a man seated alone on the couch.

"Right on time," said Andie.

"Excuse me?" said Jack.

"That's Drew Thornton. Ashley Thornton's widower. He comes every Tuesday and Thursday at two o'clock."

The man on the other side of the glass wall couldn't possibly hear their conversation, and he didn't seem to notice Agent Henning standing near the reception booth. Jack asked her, "You two have a standing appointment?"

"No," said Andie. "He just shows up twice a week. Sometimes I have absolutely nothing to tell him, but that doesn't seem to faze him. I guess he thinks that so long as he keeps coming, I won't ever let his wife's case get cold."

Jack's gaze shifted back to Thornton, and he stole a more discerning look. He was perhaps a few years older than Jack, but the worry lines seemed carved in wax. His eyes were devoid of any sense of hope, just dark pools of grief. He was sitting on the edge of the couch, elbows on his knees, chin resting on his tightly laced fingers. It was a pensive pose that seemed to be asking *What if?* What if I'd called the police sooner? What if I'd paid more ransom money? What if I'd taken a little more time to figure out "what she's worth"?

Andie said, "I'm told that Thornton was absolutely devoted to his wife."

"Is that so?" said Jack.

"Met when they were in college. Got married their junior year. This coming June would have been their twentieth anniversary."

It probably wouldn't have happened if his own marriage hadn't tanked, but for a split second Jack almost envied the guy. The pained expression on Thornton's face, however, renewed the surge of pity. "This must have been devastating for him," said Jack.

"It always is. I wish I could tell you that Ashley Thornton was the final victim. I wish I could say that Mia Salazar will mark the end of this serial kidnapper's run. But that doesn't fit with his psychological profile. Our sense is that he's just getting started."

"Unless we stop him."

"Yeah," she said, a hint of a smile coming to the corner of her mouth. "*We*. I like the sound of that."

Jack took another look at Thornton, that tragic face of sorrow and regret. He still questioned Salazar's motives in volunteering "his attorney" for the job, but if the FBI needed a bagman to make its plan work, he had to believe that Agent Henning wouldn't let him do anything too stupid.

"Actually, I think I've had enough time to consider your request."

"You'll be our deliveryman?" said Andie.

"Yeah," he said, watching Thornton through the glass. "I'll do it."

9

Andie Henning and a tech agent planned to spend the entire weekend at the Salazar mansion in Palm Beach. The FBI was expecting a phone call.

No two kidnappings were ever identical, but it was reasonable to anticipate certain parallels between the Salazar case and prior Wrong Number kidnappings. In the Thornton case, the first contact had been by e-mail, much like the e-mail Mr. Salazar received. The kidnapper followed up with a cellular phone call to the Thornton residence less than five days later. If the same pattern held in Mia's kidnapping, Andie wanted to be on location to make the intercept. By early Friday evening, however, she was on her third pot of coffee, and her tech agent was stretched out on the leather sofa, well into his fifth crossword puzzle.

"What's an eight-letter word for a recurrent throbbing headache that starts with *m* and ends with *e?*"

Andie didn't even look up from her magazine. "Marriage?"

It was a little routine they'd developed to kill the boredom, the techie posing questions and Andie feeding him wise-ass responses. "Migraine," he said as he penciled in the correct answer.

Andie tossed her magazine aside, crossed the spacious family room, and stopped at the two-story wall of windows that faced the Intracoastal Waterway. The sun had just set, and the choppy wakes had calmed. A slow parade of boats was returning to the yacht club, and the city lights were aglow to the west. Salazar had made his fortune buying and selling waterfront real estate, and his first acquisition was a choice little peninsula that projected like a golden finger into Biscayne Bay. Having moved from California, he was quick to realize that Miami wasn't like Laguna Beach or other oceanside communities where tier after tier of hillside homes offered ocean views. Florida was as flat as the ocean itself, and only a house that sat directly on the coastline commanded a view of the water. He kept buying through the eighties and nineties, and by his third wife he'd earned enough money to live anywhere in the world.

Mia chose Palm Beach.

"More coffee?" asked Salazar.

Andie turned, a bit startled to see him standing just a few feet away. It wasn't easy to sneak up on an FBI agent, but the view was that captivating. Or perhaps she was just that tired.

"No, thanks," she said. "I've had more than enough caffeine."

Salazar cast his gaze toward a sailboat in the channel. "You still think he's going to call?"

"We'll stay here until he does. As long as you want."

He didn't answer. Dusk was turning into night, and the boats along the Intracoastal were suddenly nothing more than a string of colored running lights. Finally, Salazar asked, "Why do you think Mia's kidnapper sent a copy of the ransom note directly to the FBI?"

"It's an interesting move," said Andie.

He looked at her and said, "That's an interesting answer."

She nodded, as if to acknowledge that she owed him more. "He didn't do that in the Thornton case. We didn't know anything until Mr. Thornton called and showed us the e-mail."

"So why did he do it in my case?"

"Obviously he wants the FBI involved. For some reason, he must have feared that you wouldn't call the police."

"His fears were justified. I wouldn't have called you."

"Why not?"

"I've got my reasons. But it's the other question that intrigues me more: Why does the kidnapper want the FBI involved?"

"This tells us that he wants some level of notoriety. The guy's not a media hound who plays to the newspapers, but he wants to be noticed and respected by law enforcement. And he's probably trying to make a statement of some kind through his ransom demands —kidnapping the wife and then telling the husband to pay what she's worth. At least that's the psychological profile we've constructed so far."

"That scares me," he said.

"That's understandable."

"People with motives other than money always scare me," he said, his expression deadpan.

"It does complicate the equation."

He looked away, staring at nothing. "As if the situation weren't complicated enough already."

She sensed that he was finally ready to open up a little. "Mr. Salazar, is there something you should be telling me?"

He stepped away from the window and turned toward the fireplace. A large painted portrait of Mia hung over the mantel, but he didn't look at it. "The other day you asked about delivering a proof-of-life payment to the kidnapper. You obviously didn't realize it, but I was being somewhat facetious when I told you to call Jack Swyteck."

"He did act rather puzzled when I talked with him. He didn't even seem to know whether he was actually your attorney."

"That's because he's not my attorney."

"What is he then?"

"My wife's lover."

Andie caught her breath. "When you told me Mia was having an affair, I didn't realize it was with Swyteck. Are you sure about this?"

"No question about it."

"That explains a few things. I thought Swyteck was acting strange, but I figured it was because he suspected or maybe even knew about Mia's affair. Never did he let on that it was *him*."

"I don't think it's something he's particularly proud of."

"There's no room for pride here. Your wife has been kidnapped. I need to know everything there is to know. That goes for you as well as him."

"I think that's finally been resolved. Swyteck and I talked after you met with him. We agreed that you should know the whole story, and that I should be the one to tell you."

"That's fine and dandy, Ernesto. But damn it, why are you just now getting around to it?"

"I needed time to think it over."

"Think what over?"

"Whether I still want Swyteck to deliver the proof-of-life payment."

Andie scoffed. "Do you seriously think that's still on the table after telling me that he slept with your wife?"

"It actually makes perfect sense. Swyteck feels like he owes me something, so I'll let him be the delivery boy. If he succeeds, he can have the peace of mind that comes with making amends for his indiscretion. If he fails and ends up on a slab in the morgue—well, it's not like I've lost a friend. It's a classic win-win situation."

"In your mind, perhaps. But from my standpoint, it changes everything."

"I'm not doing your plan any other way."

"What are you saying, it's Swyteck or nobody?"

"Precisely," said Salazar. "I'm certainly not going to put one of my friends in danger."

"We'll use an FBI agent. That's the safest way."

"I thought we already dismissed that idea."

"No question, the kidnapper is more likely to go along with the plan if it's obvious to him that the delivery person is not law enforcement. That's how Swyteck's name came up in the first place. But we have convincing undercover agents."

"I don't want the FBI. Like I said: Swyteck or nobody."

"Then I say nobody. I don't like the personal history here."

"That's really too damn bad," said Salazar, his voice taking on an edge. "I'm in control, not you."

"Excuse me?" she said.

"When that kidnapper calls, I'll be doing the talking. And I'm going to tell him that my attorney, Jack Swyteck, will deliver ten thousand dollars in exchange for some proof that Mia is alive. It can be my ten thousand dollars, and you can stay out of it. Or it can be the FBI's ten grand, and you can have your finger right on the pulse. It's up to you."

Andie studied his expression. Behind the dark, piercing eyes surged a controlled sense of anger—*barely* controlled. "Mr. Salazar, just how disappointed would you be if something did go wrong with Swyteck's delivery?"

"I would never wish any harm on anyone."

Why do I doubt that? thought Andie.

The telephone rang. Immediately, the tech agent sprang from the sofa and checked the monitor in front of him. "Could be him. It's a voice over Internet Protocol."

Andie wasn't expecting that from a conventional phone, but she was conversant enough in techspeak to understand that the digitized signal was being compressed into an IP packet that moved between gateways from the caller's computer to a telephone. "Can you trace it back to him?"

The phone continued to ring as they spoke, a reminder that there was no time to think.

"I'll try," the tech agent said. "But he'll be long gone before we even get beyond the servers." They stood mute through a fourth and fifth ring. "Somebody needs to answer," the tech agent said as he pulled on his headphones.

Salazar shot Andie a look and said, "My rules."

Andie could only watch in silence as he answered on the seventh ring. His clipped "hello" was met by a stretch of dead air that seemed much longer than it actually was. Andie listened through her own set of headphones, waiting. Finally, a response came.

"You alone?" The voice was distorted by a mechanical device. It sounded as if the caller were talking underwater—an eerie coincidence in light of what had happened to Mrs. Thornton.

"Is this who I think it is?" said Salazar.

Another delay, but Andie figured that this one was due to the Internet transmission. "Yeah. Your wife's new best friend. That's what you were thinking, right?"

Salazar paused, seemingly mindful of the key point Andie had repeated over and over again in their hour-long coaching lesson: Don't get agitated; think before you speak. "I was hoping you'd call," said Salazar.

"Hey, I aim to please."

"What do you want?"

Andie grimaced: a little too quick to the bottom line. Her tech agent was communicating by keyboard with the tracers in the field, trying furiously to narrow down the origin of the voice transmission. Andie caught Salazar's eye and made the "stretch" gesture.

"You know what I want," said the caller.

"What she's worth?" said Salazar.

"Not a penny less."

"That's fine," said Salazar. "I have a very exact number in mind."

"Good. Then we can get down to business straightaway."

"Not so fast. I want to know if my wife's still . . . with us."

"All you need to know is that if you don't pay, she's dead."

"We have to do better than that. I want proof that she's alive."

The threesome waited, but the response was slow in coming. The tech agent adjusted his volume control, and for a moment Andie feared that the connection had been lost.

Salazar said, "I'll pay you for it."

"Now you're talking," the caller responded.

"Five thousand dollars," said Salazar.

"Ten."

Salazar paused, as if he had to think about it. "All right. Ten. My attorney will handle the money. His name is Jack Swyteck. S-w-y-t-e-c-k."

Andie wanted to stuff a sock in his mouth. It was so gratuitous, so unnecessary to inject Swyteck's name at this juncture.

"Tell Swyteck he can expect to hear from me."

"When?" asked Salazar.

"When I feel like it. Now, what proof do you want? Pictures?"

"Pictures don't prove anything in a digital world. I want the answer to a question. A question that only Mia would know how to answer."

"Okay, name it."

Andie glanced at the tech agent, who shook his head, as if to say that the FBI's trace effort was going nowhere.

Salazar said, "I want to know . . ."

The pause made Andie nervous. They'd rehearsed this part a dozen times. Mia was a horse lover, and the first one she'd ever owned was a mare named Azúcar. Andie waited for Salazar to ask the question, but it was as if he'd frozen stiff, the way actors sometimes forgot lines they'd uttered a hundred times before.

Andie grabbed a pencil and scribbled a prompt on a yellow Post-it: *Her horse!*

His smugness only confirmed that he hadn't forgotten anything. An almost imperceptible smile creased his lips as he spoke into the phone. "Ask Mia this question: What does a kiss have in common with real estate?"

"What?" the man said.

What? Andie wanted to say. It wasn't even one of the questions they had considered, let alone settled upon.

"That's all I want to know," Salazar told the kidnapper. "What does a kiss have in common with real estate?"

Andie wanted to snatch the phone from him, but what could she tell Mia's kidnapper—that Mr. Salazar couldn't chat any longer because he was a very bad boy who refused to follow the FBI's plan? Her only option was to ride out this stunt and hope for damage control. As she watched Salazar scratch out a message on another Post-it, however, she was beginning to feel a bit like the victim of a hijacking.

MY RULES he wrote in all capital letters, the word *my* underlined three times.

"I'll wait to hear from you," Salazar said into the phone. The kidnapper disconnected, and Salazar laid the receiver in the cradle, seemingly unfazed by the laserlike glares from the FBI.

10

•

Theo scratched his head, pondering his friend's question. "Got it!" said Theo. "They both end up costing a shitload more then you thought they would."

"No, man," said Jack. "It's location, location, location. *Comprende?* That's what kisses have in common with real estate."

They were in Jack's kitchen, and Theo was standing in front of the open refrigerator. He wasn't hungry. It was eighty-eight degrees at 7 p.m., a near record for winter in Miami, and Jack was determined to put off his big air-conditioning repair bill until at least April. Theo rolled a cold can of soda across his sweaty forehead and said, "So it's like you and that fancy-pants attorney, William Bailey, right?"

"Huh?"

"The way you was kissing his hairy ass to get new clients before this thing with Mia blew up in your face."

"I wasn't—"

Theo got down on one knee, puckered up, and made a long, loud kissing noise. "Oh, Mr. Bailey, I just *loves* this location, location, location. Matter of fact, this here be my very *favorite* loca—"

"All right, all right. Knock it off. I wasn't sucking up that much."

Theo arched an eyebrow, no words needed.

"Fine," said Jack. "Maybe I got a little carried away with the thought of finally snagging a client who can actually afford to pay his bill. But that's beside the point."

"What is the point?"

Jack took a seat on the barstool at the kitchen counter. "I talked with Agent Henning today. She and Salazar got a call from Mia's kidnapper last night."

"He tell him to pound sand on the ransom?"

"Not yet. They wanted confirmation that Mia is still alive, so Salazar asked a proof-of-life question."

Theo popped open the soda, chuckling to himself. "What'd he ask? What's real estate and kisses got in common?"

"Yes."

"You shittin' me?"

"Henning says he completely coldcocked her. That wasn't even close to the question they'd agreed upon."

"Course it wasn't. Pretty much sucks as far as proof-of-life questions go. Anyone who knows anything about real estate could probably figure out the answer to the joke, if they thunk about it long enough. It ain't like askin' what's the inscription inside Ernesto's wedding band. Something Mia would know but that a kidnapper could never guess."

"That's the issue," said Jack. "Are we talking about a guy who's just making bad decisions? Or is he deliberately trying to sabotage the whole rescue?"

"What do you think?"

A southeasterly breeze rustled the curtains over the sink. More hot air. "Just for argument's sake, let's give him the benefit of the doubt on the proof-of-life question. You say it's not a very good one, but maybe Ernesto asked it because it was Mia's favorite joke. He made his money in real estate. Probably he's the one who told it to her."

"Or?"

Jack chased his scattered thoughts, trying to organize them into words. "Maybe it was his way of telling Mia that he knows about me and her. That he's known all along."

"How's that?"

"She told that same joke to me."

"When?"

"Just a few hours before I met her husband. That same night, in fact."

"She told you at the snobfest?"

"No. We were here in the house."

"The bedroom?"

"No. Right here in the kitchen."

It was as if an Arctic blast had suddenly cut through the room, displacing the heat. Theo made a slashing gesture across his throat, signaling "cut." He stepped away from the counter and moved to the center of the kitchen. His gaze swept the room like some kind of electronic eavesdropping detector, over cabinets and counters, around the appliances. Not that he had X-ray vision, but the wheels were clearly turning in his head as he tried to figure out where *he* would put a listening device if he were bugging this room. Finally, he zeroed in on the ceiling fan suspended over the island. Jack watched, impressed, as his friend stood on a chair and pointed toward the brass plate that connected the fan to the ceiling. It would have been virtually invisible to anyone not looking for it, but a small black nub was protruding from a screw hole in the brass.

Theo smiled, as if to say *Bingo*. He yanked out the bug and tossed it on the floor, then hopped off the chair and smashed it to bits.

"Adios, Señor Salad Bar."

Jack was about to say *Salazar*, but Theo stopped him. "There could be more," he whispered. "Let's go outside."

Jack followed him to the back patio and closed the California doors behind them. They walked toward the seawall, stopping just short of the fishing boat that Theo docked at Jack's place. Theo said, "See what you get for being too cheap to install AC, leaving your windows open all day long like that? Looks like Ernesto had one of his boys pay you a visit and wire you for sound."

"So, you don't suspect even for a minute that it could be someone else?" said Jack.

"That equipment was standard PI shit sold at any spy shop, easy enough for any schmo to install. Perfect for keeping tabs on a wandering spouse. No way the FBI uses that crap."

"I wasn't thinking FBI. I was wondering more about Mia's kidnapper."

"Has to be Salazar. Can't be a coincidence that his proof-of-life question matches a joke that Mia told you before the two of you hopped into bed."

Jack drew a deep breath and let it out. "The thought of him hearing every sound Mia and I made . . ."

"Sounds that his wife was no longer making in their own bedroom, mind you."

"So she tells me," said Jack.

"That's enough to make a married man extremely angry."

"Angry enough to sabotage the rescue of his wife from a kidnapper? I guess that's the question."

"Puh-lease," said Theo. "How about angry enough to feed her to the fishes and make it all look like a kidnapping?"

"In that case, maybe I was right after all."

"Yup. Maybe the person who bugged your kitchen *is* the kidnapper."

Jack looked toward the bay, considering it. "I think I need to have a talk with Agent Henning."

11

The sweep of Jack's house turned up no new bugs. FBI tech agents searched for transmitting devices with a spectrum analyzer. They looked behind walls and ceiling tiles with a thermal imaging camera. Phone and cable lines were tested with a time-domain reflectometer. They even checked the electrical wiring with a Fluke multimeter. Their assortment of gadgets sounded like a Dr. Seuss catalog, and Jack was beginning to wonder when it would be time for the Whoville rammer-jammer rectal thermometer.

"Who's gonna sweep to see if the FBI planted any bugs of their own?" said Theo, standing in the driveway.

"Don't be so paranoid."

"Don't be so naive," said Theo.

Jack leaned against Theo's car, thinking. Once a criminal defense lawyer, always a criminal defense lawyer. "Know anybody with the right toys?"

"Yup," said Theo.

"Bring him through tonight."

"Will do, boss."

Agent Henning was staying at the Salazar estate in Palm Beach, her center of operation until the kidnapping was solved or until Mr. Salazar kicked her out, whichever came first. By eight thirty she was supposed to head to Jack's place, but he didn't want her to show up in the middle of Theo's reinspection. Distrusting the FBI was one thing, but letting them know the exact level of your distrust was quite another. So Jack offered to save her the drive over to Key Biscayne and meet on the mainland for coffee. They agreed on Perricone's, near the Brickell Avenue financial district.

Perricone's Marketplace and Cafe was a slice of old Miami by way of New England. Like so much of Miami's history, the house that originally sat on the property had been destroyed. In lemons-to-lemonade fashion, a visionary restaurateur bought himself an eighteenth-century barn in Vermont; moved the hand-hewn beams, walls, and floor planks to Miami; and then, piece by piece, rebuilt the homey atmosphere of a long-lost My-amma. The front half was a gourmet market, and out back, overlooking a park, was a screened-in dining area beneath a forest of sprawling oaks. No one would ever guess that a coastline crowded with high-rise condominiums was just a couple of short blocks to the east. Add good food at decent prices, and in Jack's book Perricone's was one of the most welcome Yankee transplants to south Florida since Jackie Gleason.

But the Great One still used better beans to make his coffee.

"Sorry I wasn't able to make it back in time for your house sweep," said Andie.

They were outside at a corner table, alone, as every other patron had opted for inside seating with air-conditioning. "No problem," said Jack. "Getting to Miami can be a bear even on weekends."

"I'm still getting used to that. I've only been here a few months."

"Not like Seattle, is it?"

"Seattle and Miami are actually a lot alike."

"Yeah. Must be the mountains."

"I'm serious. Both are these geographic paradises tucked away in a corner of the lower forty-eight states. Both have their share of ethnic tensions. And they both get way more than their share of lunatics. You think it was pure coincidence that Ted Bundy started in Seattle and ended in Florida?"

"Never thought of it that way," said Jack.

"See, you learned something."

She had a nice smile, and she seemed more relaxed than the last time they'd met. She was dressed more stylishly, too. Perhaps it was the Palm Beach influence. In any event, Jack was getting a fuller appreciation of the initial report from his old boss that Henning was a "real looker." The raven black hair and amazing green eyes made for a striking, exotic beauty.

"So, Jack, what did you want to talk to me—"

"So, what brought you to Mi—"

They were talking on top of each other, and they both stopped in midsentence. Hers was clearly a business question. Jack's wasn't, which embarrassed him a little. *This isn't a date, Swyteck.*

The waiter brought them two lattes, then disappeared. Andie waited for him to leave, then asked, "You really want to know why I came to Miami?"

"I wasn't trying to be nosy or anything."

"It's fine. Basically, I needed a change."

"Good career move, I imagine."

"Not really. I was doing fine in Seattle. The ASAC was my former supervisory agent, and we had a great relationship."

"Just wanted something different?"

"It's hard to explain. Most people can't relate."

"To someone with a job like yours, you mean?"

"No. To a half-Indian girl who was adopted and raised by white parents. Don't get me wrong. My parents are great people, and I'm not some head case walking around with a chip on her shoulder. I just felt like it was time to move on, that I should find a place where I didn't even have to think about fitting into one culture or the other."

"You can't be the only person in Seattle with a mixed background."

"No, but I figure, why put up with the bullshit? I remember once at U-dub—University of Washington—I went to this powwow on campus. Talk about awkward. The women all looked at my green eyes and treated me like just another horny white chick looking for her big brown Indian stud."

"Interesting."

"Of course, they were basically right. But it still bothered me that they thought it."

Jack's mouth opened, but he didn't say anything.

"Are you blushing?" she said, seeming to enjoy the fact that she'd knocked him slightly speechless.

Jack shrugged it off and smiled, but he was thinking about the Cuban mother he'd never known, the half-Cuban boy who didn't eat a plantain until his sophomore year in college. They were talking about Andie, however, and he didn't want to one-up her with his story of a twenty-three-year-old mother who died in childbirth and an alcoholic stepmom who destroyed all the letters that his *abuela* mailed from Cuba. "I can probably relate to your situation more than you'd imagine," he said, leaving it at that.

The waiter checked on them again and then retreated inside. Andie stirred another packet of sweetener into her cup. The conversation turned to business, and Jack gave her the whole story without interruption, including Theo's theory that Salazar might have killed his wife and staged the kidnapping.

Andie gave it some thought, then shook her head. "It's a stretch."

"Why do you say that?"

"Like I told you from the start, the exact wording of the kidnapper's demand has never been made public. It's this kidnapper's signature—'pay what she's worth'—and we didn't want a flood of copycats using it. For Salazar to be able to fake a kidnapping and use that exact same language in a ransom note would mean that he somehow had access to police details of the previous ransom demands."

"Hey, imagine that. A leak in law enforcement."

She nodded and gave a little smile. "I hear you. I just don't think so in this case."

"Is Mia's kidnapping really that similar to the Thornton case?"

"I can't share everything with you. But there are some important differences. Here, the ransom demand went to Mr. Salazar and to the FBI. Last time, it went only to Mr. Thornton. The use of the Internet phone to avoid tracing didn't happen in the Thornton case."

"None of these differences raise red flags for you?"

"There are too many other important similarities."

"So you think it's purely a coincidence that the husband finds out his wife is cheating and then she disappears?"

"No more of a coincidence than if her lover suddenly finds out she's married and then she disappears."

Jack coughed on his latte foam. "Wait a minute. Am I on some kind of list that I should know about?"

"Let me put it this way. You're pretty much on the same list Mr. Salazar is on."

"I'm not sure how to take that."

"I'm not saying you're a suspect. I'm not barking up your tree or Salazar's, but we haven't ruled anything out completely."

"Fair enough," said Jack, though he knew the reality. Whether the cops admitted it or not, everyone was a suspect until they were ruled out. Especially the two male corners of a love triangle.

Andie set her empty coffee cup aside, seeming to shift gears slightly. "I'm not just asking this out of idle curiosity, but I would like to know. How did you feel about Mia?"

"You mean before or after I found out that she was married?"

"Let's start with before."

"I thought we were close."

"Were you in love with her?"

"Maybe. I was definitely more excited about her than anyone else I've dated since my divorce."

"How do you feel about her now?"

"How do you think I feel?"

"If the kidnapper sent you the same note—pay what she's worth— would you do the same thing Mr. Salazar is doing?"

"Not at all."

"You'd pay a ransom?"

"I didn't say that. Salazar is playing a very dangerous game. It's his prerogative to decide whether he wants to pay. But he shouldn't be toying with the kidnapper in a way that could get Mia killed."

"Now you understand my frustration," said Andie. "The FBI can only advise in these situations. It's like when the cops say don't pay a ransom, and the family does it anyway. We can't force Salazar to conduct his negotiations any certain way."

"Yeah, but at some point the FBI has to step up and say, hey, bucko, you're being a jerk, and we're not gonna let the victim be the one who suffers."

"True. And that's why you should stay involved."

"What do you mean?"

"I think you still care about Mia. And I think Salazar knows that you still care about her."

"Then you're both wrong."

"Hey, I'm a cop, but I'm still a woman. You can't fool me or yourself about these things. The feelings we have for other people are rarely rational."

Jack averted his eyes. "What does this have to do with anything?"

"I want you to deliver the proof-of-life payment."

"You do?"

"I'll admit, I was dead set against it when I first found out about you and Mia. But Salazar made it clear that he's not going to let me use an undercover FBI agent. So if you don't do it, I'm afraid he'll try and do it himself. Or worse, maybe even send one of his boys to screw things up."

"Maybe the same guy who bugged my kitchen."

"Exactly. The more aspects of this negotiation and delivery that I can take out of Salazar's hands, the better it'll be for everyone. Especially Mia."

Jack finished his coffee, thinking. "Last week, when I saw Mr. Thornton sitting in your lobby all broken up over his dead wife, I was all for helping out any way I could. But Salazar's proof-of-life question changes things. At best, he's being cute. At worst, he's trying to get somebody hurt. I'm just not sure."

"I understand. Either way, I need Salazar out of the way. I wouldn't ask just anyone. But as a former prosecutor, you must have some bone in your body that still wants to help catch bad guys."

"Yeah, I suppose. Counterbalanced, of course, by a healthy survival instinct. When do I have to decide?"

"The kidnapper said he'd follow up with instructions. Could be any day. Could be any minute."

Jack's fingers drummed across the tabletop, but the answer wasn't coming any faster. He looked at Andie and said, "I'll sleep on it," knowing that sleep was not in the cards that night.

12

•

Jack left Perricone's and had clear sailing till the traffic light changed at Miami Avenue. To his left was the official welcome to Key Biscayne, a big marquee with a life-size plastic dolphin. It was once a shark, not so many years ago. Jack imagined it dressed in pinstripes and asking *Have you been injured?*—a fitting tribute to the many wealthy lawyers who called the island home.

He sometimes wondered how his life would have changed had he put his trial skills toward plaintiff's personal injury work. It could have been the end of his money troubles. Your vintage Mustang convertible goes up in flames? No problem. Buy two more. Your marriage crashes and burns? Not to worry. Nothing that a thousand-dollar-an-hour divorce lawyer can't handle. But it just wasn't his style to juggle countless slip-and-fall cases while fervently hoping for a grieving mother to come through the door with a quadriplegic toddler who had been pushed into the street by Donald Trump, run over by a speeding FedEx truck, and then diagnosed with the flu by a drunken ER physician. Then again, trying to snag referrals from a guy like William Bailey wasn't really Jack's style either. If there was a silver lining to the Mia disaster, it was the quick death it had delivered to his idiotic pursuit of the golden handcuffs—or as Theo had put it, yanking up the FYN.

Stopped at the red light, he dialed Theo from his cell. "Your friend still there?" said Jack.

"What?" Theo shouted.

"Is your electronics guy still at my house checking for bugs?"

Jack heard music and laughter in the background. Theo said, "Oh yeah, he's still here. Brought a few of his friends over, too. Jack Daniel, Mr. Bacardi . . ."

Great, thought Jack.

He overheard Theo say something like "Come on, baby, I'm talking on the phone here." Jack didn't even bother asking. He just said good-bye and disconnected. The traffic light changed, but he didn't make his turn. Instead, he cut across three lanes to the I-95 North on-ramp, and he didn't plan on stopping until he reached Palm Beach.

It was time to pay a visit to Mia's best friend.

Jack had never met Emilia Varnal, but he had her cell number. Whenever Mia had to cut a date short or cancel plans unexpectedly, her usual excuse was that she was helping her friend Emilia through a postdivorce funk. On more than one occasion she'd actually called on Emilia's cell phone to tell Jack how much she missed him. In hindsight, Jack realized that it wasn't because she'd forgotten her own phone or because her battery was dead. She was simply minimizing the number of calls to him from her own number, avoiding a paper trail that her husband might uncover.

Jack dialed Emilia's number and caught her at what sounded like a crowded cocktail party. It wasn't an ideal time for her to talk, but Jack persisted. "I need to speak with you," he said. "It's about the kidnapping. It's urgent."

That seemed to change her tune. "I'm at the Breakers Hotel," she said. "I can slip away to meet you for a few minutes in the lobby."

"I'll see you there at nine," said Jack.

The Breakers Hotel was a Palm Beach landmark, a well-restored architectural gem that smacked of history, opulence, and (hey, it *was* Palm Beach) attitude. Its impressive towers, ornamental stonework, and iron balconies were inspired by the Villa Medici in Rome, and the grand entrance evoked the style of the Italian Renaissance. A string of black limousines was in front by the valet stand. Jack self-parked and entered the lobby behind a group of socialites who looked as though they'd just cleaned out the Chanel Shop on Worth Avenue. He was starting to feel like the proverbial brown pair of loafers in a black-tie world, his blue jeans and T-shirt having barely met the dress code at Perricone's for his meeting with Andie Henning. Casual could be chic, he kept telling himself, but for some reason the theme song from *The Beverly Hillbillies* was playing in his mind as he crossed the lobby.

"Jack?" he heard a woman say.

He turned and knew immediately that it was Emilia. She looked as he'd imagined her. Though not as pretty as Mia, she had a certain refinement about her. The emerald-and-diamond necklace around her neck seemed to suggest that she'd made out well in the divorce.

They took a seat on a Louis XVI–style couch near the fireplace, away from the crowd. Emilia was on the edge of her seat, not because she was hanging on Jack's every word, but because she seemed in need of another week or so on phase one of the South Beach Diet to squeeze into the black satin dress she was wearing. They exchanged pleasantries—how it was nice to finally meet, too bad about the circumstances—and then Jack turned the conversation to Mia.

"The FBI wants me to help with the kidnapping," he said. "I can't get into the details. But it's important, and I have to make a decision about what I'm going to do."

"So you called me?"

"Yeah," he said, struggling with how best to put it. "I don't know if it makes a difference or not. I just felt this sudden need to know . . ." He offered a look that made it completely unnecessary to say more.

"Mia was in love with you," she said, her tone soft and sincere. "You do know that, don't you?"

"All I know is that she lied to me."

She set her half-empty champagne flute on the marble-topped end table. "You have to understand Mia's side of it. If she told you she was married, there was a chance that you might get angry or spiteful, run straight to her husband, and tell him everything. You might even have blackmailed her, for all she knew. I warned her that a married woman should never sleep with an unmarried man. You have to make sure that the other person has as much to lose as you do."

"Interesting theory."

"I read it in *Cosmo*."

"I must have missed that issue."

It took a moment, but she seemed to catch on that he was being facetious. "Never mind that," she said. "All rules and every bit of logic went straight out the window when she met you. This wasn't a fling. From the very start, she was pretty much head over heels. Don't get me wrong. It isn't like you stole her from Ernesto. She stopped loving him a long time ago."

"If that's the case, she should have divorced him and *then* gone looking."

"It's not that easy for her."

"It's never easy for anybody."

"No, you don't understand the relationship."

"You're right. I don't. Why don't you help me out there?"

She glanced down the hall, toward the noisy cocktail party in the ballroom, as if debating whether she had time to explain. "The simple truth is she couldn't leave Ernesto."

"No. That's not the way it works. If she didn't leave him, it's because she wouldn't, not couldn't."

She shook her head. "Where'd you learn that, law school? Domestic Relations one-oh-one? Try living in the real world."

His gaze swept the lobby. "Mia was living in Palm Beach. It's hardly the real world."

"You think there are no women in Palm Beach who live in fear?"

"Fear of what? Coming out on the short end of divorce from an insanely rich husband?"

Her expression soured. "Look, you're obviously angry, and I don't really blame you. But do you want to know the truth about Mia or don't you?"

Jack breathed in and out. Sarcasm was never the high road, and he was embarrassed that he'd resorted to it. "Sorry. Please, go ahead."

"No question, when you look at Mia and then look at Ernesto, the first thought that pops into anyone's brain is that she married him for his money. People always talked behind her back, assumed she was doing the pool guy, the tennis pro. But I'm her best friend, and I can tell you this: You were the first."

"That doesn't make it right. She was still married."

"Oh, please. Ernesto was the one who played around. He even hit on me once."

"I hate to sound like a broken record, but why did she stay married to him?"

"I asked her the same question, many times."

"What did she say?"

"*Seguridad.* That's Spanish for—"

"Security. I know. I'm half Cuban."

"You are? I never knew—"

"It's okay, no one ever guesses, especially from my Spanish. But let's keep this about Mia and her *seguridad.* Financial security, I assume she meant?"

"That's what I thought. Till one night, we had a few drinks. I got her to talk more about it, and she started to explain. Turns out she and Ernesto didn't even have a prenup. She could have cleaned up in a divorce."

"What does that tell you?"

She leaned closer, her voice softening. "Staying with him wasn't about financial *seguridad.* It was more security in the sense of . . . *protección.*"

"Protection? From what?"

"She wouldn't say. Like I told you, we were drinking, and it was just a momentary slip that had her talking about something she clearly didn't want to discuss—not even with me. But I got the distinct impression that so long as she was married to Ernesto, she would be safe."

"Was she afraid of something in particular?"

"She didn't get into that. It was more the way she talked about Ernesto, how he's from a very powerful family. Odds are you'd know his name if you were Venezuelan, and if you're at all involved in the Latin community, you'd surely think twice about messing with him. She never told me this in so many words, but if you ask me, that's why she married him."

"That's the *protección*? She married a man who is feared by certain people?"

She nodded.

Jack looked away, considering what she'd told him.

Her date suddenly came around the corner and entered their sitting area. "Emilia, I hate to interrupt, but dinner's being served."

"I just need another minute. I'll be right there. Promise."

He looked confused for a moment and then walked away. Emilia said, "My first real date since the divorce. Guess I'd better get back."

As they rose, she took his hand. It wasn't anything untoward, but it was definitely more than a simple handshake. "Corny as it sounds, Mia met Mr. Right at the wrong time. She never should have lied, and I'm sure she regrets it. I'm not asking you to take her back. But if you're in a position to help her, please—*please* do it."

He didn't want to promise anything. "I'll have to think—"

She squeezed his hand tighter, stopping him in midsentence. "Let me just finish this conversation the way I started: Mia really did love you. Remember that."

Jack wasn't sure how to respond.

She offered a hint of a smile, as if to thank him in advance for helping her friend. Then she turned and headed back to the ball. Jack watched without really watching. He knew it hadn't been her intention, but he was certain of one thing.

He was more confused now than before he'd spoken with Emilia.

13

•

Jack didn't leave the Breakers right away. He walked through the loggia to the back of the hotel, past the swimming pool and beyond the manicured croquet lawns. He stopped at the top of the wooden staircase that led down from the bluff to the beach. Since childhood he'd been drawn to the soothing sound and smell of the ocean.

She loved me. Or so Mia's best friend said. What difference could that possibly make now? Even if she hadn't been kidnapped, Mia still had a husband. Whom she didn't love. Whom, for some reason, she didn't have the courage to leave. Maybe that was because she hadn't met the right . . .

No. No way was he going to let himself think that way. However this kidnapping resolved itself, he didn't need her. But he didn't hate her, either. There was anger, yes, but not that sickening sense of precious time wasted that was his failed marriage. Perhaps it was because he had suspected all along that Mia wasn't telling him everything about herself. Not that she was married, of course. Jack would never have let himself get caught up in that. But she did seem to have a secret buried somewhere in her past. Hearing her best friend say that Mia was afraid to leave her husband, that she had married him for *protección*, only heightened those suspicions. It made him think back to something they'd discussed only once—the first time they'd slept together.

* * *

"Today's my birthday," Mia said as Jack turned the key and opened the front door to his house.

Jack didn't even try to hide his surprise and disappointment. They'd had a nice time at dinner, but it was hardly special enough for a birthday. "Why didn't you tell me?"

"The big three-oh. Time to stop celebrating."

"That's crazy." He pulled the door shut and said, "Come on. Let's go out and do your birthday right."

"Why don't we go *inside* and do it right?"

The tingle of her kiss suddenly coursed through his body. "That's . . . an incredibly good idea," he said as he pushed the door open. She took his hand and led him inside, then kissed him again. "Let me freshen up."

"I'll get some wine," he said.

"Great idea."

She smiled and looked amazing, and Jack prayed to God that he wasn't sporting his *Yippee-I'm-going-to-have-sex!* grin.

He went to the kitchen to retrieve his best bottle of white, having put it in the refrigerator two weeks earlier in anticipation of a night like this with Mia. He felt mildly proud of himself—quite the clever planner—as he pulled a perfectly chilled bottle of Chardonnay from the refrigerator. But it was completely empty. Someone had jammed the cork back into the neck to disguise the theft.

Damn it, Theo!

He quickly found another bottle in the pantry, but it was as warm as the night air. He scrambled back to the kitchen, threw open the freezer door, and yanked out the ice bin. It caught on a two-year-old frozen pot roast, and ice cubes fell to the floor like a Texas hailstorm. He got down on his knees and started gathering them up. One at a time, two at a time, and finally handfuls of cubes were flying across the kitchen and landing in the sink.

"I'm waaaaiting," he heard Mia say. "I'm not getting any youngerrrrr."

The voice came from the bedroom. Jack was desperate to make this evening perfect, and the wine was going to be the right temperature if it killed him. There was no time to put it on ice, and the thought of serving a bottle of Kistler with an ice cube in the glass was too much to bear. He would have to *apply* ice. He grabbed three cubes in one hand and the bottle in the other. Standing over the sink, he started rubbing the outside of the bottle, top to bottom, hoping to transfer the cold. He stopped to feel the glass. Definitely colder. It seemed to be working. He grabbed more ice and continued rubbing, up and down, harder and harder, fast and furious, his breathing audible, his hand a blur as he found his rhythm and rubbed, rubbed, rubbed.

"*That* is the most bizarre foreplay I've ever seen in my life," said Mia.

Jack froze. She was standing at the kitchen's entrance, dressed in a black teddy that she'd obviously stashed somewhere in his bedroom in anticipation of the big night. Jack saw the curious expression on her face, and for a brief moment he seemed to step out of his own body and take a good look at himself—a maniac stroking a glass phallus to the point of exhaustion.

"Wine?" he said.

She just smiled and said, "Come to bed."

He left the wine in the sink and followed her to the bedroom. Music was already playing. She'd figured out how to operate his old stereo and found something by Carlos Santana. She dimmed the lights, then turned and kissed him with an open mouth. It was long and passionate, and it was as if all the stress were being sucked from his body. She removed his shirt, and the palms of her hands glided slowly across his chest and stomach. Another kiss, and his pants were suddenly on the floor. She was sitting on the bed now, and he was still standing as he felt the side of her face brush against the bulge in his underwear. He smiled and gently pushed her back onto the bed.

"No rush," he said.

He helped her off with the lingerie, and the sight of this gorgeous woman perched on his bed and wearing only black lace panties seemed like far more than he deserved. With just the tip of his finger he pressed against her bare shoulder until she was flat on her back. Her knees went up, and she took his hand, pulling him toward her. He went with the motion, and she wrapped her legs around his waist. He could have fallen inside her right then and there, but he resisted. He suspended himself over her, almost in push-up position, wanted to make this last. He kissed her on the lips, then on the neck.

"Happy birthday," he whispered, and he started working his way down. He glided over her breasts, touching lightly with his chin, his cheeks, his nose. Her stomach tightened with anticipation as he planted kisses around her navel. Her lace panties did little to cover the vaginal mound, and it was torture to wait, but Jack forced himself past it. He slid much lower, his head between her knees, now working from the other direction as he kissed the inside of her thighs.

"I'm not sure this is a good way to start," she said.

"Trust me. This is an excellent start."

"I'm just . . . not sure."

"Relax. Just relax."

He felt her body stretch, and he glanced up to see her reaching toward the lamp.

"It'll be better in the dark," she said as the light went out.

He didn't completely agree, but he wasn't going to argue. The journey continued, Jack alternating kisses between the left thigh and the right, slowly working his way to her warmth. Halfway down, he started using the tip of his tongue. The skin was so soft, so smooth. Her legs should have been parting with invitation, but she was gradually drawing them closer together. And then he felt it—the end of the smoothness. He couldn't see in the darkness, but he detected it with his tongue. It was on her left inner thigh, just inches away from her vagina. Scar tissue.

Serious scar tissue.

He tried to show no reaction, but that was impossible. It was pointless, too, since she had reacted strongly enough for both of them.

"I had a tattoo removed," she said.

Jack didn't say anything. He just lay there in the dark, his head between her legs. If this was a tattoo removal, the doctor should have been sued for malpractice. He knew she was lying.

Her body grew more tense with each passing moment. Jack wasn't sure if he should continue, but she answered the question for him. She gently took his chin and guided him up. He noticed the goose bumps on her belly as he slid across her and came to rest at her side. He lay perfectly still, and so did she. The music continued to play, and neither one of them said a word. Finally, Jack brushed the side of her face with his hand and said, "Is there something you want to talk about?"

She just shook her head.

"Are you sure?"

"Just hold me," she said, her voice breaking in the darkness. "Please. Just hold me."

The ringing cell phone ripped through Jack's memories. The wireless intrusion seemed so at odds with the tranquillity of the beach, but he succumbed to technology and checked the display. The call was identified as "Out of Area," which wasn't all that out of the ordinary, but given the circumstances, any mystery caller brought an instant rush of adrenaline. He opened the flip phone and answered with a simple "Hello."

"Your wait is over, Swyteck." The voice on the other end of the line sounded mechanical, clearly disguised.

"Who is this?"

"Osama bin Laden. Who do you *think* it is?"

Jack's question had been more of a knee-jerk reaction, something to put the ball back in the caller's court. "What do you want?"

"Salazar says it's in his attorney's hands. So we're dealing direct."

All the debate as to whether Jack should get involved in the delivery was over. He was on the line with the man who had viciously murdered Mrs. Thornton and who might do the same to Mia. Somehow, with everything suddenly on the line, the words *Sorry, she lied to me, so she's on her own* didn't exactly roll off his tongue. "I'm listening."

"One day this coming week, you'll receive an e-mail sometime before nine a.m. Open it. Your instructions will be inside. Follow them to the letter. As soon as the cash is delivered, you'll get the answer to Mr. Salazar's question."

"I can do that."

"One other thing. No FBI, no cops, no private detectives lurking in the background. Whenever more than two people get involved in an exchange, things go wrong. People get hurt. You understand what I'm saying?"

"Yes."

"Be sure you do. This exchange is between the two of us alone. You break the rules, and the one who pays is the one you care for more than anything."

The caller disconnected before he could answer, but Jack had no coherent response anyway. Whether he still "cared for" Mia wasn't the issue. A slightly different question was stuck in Jack's mind: Even if he did still care, how did the kidnapper know it?

And what made him think Jack cared "more than anything"?

Jack faced the ocean to gather his thoughts, the moonlight glistening on the gently rolling waves. He took only a moment, then flipped open his cell phone and dialed Andie Henning.

14

•

The e-mail hit on Monday at 8 a.m., sooner than he'd expected. "Go downtown to the corner of Miami Avenue and Flagler," it said. "Find the bench across from the drugstore. Sit as far to the north end as you can. Then wait."

Jack immediately called Andie Henning with the message. Although the kidnapper had warned him not to call the cops, Jack was taking no chances, especially with such curious instructions: "Sit as far to the north end as you can." What was the guy trying to do, line him up for the perfect sniper shot? Jack was glad he'd called in the FBI, if only because he was equipped with a Windbreaker that was actually lined with Kevlar—not to mention a briefcase filled with ten thousand dollars in marked bills, compliments of the U.S. Treasury Department.

Jack was out the door in less than ten minutes, but with the morning traffic, it was almost nine o'clock by the time he parked his car in a downtown lot and walked to the designated intersection. He found the right bench and took a seat on the north end closest to Flagler Street, as instructed. Then he waited. And waited.

There were certainly worse places to while away the morning, but even in downtown Miami, people-watching inevitably turned boring. The old man selling bags of key limes to passing motorists was entertaining for a while, the way the same bag went for a buck to a Chevy, five bucks to a Volvo. At the corner espresso bar, a group of old Cuban men were in the thick of their unending debate over Cuba without Castro. Across the street, a film crew spent a good two hours shooting a commercial with a Latina model, patiently waiting for the perfect gust of wind to send her red dress flying in Marilyn Monroe fashion. Apparently, research had shown that a twenty-year-old goddess with no tan lines was the trick to selling car insurance.

The film crew left around eleven o'clock, and from then on it was just Jack, the key lime salesman, and the usual flow of morning traffic. Music was coming from the nearby electronics store, which evidently owned just one CD. The same old salsa blaring over the speakers, over and over, was getting annoying. By twenty minutes past noon, he was almost happy to see the homeless guy take a seat on the other end of his bench.

The man just sat there, seeming not to notice Jack. He reeked of vomit and urine. His tattered and faded old army jacket was far too warm for the midday sun, but it looked and smelled as though he hadn't removed it since the big south Florida freeze of 1989. His left pant leg was smeared with what could only have been dried feces. Jack's olfactory senses could adjust to nearly anything—his best friend was Theo Knight—but in this case it might take hours instead of minutes. The man started mumbling to himself, then finally managed to put together an audible sentence.

"The son has cursed the father," he said in a matter-of-fact voice.

Jack made a conscious decision not to acknowledge him.

"Hey, did you hear what I said?" the man asked.

Jack glanced over, but the man was speaking to the purely imaginary figure before him, his tone turning harsh. "Listen to me! I said, the son has cursed the father!"

He was bobbing his head like a plastic toy dog in the rear window of a car. His hands began to shake uncontrollably. The man was obviously angry, but the quivering seemed more like signs of withdrawal from a drug addiction. His face reddened, as if someone had insulted him. He sprang to his feet and pointed an accusatory finger at no visible being, shouting, "Yeah, fuck you, too, buddy!"

The lunch crowd was streaming down the sidewalk, mostly businesspeople who passed without a word, ignoring him. The man cast a suspicious eye toward all the suits, but eventually his shoulders slumped, and more mumbling poured from his lips. He stayed put, however, his feet planted on the sidewalk. Finally, he faced Jack squarely and said, "Hey, move."

Jack looked at him out of the corner of his eye. This time, it appeared that he was indeed speaking to him.

"Move it," the man said. "I gotta take a piss."

"This isn't a bathroom."

"I don't give a crap about no bathroom. Some guy gave me fifty bucks to piss right where you're sitting, so move or I'm gonna piss all over you."

What? Jack started to say, but the answer was obvious before he could even ask the question: The homeless guy was a messenger. Jack opened his wallet and said, "I'll give you a hundred bucks to describe the person who hired you."

He grabbed the bill. "White guy. That's about all I can tell you."

"Where did you meet him?"

"Cardboard city under the I-ninety-five ramp."

"When did he hire you?"

"Last night around midnight. It was dark, man. Didn't get a good look. He just says come here at noon and piss on the bench right where the guy is sitting." The man started to squirm, and he suddenly sounded as if he were in pain. "That's all I know, man. Now move so I can piss. I got twelve cans of beer in me."

Jack rose and stepped aside. The man hurried over, unzipped, and then urinated exactly where Jack had been seated. A few passersby glanced over in disgust, but the crowd kept moving. Jack didn't want to stare, but he realized that it probably was no accident that the kidnapper had given him such explicit instructions on where to sit—and equally explicit instructions to the homeless guy on where to relieve himself.

As he finished his business, the homeless man snorted and said, "What the hell?"

Jack glanced at the bench. Something strange was happening. The urine had brought up colored lettering, like those litmus papers in science class that turned blue or green, depending on whether the liquid was alkaline or acid.

The message read, I'M PISSED.

A half block north on Miami Avenue, Andie Henning stepped away from the espresso bar and merged into the flow of pedestrian traffic. She spoke into the microphone clipped to her collar, appearing no different from at least a dozen other businesswomen who were talking on their hands-free cell phones while walking to their office. Except that Andie was connected to her surveillance team in the field.

"What's he doing now?" asked Andie.

"Homeless guy just took a piss," came the response.

"What?"

"No kidding. Swyteck gave him some money, and the guy took a piss right where he was sitting."

"You're saying that Swyteck *paid* the guy to urinate?"

"That's what it looks like. Hell, give a guy a briefcase full of money, you never know what he's gonna do."

Andie stopped at the crosswalk. She couldn't imagine why Jack would pay a homeless person to urinate on the bench. They'd decided against fitting up Jack with a wire for fear that the kidnapper might have some electronic equipment in place to detect it. In light of this, however, Andie wished they hadn't been so cautious.

"What's happening now?" she asked.

"Believe it or not, it just keeps getting weirder. Either Swyteck has an unhealthy fascination with human waste, or there's something else of interest on that bench."

"Can somebody zoom in for a look?"

"I can't but . . . Wait. Rooftop post says he sees something. Some kind of lettering, like a message."

Still bizarre, thought Andie. But it was starting to make sense. "Sounds like our homeless guy is some kind of messenger."

"Yeah. Total loser, from the looks of him. I'd say he was picked at random."

"Follow him after he leaves. Let's pick him up for questioning. Indecent exposure."

"Not sure that's a federal crime."

"Make it one," she said.

"Roger."

Jack was still staring at the message on the bench, waiting for something more to appear. But those two simple words seemed to be the full extent of the message: I'M PISSED.

The homeless guy pulled up his zipper. "For another fifty bucks, I'll shit on your shoes."

"No, thanks anyway, pal. But don't go anywhere for a minute."

"You telling me what to do, asshole?"

"Just stay put."

The man's eyes narrowed, and after about ten seconds he seemed on the verge of an explosion. He raised his arms to the sky, as if he were about to proclaim something of biblical importance, then shouted, "The son has *cursed*—"

"Yeah, yeah," said Jack. "Heard you loud and clear the first time, chief."

"Are you Jack Swyteck?" another man asked. He was a short Latin guy with a completely gray mustache that belied his jet-black toupee. He was standing on the sidewalk in front of the electronics store, a cordless telephone in hand.

"Who wants to know?" asked Jack.

"Didn't give a name. Just said he wanted to talk to the guy outside the store named Jack Swyteck."

Smart move, Jack thought. No way law enforcement could have

been prepared to trace a call coming into a randomly selected business establishment. "Yeah, thanks, I'm Swyteck," he said as he reached for the phone.

The guy pulled back. "Not so fast. Your friend said you'd give me fifty bucks if I let you use my phone."

Jack reached into his wallet and gave him three twenties. The store owner didn't offer any change. Jack took the phone. "Swyteck here."

"I'm still pissed," the caller said. It was that same mechanical-sounding voice of Mia's kidnapper.

"What are you talking about?"

"You'd think that if the FBI was going to watch, they'd at least have the brains to rotate out the agents every hour or so, or at least change clothes. Four hours is a long time for a hot-dog vendor to work straight through, never going for a cup of coffee, never going to the bathroom, never budging from the hot-dog cart. He's got FBI written all over him."

Jack glanced at the cart on the corner. He hadn't realized that it was manned by an undercover FBI agent, but obviously the kidnapper had a sharp eye. Jack didn't see any upside to arguing the point, so he launched into the backup plan he and Andie had worked out in advance. "Look, I never called the FBI. I did exactly what you said: no cops. If they're here, it's because they're following me. Not because I called them."

"Or because your client called them."

Jack had to think for a second or two, then realized that by "your client" the caller meant Salazar. "No, Ernesto wouldn't do that."

"Yeah, sure."

"Look, I don't know how this happened, but I'm sorry."

"Sorry doesn't solve it, does it? The FBI is still here. So that leaves just one thing to do."

"Please, don't take it out on Mia."

"We gotta lose 'em, Swyteck."

Jack felt a slight sense of relief. "Whatever you say."

"Here's the drill. Turn around and go two blocks to the Miami-Dade County Courthouse. Enter the building through the south entrance.

Go straight through the lobby and come out the north exit. Go down the north steps, and there's a vending machine for the *Miami Tribune* on the corner. Put in your quarter and reach inside. Go all the way to the bottom of the stack. The message is in an envelope underneath the last newspaper. You got it?"

"Yeah."

"Now go! Don't run, but you'd better walk fast. I could change my mind about all this."

Andie was coming up on Miami Avenue when she spotted Jack across the street. He was walking at a brisk pace, headed away from his original location. "He's on the move," she said into her microphone.

"We got it," the rooftop post responded.

"I'm in pursuit," said Andie.

The lunchtime crowd was at its peak, making it difficult to travel in a straight line. With vendors hustling everything from jewelry to sugarcane, from ferrets to sunglasses, the sidewalks along Flagler Street could feel like a Union Square flea market, but with a Latin beat. Andie wove her way through pedestrians, around street musicians, over a homeless guy who obviously had no trouble sleeping through all the commotion.

"Can't see him," said Andie, working her way up a crowded sidewalk. "Where's he now?"

"Crossing to the north side of Flagler Street. Looks like he may be headed for the courthouse."

Andie's pace quickened. "That's not good. If he goes inside and gets stopped by security, it's sure going to look as though Jack called in law enforcement—which is exactly what the kidnapper told him *not* to do."

"They don't routinely open briefcases. The money inside should just show up on X-ray as a bunch of typical lawyer papers."

"Yeah, but they'll detect the Kevlar lining for sure. Possibly the GPS."

They had decided against the wire, but at a minimum, it had seemed prudent to equip the jacket with a tiny Global Positioning System tracking chip that would allow the FBI to monitor his movements wherever he went.

"Not much we can do about that."

Andie kept walking. "Crenshaw, you're nearest the courthouse. Go inside, flash your badge, flex your muscle—do whatever you gotta do to make them turn off their machines and let Swyteck pass."

"Let's not overreact," said Crenshaw. "So what if the security guards get all excited about Swyteck's Kevlar Windbreaker or GPS locator? That doesn't necessarily send a message to the kidnapper that he called the FBI."

"You want to explain that one to a sociopath? We have to assume he's watching Swyteck at all times. Come on, Pete. I need you on this. Get moving."

15

•

Once the tallest building south of the Washington Monument, the eighty-year-old courthouse was quite possibly the only architectural gem in Miami that would have looked just fine in the nation's capital. It was a quintessential government building, an imposing limestone skyscraper with massive fluted columns and Doric capitals, signatures of the neoclassic revival design. Visitors had to climb not one but two long tiers of gray granite steps made smooth by decades of foot traffic. Jack gobbled up the first tier quickly, then slowed about halfway up the second—and not because he was tired.

On the other side of the glass entrance doors was a team of security guards with metal detectors. His Kevlar vest was certain to raise some eyebrows, to say nothing of his GPS locator. And if they opened the briefcase . . . well, it wasn't illegal to carry that much cash, but it wouldn't exactly lower the guards' antennae. He didn't have much choice, however. The caller had told him to enter through the south side and exit through the north. Turning away would only fuel the kidnapper's paranoia. Jack's only hope was that the FBI was on top of things and that he could pass through smoothly.

A steady stream of visitors, employees, and lawyers dressed in suits entered through the center revolving glass door. Jack jumped behind a team of reporters from a local news station, figuring that the courthouse guards might be too preoccupied with the cameras and other gear to notice him. The layout was no different from airport security, an X-ray machine to one side and the metal detector beside it, like the frame of a doorway. Jack watched as the camera crew got the full treatment—bags opened, equipment X-rayed, bodies searched with the handheld electronic wand. For a moment, Jack considered leaving, certain that they were going to detain him and that the kidnapper would go ballistic.

"Next," the guard called.

Jack stepped forward and placed the briefcase full of cash on the conveyer belt. To his relief, the guard didn't pop it open. He just pushed it through the X-ray machine.

"Step through, please," he told Jack.

This was the hard part. Jack held his breath, but it didn't help. The alarm sounded the moment he entered the metal detector, and a shrill chirping noise echoed off the stone arches of the cavernous lobby.

"Step over here, please," the guard said without expression.

Jack did as he was told, putting his arms up and feet apart. He started working up explanations in his head, but they all waxed hollow. *Don't volunteer anything,* he told himself. *Just answer their questions and maybe you'll get through.*

The guard waved the handheld wand from his shoulders to his feet. It made no sound at all. Nothing was detected. "You're clear," said the guard, still stone-faced.

The words didn't quite register for Jack. He didn't move.

"I said you're clear." This time, the guard gave a little jerk of the head, as if telling him to move on. At that moment, Jack knew: Somebody from the FBI had indeed made a phone call. And someone else had turned off his electronic wand. Relieved, Jack grabbed his briefcase and started across the lobby. He glanced back once to see the guard hassling a seventy-year-old Latin woman. Another juror/terrorist for sure. The wand was back in working order.

The north entrance to the courthouse was directly across the rotunda, but it was nowhere near as busy. Jack exited through the revolving door and continued down the granite steps. As the kidnapper had said, a vending machine for the *Miami Tribune* was on the corner. Jack fished a quarter from his pocket and put it in the slot. About half the newspapers had already been sold, and he reached to the bottom of the stack. True to the kidnapper's word, an envelope was lying facedown on the bottom. Jack let the vending door slam shut, opened the envelope, and read the typed message inside.

It read: "Kwick-e Copy Center, south of Flagler on First Street. A computer has been rented in your name. And yes, you can run now. I would if I were you."

Jack tucked the message in his pocket and ran as fast as he could, around the west side of the courthouse. He made a sharp left on Flagler Street and then headed east. The crowded sidewalk was slowing him down, so after about a hundred yards he took to the street. On a dead run, he covered the final two blocks going against traffic, trailing behind a death-defying messenger on a twelve-speed bicycle. He spotted the Kwick-e Copy Center just around the corner and ran inside.

"I'm Jack . . . Swyteck," he said, catching his breath as he reached the counter.

The desk attendant appeared to be about six months out of high school, undoubtedly years ahead of Jack in computer expertise. She removed her headset, and Jack could hear the rap music blaring from her headphones. "What did you say?" she asked.

He flashed his driver's license. "Do you have a computer reserved for me?"

She checked the name against her list. "Yup. Pod number three. It's yours all day."

Jack thanked her and went straight to his assigned space. The computer center was compartmentalized into a dozen different workstations, each separated by chest-high dividers that offered some degree of privacy. Jack laid his briefcase on the desktop and pulled up a chair on wheels. The PC was already running, but the monitor was off. With a flip of the power switch, the screen flickered and then came into focus. The desktop was already opened to a word-processing program. Someone had obviously been there earlier, typed a message, and then switched off the monitor. The same message was now before Jack's eyes.

It read: "CD beneath your chair. Insert it. Put on the headphones. Watch and listen."

Jack reached under the chair. His fingertips found a plastic jewel box taped to the bottom. He pulled off the tape, opened the case, and inserted the CD into the D: drive. The computer hummed as it processed the new data. Jack watched the hourglass on the screen, his mind awhirl. He knew this had to be it. The answer to the question— the proof that Mia was alive.

If she's alive.

The screen flickered yet again, and he put on the headphones.

The flickering stopped, and Jack found himself staring at seventeen inches of blackness. Nothing. He adjusted the brightness, but to no avail. Maybe something had gone wrong with the computer. Maybe this was the kidnapper's idea of a joke. A minute later—it seemed much longer—a message in large white letters began to scroll across the screen.

"Question: What do real estate and a red-hot branding iron have in common?"

The black screen and white letters suddenly disappeared, and the CD switched to streaming video. It was a close-up of Mia's face. She was conscious, staring straight into the camera. Jack's heart pounded as he looked into her eyes, those amazing eyes that were red and tired and wide with fear. Something in the back of his mind was telling him to look away, but he didn't dare miss anything. Then, without any warning, Mia's face became almost unrecognizable as she let out a blood-curdling scream that nearly rattled Jack's headphones, a scream unlike any Jack had ever even imagined, let alone heard, in his lifetime. It continued for an insufferably long time, tears streaming down her contorted face, her voice straining for some relief. Her cries of agony never came to a discernible end, but the video suddenly ended. Her image was gone, the editor having cut away from her suffering, as if satisfied that he'd made his point. The screen went black, and more white letters scrolled across the screen.

"Answer: Location, location, location."

Jack had instinctively covered his nose and mouth with both hands. His breathing was in gasps, like a man on the verge of hyperventilation. That was their proof of life—a sick monster's perversion of a cute joke about kisses and real estate. There was no denying that the woman on the screen was Mia. The pain on her face was real. The horror in her screams was too real, almost more than he could handle.

But it wasn't over. Another string of words appeared on-screen, and Jack read the rest of the message.

"Keep your paltry ten thousand. Stop stalling. Pay me what she's worth."

The screen went black. Jack fell back in his chair, then drew a deep breath and pushed himself away from the computer, taking extra care not to touch anything else.

He was certain that Andie Henning and her forensic team would want to take a very good look at Kwick-e computer pod number 3.

16

.

The copy center remained a secured crime scene the entire afternoon. A yellow line of police tape stretched across the storefront, though pod number 3 was naturally the forensic team's primary focus. The computer, keyboard, and surrounding area were checked for fingerprints. Hair and fiber specialists collected specimens, everything from microscopic traces to the electrical tape that held the CD jewel box to the chair bottom. Computer experts checked the hard drive for technological clues that the kidnapper might intentionally or unintentionally have left behind. A senior agent interviewed the homeless guy, but he added nothing to what he'd already told Jack on the street. The interview of the desk attendant yielded only a general description of a white male over thirty years of age, around six feet, medium build. A baseball hat and sunglasses concealed his hair and eye color. He had dressed like a homeless guy, apparently wearing the same costume in both the copy center and the homeless shanty. The one thing she did remember was that the man paid cash to rent pod number 3 in the name of Jack Swyteck.

In a separate pod, Andie debriefed the real Jack Swyteck for almost ninety minutes before sending him home.

Forty-five minutes later, Andie was in the audiovisual lab of the FBI's Miami field office, analyzing the digital images and voice recording of Mia Salazar. A technical agent was seated at his desk in front of a wall of electronic equipment. Andie stood and watched over his left shoulder as he played with various zooms, color adjustments, slow motion, volume control, and other functions. Paul Martinez, Miami's special agent in charge (SAC), peered over the tech agent's other shoulder.

"Tough not to tear your eyes away, even without sound," said Martinez.

No one disagreed. The tech agent had digitally separated and muted Mia's screams to see if background noises could be detected.

"Anything?" asked Andie.

The tech agent was wearing headphones, but he was relying more on a sight check of the needles on his instruments to detect extraneous sounds that might be picked up and amplified. Certain sounds could offer clues as to the victim's whereabouts.

"We may have something around ten to fifteen decibels," he said.

"What would be in that range?" asked Andie.

"Normal conversation is around sixty. So this could be anything from a squeaky mouse to a herd of charging elephants two hundred yards away."

"But you do hear something?"

"No promises, Andie. Could be static. I really need to clean this up and work with it to give you a definitive answer. Maybe by tomorrow morning."

"No chance of something before the joint task force meeting this evening?" she said, hopeful.

"As soon as I have something, I'll let you know."

Andie thanked him, and then she and the SAC left him to do his work alone. The task force meeting was scheduled for 6 p.m. The idea was to enhance cooperation between the FBI and various state and local law enforcement agencies. Andie was named task-force coordinator, not only because she was a field agent held in high regard by the FBI's elite Critical Incident Response Group, but also because of her hands-on experience with the Wrong Number Kidnapper in the Ashley Thornton case. This evening, it would be Andie's job to bring everyone up to date and coordinate further strategies.

"You ready for tonight's meeting?" asked Martinez. They were walking down the hallway toward his office. Martinez had once been a collegiate star in the eight-hundred-meter run and was now an aspiring triathlete in the over-forty club. A simple walk down the hall with him felt like a miniworkout, a good bit faster than the usual office stroll.

"I will be," said Andie.

They stopped outside the SAC's office. Martinez leaned against the door frame, his hands in his pockets. "Andie, I know that the CD was terribly disturbing to watch, but whatever that monster did to Mrs. Salazar is not your fault. You realize that, right?"

"Yeah, I do," she said without heart.

"Hey, I'm serious. Asking for proof of life was good strategy. Don't second-guess that."

"I had a bad feeling about it from the moment Mr. Salazar surprised me with that location, location, location riddle. I still can't believe I got sandbagged like that."

"Again, not your fault. You reacted appropriately. You brought in Swyteck. Not an ideal situation, but this is one tough case. You got a kidnapper who has killed once before. You got a jealous husband who isn't exactly making things easy for you. And your go-to guy is Jack Swyteck, who was sleeping with the victim. As if that's not confounding enough, he's a criminal defense lawyer who . . . well, he's a criminal defense lawyer. 'Nuff said, right?"

That almost elicited a smile. "In fairness, he is a former prosecutor."

"The key word there is 'former.' Use him, but don't trust him too much."

"I hear you."

"You're doing a great job. From what I see, everything the folks in Seattle said about you is true. I think you found a home here in Miami."

"Thank you, sir."

He offered a little mock salute as he disappeared into his office, and Andie started down the hall toward hers. Praise from a supervisor was always nice, but it was especially gratifying for Andie to hear that she still had the backing of some hometown friends. More than anyone, that had to mean Isaac Underwood, the number two man in the Seattle office. Isaac had been her biggest supporter—from her first job on the bank robbery squad, to the dangerous undercover work that put her on the fast track to stardom in the bureau. It was Isaac who'd steered her toward hostage negotiation. He would have been the first to admit, however, that he hadn't planned on saying good-bye to a friend so soon.

Neither had she.

She shook it off, not letting all that personal history spoil the pat on her back from a new boss. In fact, the kind words had given her exactly the kind of lift she needed to deal with Pete Crenshaw, the undisputed malcontent on her team. She had the good sense to realize that today's exercise had ruffled the old rooster's feathers. She'd tried to be as diplomatic as possible about ordering him into the courthouse to arrange for Jack's smooth passage through security. But Pete wasn't easy. Just two years shy of mandatory retirement, he'd never gotten that high-profile case he'd always wanted. The word around the office was that he'd practically exploded when it was announced that the head of the kidnapping task force would be a thirty-two-year-old woman who'd just moved to Miami from Seattle.

As she neared the end of the hallway, Andie spotted Crenshaw making his way toward the kitchen. She followed him inside with hopes of doing damage control. He was standing at the counter stirring extra sugar into his coffee.

"Hey, Pete, thanks for taking care of the courthouse guards," she said in a breezy tone.

"Should never have been necessary," he said, grumbling.

"What do you mean?"

He tossed a couple of empty sugar packets into the trash, then looked straight at her. "It's called anticipation, Henning. If you'd thought through the various possibilities, courthouse security could have been put on alert twenty-four hours ago. In case you haven't heard, that's what a multijurisdictional task force is for."

"Are you saying that I should have anticipated that the kidnapper would send Swyteck four blocks away to the courthouse and have him walk through security?"

"Hey, I'm not saying anything. You're the one in charge, right?"

A snide remark like that definitely required a response, but she took a moment to measure her words. She wasn't the type to cry sexism every time she suspected it, so she took a less accusatory tack. "Look, I totally respect the fact that you have almost twenty years more experience than me, but—"

"This isn't about age or experience. It's about you being a woman."

Her words were on a momentary delay. That was about as blunt as it got. "Okay . . . and what about me being a woman?"

"I think it's a mistake for you to be the team leader. If you ever have to talk directly to this kidnapper, it will be a disaster."

"Because I'm a woman?"

"In a word: yes."

"Don't you think that's a little—"

"Sexist? No way. It's reality. You've seen the psychological profile from our friends up in Quantico. This kidnapper obviously sees women as nothing but a liability, and he wants the husbands of his victims to see them the same way. Basically, he's a woman hater. So it kind of makes you wonder: What the hell is a woman doing in charge of the investigation?"

"Are you saying I can't do the job?"

"Don't get defensive about it. If a rape victim wanted a female counselor, would you force her to talk to a man just because some idiot up in Washington wants to prove that men are equally competent?"

The situation hardly seemed analogous, but it was an unwinnable argument. "If I understand your point, I honestly don't see how my gender has any bearing on the vast majority of my responsibilities as team leader. But if there ever comes a time for an FBI negotiator to speak directly to the kidnapper, I'll definitely consider your input as to who should do the talking. Fair enough?"

She thought she was offering an olive branch, but his face showed even more anger. "Don't patronize me," he said, then walked away. He got halfway to the door, then wheeled around and stepped toward her, standing closer than before. "Just so you know," he said, his voice low but forceful, "I've done some checking on you, Henning."

"So has the rest of the FBI."

"Not like I have. I know why you left Seattle. Not the bullshit 'I-needed-a-change' excuse. The real reason."

Andie tried to show no reaction.

He was almost glowing. "So if you're not up to this, you'd best step aside now. Because sooner or later people around here are going to realize that this case is far too important to be in the hands of someone who doesn't have a clear head."

"Don't worry. I'm up to it."

"I hope you are. Truly. I mean that." He couldn't have sounded less sincere. He raised his coffee mug, as if toasting her failure, and left the lounge.

Andie didn't move. She stood there, thinking, trying to get a better handle on what had just happened.

Crenshaw knew the real reason? *Yeah, right.* Everyone thought they knew the real reason she'd suddenly chucked everything and left her hometown of Seattle. She had an affair with the special agent in charge. Her ex-fiancé was stalking her. She got passed over for promotion to Quantico. All those rumors and many others ran up and down the grapevine. Truth be told, no one knew the real reason. No one but Andie.

And she wasn't about to share that secret with anyone.

Ever.

Andie had a meeting to prepare for. She poured a cup of coffee and walked back to her office, albeit with a little less spring in her step.

.

17

Jack didn't touch his midafternoon lunch. Theo ate it for him.

A Windbreaker lined with Kevlar and a troop of FBI agents notwithstanding, Jack wasn't about to put himself in the crosshairs of a kidnapper and known killer without having his friend Theo Knight somewhere within shouting distance. After the debriefing with Agent Henning, Jack and Theo went for sandwiches at Gruenberg's Deli, downtown Miami's version of a New York delicatessen, complete with matzo balls the size of a grapefruit. They found a table by the plate-glass window overlooking the sidewalk. The lunch crowd had long since passed, and Gruenberg's wasn't open for dinner. Inverted chairs rested atop the other tables, and the janitor was mopping the tile floors, almost ready to close.

"This maniac is going to kill her," said Jack. "I can feel it. Somebody has to come up with some ransom money."

Theo polished off a pickle spear. "What about the FBI?"

"No way. The bureau put up ten grand for a proof-of-life payment, but that was in marked bills used as bait to trace back to the kidnapper. The Justice Department isn't in the business of paying ransoms, especially not the big number we're probably talking here. Hell, when I was with the U.S. attorney's office, we were lucky to get twenty or thirty grand for an entire undercover operation."

"What about tapping Mia's husband? You think Bailey's got leverage on Salad Bar?"

Jack was beyond correcting him about Salazar's name. "Maybe he can reason with him. Especially if I tell him what I just saw on that CD."

"Then let's you and me go pay Mr. Bailey a visit."

"Thanks, but this is something I should do."

"Just let me walk you over there. Could be the kidnapper is still watching you. Doesn't hurt your profile any to be seen in the regular company of a former death row inmate who's built like Governor *Ahh-nuld* in his prime."

"I guess that makes some sense. Come on. Bailey's office is right across the street."

Bailey Benning & Langer occupied the top six floors of the fifty-five-story Financial Center. Jack and Theo cut through the breezeway, a huge covered area where palm trees and pedestrians soaked up the sunshine beneath a clear Plexiglas canopy that connected the office tower to the parking garage. It was a popular spot for the lunch crowd, people-watchers, and employees in need of a nicotine break. Anytime Jack passed through it, however, he was reminded of the poor construction worker who'd taken a seat on a steel crossbeam and leaned back to relax against the Plexiglas, only to discover that his crew had yet to install that particular panel. A fifteen-story fall onto solid granite had to hurt, but he didn't live to tell anyone about it.

"I think I can take it from here," said Jack.

"Nah, I'll go up with you."

Jack hesitated, naturally suspicious of Theo's desire to actually enter a law firm like BB&L. But he was too worn out emotionally to argue about it. "Just behave yourself, all right?"

"You're hurtin' my feelings, buddy."

The escalator carried them up to the main lobby. They passed through security to an express elevator that would take them nonstop to the reception area for the BB&L office suites. The chrome doors closed, and Jack and Theo stood side by side, watching the illuminated numbers blink as the car rose. Annoying symphonic Muzak played over the speaker; Jack recognized it as a string-and-woodwind abomination of the old Rolling Stones hit "Satisfaction."

Theo said, "You think thirty years from now they'll turn rap music into Muzak?"

"Do what?" said Jack.

"Years ago, did anyone think that these sickeningly sweet versions of classic Stones songs would be playing in elevators? It makes me wonder if when we're old, maybe we'll step inside an elevator and some DJ with a smarmy voice will say, 'This is WOLD, all oldies, all the time, and you just heard the Mormon Tabernacle Choir singing "Back That Big Ass Up, Bitch." ' "

Jack couldn't even crack a smile. "Theo, I appreciate what you're trying to do, but it's not going to work. Not after what happened this morning."

"That bad, huh?"

"Unbelievable," said Jack.

"You think it hit you that way because you know her, maybe even still have feelings for her? Or was it just that bad?"

"Could be the worst thing I've ever seen, period. And you don't do death penalty cases for four years without seeing some pretty horrific stuff."

Theo was silent, as if not sure what to do when humor didn't work. He just laid a big hand on Jack's shoulder and said, "I'm sorry, man. Really."

"Thanks."

At the fifty-first floor the elevator doors opened to a two-story cherry-paneled lobby. The firm name was displayed prominently in polished brass letters. A wall of windows to the east made it seem entirely possible to leap off the building and fly to Jack's house on Key Biscayne. Jack approached the pretty blond receptionist behind the antique desk and asked to see William Bailey. She smiled and placed a phone call, then instructed Jack and Theo to please have a seat in the waiting area. Jack went past the leather couches and stood at the floor-to-ceiling window.

He was staring out at paradise, but he was barely aware of the view.

Theo came up behind him and said, "Calling the FBI was the right decision. You know that, right?"

"I feel like I don't know anything anymore."

"What you saw on that CD wasn't payback for bringing in the FBI. The CD was burned before this creep had any idea you called the cops. He's pissed about the stalling with the proof-of-life question. That wasn't your idea."

Jack's gaze settled on a schooner headed toward Miami Beach. It made him think of the time he and Mia sailed overnight to Bimini. Seas so rough that John Paul Jones would have gotten seasick. She never blamed him, but he owed her big-time for that disaster. Not that these little personal debts mattered anymore. She was another man's wife. She'd been kidnapped. And now she was being tortured.

Tortured. It was one of those words that could rip right through the soul and make *kidnapping* sound almost benign.

Jack lowered his eyes. "I wonder what the FBI isn't telling me."

"What makes you say that?"

"Saturday night I went to see Mia's best friend, Emilia. We were talking about the reason Mia stayed married to Ernesto, and she said it was about protection."

"Protection? You mean like keeping her safe?"

"Yeah, except she didn't say 'safety.' They were speaking in Spanish, and according to Emilia she used the word *protección*, which is Spanish for 'protection.'"

"Protection from what?"

"That's what Emilia couldn't answer. Mia never told her."

"She ever mention anything like that to you?"

"No, of course not. But here's what nags at me. Whenever I look back and wonder why I never even suspected that she was married, the thing that amazes me most is how she managed to avoid talking about herself."

"You dated all that time and never had a deep conversation?"

"Yeah, plenty of them. But with Mia, it was never about where she came from. It was about where she wanted to go. Hopes and dreams, that kind of thing."

"Girl stuff," said Theo.

"If that's what you want to call it. But . . ."

"But what?"

Jack didn't want to get into the scar on her leg, the night of her birthday when their first attempt at lovemaking turned into Jack holding her in his arms until she fell asleep. "I just don't have many details about her. Sure, I have a general idea that she grew up in Venezuela, but I couldn't give you the name of a city or even a state. I don't know how many brothers and sisters she has, whether her parents are alive or dead, what jobs she used to have. Don't you think that's weird?"

"Not really. Friend of mine eloped in Las Vegas and didn't know his bride was adopted till he came home from the honeymoon and met the snow-white parents."

"Leave it to you to come up with an extreme example."

"Just trying to help. My take on it: Mia was probably being coy so you couldn't find out she was married."

"That was my initial thought," said Jack. "But now I'm starting to lean in a different direction."

"She hiding something specific in her past, you think?"

He gave Theo a serious look. "I'm thinking she might be hiding her *entire* past."

"What, like a secret agent?"

"No. I come back to that word—*protección*. Maybe it's because I'm a criminal defense lawyer and a former prosecutor, but when someone is vague about their past and starts using words like *protección*, I start to think about a very specific kind of protection."

"Something tells me you ain't talking condoms."

"Not even close."

"You mean witness protection?"

The receptionist approached and interrupted, hands clasped demurely behind her back, bony ankles together, her soft tone bordering on the obsequious. "Gentlemen, I am so very sorry, but Mr. Bailey had to leave the office on an emergency. I'm afraid he won't be able to see you today."

"Or any other day, I'm sure," said Theo.

The receptionist seemed befuddled, her puckered lips in search of words.

Theo started toward the elevator. "Come on, Swyteck. We've got some protection issues to sort out."

18

·

The meeting of the multijurisdictional task force was held in a brightly lit conference room at the Palm Beach County Sheriff's Office, PBSO for short. Andie sat at the head of the long rectangular table, flanked by senior supervisory agent Peter Crenshaw and an FBI technical agent. To keep things manageable, she'd requested that each state and local agency working the Salazar kidnapping or the Ashley Thornton kidnapping-murder send no more than four representatives to tonight's gathering. To Andie's left was Major Lew Collins, head of the PBSO's Investigative Services, and his three subordinates in charge of the Special Investigations Bureau, the Violent Crimes Bureau, and Technical Services, the latter being a rather unglorious title that covered everything from crime-scene analysis to serology. Filling out the right side of the table were representatives of the Palm Beach Police Department, the Florida State Troopers, and the Florida Department of Law Enforcement. Directly opposite Andie, at the short end of the rectangle, sat Sheriff McClean (the boat driver on the night Ashley Thornton's body was recovered from Devil's Ear) and his two lead investigators. Reps from the Miami-Dade Police Department and the City of Miami Police took the extra seats in the back. They were new to the team, their involvement triggered by the kidnapper's choice of downtown Miami for the proof-of-life exchange.

"Thank you all for coming," said Andie. "We have a number of developments to bring you up to date on."

She rose and went to a big map of Florida that nearly covered the entire wall behind her. A blue pushpin marked the suspected point of abduction for Ashley Thornton in Ocala—"suspected" because her horse returned to the barn without her, and a field examination was unable to identify the exact point of attack along the wooded eight-mile trail. Another blue pushpin marked a similar approximation in Palm Beach for Mia Salazar, who vanished while jogging. Numbered yellow pushpins identified specific locations that the kidnapper had probably visited. Number five—the highest number—marked the Kwick-e Copy Center in Miami.

A single red dot on the Sante Fe River punctuated the recovery of Ashley Thornton's body.

"As you can see," said Andie as she pointed to the map, "the kidnapper's zone of comfort continues to expand geographically."

"Assuming we're talking about one kidnapper," said Crenshaw.

Andie paused, not sure what her senior colleague was up to. "That's correct, Peter. We continue to believe the person who kidnapped and murdered Ashley Thornton also kidnapped Mia Salazar."

"Just so we all understand that this is an assumption on our part," said Crenshaw.

"Yes, we're making it based on the evidence gathered so far," said Andie. "Which leads me to the first order of business: new evidence. We've prepared a notebook for everyone, which most of you have perused by now. The first new item is a composite sketch of the suspect prepared from information obtained from the desk attendant at the copy center and the hired homeless man who served as the kidnapper's messenger."

Major Collins from the PBSO opened his book to the sketch, then scowled. "Looks like that old rendering of the Unabomber—the one of that man in a hood and dark sunglasses that yielded exactly zero useful leads in seventeen years."

Andie said, "It's not great, you're right. But until we nail down something better, we do plan to go with it."

"Weren't there any security cameras in that copy center?" asked Collins.

"There were," said Andie. "But it was store policy not to turn them on. Some of their Internet-surfing customers threatened to sue for invasion of privacy."

"Ah, the time-honored constitutional right to porn," said another officer. "Thank you, ACLU: making the world a safer place for serial killers and child molesters alike."

A light chorus of combined chuckles and grumbles followed—*chumbling*, Andie called it, something cops seemed to do a lot of.

Andie said, "I also want to update you on the scuba search. The fact that Ashley Thornton's body was found inside the Devil's Ear led us to believe that her kidnapper was not only a licensed scuba diver, but someone with specialized training in cave diving, perhaps even CDS-qualified. That's Cave Dive Section, National Speleological Society. They certify cave divers and instructors. Obviously, cave divers would be a narrower field of suspects."

"People cave-dive without proper training every day," said Sheriff McClean. "That's why we've pulled so many bodies out of the aquifer over the years."

"You're exactly right," said Andie. "That's why we did our research against the broader nationwide list of certified divers. Fortunately, we didn't have to reinvent the wheel, since this same information is of serious interest to our antiterrorism people since nine-eleven."

"Yeah, except Joe Terrorist probably isn't going to be on the list, since strapping a bomb to the bottom of a cruise ship isn't part of the Club Med certification program."

Another round of chumbles followed.

"You raise a good point," said Andie. "This task force faces a similar problem. We're not looking for a terrorist, obviously. But our kidnapper could have learned to dive in a foreign country, or rather than seek formal certification he may just have kept a logbook, which is sufficient in some places. Still, we figured it was worthwhile to cross-check a list of certified divers with a list of convicted felons."

"Let me guess," said Collins. "You discovered that a lot of divers like to smoke pot."

Andie said, "Anyone who's been to the Florida Keys could probably tell you that much. But more important, your notebook contains personal data and the last available photograph of certified divers convicted of similar crimes in the last seven years. Kidnapping, obviously. Sexual assault, battery. Of course, we factored out anyone who is dead or presently incarcerated."

Collins thumbed through the considerable stack. "Why not just give us the phone book?"

"It's not as intimidating as it looks," said Andie. "The first section is the entire list. We then took that raw data and compared it with Quantico's psychological profile of the kidnapper. Age was a defining characteristic. Education another. The bottom line is, we're left with fewer than a hundred subjects of interest."

"So, you think one of these hundred or so men in this notebook kidnapped Ashley Thornton and Mia Salazar?"

"It's very possible," said Andie.

"Assuming the same man kidnapped both women," said Crenshaw.

Major Collins shot Crenshaw a curious look. "That's about the third or fourth time you've said that—'Assuming it's the same kidnapper.' Is the FBI suggesting there might be two different kidnappers at work here?"

"That's not what our profilers are telling us," said Andie.

Crenshaw shook his head and said, "But when you've been around for thirty years, you know that profilers are sometimes wrong."

Several others nodded. It didn't take much to convince the locals that the FBI's most "elite" unit was, at worst, a bunch of know-it-alls, or at best, certified workaholics who spread themselves too thin.

Major Collins said, "I'd like to hear more. What makes you think the experts up in Quantico might have missed something?"

Andie was about to interject in an effort to keep the group focused, but Crenshaw was all too eager to run with his theory. "Be glad to," he said as he rose from his chair. "First thing you have to look at are the glaring differences between the two kidnappings. For example, in the case of Mia Salazar, the ransom demand went to the FBI as well as the family. It only went to the family in the Thornton case."

"That's accounted for in the profile as an increasing appetite for notoriety," said Andie.

"I'm only getting started," said Crenshaw. "In the Thornton case, the kidnapper never revealed himself to anyone. Now all of a sudden he's out in the street dressed like a homeless guy, renting computers and hiring street people to piss on public benches. And that urination stunt? Too cute, too clever. Didn't see any of that in the first kidnapping."

"It's not uncommon for serial criminals to grow bolder over time," said Andie.

"True," said Crenshaw. "But if a profile is to have any validity at all, we have to assume that the work of a sociopath reveals something about his psychology that is virtually unchangeable. It's his personality, or signature, if you will. And that's where this single-kidnapper profile falls apart in my book."

"How so, specifically?" asked one of the officers.

Crenshaw seemed grateful for the question, like a teacher who's finally captured the class. "Torture of the victim. The autopsy protocol revealed nothing on Ashley Thornton's body to indicate she was harmed in any way before she was murdered. As we know from today's CD-ROM—and of course, if we assume that Mia Salazar is still alive— it's a whole different ball game with his current victim."

Sheriff McClean said, "You don't consider it torture to drag a woman into an underwater cave, remove her breathing apparatus, and leave her there to drown?"

"I call that a cruel, heinous homicide. That's different from a guy who inflicts nonlethal wounds for the fun of it so that he can keep his victim around for another day of fun and games. It's a subtle difference, but it's a difference."

The team fell quiet, as if in need of a moment to ponder the distinction. Andie said, "Let's take a break. There's plenty more to cover. See you all in ten."

The group splintered into smaller clusters of conversation, some drifting toward the coffee machine, others headed for the restrooms. Andie followed Crenshaw down the hall and pulled him aside. It was just the two of them standing in an alcove near the drinking fountain, far enough from the others not to be overheard.

"What are you trying to do in there?" said Andie.

"What do you mean?" said Crenshaw.

"This two-kidnapper theory you're suddenly pushing on the task force. Where did that come from?"

"Are you telling me that I don't have a right to my own opinion?"

"It would have been nice of you to run it by me beforehand."

"I'm running it by you now. What do you think?"

"I think—" She stopped herself.

Crenshaw answered for her. "You think I'm a pain in the ass, don't you?"

She didn't say anything.

"Okay, you're right. I am. I'll be the first to admit that I'd be a profiler in Quantico right now if it weren't for my so-called attitude problems. But consider this. If someone like me can make it onto the short list of candidates for the ISU, it must mean only one thing. Yes, I'm a pain in the ass. But I'm usually right."

Andie watched in silence as he turned and headed back toward the conference room. She couldn't say she liked him, but she couldn't dismiss him, either.

Like it or not, Crenshaw had given her one more thing to think about.

19

•

Ernesto Salazar walked straight down the middle of the gray wooden pier at Key Biscayne Marina, toting a suitcase-on-wheels. The sun had set hours earlier, replaced by moonbeams from a low-hanging crescent that glistened against the black water. Most of the boats in the slips were completely dark, no signs of life. A big yacht at the deeper end of the marina was a notable exception. The happy crew was either partying after a day on the ocean or warming things up before going out for the night. The hell-raisers were too far away, however, to rob the marina of its eerie peacefulness. Even the most gentle breeze from the bay could set off a veritable chorus among the sailboats, the sharp, hollow sound of taut halyards slapping against bare aluminum masts.

Ernesto checked his watch. Ten p.m. He was right on time. Now all he had to do was find a boat called *Mega-Bite.*

Agent Henning had warned him about the disturbing video of his wife, but Ernesto watched it anyway. Once. That was enough. He went straight home and tried to put it out of his mind, but evidently the kidnapper had no intention of letting him stay above the fray. The succinct instructions came via e-mail, midafternoon. "No more cops, no more Swyteck, no more fucking around. I'm dealing with you now. Put as much cash as you can inside a watertight suitcase. Go to Key Biscayne Marina at ten o'clock. Find a fishing boat called *Mega-Bite.* The captain will know what to do. In case you're wondering, the size of the suitcase and the denominations of the bills are up to you. But this is your last chance. Pay me what she's worth."

Ernesto found the *Mega-Bite* at the end of the south pier. The running lights were on. Twin inboard diesel engines churned the seawater beneath the vessel's hand-painted name.

"You Mr. Salazar?" the burly man at the controls asked. He had a fisherman's build, soft around the middle but arms big enough to reel in a Buick from the depths. The sleeves of his denim shirt were torn off at the shoulder to show off the intricate tattoos on both biceps. Not even for a second did Ernesto entertain the possibility that this guy was Mia's kidnapper. He was clearly an intermediary, a pawn hired by the kidnapper for his own purposes, like the homeless guy who had urinated on Swyteck's bench.

"That would be me," said Salazar. "Ernesto's the name."

"Let me take your bag."

Ernesto stepped back, as if guarding the suitcase. "That's all right. I got it."

The captain shot him a curious look and went back to the controls. "Suit yourself. Toss me that line and climb aboard."

Ernesto untied the bow line and stepped down into the boat. He took a seat in the stern behind the captain, keeping his suitcase with him at all times. Diesel fumes assailed his nostrils as the captain slowly maneuvered the forty-two-footer backward, then forward, away from the dock. In just a few minutes they were out of the marina and beyond the no-wake zone. The captain idled the engines and went down into the galley. Ernesto couldn't see what he was doing, but the sound of Lucille Ball's voice was a fairly strong clue.

"I don't need television," said Ernesto as the captain returned to the controls.

"Neither do I. But the dude who paid for your ride said the television stays on from the moment we leave the marina. So it's on."

That seemed like a strange request, but Ernesto didn't have much time to consider it. The captain opened the throttle, and the sound of

Desi Arnaz singing "Babalú" was completely drowned out by the roar of over a thousand horsepower. The seas were calm, and the boat skimmed across the gentle waves at a good twenty-five knots per hour. They maintained that speed for almost forty-five minutes, but they didn't seem to be traveling in any particular direction. Twenty minutes due west. Five minutes south. Two minutes to the northeast, then south again.

"Where are we?" asked Ernesto, shouting over the engine noise.

"Can't tell you."

"Let me guess. The man who hired you said not to tell me."

The boat hit a swell, and foamy ocean spray soaked the captain's face. "Well, yeah. He did tell me that. But even if I was free to run my mouth, I still couldn't tell you *exactly* where we are. Not with that damn television playing. Knocks out my GPS."

"What?" Ernesto said.

"The powered antenna creates interference for the satellite signal. GPS either goes screwy or shuts down altogether when the TV is on. I could get a different marine antenna that doesn't mess up my GPS, but I never watch television except when I'm in the marina. So why bother with the expense?"

Ernesto suddenly realized what all the cruising around was about— and why the kidnapper had told the captain to keep the television playing.

He thinks there's a GPS tracking chip in the suitcase that needs to be disabled.

They reached another no-wake zone. The captain cut their speed, the bow dipped, and the engines became much kinder to the ears. In the cabin below, the television continued to play. It was Nick at Nite, or some such all-rerun station, as Ernesto recognized the whistler's theme song from the original *Andy Griffith Show*. As far as he could tell, they'd done almost a complete nautical loop, and they were approaching a marina near Coconut Grove, just a few miles from where they'd started. This marina, however, wasn't just boats in slips, one neat row after another. Rather, scores of vessels were moored offshore, scattered across the open harbor, accessible only by dinghy, not by piers. Some were houseboats, and this was home for the winter months. Others were impressive sailboats, stopping in Miami for a few days before continuing on to Martinique, the Virgin Islands, or countless other Caribbean paradises.

Ernesto walked quietly toward the bow as the captain maneuvered between and around moored vessels. Their wake was minimal but big enough to give other boats a gentle roll. Even that slight motion made the halyards sing, and all those bare masts swaying in the moonlight gave the illusion of a vast wintry forest.

The captain killed the engines, and the boat started to drift. The television continued to play. Some surrounding boats, Ernesto noticed, also had television. There was GPS interference all around. *One smart, sick bastard*, thought Ernesto.

"This is the spot," said the captain.

"What spot?"

"Throw the suitcase over."

"Into the water?" Ernesto said, incredulous.

"Yeah. Those were his instructions. Drive you around the bay for an hour, keep the television playing, and then stop just outside the Coconut Grove Marina thirty feet north of *The Whispering Seas*.

Ernesto glanced to starboard and saw *The Whispering Seas*. Then he looked at the captain and said, "Do you have any idea what's in this—"

"I don't know, and I don't care," said the captain, holding up one hand in the stop position. "All I know is that the guy paid me two thousand bucks to do exactly as he says. That's a very good two hours of work for me. Now throw the suitcase over."

Ernesto wasn't sure what to do. It sounded crazy, but it seemed unlikely that the captain was making this up. He lifted the suitcase by the handle and rested it atop the boat rail. He paused, wondering if this really made sense. *Don't overanalyze things*, he told himself. Then he drew a breath and pushed it over the side.

The suitcase landed with a splat, then floated away from the boat. It would take a while to sink, as the kidnapper had specified a waterproof suitcase. Ernesto watched it closely, barely allowing himself to blink. Then, suddenly, he noticed a change in the water around the suitcase. Bubbles. It was difficult to see much of anything in the darkness, but those were definitely bubbles rising to the surface.

The suitcase bobbed to the right, then to the left. A second later, it vanished, as if sucked into the black water. Small rings of water rolled out to mark the spot, the way a pond rippled when swallowing a stone. Ernesto stared for a moment, saying nothing. With his gaze riveted on the fading trail of bubbles, he asked, "Does GPS work underwater?"

"Some of the new ones do. Most don't."

He nodded, realizing that even the ones that did probably didn't when surrounded by five hundred other boats with television and marine antennae.

"Why do you ask?" said the captain.

"Just curious," he said, realizing that, in all probability, he'd just gotten way too close to the man who'd murdered Ashley Thornton—and the man who'd kidnapped Mia Salazar.

Or worse.

20

.

Mia Salazar feels no pain.

    Curled up in the corner of a dimly lit room, she kept thinking that same thought over and over again. The words fixed in her brain like a mantra, a technique she'd developed years ago in her first half-marathon race, when a nasty side stitch had brought her to the verge of collapse. Running was often a matter of mind over body, and her little trick had worked beautifully in every race since. Today, however, it wasn't working at all.

Mia Salazar feels—damn, this hurts!

She wasn't crying, but it was only because her body seemed incapable of producing more tears. The pain had triggered the release, to be sure, but the emotion had been building up inside her for days, since this ordeal began. She'd awakened from an incredibly deep sleep with absolutely no idea where she was or who had taken her. Her last memory was of her morning run. It was sunny and cool, and she was making good time through her favorite part of her three-mile course, weaving through sand dunes and sea oats along the beachfront. Although this isolated part of the trail could be a little scary after dark, in daylight she'd never felt threatened—until this time. Seemingly out of nowhere, a man leaped from behind the dunes and wrestled her to the ground. She resisted and tried to scream, but everything was a blur. A thick blanket of blackness nearly smothered her. She was flat on her stomach, her face in the sand, as the weight of her attacker's body nearly crushed her kidneys. The prick of a needle pierced her right thigh, followed by a burning sensation that ran the length of her leg. In a matter of seconds her body went numb, and she blacked out.

Next thing she knew, she was a prisoner, her hands and feet bound, her mouth taped shut. She allowed herself a few tears out of fear and loneliness, the utter sense of helplessness that comes with such complete uncertainty. Then she tried to sharpen her senses. She felt the sting of bindings too tight around her wrists and ankles, the chill of a musty room, the discomfort of a bulging bladder. Those initial pains and inconveniences were about the only thing that made her feel totally awake, as her blindfold made it difficult to distinguish dreams from reality. When she closed her eyes, she saw nothing. Eyes open, nothing still. It was yesterday, or maybe the day before—she couldn't be certain—when the blindfold came off for the first time. A light was shining directly in her eyes, which made it impossible to see who had removed it. She saw only a silhouette standing behind the glowing lamp. Just the sight of that menacing human form made her want to scream, but she couldn't. The gag prevented it.

By the third or fourth encounter, the removal of the blindfold and bright light in her eyes had become something of a ritual—not a welcome one, but at least a reminder that she was still alive. The silhouette would hand her a bucket for a sponge bath, another bucket for her waste, and a plate of cold food. He never unfastened the bindings on her ankles, but for ten much-needed minutes her arms would be free to wash and feed herself, albeit in the company of the silent stranger. That same routine continued for several days.

Then everything changed.

Almost immediately, she'd realized something was different. She heard the door open and the sound of her captor's footfalls across the room. The blindfold came off, and the light was shining in her eyes. This time, however, he brought no buckets, no articles of personal hygiene, no food. Instead, she noticed another light, a more focused beam that was not as blinding as the other one. Squinting, she was able to determine that this second light emanated from some kind of electronic equipment. Then she heard a short beep, and she realized what was happening. She was being filmed, and all kinds of terrible reasons for it raced through her mind.

"On your back," he'd told her, speaking through wads of cotton that disguised his voice.

Those three words sent chills coursing through her body. She was certain that her worst fears were about to be realized, that her captor was at best a rapist, and at worst . . . she didn't want to think about it.

"Do it!" he said sharply.

Trembling, she lay back onto the mattress. She tried not to let her imagination run wild, but it was impossible to shut down her mind entirely. Her body was tense with anticipation, the muscles instinctively recoiling at the mere thought of his touch. Slowly, the white light came toward her, and the discerning lens of the video camera came into view. The cold, mechanical eye was staring at her, pointed directly at her face, which could not bode well. She closed her eyes, but that brought the quick reproval of her captor. "Eyes open!" he told her, and her lids quivered with obedience. She lay still, her heart pounding, her eyes growing wider with fright as they adjusted to the lighting. And then she felt it.

It was unlike any pain she had ever experienced in her life. Something—pliers, perhaps—had taken hold of her big toe and squeezed so hard that it felt as if her eyes might pop from her head. She screamed until her throat was raw, but the squeezing only got worse. Finally, it stopped. She could only guess how long it had actually lasted, but it felt like an eternity. The camera light blinked off. The dark silhouette stood over her, his form backlit by the sole remaining light in the room. He handed her a wash bucket with a sponge and a bandage. She took it and cowered in the corner.

Hours later, her toe was still throbbing. She tried to take her mind off the pain by replaying favorite songs in her head or recalling her favorite places. She thought of her husband and wondered if he'd pay a ransom. She wondered if Jack Swyteck knew what had happened to her, and if he even cared. That kind of thinking only seemed to make her head hurt as much as her toe. She returned to escapism—recounting the ingredients in her favorite foods, then a lightning round of movie trivia. *Name every film in which Humphrey Bogart played against an older female lead.* The movie game seemed to help a little. Her toe was killing her, but she seemed to recall that a similar technique had been used to get a fifteen-year-old Brooke Shields to simulate an orgasm in *The Blue Lagoon*—though whoever was standing off-camera squeezing the "unaware" young actress's big toe probably wasn't using the tools of a psychopath. Mia surely wasn't going to be running anywhere soon, and it suddenly occurred to her that perhaps that was precisely the idea. Long ago, slave owners sometimes maimed runaway slaves to keep them from running again. Evidently, her captor had stolen an ugly page from U.S. history books.

A *slave*, she thought. *Is that what I am?*

The prospect chilled her, but that slave imagery stuck in her mind. The past several days had been unlike anything she'd ever experienced, but this wasn't the first time she'd felt trapped and helpless.

The door creaked open, and she was suddenly alert, listening. The blindfold prevented her from seeing him come toward her, but her hearing was sharper than ever before. She knew his footsteps. She braced herself as he drew near. This time, would he bring the bucket and the plate of food? Or would it be the lights, the camera, and . . . and God only knew what kind of action.

"Sit up," she heard him say, his voice thick with wadded cotton.

The pain in her foot suddenly sharpened, but only from anticipation. Slowly, she pushed herself up from the floor, as he'd commanded. And then she waited. She couldn't see him, and she heard nothing, but somehow she knew how much he was enjoying this.

Mia Salazar feels no pain, she told herself, sensing the heat of the white-hot spotlight. But she wasn't fooling herself.

She'd never known pain like this.

21

The telephone rang just as Jack was falling asleep. He rolled to the edge of the mattress, fumbled for the phone in the darkness, and answered on the fifth ring. It was a voice he hadn't heard in a long time.

"Swyteck, hey. It's your old buddy, Eddy Malone."

His grating voice alone was enough to give Jack insomnia. Ironically, Jack used to enjoy Malone's articles in the *Miami Tribune*, but that was in the bad old days when Jack wasn't speaking to his father and Governor Harold Swyteck was one of Malone's favorite whipping posts. Even when things were at their worst, however, Jack had never stooped so low as to feed Malone's repeated requests for dirt on the governor. Finally, after father and son reconciled, Malone stopped calling him, and he hadn't printed anything about the Swytecks since the end of Harry's second term. Nonetheless, a phone call from Malone just minutes before deadline could never be good news.

"I'm hanging up now, so don't call back," said Jack.

"Wait. I have it on good authority that you were sleeping with Ernesto Salazar's wife."

Jack sat up in his bed. Ordinarily he would have hung up, but after watching Mia's torture and knowing the danger she was in, he couldn't ignore anyone who claimed to know her secrets. Besides, there wasn't a criminal defense lawyer alive who didn't think he could handle a reporter—even the likes of Eddy Malone. "Let's slow down a little," said Jack. "Assume I choose to dignify that question with a response. What does it have to do with anything?"

"I'm not looking for a debate. A simple confirmation or denial will do."

"Mia Salazar has been kidnapped. For her own safety, it's simply not appropriate for me to comment on anything."

"Very interesting. First you say it's inappropriate to comment on anything, and then in the same breath you confirm that she's been kidnapped."

"That much is public information."

"And by tomorrow morning, plenty more will be public."

"Come on, Malone. For once in your life, act at least half human. I don't know what your angle is, but is this alleged affair really that important to your story?"

"First of all, it's not an *alleged* affair."

"It is until I've confirmed it."

"Wrong, my friend. I've heard the audiotapes."

That one hit him like a 5-iron. Malone had to be talking about the eavesdropping tapes from Jack's kitchen—which meant that Malone's "source" could only have been Ernesto Salazar himself.

Malone continued, "Second of all, the affair is *very* important to my story. How else will my readers understand why you're paying Mia's ransom?"

"I'm *what?*"

"I got my sources, Swyteck. You were Mia's lover, and you've agreed to pay the ransom. That's my story. So, how much is the demand? A hundred grand? More?"

Jack struggled to keep his wits. Thus far, the FBI had prevented the media from uncovering the kidnapper's signature demand, "Pay what she's worth." Malone's question—"How much is the demand?"—suggested that he was still unaware, and Jack didn't want to blow it here. "This is very dangerous territory," said Jack. "You have no idea what you're doing."

"I'm doing my job, that's what I'm doing. The least you can do is tell the truth. Were you sleeping with Mrs. Salazar or not? If you deny it, I swear I'll quote verbatim and extensively from the tapes. If you admit it, I promise to spare you that embarrassment."

The thought of negotiating with Malone repulsed him, but Jack recognized a good deal, even when it was offered by a snake. "All right. I'll give you that much. I was seeing her. But I didn't know that—"

"What about the ransom?"

"Let me finish," Jack said in a stern voice. "I didn't know she was married."

"Yeah, yeah, sure. Got it. Now as for the ransom. Are you paying it or not?"

"I can't comment on the ransom."

"You'd better. Because I'm not giving you another chance."

"Listen, just hold your story for one day, all right? I'll give you a quote just as soon as I clear it with the FBI."

Malone laughed. "I got my sources. I can live without your quote."

"Just one day, Malone."

"In my business, one day is an eternity. I got page one tomorrow, and my sources tell me that Jack Swyteck will pay Mia Salazar's ransom. Do you confirm or deny it?"

Jack swung his legs across the mattress and sat on the edge of the bed, not sure what to say.

"I need an answer, Jack. I'm on deadline."

"Don't do this, Malone. You're putting Mia's life in danger."

"No, *you* are. It's a safe bet that her kidnapper is going to read this article. I want to print the truth, and you're feeding me bullshit. So, let's try this one last time: My sources say you're going to pay Mia's ransom. Do you confirm or deny?"

Jack gripped the phone, the other hand running anxiously through his hair.

"Confirm or deny, Swyteck?"

Jack had no idea where the answer came from, but it popped like a reflex. "Deny."

"So you steal another man's wife, she gets kidnapped, and your position is 'Too bad, so sad, you're on your own, baby'?"

"Don't insult me. It's more complicated than that."

"It's complicated," Malone said, mocking him. "Good quote, Swyteck. I'll be sure to use it. Just do me one last favor, will you?"

"What?"

"Buy a paper tomorrow."

The line clicked, and Jack heard only the dial tone.

22

.

At 2:10 a.m., Andie Henning was riding in the back of a box truck, shoulder to shoulder with six members of FBI SWAT from the Miami field office and two other agents. To maintain the element of surprise, they were traveling in a rented moving van rather than the big black Suburban, the usual FBI vehicle of choice. The team leader, Supervisory Agent Michael Harland, sat nearest to the steel barn-style doors. The tactical team was dressed in full SWAT regalia with Kevlar helmets, flak jackets, and night-vision goggles. Five were armed with M16 rifles and 45-caliber pistols. The sixth, a sniper, toted a .308 sniper rifle. The compartment was silent, save for the steady hum of the truck's engine and the drone of rubber tires rolling on pavement. Each agent was deep in thought, recounting the plan, calming the nerves, trying to bring that pulse rate down to the optimum firing level of sixty to seventy beats per minute. Any higher rate was a marksman's liability. It wasn't just the bad guys who killed more efficiently with cold blood.

Andie checked her GPS locator. Less than five miles from their target. It wouldn't be long now, though she still had reservations about a SWAT launch. She would catch some heat in the morning, but rather than alert the entire task force, she'd decided to keep the latest breakthrough within the bureau. It was difficult enough for a negotiator to rein in the enthusiasm of an FBI SWAT squad, let alone those of other agencies.

The sharp ring of her cell phone pierced the silence. Paul Martinez, Miami's SAC, was on the line with the call they'd been expecting. Andie switched to speakerphone so that both she and Harland could participate in the conference.

"Just got off the phone with the AUSA," said Martinez, his voice tinny over the cellular speaker. "We've got a no-knock warrant. Tactical Operations Center has granted clearance and compromise authority to conduct this as a weapons-drawn rescue, if that's what we deem necessary."

"Of course it's necessary," said Harland. "We're dealing with a kidnapper who has nothing to gain by turning himself in. He's already killed one victim."

"How sure are we that we've got the right house?" asked Martinez.

"Sure enough," said Harland.

Arguing against SWAT in the presence of the entire team was a touchy situation, so Andie stuck to the facts. "That depends on your comfort level," she said. "We have to remember that this lead came through a technical agent's analysis of the hard drive in that computer from the Kwick-e Copy Center."

"I've seen the report," said Martinez. "I understand that the Kwick-e computer was in communication with a computer at the target address not long before Swyteck reached the copy center. But I'm not sure how we reached the conclusion that the kidnapper was using the Kwick-e computer to access some kind of remote Internet camera that allowed him to check on his prisoner back at a target address. Do we have actual images to that effect?"

"No images," said Andie.

"So the notion that our kidnapper was monitoring his prisoner while he was out and about is just a theory?"

"That's correct," said Andie.

"We also can't rule out the possibility that the kidnapper was communicating with a partner," said Harland. "I understand that Agent Crenshaw made a convincing case at the joint task force meeting that there are two kidnappers operating here."

"Again, just a theory," said Andie.

"Sir, the Kwick-e computer was in contact with the remote computer less than an hour before Swyteck arrived at the copy center. It was reserved in the name of Jack Swyteck all day, so it's fairly obvious that the contact was initiated by our kidnapper. And let's not forget that the remote computer is in the house of a convicted sex offender."

"We're sure of that?" asked Martinez.

"Yes," said Harland. "He was convicted of sexual assault at the age of twenty-two."

"Does he otherwise fit the profile out of Quantico?"

"Yes," said Harland.

"But it's a fairly general profile," said Andie. "And we don't have any confirmation yet as to whether he's a trained scuba diver who could have dragged Mrs. Thornton into the Devil's Ear."

"We don't have confirmation that he's not, either," said Harland.

"Sir, I'm not trying to dismiss the utility of SWAT, but if the kidnapper gets the slightest inkling that his house is under attack, we'll have a dead hostage on our hands. Guaranteed."

Harland said, "With all due respect, if Agent Henning posts up on the lawn with a loudspeaker and tries to negotiate, we'll turn a kidnapping into an active and even more volatile hostage crisis. And we will have completely lost the element of surprise."

The SAC did not respond immediately, seeming to take the time to weigh a difficult decision. Harland edged closer to the phone, his voice deepening with concern. "Sir, what are we going to do when he sends us another torture video, along with a demand to lay down our weapons and let him go?"

There was only silence over the line for a moment longer. Finally, Martinez said, "No slight to you, Henning. We're going in with SWAT."

23

.

Across the street from the target residence, Andie Henning drew a deep breath and waited for the signal. She was crouched in a ravine alongside a technical agent and a forensic specialist. Directly in front of them was SWAT commander Michael Harland, flat on his belly. The other SWAT agents had fanned out along the perimeter, virtually invisible beneath the black shroud of a cloudy night. Andie was armed with only her standard Sig Sauer 9 mm sidearm, but she and the other non-SWAT agents had donned Kevlar vests and helmets since leaving the truck, as the odds seemed pretty fair that larger-caliber bullets might soon fly.

Peering through night-vision goggles, Andie locked onto an old ranch-style house. No interior lights were visible through the windows, but a yellow bug light cast an eerie amber pall across the front porch. The house was nestled in a wooded area of northern Palm Beach County, surrounded by mature olive trees and Australian pines. Not a single blade of grass graced the twenty-five-yard stretch from the street to the front door, but the soft blanket of fallen pine needles would ensure a stealthy approach for the SWAT team.

Andie gestured toward the loudspeaker on the ground beside her. "Don't suppose there's any last hope of talking you into using this, is there?"

Agent Harland shook his head once, unamused. Andie listened

through her audio headset as Harland checked in with each of his team members. The final exchange was with site surveillance, a two-man team who had the important job of approaching the house and scoping out the scene before the others made their move.

"Two bedrooms, both on the west side of the house," the surveillance agent reported. "Kitchen, dining, and TV room on east side. One subject confirmed in the master bedroom. Large, probably male. Appears to be asleep. There's a large room in the northwest quadrant, a converted garage. Can't get a visual. Old garage door is gone and replaced with drywall. No windows. Infrared camera scan shows what appears to be a smaller subject with no visible arms or legs, as if curled into a ball. Possibly a woman in the fetal position."

Andie listened with interest. An infrared camera picked up body heat, effectively looking through walls to find a living and breathing human being. A body lying in the fetal position, curled into a ball, sounded entirely consistent with a woman who'd just been tortured. Then again, so did a body with no arms or legs. Either way, there was no guarantee that Mia was still alive. Andie knew that Mia's body would still give off detectable levels of warmth at least two or three hours after death, losing on average one and one-half degrees per hour.

"Good work," Harland said into his bone microphone, speaking without emotion. "On three we're yellow."

Andie didn't live and work beneath the SWAT rainbow, but she knew that yellow was code for the final position of cover and concealment. Green was the assault, the moment of life and death, literally.

"One . . . two . . . three." Harland sprang from the ravine and moved quickly toward the house. Andie remained under cover, watching with the aid of night vision as the SWAT members executed their well-choreographed movements in a wave of utter silence. They moved toes first, then heels, knees bent to absorb recoil in case they had to fire. Two agents approached from the east to cover the back door. Two others closed in from the west and assumed positions in front of the house, but not too close, strategically stopping just beyond the reach of the glowing yellow porch light. Harland continued around the west side of the house and joined up with the agents in the rear. The plan was for the point agents to enter from the rear of the house, where there was only darkness, and flush the occupants out the front door, into the light, and straight into the sights of two SWAT members with M16 rifles. If that wasn't enough, somewhere in the trees, invisible even to Andie, was a trained sniper who could shoot the cap off of a beer bottle at two hundred yards.

Andie couldn't see the back of the house, but she heard their maneuvering with the aid of her headset.

"On three we're green," Harland whispered, his voice breaking the radio squelch in Andie's ear. He counted slowly, deliberately, a man with ice water in his veins. At the count of three, Andie's headset resounded with the crash of a door and shattered glass. She braced herself for the crack of gunfire, but she heard only the shouts of Agent Harland and his team as they swept through the house.

"Down, down! Get down on the floor!"

There was a crackling over the radio and more shouting. Outside the house, directly in Andie's line of sight, the agents in the front yard moved from their yellow positions of cover and approached the porch. Then, suddenly, they both hit the ground as a gunshot erupted inside the house. It was so loud that Andie would have heard it without the headset. The outside agents resumed cover behind trees. Andie ducked back into the ravine, cautiously raising the night-vision binoculars just enough to see what was going on inside the house.

A minute later, the front door opened and Harland stepped out. Standing on the porch, he gave a hand signal as he announced over the radio, "All clear."

Andie jumped to her feet and ran toward the house. The technical agent and forensic specialist were right behind her. If Mia was inside, Andie wanted to do the talking. If her kidnapper was there and still alive, Andie didn't want some clever defense lawyer arguing that he had confessed to a crime with a gun pointed at his head. She hurried through the front door and found Harland in the back room. He and another SWAT agent were standing over a large man who was facedown on the green sculptured carpet. He was wearing only boxer shorts. His hands were clasped behind his back with plastic cuffs, but he appeared to be unharmed.

"Where is Mia Salazar?" Harland shouted.

"I got no idea what you're talking about!" the man said, his voice shaking.

"Where is she?" said Harland.

Andie said, "What about the other subject in the converted garage?"

"A Rottweiler," said Harland.

"They shot my dog!" the man said, still facedown on the carpet. "What'd you go and shoot my dog for?"

"Shut up!" said Harland.

"You shot the man's dog?" said Andie.

"It was a monster. Big enough to look human in the Infrared camera. Went right for my throat when we broke down the door."

"I'm gonna sue you bastards, I swear!" the man shouted.

Harland continued to bark out orders to his team. "Check the attic. Crawl space, too. If Mia Salazar is here, we need to find her—*now!*"

"She's not here," said the technical agent as he entered the room.

Harland shot him a look of annoyance. "I don't think that's for a techie to say."

"Fine. Keep searching," said the technical agent. "Henning, you need to have a look at this guy's computer."

Andie followed him into the TV room. The light from a glowing computer monitor reflected off the little sparkles in the popcorn ceiling. "He's fairly high-tech," said the technical agent. "Twenty-one-inch flat-screen monitor. A favorite of gamers and porn addicts."

"Which one is he?"

"Both, judging from the cookies on his hard drive."

"So, is he our man?"

"Nah. He's a host, not the parasite."

"What do you mean?"

With a click of the mouse, the tech agent brought an image to the screen. "Here's what our kidnapper transmitted from the Kwick-e Copy Center this morning. Probably came under the cover of a free porn e-mail, which invaded the guy's hard drive when he opened it. It's parked in the system subfile of Windows, a fairly typical way for any virus transmitted by Internet to invade another computer. Except it's not technically a virus. It's purely a data file. Have a look for yourself."

He clicked on the folder, and Andie read the taunting message:

> Fools! You make this so easy! All I have to do is send an infected
> e-mail to a convicted sex offender, and you morons are all over him.
> You got the wrong man. Be sure you get the right number. Payment
> is due in five days. Delivery instructions to follow.
>
> P.S. Mia and I are already working on a sequel. The ending is guar-
> anteed to make her cry.

For several chilling moments, Andie was unable to tear her eyes away from the screen. She was reading it for the fourth time, exploring the mind of a sociopath, when the technical agent broke her train of thought.

"You want to tell Martinez, or you want me to call him and test the waters first?"

Andie suddenly felt as if her neck were on a chopping block. It hadn't been her idea to go in with SWAT, but this was her team, and the captain always went down with the ship.

"I'll tell him," she said, her voice tightening with an acute sense of dread.

24

Jack was one of the first people in Miami to get his hands on the morning paper. He was waiting outside the *Tribune* headquarters, well before sunrise, when the first delivery truck rolled onto the street. Alone in the front seat of his car, he devoured the page-one story beneath the steadily weakening glow of a yellow dome light, his hands trembling as he read and reread the disturbing headline: KIDNAP VICTIM'S LOVER REFUSES TO PAY RANSOM.

In at least one respect, Eddy Malone had been true to his word. To Jack's relief, there were no lurid excerpts from the ill-gotten audiotapes of his most private moments with Mia. On the other hand, the article didn't exactly go out of the way to exonerate him:

> In an exclusive interview with the *Tribune*, Jack Swyteck, son of former governor Harry Swyteck, has confirmed reports that he was having an affair with the thirty-year-old wife of Ernesto Salazar prior to her kidnapping. Swyteck—a savvy criminal defense attorney and respected former prosecutor—claims he had no idea that Mia Salazar was married to the multimillionaire developer, even though they saw each other extensively over a two-month period while Mr. Salazar was out of the country on business.

It went downhill from there, making it seem highly unlikely that anyone would actually believe his claimed ignorance. He was ashamed, only slightly consoled by the fact that his *abuela* still couldn't read an English-language newspaper. But he had to separate the embarrassing from the truly life-threatening, because the meat of the article was indeed dangerous—for Mia.

What would the kidnapper do now that it was printed in black and white that *no one* intended to pay a ransom?

Seeing his refusal to pay splayed across the front page was painful, but the facts were the facts. Mia was another man's wife. Jack had let himself fall for her only because she'd deceived him. How did that make it *his* responsibility to pay a ransom? Wasn't it enough that he'd put his life in danger and tried to deliver the proof-of-life payment? Of course, none of those details made their way into the article. Jack had called Agent Henning last night, immediately after hanging up with Malone, and she'd confirmed that the entire proof-of-life episode was one aspect of the kidnapping that the FBI had succeeded in keeping out of the media. Secrecy was good for the investigation, but the immediate result was a story that was in keeping with the tone of Eddy Malone's remarks to Jack on the telephone: "So you steal another man's wife, she gets kidnapped, and your position is 'Too bad, so sad, you're on your own, baby'?" Those weren't the exact words in print, but the implication was undeniable.

Jack folded the newspaper in half and tossed it onto the passenger seat beside him. The sun had begun its climb above the bay, and the many thousands of lights that had brightened the nighttime cityscape seemed to dissolve into a blue morning sky. With the early rush hour just under way, Jack knew that if he hurried, he could reach William Bailey at his house before he left for work. He zipped onto the I-95 on-ramp and took the first exit to historic Bayshore Drive. It was Jack's good fortune that the housekeeper answered the door and let him in. He found Bailey having coffee in the breakfast nook, the *Tribune* article spread across the round glass tabletop in front of him.

"My, what a coincidence to see you," said Bailey, looking up from his newspaper. With a wave of the hand, he invited Jack to join him.

"It's no coincidence," said Jack as he took a seat.

Confronting Salazar's attorney at his home was arguably impulsive, but the one-two punch of the late-night telephone interview with Malone and this morning's distressing front-page article had Jack feeling the need to take action. Bailey seemed like a logical place to start.

"You want to tell me how Eddy Malone got his hands on the Jack and Mia audiotapes?" said Jack.

"Tapes?" Bailey said as he spread strawberry marmalade atop his bagel and cream cheese. "What audiotapes?"

"That's a pretty unconvincing denial," said Jack. "Malone threatened to quote from some tawdry audiotapes of me and Mia unless I admitted to the affair. So I admitted to it."

Bailey chewed his bagel, saying nothing.

Jack said, "You should at least thank me. I could have gone on record and accused your client of breaking and entering my house to record our conversations."

"I can assure you that Ernesto Salazar had nothing to do with those tapes."

"Cut the crap," said Jack. "How else could Salazar have coldcocked the FBI with that surprise proof-of-life question? You know what I'm talking about. The joke—location, location, location. There's no way Ernesto would have known about that if he hadn't bugged my house."

Bailey laid his half-eaten bagel aside and neatly brushed away the crumbs. Without a hint of emotion in his voice, he said, "Are you willing to agree that this conversation never happened?"

"Only if that's what it takes to get a straight answer from you."

Bailey nodded, then looked Jack in the eye and said, "We never gave Malone the tapes."

"Don't get cute with me," said Jack. "What did you do, give him a *transcript* of the tapes?"

"Malone called Ernesto and asked for the tapes. It was out of the blue. I'm not sure how he found out about them, but we refused to give them to him. We refused to talk to him. We refused to acknowledge in any way that Ernesto's wife was sleeping with another man."

"So you deny telling Malone that I was going to pay Mia's ransom?"

"I more than deny it. I give you my word that it didn't come from us."

"I'm afraid your word's not good enough."

Bailey bristled, yet he somehow seemed to know better than to feign too much indignation. "Then let's deal strictly with the practicalities. Breaking and entering into a private residence to plant an eavesdropping device is a felony. Do you think for one minute that Ernesto would risk jail time by sending those tapes to a reporter?"

"A journalist's sources are confidential," said Jack. "A judge could set his balls on fire, and Malone still wouldn't say who made the tapes."

"I suppose that's so," said Bailey. "All I can tell you is that Malone didn't get the tapes from us."

"But you can't prove it."

Bailey fell silent, then leaned forward, as if a thought had just come to him. "Just think about it for a minute. Ernesto Salazar is a powerful and handsome Latin man, the don of all Don Juans. When you open up *el diccionario,* his picture is right there next to the word *machismo.* Do you think he would send audiotapes to a reporter and, in effect, reveal to the world that his young wife had to look outside their own bedroom for sexual gratification? *That,* I assure you, is not an image that Ernesto Salazar would cultivate."

Jack was hard-pressed to argue with that kind of logic. "You may have a point."

"Of course I do," said Bailey. "Which means that you have a new question. If Ernesto Salazar wasn't Eddy Malone's source, then who was?"

25

·

Andie heard gunshots on the other side of the door. She took a deep breath and entered the firearms training room, thankful that Paul Martinez wasn't packing live ammunition.

The Miami field office had a state-of-the-art training facility, with simulated laser weapons that could satisfy the most exacting virtual-reality enthusiast. The guns looked, weighed, and felt like the real thing. Sound effects provided the authentic crack of gunfire. Shooters had to change magazines when ammunition ran out, and air pressure created a convincing recoil. Shrouded in darkness, the agent faced a display screen where he could pretend to be on the academy's firing range in Quantico, while more complex "situation" DVDs tested snap decisions in various life-or-death situations, such as a face-to-face confrontation with a hostage taker.

Martinez was standing in the classic marksman's pose—feet apart, knees slightly bent, two hands on the pistol—squeezing off one precise shot after another in the simple target-practice mode. It was a surefire method of working out anger, and the SAC's anger had been obvious from beginning to end of his morning meeting with Andie. The tongue-lashing had lasted all of five minutes, and Martinez had done almost all of the talking. The SWAT disaster was his headache. By default, it was Andie's, too, because she hadn't done a better job of talking him out of it. Not an entirely fair system of accountability, but that was the reality of the situation when you were the new kid in town. She dreaded the thought of interrupting his cooling-off period, but developments in the Salazar case left her no choice.

"Excuse me, sir," she said as he changed mock magazines on the simulated .45-caliber pistol.

He turned and dropped his earphones down around his neck. "What is it now, Henning?"

Andie said, "I just got off the phone with Ernesto Salazar. He made a delivery to the kidnapper last night."

That got his interest. Martinez slid the gun simulator into its plastic cradle and said, "How the hell can that be?"

She relayed exactly what Ernesto had told her about the call from the kidnapper, the trip to the marina, and the delivery of the suitcase.

"Why didn't he call us before the drop?" asked Martinez.

"Kidnapper said he was pissed that Swyteck called us in. Salazar didn't want to make the same mistake."

"How much ransom did he pay?"

"He wouldn't tell me. Says it's confidential."

"That's understandable. No wealthy family wants the word to get out among would-be kidnappers that they're an easy mark."

"I suppose that could be what this is all about," said Andie. "But after the conversations I've had with him, this sudden decision to pay a ransom is a radical change of heart."

"Must have been the video. Seeing his wife tortured had to affect him."

"That was exactly what he told me," said Andie. "But I'm still not sure what he's up to."

"What do you mean?"

"Again, from the very beginning he was adamant about not paying a ransom. His wife cheating on him and all. And even after talking to him this morning, he didn't seem convinced that any amount of money could possibly save Mia."

"Then why would he pay a ransom at all?"

"Like you said, it's possible the video did affect him. Maybe he can't stand to see her suffer. On the other hand, he's probably not willing to give up his entire fortune to save her—to pay what she's worth. So he pays a ransom on the quick, knowing that it will be rejected. And then . . ."

"And then the kidnapper kills Mia, just like he killed Ashley Thornton. Her suffering is at an end."

Andie didn't answer right away. That was precisely her theory, but hearing the SAC articulate it made the whole thing seem almost too cold and calculating. *Almost.* "It's a thought that crossed my mind," she said.

Martinez nodded. "I'm not saying you're right, but I do like the way your suspicious mind works, Henning."

Andie did a double take. After the way he'd chewed her out in his office just minutes earlier, she would have bet her FBI shield that her next compliment was months in the offing. "Thanks."

Martinez retrieved his weapon and resumed firing, talking between shots. "Not to shift gears too abruptly, but the very notion of a phone call directly from the kidnapper to Salazar is a very interesting turn of events. Especially when you consider it in light of Crenshaw's two-kidnapper theory."

"How do you mean?"

He squeezed off three shots, *pow-pow-pow,* in rapid succession. "You might say we have conflicting developments here. The e-mail message you found on that computer in the SWAT raid said 'Payment is due in five days. Delivery instructions to follow.' Now Ernesto tells us that he got a phone call that same afternoon, and the kidnapper told him to make the delivery last night. It seems to support Crenshaw's view that we're dealing with two kidnappers, one of whom is an imposter."

"I don't see it that way," said Andie. "The messages conflict because the kidnapper changed his mind."

"And you would know that because . . ."

"Because the e-mail message was sent from the Kwick-e Copy Center first thing in the morning, long before the kidnapper knew that Jack was being followed by the FBI. Only after Jack went through the courthouse metal detectors and that whole rigmarole did the kidnapper decide that he didn't want to deal with Jack anymore. So he contacted Salazar directly that afternoon. By then it was too late to retract the e-mail he'd sent in the morning."

Martinez switched from target practice to crisis-situation simulator. On-screen, a heavyset thug was ordered to put his hands up and come out of his bedroom. He started walking toward the agent, but from the shooter's perspective, it was like looking into a tunnel, the field of vision defined by the open doorway.

"Plausible explanation," said Martinez, keeping his gun trained on the simulation suspect. "But not dispositive."

"Shoot!" Andie shouted, but Martinez held his fire. He'd failed to notice that the bad guy had grabbed a gun from a high shelf on the bedroom wall, which was hidden from the shooter's view. In the world of FBI simulation, Paul Martinez was a dead man.

Andie raised an eyebrow impishly. "You should listen to me more often, boss."

He said nothing, but she thought she detected just a hint of a smile.

The phone on the wall chirped, giving Andie a start. Martinez was standing nearest to it and answered on the third ring. Andie wasn't trying to eavesdrop, but when the SAC made eye contact with her and said, "Yeah, Henning's standing here with me right now," she made it her business to catch his end of the conversation.

"Interesting," Martinez said for the third time, speaking into the phone. "We'll be right up. Meet us in the east conference room."

As he hung up, Andie laid open her hands, as if to say *Tell me.*

"Our search of scuba divers has turned up a lead," he said.

"I hope it's better than the one that led to our SWAT raid."

"Much better," he said, his voice deadly serious. "This one actually has a motive."

26

It was still early when Jack left Miami, but with morning traffic he didn't reach Palm Beach until the very civilized hour of nine o'clock. Worth Avenue was one of the most exclusive shopping streets in the world, one designer boutique after another, the perfect place to drop eleven thousand dollars on an evening bag or trash your best friend's plastic surgeon behind her back. The Hermès shop didn't open until ten, so Jack waited outside the front door, coveting the classic Silver Shadow convertible parked next to the Maserati across the street. Mia's friend Emilia was an assistant store manager, and at nine thirty she arrived with the door key in hand.

"Jack, what brings you here?" she said, shoving her tortoiseshell sunglasses above her hairline.

He handed her the *Tribune*. "I thought I'd deliver the Miami paper. Just in case you don't get it up here."

Her eyes were drawn immediately to the headline, and Jack watched as she quickly read the article. About halfway through, her mouth fell open.

"Something wrong?" said Jack.

A noise came from her throat, something between a sigh and a groan. This was the kind of reaction that Jack could never have gauged over the telephone, making the drive worth the effort. "What is it?" he asked.

She read further, then said, "I can't believe he printed this."

"So, my instincts were right? You did talk to Malone?"

She handed the newspaper back to him, her eyes glinting. "Yes. He called me last night, pretty late. I thought for sure the article would be in tomorrow's paper, not today's."

"What did he want?"

"At first, I thought he only wanted me to confirm that you and Mia were having an affair. I told him I didn't know anything about it, I swear. But then he played some tapes for me. It was clearly you and Mia. I couldn't deny it at that point. Obviously you couldn't, either. You admit it right here in the article."

"Yeah, but that's not the part that interests me anymore. What I want to know is, how did Malone get it in his mind that *I* was going to pay Mia's ransom?"

She swallowed so hard that Jack could actually see the lump bobbing in her throat.

"Emilia, I need to know what you told him."

"I wasn't trying to railroad you into anything. I was just trying to protect Mia."

"Protect her how?"

"Malone said that he had it on good authority that Ernesto was refusing to pay a ransom. I was afraid for Mia. I figured that if it was printed in the newspaper that she was having an affair and that her husband refused to pay a ransom, she'd be dead as soon as the kidnapper picked up the newspaper."

"So you told him I would pay the ransom?"

"I didn't say *for sure* you'd pay the ransom. I told him I thought you cared very deeply for Mia and you might pay something if Ernesto didn't. That's all. I wasn't trying to force you into anything. He twisted my words if he made it sound like more than that."

Jack studied her expression, and the welling in her eyes seemed sincere. He couldn't blame her for trying to protect her friend, and he didn't doubt for a moment that Malone would manipulate her words. "It's all right, Emilia. You didn't do anything wrong."

"Yes, I did."

"Really, it's not your fault."

"After I talked with Malone, I should have called you and made sure we were on the same page. But I never thought—" She stopped herself, as if debating whether to say more.

"You never thought what?" said Jack.

"I can't say I ever had much faith in Ernesto," she said, her voice shaking, "but I always hoped that if someone had to step up and help Mia, you would do it. I never thought you'd flat-out refuse to pay a ransom."

Jack folded the newspaper in half, as if hiding from his own words.

Emilia said, "And I never dreamed that you'd tell it to a newspaper reporter for all the world to see. For *the kidnapper* to see. How could you do that?"

Although a little voice inside was telling him that he'd done enough for Mia, that he'd done far more than most men would, he suddenly felt as if he were shrinking right before Emilia's eyes. "I'm sorry," said Jack, not sure what else to say.

"Do you care about Mia or don't you?"

"You think I'd be here right now if I didn't care?"

"Then act like it." She aimed her key at the lock and opened the store door, then stopped. Her voice took on a slight edge, equal parts anger at Jack and concern for her friend. "I won't even try to defend the lie she told you, Jack. It was a terrible mistake. But what are you going to do about it now, make her pay with her life?"

Jack watched from the sidewalk as Emilia turned her back and disappeared into the store.

27

He was naked, except for the white bath towel wrapped around his waist. The shower awaited, and the scent of the ocean was still with him. A black wet suit lay flat on the tile floor, not quite dry after last night's dive. Atop the round kitchen table was a waterproof suitcase, cracked open like a book.

He pushed away from the table, rose slowly, and walked to the stove. The Mexican tiles felt cool beneath his bare feet. The dark panels of tinted glass on his sliding doors were like mirrors in the morning, allowing him to admire his reflection as he crossed the room. The usual adjectives came to mind. Cut. Ripped. He was especially proud of his well-defined abs: six-pack all the way. He worked hard at his body, and the results were obvious. It had started with the rehab—no drugs, no alcohol, no cigarettes—but now it was a lifestyle. He was a walking transformation, tight skin over solid muscle, driven to the brink of obsession. His friends at the gym called him the Machine.

They had no idea.

He removed the whistling kettle from the burner and poured himself a steaming cup of herbal tea. Chamomile with lemon made him sleepy, and he needed rest. Since Mia's kidnapping, he hadn't slept for more than four hours at a stretch. Part of it was the sheer excitement of having her around, but mostly it was the paranoia of an attempted escape or suicide. He felt the need to check on her regularly, like a mother with her newborn, which seemed only normal to him. In the last thirty-six hours, however, he hadn't slept at all—which was *not* normal. The anticipation of Mr. Salazar's delivery had kept him awake. Naturally, the drop-off was always the most thrilling part of the game. It raised such intriguing questions. How much ransom would the husband pay? How much was a man's wife worth to him?

Best of all, what would be the penalty for paying too little?

He returned to the table, teacup in hand. Beside the suitcase was a small tape recorder. He reached for it, then stopped short of hitting the Play button. He'd been listening to the recording since late last night, and he couldn't bring himself to hear it yet again.

He leaned back in his chair and studied the open suitcase. Ernesto Salazar had selected a fine one indeed, completely watertight and big enough to hold plenty of cash. It was actually larger than the suitcase Drew Thornton had chosen, and that one had held a cool million dollars. Salazar, however, had delivered more than just money. This one also held a tape. *Jack and Mia, Jack and Mia, Jack and Mia.* How many times could he listen to their inane conversation, their playful banter, the stupid jokes of lovers?

He listened to all of it—not just once or twice, but many times. The part where she said the kitchen countertop felt cold on her bare ass was mildly interesting, almost titillating, but he quickly slapped down that emotion. He wanted to feel nothing but anger, and by breakfast time he'd heard enough. Mia's husband had made his point. He was married to an adulteress. The handwritten message inside the suitcase left no doubt that the ransom payment had been adjusted accordingly.

What she's worth, Salazar's note read.

He drummed his fingers across the tabletop, thinking. So far, he'd played the game straight, going back to his first kidnapping. When that Georgia auto mechanic hocked everything he owned to come up with a nineteen-thousand-dollar ransom, he'd earned his wife's release, unharmed. But when a multimillionaire like Drew Thornton tried to get off cheap for a measly million bucks, he got exactly what he'd paid for.

The Salazar situation was far more tricky. In some ways, this was business, and a deal was a deal. He'd promised to let Mia go if her husband paid what she was worth. Arguably, Salazar had done just that. You almost had to respect the guy.

He finished his tea with two more swallows. He didn't need to listen to the audiotape again to convince himself that he'd made the right decision last night. He hadn't acted rashly. Sending the audiotapes with an anonymous note to Eddy Malone at the *Tribune* had been the smart thing to do. Now it was time to call Jack Swyteck.

He rose and poured himself another cup of tea. This was no time to rush things.

He wanted to find the exact right words.

28

Nothing quite lit up the little orange lights on a telephone like having your name linked to a sex scandal in the morning newspaper. Jack got the full effect as he entered his office.

"You have twenty-seven messages, Mr. Swyteck." Dani Gilbert was on spring break from Yale, filling in for Jack's regular secretary, who was on vacation. She had the trifecta—brains, beauty, and personality—which had earned her everything from an internship with a prominent U.S. senator to the role of Ophelia in a critically acclaimed production of *Hamlet*. Yet she was mature enough to realize that being a secretary was no walk in the park. Jack and Dani's father were friends from way back, and Jack figured that her one-week stint at Jack Swyteck, PA, was Mark's way of ensuring that his daughter would decide never to become a criminal defense lawyer and would instead choose a more stable career path—like acting.

"Thanks," he said as he took the stack of messages. "But do me a favor, okay? Stop calling me Mr. Swyteck. I keep thinking my dad's here."

"Sorry. I put them all in alphabetical order, except that one on top with the gold paper clip. It requires your immediate attention."

Jack noticed that the "urgent" message was from Theodopolis Knight III—Chief Justice, Florida Supreme Court.

"Uh, Dani. Theo Knight is *not* the chief justice of the Florida Supreme Court."

She shrank with embarrassment, a total overreaction, as if she'd just hiccuped in the middle of her own wedding vows. "I'm *so* sorry, sir. He said that's who he was, I swear. Who is he?"

"He's—" Jack stopped himself. She was trying so hard to be a good secretary, alphabetized messages and all. Even a minor reprimand might crush that amazing youthful spirit. "He's actually an *associate* justice," said Jack. "Minor mistake. Don't worry about it."

"Thank you," she said, breathing a sigh of relief. "But in that case, probably the second message in that stack is most important. There's an FBI agent who wants to see you immediately. Andie Henning. It's Andie a woman, not a man. Don't you think that's odd?"

This, coming from a young woman who called herself Dani. "Only if you do," said Jack.

"She went across the street for coffee," said Dani. "She said to call her and she'd pop back in as soon as you returned. You want me to give her a ring?"

"Sure. I'll wait in the conference room."

The conference room, despite its name, was only occasionally used for conferences. It also served as Jack's library, computer room, and lunchroom. Every now and then Jack even slept there. At the perfunctory one-man annual partnership meeting, it served as the boardroom. And on one special occasion, Mia had interrupted his late-night trial prep with a bottle of wine in hand and officially christened it "the playroom."

Five minutes later, Dani was showing Andie into the conference room. Andie was talking before Jack could even say hello.

"Ernesto paid a ransom last night," she told him. *That* had not been in Malone's newspaper article, and it explained why Andie had dropped in for a face-to-face discussion. Jack had to reel in his surprise as she gave him the short and sanitized version, the one reserved for non-FBI.

"How much did he pay?" asked Jack.

"I couldn't tell you even if I knew."

"Is it enough to get her released?"

"I can't discuss the details with you. In light of this morning's newspaper article, I just thought you should know that he did pay something."

"Please, don't feed me that police-ears-only party line. We both know that he did it to save face, not to save *her*."

"I'm not saying I disagree, but I am curious to know why you think that."

"I talked to William Bailey this morning. The only thing those jokers care about is how it might impact Ernesto's playboy reputation if it came out that his wife was cheating on *him*."

"Bailey told you that?"

"Basically. Even Mia's best friend told me that Salazar tried to hit on her. As far as I can tell, the guy must be an egomaniac. And now he's just doing image control. After seeing that streaming video of Mia's torture, he probably started to worry about how his continued refusal to pay a ransom might play in the newspapers. So he paid one." Jack ran a hand through his hair, exasperated. "He doesn't give a shit about Mia. There's no doubt in my mind about that."

He paused, giving Andie an opportunity to disagree. But she didn't.

Her voice softened as she said, "That's why I'm here talking to you, and not to him."

"We have to do more than just talk," said Jack. "If Salazar didn't pay enough ransom, this creep will kill her, just like he killed Ashley Thornton."

"The best thing we can do right now is go full speed ahead with our efforts to figure out who the kidnapper is. If we act fast enough, maybe we can find him before he has the chance to harm Mia. That's what I'm here for. I need your help. Sit down, please."

The adrenaline wanted him to keep pacing, but he forced himself to take a seat opposite Andie. "What do you need from me?"

"I'm trying to find out something about Mia. It's extremely personal. Something I think that only a man who has been intimate with her could tell me."

That rules out her husband, Jack thought, but he kept the snipe to himself.

Andie asked, "Do you have any reason to believe that Mia was the victim of a sexual assault?"

"You mean other than the CD we got from the Kwick-e Copy Center?"

"I mean in her past. Before you met her."

The question didn't shock him, but it was the first time anyone had come right out and asked, and it forced him to confront something he'd wondered about for quite a while. "Mia has a scar on her leg. Inside the right thigh. I noticed it the first time we were in bed together. She said it was from a tattoo removal, but I didn't believe her."

"Did you talk about it?"

"She didn't want to."

"So you just dropped it?"

"That night I did. She slept over, but we didn't do anything. She asked me just to hold her. So I did."

"Did it ever come up again?"

"I made a few remarks here and there, probably for a couple of weeks afterward. I didn't push it, but if she felt like talking, I wanted her to know that I was willing to listen. She just never seemed to want to go there. And honestly, after that first night, she seemed very comfortable with what we were doing. As far as intimacy goes, I mean."

"I'm not sure I'm understanding you. Are you saying that you do or you don't think she was ever the victim of a sexual assault?"

"I don't know. Why are you asking?"

"I really can't say," she said.

It obviously hadn't been her intention, but given the context, her coyness was telling him plenty. Jack just had to read between the lines more closely. "You think there's some connection, don't you? This kid-napping has a link to her past. Is that the FBI's theory?"

"Look, Jack, if I could tell you more, I would."

"Does your suspect have a name yet?"

"Can't tell you."

"How did you focus on him?"

"Can't tell you that, either."

"He must be a scuba diver, right?"

She averted her eyes, but his persistence seemed to be breaking down her barriers—albeit slowly. "Naturally, any cop in an investigation of this nature and with a brain in her head would be looking for a scuba diver who is a known sexual offender."

Jack narrowed his eyes, thinking. "There has to be more to it. Something that would make the FBI zero in on a guy as an actual suspect. I'll bet it's his MO, isn't it?"

She didn't answer, but Jack immediately noted the absence of a denial.

"So," said Jack, "you found a sex offender who knows how to scuba dive, and his modus operandi bears some resemblance to that of a kidnapper whose ransom demand reads 'Pay me what she's worth.' That's impressive work, Agent Henning."

"It's highly confidential at this point."

"Why? It seems to me that if you have a suspect, it's time to tell the world his name. Get his face plastered on television, issue a be-on-the-lookout, get everyone into the hunt."

"Going public might jeopardize some important leads we're following up. We're not ready to release any information yet. Not even to you. I'm sorry I can't answer your questions."

"Fine. Let's scrap my questions. I'd be just as happy to hear you answer your own questions. Tell me: Do *you* think Mia was the victim of a sexual assault?"

"I can't . . ." She stopped herself, as if it suddenly seemed pointless to continue the game. "All right, Swyteck. I'll tell you what I think. If you ask me, it's an either-or situation. Either she was the victim of a sexual assault before she was married . . ."

"Or?"

"Or she was the victim after."

Their eyes locked, and Jack tried to read as much from her expression as he possibly could. "Do you mean by a stranger, or are we talking spouse abuse?"

She didn't answer.

Jack said, "That's the real reason you're talking to me and not Salazar, isn't it? You still haven't ruled him out."

Again there was no answer, but Jack didn't really need one. He said, "I assume the focus of your investigation shifts dramatically, depending on which way your either-or situation cuts."

"Very definitely."

"So, you would really like me to tell you where Mia got her scar."

"Yes, I would."

"All I can say is, I wish I knew."

"I wish I believed you."

Jack was taken aback. "Hey, I've got nothing to hide here."

"Really?"

"Yes. Really."

She folded her hands atop the table and leaned forward slightly, as if sizing him up. "You seem like such a smart man. A nice enough guy, too. But your ostrich imitation is getting pretty hard to swallow."

"What are you talking about?"

Her voice tightened, and the words came faster. "You dated a woman for two months, slept with her, apparently fell in love with her. The first time she spent the night, you ended up just holding her, no sex, because you found a scar on her leg. But as we sit here today, you can't even venture a guess as to whether she was ever the victim of sexual assault, even though her scar obviously has some history to it, or she would never have lied to you about what caused it. And to top it all off, as recently as this morning you still expected a half million readers of the *Miami Tribune* to believe that you didn't know Mia was married. So I say this with all sincerity and with the best of intentions. I hope you *are* trying to hide something here, Swyteck. Because if you're not, it has to be a living hell to go through life so positively clueless."

Jack felt his body heat rising, but with cops you always had to be careful. They sometimes angered you just to see your reaction. "What's this all about?"

She took a deep breath, then shook it off. "Sorry. That was a good bit more personal than intended."

"You *think?*" he said, doing nothing to mask his incredulity.

"I said I was sorry."

Jack considered it, then said, "Apology accepted. I guess we can still be friends."

She smiled just enough to keep it light, then almost chuckled.

"What?" asked Jack.

"Your 'friend's' remark. It reminded me of a line from a book I read, or maybe it was an old movie. How men and women could never really be just friends."

"You think that's true?"

"Let me put it this way. Perhaps my remarks were out of line, but I'm not going to pretend I didn't mean it. You really can be . . . I don't know. Frustrating. Take that as a little friendly advice."

"I was just being nice with the friends thing, okay, Henning?"

"Great," she said, rising. "Sounds like we finally understand each other."

They shook hands, a little firmer than usual, as if each was sending a message that kicking the other's ass would be no problem at all. Jack led her from the conference/bed-/lunch-/playroom, and Andie thanked Jack's secretary as they reached the reception area. Jack opened the door for her.

Andie said, "Call me when you're ready to pluck that head from the sand, will you?"

She seemed to be teasing, but it wasn't entirely clear. Everything about her was puzzling now, and Jack wondered if he was finally seeing the real Andie Henning—or if it was all just a calculated change in FBI strategy.

"I'll be in touch," said Jack. "But only if you promise to call me as soon as you have anything on Mia. Salazar's ransom payment has to prompt a response of some kind. One way or the other, I want to know."

Her expression changed, a bit too somber for Jack's comfort. "Deal," she said.

Jack said good-bye and closed the door, watching through the window as one very perplexing woman walked quickly to her car. She'd definitely pushed his buttons with her remarks. Clearly she was trying to get under his skin. But why? Then it came to him: She wanted him to confront Ernesto Salazar and find out just how much he was trying to help—or hurt—his wife. But if that was her angle, she'd badly misread Jack. He didn't need to be goaded by Andie or anyone else into a showdown.

He knew he was long overdue for a talk with Mia's husband—mano a mano.

29
·

What a house, Jack thought as he drove up to the wrought-iron gate. A life-size pair of stone lions stood guard outside the entrance. Ivy-clad walls ran the length of the estate like a medieval fortress. Jack stopped his car but left the motor running, taking it all in. The feeling was unlike anything he had anticipated, a strange and powerful mix of emotions. It was as if Mia's other life—her life as Ernesto Salazar's wife—hadn't fully materialized for him until this moment. This was the place she'd called home, the place her husband had built specially *for her.* It was a multimillion-dollar monument to her personal tastes, her decorating likes and dislikes. Here she ate breakfast, walked in the gardens, and lounged by the pool. Jack could only imagine the parties they'd thrown, the countless guests that Mr. and Mrs. Salazar had greeted in the name of business, charity, or friendship. This was where she'd awakened each morning and gone to bed every night.

Well . . . almost every night.

He lowered the driver-side window and rang the intercom button.

"Who is it?" asked the butler, his tinny voice rattling in the outdoor speaker.

Jack hesitated. *Mia's lover? Her, uh, friend?* "It's Jack Swyteck. I'm here to see Mr. Salazar."

There was a long pause, and Jack half expected the sentries to pop up from behind the wall and douse him in boiling oil. Instead, the gates yawned open, and Jack drove up the long curving driveway to the front entrance. The butler stepped down from the porch and escorted him around the side of the house, through the garden, to the pool area in back. Ernesto was seated at a glass-topped table in the shade of a large canvas umbrella. He offered a chair with a gesture, but he did not rise to shake Jack's hand. The butler retreated to the loggia, out of earshot.

"You surprise me," said Salazar. "I didn't think you'd have the balls to come here."

Jack settled into his chair facing the pool. It was more of a water feature than a conventional swimming pool, with man-made streams of crystal clear water rushing through lush tropical gardens. It was built to resemble a lagoon, neither angular nor kidney shaped, and the black finish created a mysterious illusion of depth. Across the way, beside a huge gumbo-limbo tree, a twelve-foot waterfall produced the soothing sounds of water in sheets cascading over limestone boulders. Jack couldn't help but notice the replica of Michelangelo's statue of David standing on a pedestal. Somehow it didn't seem like a good time to bring up his own litigious battle of the bulge, so to speak, and Theo's rendition of "Suwannee River."

"I didn't come here to trade insults with you," said Jack.

Ernesto's gaze shifted away from the pool, and he was looking straight at Jack. "Why *did* you come here?"

"Because I heard a rumor that you paid a ransom."

"Rats," he said, his voice laden with sarcasm. "The FBI can be such a sieve."

"Cut the crap, Ernesto. I don't believe for one minute that this is something you want to keep secret."

"Then you don't understand the constant threat of kidnapping. That's the reality when you live like this. If it becomes known that I'm an easy touch for a hefty ransom, I might as well start leaving a stack of blank checks in my mailbox."

"Interesting word choice," said Jack. "Is that what you paid for Mia last night? A *hefty* ransom?"

"What I paid is none of your business."

Jack glanced toward the black water. Would that be Mia's fate, he wondered, trapped somewhere beneath the surface in some black, watery grave like Ashley Thornton? "I'm making it my business," he said.

"I find your nobility truly quaint, but it's hardly necessary. I have always protected Mia, and in the end, I've done it again."

"Do I detect a change of heart? Now you're suddenly Mia's protector?"

"Nothing sudden about it. Even before we were married, she called me her protector."

Jack recalled the comments of Mia's friend Emilia—how Mia once remarked that she'd married Ernesto for *protección*. "What were you protecting her from?"

"Her past, I suppose you'd say."

"What about it?"

A warm breath of wind stirred the trees around them. A handful of leaves fluttered downward and landed gently in the pool. "By now I'm sure you're aware that there was no Mia before I met her."

"That has to be the most egocentric statement I've ever heard from a married man."

"Ego has nothing to do with it. I mean it quite literally. Try to do a background check on Mia. It will lead you nowhere."

"That's not unheard of among immigrants. It was my understanding that Mia was living in South America before she married you."

"That has nothing to do with it. I'm telling you straight: There was no Mia."

Jack studied his expression, those mysterious dark eyes. Finally, he asked, "Who is she?"

"What?"

"Tell me who Mia really is."

"Mia is my wife, Mr. Swyteck. That is all you've ever needed to know."

Jack ignored the jab. "Agent Henning has her own theory. She thinks Mia may have been the victim of a sexual assault. That could jibe with her apparent lack of a past. Occasionally, victims do assume new identities."

Salazar was staring off toward the waterfall, avoiding Jack's gaze. "Is that who you think Mia is? A victim?"

"I don't know. Maybe it's because I'm a criminal defense lawyer, but I never find myself buying into everything the FBI tells me. In my own mind, I still haven't ruled out the witness-protection program."

Jack watched closely, but he detected no reaction whatsoever. If his hunch about the witness-protection program was correct, Salazar wasn't taking the bait.

"Do you love her?" asked Salazar.

The delivery was matter-of-fact, but the question hit Jack like a slap across the head. It wasn't a complete change of subject. Still, whatever feelings he had for Mia, he wasn't comfortable describing them to her husband. "Do you?"

"I'm the one who paid the ransom, not you."

"Hate to break this to you, Ernesto. But when it comes to ransoms, size does matter. Especially if Agent Henning's alternative theory is correct."

"What alternative theory?"

Jack hesitated to attribute the entire theory to Agent Henning, but he was fairly certain that he had decoded her line of thinking. "A rich husband, an abused wife, and no prenuptial agreement. Financially, you're better off if the kidnapper rejects the ransom."

Salazar's face flushed with anger. "I'm so sick of this. The accusations from the FBI, now from you. Do you think I'm some kind of monster? This woman was my wife. How could any human being see her suffering on that CD and simply ignore it?"

"I didn't say you ignored it. I just want to know if you paid enough to save her."

"Who the hell made you my conscience, Swyteck? I paid plenty. There was five hundred thousand dollars in that suitcase, all right? Half a fucking million for a wife who was sleeping with another man. How many husbands would show that much compassion toward a cheating spouse?"

Jack didn't answer. He was still processing the amount, which was genuinely surprising.

"So don't presume to judge me," said Salazar, "because I sure as hell don't see you coughing up any money. As I recall, you went on record in the newspaper to state that opening your own wallet was completely out of the question. How compassionate is that, lover boy?"

"I've done all I should," said Jack, though compared to Salazar's half a million dollars, it didn't quite ring true.

"And I've done far *more* than I should. Anyone who thinks otherwise can kiss my ass." Salazar shifted his chair, not quite showing his back to his guest, but making it clear that the conversation was over. "Now get lost, Swyteck. I've done my part, and I'm expecting a phone call."

The thought of a call and a final decision from the kidnapper chilled him, but for now there was nothing more to say. Jack rose and started toward the iron gate to the garden, leaving Mia's husband alone with his anger by the black pool of water.

30

·

Jack's drive back to Miami was even more disorienting than usual. The never-ending construction had things so completely twisted around that a stretch of southbound traffic was temporarily rerouted to the east of northbound lanes. It was like driving in the United Kingdom, which reminded Jack of one of his father's favorite old sayings: If everything is coming your way, you must be speeding down the wrong lane. It was about the most optimistic spin he could put on his feelings at the moment. Clearly, the conversation with Salazar had not gone as expected. Jack needed to rethink his basic assumptions about Mia and her kidnapping. Was he really her only hope, or was he sticking his nose someplace it didn't belong?

"Sexual Healing" suddenly blared from Jack's cell phone. The old Marvin Gaye song was his customized ring, thanks to Theo and his technological practical jokes. It wasn't exactly Jack's style, but it sure beat the first song Theo had surreptitiously downloaded for him—Helen Reddy's "I Am Woman."

"Hello," he said, steering with one hand while grasping the flip phone in his left. He answered a split second before the call would have been lost to voice mail, though the delayed response made him think for a moment that he had indeed missed it.

"It's me again, Swyteck."

Jack immediately recognized that chilling, mechanized speech—the altered voice of the kidnapper. Without even realizing it, Jack slowed his vehicle from seventy to forty-five miles per hour. "I'm surprised to hear from you," said Jack.

"You shouldn't be. You're Mia's last chance. Don't you know that by now?"

"Are you telling me that I'm in a position to help her?"

"Wow. You don't miss a beat, do you?"

"I just don't make assumptions. I like things to be explicit. This will work a lot better if you tell me exactly what you want me to do."

"First, I want you to tell me that what I read in the newspaper this morning was a misprint."

"You mean Malone's article?"

"I don't mean Dear Abby."

Jack was cruising in the middle lane, vehicles on both sides of him flying by at much higher speeds. A quick shift to the right saved him from getting flattened from behind by a speeding dump truck. "Exactly which part of Malone's article do you hope was a misprint?"

"Obviously not your admission that you were fucking Salazar's wife. That's pretty undeniable in light of the audiotapes he sent me."

Jack was surprised but not shocked. "Ernesto Salazar sent you the tapes?"

"Yeah. Along with the ransom payment."

Jack hesitated. He didn't want to provoke the guy, and prying into the amount of the ransom might do just that. But Jack didn't see another opportunity coming along any time soon. "You mind telling me how much he—"

"A crisp Andrew Jackson."

"What?"

"The ransom. You wanted to know how much he paid. One twenty-dollar bill."

"I'm not sure I heard you right. Are you saying that the entire sum of cash Ernesto put in the suitcase was—"

"Yeah. Twenty dollars. The price of a cheap whore. That's what his wife is worth."

Jack wasn't sure what to say, or if he should say anything. Either Ernesto had lied to him to the tune of a half million dollars, or the kidnapper was lying to him now. He couldn't waste time trying to sort it out in this phone call. "All I can say is, please don't hold it against Mia."

"I'm not holding it against anybody. Ernesto and I are square, as far as I'm concerned. He paid me what she's worth—to *him*. It's you I'm dealing with now."

It suddenly felt much warmer in Jack's car. "All right. But like I said before: Just tell me what you want."

"First, I want a straight answer. Did you tell that reporter from the *Tribune* that you are not going to pay a ransom for Mia?"

"Look, what I tell a reporter is not necessarily—"

"Shut up! Listen to my question. Did you tell that to the reporter?"

Jack feared the consequences his answer might bring, but telling a lie in these circumstances seemed even more stupid. "Yes, I told him that."

"Was it a misprint?"

"No."

"Now, just so we understand each other, if this conversation ends right now, Mia will be in serious pain in a matter of minutes and dead before sundown. Is that the way you want it?"

"No. Of course not."

"Then tell me, Swyteck. What are you willing to do to change all that?"

"I'm . . . you name it."

"No. I want to hear you say it. Tell me what you're willing to do."

"I don't know what I'm supposed to tell you."

"Tell me what you couldn't tell that reporter."

"Okay," said Jack, collecting his breath. "I'm willing to pay a ransom."

"How much?"

"How much do you want?"

He chuckled, but there was no humor in the mechanized tone. "Have you not been paying any attention at all, Swyteck?"

"I'm listening to every word you say."

"No, you're *not* listening! If you were listening, you'd know how much I want."

"I don't like guessing games. Just make some kind of a demand that I can get my arms around."

"My demand will never change. The only thing you have to ask yourself is whether you're willing to pay it."

"I just want Mia back safe."

"That's great. But that's not what I want to hear. And if I don't hear the magic words in the next few seconds, this call is over, and Mia's a dead woman. So say it, Swyteck."

"Okay, okay. I'll do it."

"You'll do what?"

"I'll pay."

"Pay me what?"

Jack paused, then said, "What she's worth."

"Now say it all together in one nice sentence, like you mean it."

"I'll pay you what she's worth."

The caller's voice flattened, almost deadpan in delivery. "Congratulations. You just bought your pretty girlfriend another twenty-four hours of living hell."

The line disconnected. Jack dropped the phone into his lap and steered his car onto the shoulder, too drained to drive any farther.

31

·

The FBI field office was right off I-95, a plain white building with plenty of equally unremarkable American-made sedans in the parking lot. The kidnapper hadn't explicitly told him no cops. Regardless, Jack had no doubt in his mind that it was time to pay Agent Henning another visit. They met in her office behind a closed door, where Jack recounted the entire telephone conversation while trying not to move around too much in the squeaky office chair that faced Andie's desk.

She listened carefully and took a few notes until it was clear that he was finished. "I'm sorry you had to go through that," she said.

"I appreciate that."

"And I'm also sorry for having been so hard on you earlier this morning. I said some things I probably shouldn't have."

"It's all right. I'm over it. But if your intent was to shame me into a confrontation with Mia's husband, it may have worked. I met with him right after you and I talked."

Andie cringed, but it wasn't triggered by Jack's remark. She'd forced down a half swallow of cold coffee, then dumped the rest of her cup into a potted ficus in the corner. From what Jack could tell, Henning seemed to be doing a much better job of surviving on caffeine than her plant did.

"You're going to kill that plant," said Jack.

"It's a fake."

"No it's not. The leaves are turning yellow."

Andie plucked one off, examined it. "I'll be damned. It is real. Never noticed."

Jack took a gander at all the files and reports scattered across her desk, her credenza, even the office floor. *This girl works too much.*

"Anyway," said Andie, "you were saying what again?"

"I met with Mia's husband this morning."

"Yeah, I know all about that. Ernesto called to tell me that you two had spoken."

"Did he tell you how much ransom he paid?"

"Yes. He said he blurted it out after you made him mad, so he figured he might as well come clean with me. Half a million is what he told me."

"So how do we reconcile his figure with the kidnapper's claim that it was all of twenty bucks?"

"You heard both of them firsthand. Who do you believe?"

Jack's gaze drifted vaguely toward a marksman's trophy on Andie's credenza. "Both of them have reason to lie, I suppose. I don't know."

"Then let me start with a simpler question. What exactly made you change your mind and decide to pay a ransom?"

Jack shook his head. "Not sure I know that, either."

"Well, let's think about it. One possibility is that you decided to pay a ransom when you found out that your girlfriend's husband had just paid half a million dollars to rescue the woman who was cheating on him. I'd call that your mindlessly competitive male ego talking. Another possibility is that you came to your decision after the kidnapper stated in no uncertain terms that someone was going to have to cough up some real money to save Mia."

"And that second scenario, that would be what? My sensitive male side talking?"

"Something like that."

"Truthfully, I don't know when I reached a decision. I think maybe it was this morning, when I read my own words in the newspaper. It sort of hit me that Malone had blindsided me, and unfortunately I made the wrong decision."

Andie gave him a serious look. "I'm not sure it was the wrong decision."

"You're telling me I shouldn't pay a ransom?" She didn't say a word, but Jack could read her expression. "You're telling me it doesn't matter what I pay, aren't you? This maniac is going to kill Mia no matter what."

She gave a slow, rolling shrug, as if reluctant to speculate. "In my opinion, our strategy has to be to string out the negotiation. If it's your decision to pay a ransom—irrespective of the amount—we have to play that angle to get the time we need to catch this guy before you're forced to hand over the cash."

"He told me I'd just bought Mia twenty-four more hours."

"That's good. Now we have to figure out how to buy twenty-four more, and then maybe even twenty-four more after that."

The torture video from the Kwick-e Copy Center was suddenly replaying in Jack's mind. "I can't keep buying time. Mia's the one who pays for our stalling. We need to find this guy fast."

"I'm working on it."

"I think we should both be working on it."

"That's not your best use, Jack."

He leaned forward in his chair, his hand on the edge of Andie's desk, until he realized that he was probably coming across like one of his own desperate clients. He backed off and said, "I'd just like a little information, that's all. I think it would be helpful for me to know something about this suspect you're pursuing."

"I can't talk to you about that. Just two minutes ago, you admitted that you said something to a reporter that you wished you hadn't said. I can't take that risk."

"Now you're making excuses."

"You're right. I am. It doesn't matter if you're talking to reporters or talking in your sleep. I can't share any information about the suspect until I've closed out a couple more leads. Then we'll issue a BOLO nationwide, and we can talk all you want."

"Is he someone Mia met in the past? Someone who raped her?"

"I'm not answering those kinds of questions."

"Ernesto told me that there was no Mia before he married her. My own investigator hits a dead end every time he runs a background check. What's that all about?"

"I wish I could tell you."

"Look, I'm the one who has the direct line of communication to the kidnapper. I should know more about the man I'm dealing with and the woman I'm trying to save."

"Those are distractions at this point. You need to stay focused. We'll do practice runs this afternoon. What matters most right now is that you know how to handle yourself when the next phone call comes."

"So I'm just supposed to be a good boy and do as I'm told. Is that it?"

"The more information I give you about possible leads, the more likely you are to do something counterproductive. It's a simple fact that people make bad judgments when they have an emotional stake in something like this."

"It's also a simple fact that the kidnapper's next phone call isn't coming to you. It's coming to my house, my cell, maybe my office. So if you stop to think about it, the FBI needs me more than I need the FBI."

"What are you saying? You won't cooperate with the FBI unless you're privy to everything in the investigation?"

"Not everything. Just certain things I need to know."

"I can't operate on those terms."

He rose and said, "Then I'm outta here."

"You're bluffing," she said as he started for the door.

He stopped and turned. "I'm very serious."

She let out a mirthless chuckle. "Okay. You're right."

"Glad you see it my way."

"No, I don't see it your way. What I see is the same thing I see in my head every night before I go to sleep. Over and over, I watch them pull Ashley Thornton's body out of the Florida aquifer after her husband paid a million-dollar ransom. So, yes: We need you more than you need us. But *Mia* needs the FBI more than she needs Jack Swyteck. Much more. I can assure you of that."

He stood silent for a moment, then noticed the clock on Andie's desk. Just like that, sixty minutes had passed since the kidnapper's last call. One of the precious hours he'd bought for Mia was already gone. And the next conversation promised to be worse than the last.

"Please, have a seat, Jack. It's time we did some role-playing."

Yet again, she was pissing him off with her stonewalling. This time, however, he knew she was right.

"By the way, how much ransom are you willing to pay?" she asked.

The blood seemed to drain from his head as he returned to his seat. "I have absolutely no idea."

32

·

Around four thirty, Andie had to cut Jack's prep session short. It was their first big break linking Mia to their suspect—one of the crucial leads that had to be explored before the FBI could go public with its information.

"Who is she?" asked Andie. She was on the telephone with an agent in the Atlanta field office.

"Her name's Cassandra Nuñez. Lives in Newnan, just a few miles down the interstate from our office. You want me to interview her?"

Andie thought for a second, but she never really considered the possibility of letting another agent handle the most important interview to date in the case of the Wrong Number Kidnapper. She was just trying to figure out a way to respond without sounding like a control freak. "Even if I took the time to bring you up to speed, there's probably still something we'd miss. I'll be on the next flight out of Miami International. Meet me at the gate. We'll go together."

Three hours later, Andie was riding shotgun in an unmarked vehicle, Atlanta agent Dwayne Carmichael behind the wheel. She'd caught a glimpse of the Atlanta skyline from the airplane, but they were now far from the city lights, in a residential area that could have been just about anywhere. Anywhere except Miami. Atlanta was much colder than Andie had expected, and she'd dashed off to the airport with no time to stop by her house for a coat. Carmichael parked at the end of the cul-de-sac and switched off the headlights. It was a new subdivision, darker than it might have been, as several unsold spec houses were as yet unoccupied. It was typical suburban tract construction, beige or gray paint being the major distinguishing feature between units. Each lot was virtually identical to the next, right down to the same number of needles allocated to the lone six-foot pine tree that graced the front yard in the name of landscaping.

Andie's breath steamed as she stepped onto the concrete driveway, and she folded her arms tightly for warmth.

"You sure you don't want my coat?" said Carmichael. He was a tall African American with a shaven head that was collecting droplets of moisture in the misty night air. Neither of them had thought to bring an umbrella.

"I'm fine. I lived in Seattle till about six months ago."

"Great city. You must have hated to leave."

She didn't bother telling him that it had been impossible to stay. "Yeah, it was tough. Worse places to land than Miami, though."

They approached the house with the usual caution, nothing out of the ordinary, nothing taken for granted. Their guns remained holstered but within reach. From all indications, this would be a friendly witness. Ever since their list of potential suspects had narrowed to a particular sex offender whose MO was curiously similar to that of the Wrong Number Kidnapper, the FBI had been searching for a woman named Cassandra—albeit under a different surname. It turned out that she'd married a man named Nuñez, and even though the name wasn't particularly distinctive, they had enough information to confirm that this was the right Cassandra.

Andie stepped onto the front porch and rang the doorbell. After a minute or so, the porch light switched on, but the door remained closed.

"Who is it?" a woman asked from inside the house.

"FBI, ma'am."

There was a long pause, and the woman again spoke from behind the closed door. "What do you want?"

"It's nothing to be alarmed about. We're just here to speak with Cassandra Nuñez. Purely routine."

Another long pause. "Okay. Give me a minute."

They waited, and Andie heard people talking inside, though it was impossible to make out what they were saying. The conversation was suddenly drowned out altogether by louder voices. Andie quickly realized that either the entire cast of *Friends* had coincidentally come to visit Cassandra, or someone inside had cranked up the volume on the television set. She and Agent Carmichael exchanged glances, their figurative antennae on alert.

Both agents started at the sound of what was surely the back door slamming. Instinctively, they drew their weapons and gave chase, Andie going around the two-car garage and Agent Carmichael taking the other way around the house. Andie was first to reach the backyard. She crouched behind a log pile, then signaled to Agent Carmichael on the opposite side of the yard. He returned the hand signal, then made his way toward the door, his shoulder blades flat against the clapboard siding. He was halfway across the wooden deck when he stopped short and listened. Andie heard it, too. Voices. They were coming from the wooded area beyond the chain-link fence that ran the length of the property.

The agents locked eyes and, without a word, made the same decision. They sprinted across the lawn, flew past the swing set, and hopped over the fence. The ground was soft and slippery with the decaying leaves of many autumns past. Low-hanging branches were the real hazard in the darkness, and Andie felt their stinging slap across her face as she sliced through the forest. Agent Carmichael was keeping pace to her left.

"Hurry!" a woman shouted, and it sounded like the same woman who had refused to open the front door. Her voice gave Andie a specific point of reference, and she was able to discern three silhouettes scaling the slope ahead of them.

"Stop, FBI!" Andie shouted.

The threesome only accelerated, but one of them stumbled and fell to the ground. The leader kept running, but the other returned to help. Andie did a runner's gut check, found another gear inside herself, and quickly caught up with them. "Hold it right there," she said, training her gun on them.

It was two women. The older one was sitting on the ground and trying to catch her breath. The younger woman was on one knee, embracing her and giving comfort.

"Hands over your heads," said Andie.

The younger woman complied, then said something in Spanish, and the old woman did likewise. "She speaks no English," she told Andie. "Don't shoot!"

Agent Carmichael burst through the brush, a few seconds behind. "Should I pursue the other one?" he said, his breath steaming in the cool night air.

"No," said Andie. Even in the darkness, she'd seen enough to recognize the third one as a man, obviously not the person they were looking for. She asked the younger woman, "Are you Cassandra Nuñez?"

"Yes."

"Why did you run?"

She glanced at the old Hispanic woman beside her. "Why do you think?"

Andie quickly surmised that it was an immigration issue. "Do you have relatives staying with you?"

"My husband's aunt and uncle."

"Okay. That's all I need to know about that. I'm not here on immigration. I want to talk about your sister."

"My sister?"

"You can put your arms down now," said Andie. Cassandra complied, and with a quick translation from her niece, the older woman did the same. Then Andie signaled to Carmichael. He pulled a photograph and penlight from inside his trench coat, took a few steps closer, and showed the picture to Cassandra.

"Do you recognize this woman?" asked Andie.

Cassandra looked closely, studying it for what seemed like too long.

Andie could suddenly hear herself breathing—not from the run, but from anticipation. A positive ID from Cassandra was the confirmation she needed to support her entire theory on the Wrong Number Kidnapper. It was a photograph of Mia.

Cassandra returned the photograph and said, "Never saw her before."

Andie's heart sank. "That's not your sister?"

"No. My sister is dead. Killed by the monster who raped her seven years ago."

Andie paused, choosing her words carefully. "I don't mean to sound cold, but if I'm not mistaken, the police never recovered a body, did they?"

"No."

"Then how do you know your sister is dead?"

"Because we were sisters. Family." She leaned closer to the old woman. "We look after our family."

"I understand."

"No, you could never understand," she said, her voice shaking. "My sister was all I had when we came to this country. She would never cut me out of her life if she could help it. Somehow, sometime in the last seven years, I would have heard from her. She's not alive. She's dead. So if you want to make good use of your time, look for the creep who killed her."

Andie breathed in the cool night air, confused. But not *totally* confused. "Can we go back to the house and talk, please? Something tells me we may have found the man you're talking about."

33

Cassandra went to bed at 12:30 a.m., but she didn't sleep. She lay awake in her darkened room, her thoughts consuming her.

After the FBI had chased her down, she and Agent Henning went back to talk in Cassandra's kitchen. Agent Henning did most of the talking, and at her request, Cassandra retrieved some old photographs of her sister. Henning laid them side by side against the FBI photograph of Mia Salazar. There were similarities, to be sure, which Agent Henning emphasized repeatedly. But Cassandra easily saw the differences.

It wasn't nearly so easy, however, to dredge up the past all over again.

Cassandra glanced at the clock on the nightstand. The green liquid crystal numbers glowed in the darkness. It was approaching 1 a.m., and she was reminded of the bad old days. Back then, when her sister had disappeared, Cassandra had routinely seen 1 a.m., 2 a.m., 3 a.m. Sleep was an ever-elusive escape from the harsh reality. Counseling finally helped her to control the awful nightmares, but the memories were still there. She was fighting with the past again, and despite the two-hour conversation with the FBI about her sister, she'd somehow managed to keep the demons at bay. Until now. Maybe it was the quietude of morning's smallest hours. Or maybe it was the gaping emotional wound inside her that had never really healed. Whatever the catalyst, she could feel her defenses weakening. Her grip on the present was failing, and her mind was taking her back to another place, another time—to a time in her life when she idolized her beautiful older sister, Teresa.

"Lookin' hot, ladies," said the muscular young bouncer standing at the entrance to Club Vertigo II. His rock-solid frame was the proverbial keeper of the gate to the hottest new dance club on the Atlanta night scene. The waiting line extended down the sidewalk, around the corner, and halfway up the block again. Three-fourths of the hopefuls would never see beyond the bouncers. Fat chance for the khaki-clad conventioneer from Buffalo who was dressed to sell insurance. The Latin babe in the stiletto heels was a shoo-in. Most of the rejects would shrug it off and launch Plan B. Others would plead and beg to no avail, only embarrassing themselves. A few would curse at the bouncers, maybe even come at them, driven by a dangerous combination of drugs and testosterone, only to find out that the eighteen-inch biceps weren't just for show.

Cassandra was standing at the velvet rope with her sister Teresa.

"You're looking pretty good yourself," Cassandra told the bouncer.

"Thanks," he said. "Who's your friend?"

"My sister. Teresa."

"Lookin' *really* good."

Teresa was wearing black high heels and leopard-print Lycra. She cut a deadpan expression and said, "Got a keen eye for the obvious there, don't you, big guy?"

"Ooh, and attitude too. Guess I'll just have to waive the cover," he said as he pulled the velvet rope aside. "Have a good time, ladies."

The main doors opened, and the two young women were immediately hit with a flash of swirling lights and a blast of music. They were just beyond the bouncer's earshot when they broke into laughter. Cassandra said, "I told you to be cool, not the ice princess."

"You want in, you have to play the game," said Teresa.

As the name implied, Club Vertigo II was the second of its kind. The owner had enjoyed a good long run with the original Club Vertigo on Miami Beach, and he was cashing in all over again at a new

Buckhead location. The look and feel of the place were the same, the inside of the four-story warehouse having been gutted and completely reconfigured with a tall and narrow atrium. The main bar and dancing were on the ground floor, and several large mirrors suspended directly overhead at different angles made it difficult at times to discern whether you were looking up or down. With even a slight buzz, the pounding music, swirling lights, and throngs of sweaty bodies were enough to give anyone a sense of vertigo. The sensation worked both ways, with hordes of people-watchers looking down on the dance crowd from the balconies.

Cassandra and her sister found a place at the bar and checked things out over apple martinis. They could feel the vibration in their feet, almost smell the mix of perfume and perspiration wafting up from the crowd. It wasn't long before they were invited to show their stuff on the dance floor. After two numbers, the guys followed them back to the bar and obviously wanted to hang out, which was when Teresa pulled out her cellular phone and pretended to take an emergency call from her supervisor at the Drug Enforcement Administration. She didn't really work for the DEA; there wasn't even an incoming call. But it worked every time.

"See you later, boys," she said as they disappeared into the crowd.

They bought themselves another round of drinks, beholden to no one. "Fire Girl" was onstage, a Vegas-style act in which a ballet dancer with a body even better than Teresa's managed to keep time to the music while tiptoeing around flames. The sisters watched from their barstools. At the end of the routine, Cassandra noticed that the bouncer was headed straight toward them. A mild wave of panic washed over Cassandra, as if somehow their secret was out and management had learned that they weren't nearly as cool as they pretended to be—and that Cassandra was underage.

The bouncer showed no expression as he approached and placed a card on the bar in front of Teresa. He kept walking, leaving without a word.

Cassandra's mouth was hanging open. "He gave you a card."

Teresa swirled her martini glass, coating the inside with what remained of her martini. "So?"

"Do you know what that means?"

"He's actually a lawyer and wants to know if I've been injured?"

"Cut it out, will you? Look at it."

The business card was facedown on the bar, the back plain white. Teresa gave it to Cassandra, who read it to herself.

"Oh . . . my . . . God," said Cassandra, punctuating each word.

"What's the matter with you?"

She turned the card so that Teresa could see the message: GOT THE LOOK. 2 a.m. THE SUITE.

"What's that supposed to mean?" said Teresa.

"Don't you see the initials, GM, handwritten in the corner? That's Gerard Montalvo."

"Who's that?"

"*Hel-lo.* He only *owns* the club. You've been invited to his private suite."

"Why would I want to meet him?"

"*Why?* Why does anybody do anything in a place like this? So you can say you did, genius."

Teresa arched an eyebrow. "I don't think so. This may be the new hot spot, but call me old-fashioned. I don't show up in the club owner's private suite just because a business card lands in front of me."

"Teresa, *please.* This has to be an amazing party. I'll bet there's even movie stars in there. People would probably kill for these invitations."

"Fine," she said. "You go. Take my card."

"Oh, sure. So they can humiliate me and turn me away when I try to use a borrowed invitation? Just go, all right? Even if it's for five minutes. Then I promise, I'll pay for the cab home, and you can tell me all about it."

"You really want me to do this?"

"Yes. Definitely. But only because you've got the look." ·

"Yeah, right," she said with a light chuckle.

"Please?" said Cassandra. "For your little sister?"

Teresa checked her watch. Almost two o'clock anyway. "Oh, all right," she said, grumbling. "I'll go."

Cassandra's face lit up, and she gave her sister a quick hug. Locked in that brief embrace, peering over Teresa's shoulder, Cassandra caught sight of the bouncer across the crowded dance floor. His stonelike expression seemed to crack ever so slightly, just a hint of a smile. Cassandra didn't look away, not because she was drawn to him, but because she wanted to be sure that she was reading him correctly. She didn't have much to go on, but it was as if the little voice in her head were trying to tell her something.

Maybe this invitation wasn't exactly what she'd thought it was.

34

•

A t 8 a.m. Andie did one final review of the draft BOLO (be on the lookout) that the FBI planned to issue for Gerard Montalvo. She had a few leads to check out before Paul Martinez would give her the green light, but she was confident that the BOLO would issue before the end of the day.

Andie's meeting with Cassandra had not been the home run she'd hoped for. Part of the problem was that she couldn't tell Cassandra why the FBI had focused on Cassandra's sister in the first place. To do that, Andie would have been forced to reveal details about the kidnapper's MO—in particular, his signature "pay what she's worth" ransom demand—which the FBI had assiduously guarded from public disclosure. Those details would not be part of the BOLO, either. By playing the investigation that close to the vest, Andie realized in hindsight, she'd set the wrong tone for their discussion. Cassandra seemed suspicious, unwilling to agree with Andie on virtually anything. Most important, she wasn't buying Andie's theory that Mia Salazar was Teresa Bussori.

There were other ways to prove her point.

Around nine o'clock Andie caught up with Ernesto Salazar at one of his job sites. It was a $12.5 million British Colonial estate gracing the Intracoastal Waterway in Palm Beach, a far cry from Cassandra's tract house in Newnan, Georgia.

Salazar's latest megamansion was 99 percent completed, and Andie could still smell the fresh paint in the formal living room. The floors were Brazilian cherry, offset by white wainscoting and enough custom millwork to keep a skilled craftsman busy for life. Five sets of French doors offered unobstructed views of a stone fountain, lush gardens, and the waterway beyond. It was eleven thousand square feet of opulence, and Andie had to wonder what a developer's profit was on a palace like this. She wondered, too, if a five-hundred-thousand-dollar ransom—if he had indeed paid it—was anything more than chump change to Ernesto Salazar.

"You here to make an offer, Ms. Henning?" said Salazar as he entered the living room.

Andie turned to greet him. "A thousand dollars a square foot is a little much on my government salary."

"Eleven hundred, actually, unfurnished. But who's counting?" His polite smile faded, replaced by his business face. "How can I help you?"

Andie could have eased into it, but she sometimes liked to catch people off guard by cutting to the chase. "Does the name Teresa Bussori mean anything to you?"

"Mmm. Nope. Should it?"

"Teresa was the victim of sexual assault seven years ago. We think her attacker may be the Wrong Number Kidnapper."

"I'm happy to hear you have a concrete lead. But what makes you think I would know this Teresa?"

"Because we have reason to believe that Teresa and Mia are the same person."

He let out a cross between a cough and a chuckle, a kind of nervous reaction that Andie often saw in people who didn't know what to say. "Why do you think that?" he asked.

"Mr. Salazar, if you don't mind, I'd like to ask the questions. Some hard questions." She cut her eyes toward a carpenter in the hallway. "Can we go someplace more private?"

"Sure. Follow me." He led her to the butler's pantry—which was bigger than Andie's kitchen—and closed the door. "What do you want to know?"

"Do you remember the first conversation we had, when I asked you if your wife had any significant identifying features—scars, tattoos, birthmarks?"

"Yeah, I remember."

"Why didn't you tell me about the scar on the inside of Mia's thigh?"

He paused, then said, "I thought I did tell you."

"No, you didn't."

"You were asking me a million questions. I had just found out she was sleeping with Swyteck, then I found out she was kidnapped. My head was spinning. I guess I forgot."

"You forgot about it?"

He looked suddenly irritated. "My wife and I stopped having sex two years ago, okay? I don't remember the last time I saw the inside of her thighs."

"Was your wife ever the victim of sexual assault?"

"Don't change the subject on me. If it wasn't I who told you, how did you find out about her scar?"

She didn't want to answer, knowing that it would further annoy him. "Swyteck told us."

"Swyteck," he said, using a tone to be expected when referring to a man who knew the inside of his wife's thighs.

Andie said, "He doesn't know how she got it, but I thought you might."

"Why does it matter?"

"It's just a simple question, Mr. Salazar. Do you know how she got it?"

"No, she never told me."

"Did she get it before or after you were married?"

He paused, as if he didn't like the way the conversation was headed. "Before."

Andie studied his face. She sensed that he wasn't telling her something, but she needed his cooperation and couldn't risk alienating him. "I have a favor to ask you," she said. "I need to collect a personal article that belongs to Mia. I'm looking for a DNA sample."

"For what?"

"Unfortunately, we don't know of any record of Teresa Bussori's fingerprints. But we're checking to see if the lab that processed the evidence in her rape case retained any of her DNA. If they locate some, and if we get a match, we'll know for certain that Teresa is Mia. Then Teresa's attacker goes from suspect to prime suspect in the Wrong Number kidnappings."

He showed little reaction. He just stood there, his eyes narrowing. "I'm not buying it."

"Buying what?"

"Any of this Teresa and Mia thing. This is just a ruse."

"A ruse for what?"

"This is all part of the thing Swyteck threw in my face the last time we talked."

"I'm not following you."

"Don't play dumb. He told me the FBI's theory: Ernesto the abusive husband is far better off with his cheating wife dead. What else did Swyteck tell you? That I couldn't get it up and have sex with her, so I sliced her leg open to get my rocks off?"

"No one is accusing you of anything."

"Not officially. But I watch enough television to know that the husband is always a suspect. I'm not about to help you scrounge up DNA samples only to help you pin Mia's disappearance on me." He gave the door an angry shove and stormed out of the pantry.

Andie followed him through the living room. "You're misunderstanding my point."

He stopped in the foyer. "You know what? I already delivered my ransom. I paid what my wife is worth, and now I'm done with you people. Just call my lawyer."

"All I'm asking for is something on the order of a toothbrush or hairbrush. This is very straightforward."

"Good. Then you should have no trouble persuading a judge to give you a warrant."

"You're putting up roadblocks where they don't belong. DNA analysis is time-consuming as it is. Don't you get it? Every minute could make a difference to Mia."

"Fine. You want a quickie DNA sample? Why don't you go wipe her lipstick off Swyteck's dick?"

It was the bitterest tone she'd heard Ernesto use since the start of the investigation, but Andie was taken more with his logic than his attitude. She thanked him and said good-bye, conveying nothing to indicate that his crude remark had just sparked a fabulous idea.

35

After an early calender call for an upcoming trial, Jack checked his phone messages while searching for his car in the courthouse parking lot. He was retrieving the third voice mail when the little bleep on the line indicated an incoming phone call. Just yesterday morning, the kidnapper had congratulated him on buying another twenty-four hours of living hell for Mia. With that deadline in mind, Jack wasn't about to let any call go unanswered—especially when he didn't recognize the displayed telephone number. He hit the Flash button and said hello.

"Mr. Swyteck?" the woman said.

"Yes. Who is this?"

"You don't know me, but the FBI thinks I might be Mia Salazar's sister. I'd like to talk to you."

An answer like that could easily have spawned a dozen follow-up questions. "What do you mean 'thinks'? Are you Mia's sister?"

"That's what I want to talk to you about."

"I didn't even know Mia had a sister."

"Let me explain, please. I have some photographs I want to show you. They're of my older sister, Teresa. She went missing seven years ago, and now the FBI thinks Teresa is Mia. I was hoping you and I could sit down and maybe sort this out."

More questions came to mind, but Jack's better judgment took over.

She wants to meet with you, Swyteck. Don't scare her away. "Sure, love to get together with you. Just tell me when and where."

"Actually, my flight from Atlanta just landed. I'm at the airport here in Miami."

"I'm in my car now. I'll pick you up."

"Great. I'll wait outside the Delta concourse. My name's Cassandra. Cassandra Nuñez."

"Nice to meet you, Cassandra. I'm driving an old black Saab. How will I recognize you?"

"I'm wearing . . ." She paused, then said, "People always used to say I resembled Teresa. So why don't you just look for a woman who could pass for Mia's younger sister?"

It was a strange answer, almost a little creepy. "All right. I'll see you in about fifteen minutes."

The trip actually took Jack closer to half an hour, though most of that time was spent inching from the airport entrance to the Delta concourse, the very last one at the domestic terminal. Jack steered around a courtesy van that was blocking traffic at curbside check-in, but he drove slowly enough to scan the crowded sidewalk for Cassandra. As it turned out, Jack didn't have to make a judgment as to whether the attractive young brunette at the curb bore any meaningful resemblance to Mia. She signaled to the black Saab and gave herself away before he could even get a good look at her face. Jack stopped the car and left the motor running. He was about to step out to greet her when she opened the passenger door herself and hopped into the bucket seat.

"You must be Cassandra," he said.

"Everyone calls me Cassie." They shook hands, and he told her to call him Jack as he lifted her small overnight bag into the backseat. Then he pulled back into the slow flow of airport traffic, headed toward the exit.

"My office is right in Coral Gables," he said. "It just takes a few minutes to get there."

"Would you mind if we went somewhere else?"

"What's wrong with my office?"

"Nothing, I'm sure. But I should tell you that I met with the FBI for almost two hours last night. A woman named Henning and a man named Carmichael came to interview me."

"I know Henning."

"Anyway, if you're as central to the kidnapping as the FBI says you are, it seems possible that your office is being watched. I'd rather not make it so easy for someone to find out that I came to see you."

"By 'someone' do you mean the kidnapper?"

"No. I mean the FBI."

The answer was surprising enough to force his gaze from the road to his passenger. "Are you hiding something from the FBI?"

"Let's just say I don't completely trust them."

Interesting, he thought. This Cassie was starting to sound less like Mia's sister and more like one of his many guilty clients. "There's a little restaurant over on LeJeune. You hungry?"

"I flew coach. What do you think?"

"Good. We can talk there."

36

•

His name was Gerard Montalvo," said Cassie. "They called him the Got the Look Rapist."

Jack gave her his complete attention as Cassie talked between bites of a toasted whole-wheat bagel with melted honey butter. The LeJeune Diner wasn't one of Jack's regular spots, but he remembered it from his days as a prosecutor, when an airport baggage employee agreed to meet him there and blew the lid off a currency-smuggling ring. It was a small joint with a few tables in the middle and booths on the left. A long Formica-topped counter separated customers from a short-order cook and the collective grease of four decades and over a million strips of bacon. Directly overhead, a pair of noisy ceiling fans wobbled out of plumb, like a couple of whining old synchronized swimmers who'd forgotten their routine. Jack and Cassie were seated opposite each other at a booth large enough for eight dockworkers, which made Cassie seem even more petite than she was. She told him all about the visit from Agent Henning and the FBI's theory that Teresa was now Mia. She told him, too, about that night at Club Vertigo II, when Teresa got the calling card from the club owner. Even as Jack listened, he was searching for physical similarities between Cassie and her alleged sister. With flawless olive skin and big, dark eyes, both were undeniably attractive Latin women.

It wasn't until Cassie identified her sister's rapist by name that Jack interrupted. "His nickname—the Got the Look Rapist. Was that a name Montalvo got because he'd used the same pickup line with other women in the past? Or did it start with this case, when he gave that card to your sister?"

"I'm not sure."

"Okay. Tell me more about that night."

"Like I said, we went to that bar, Club Vertigo two. I didn't go with Teresa to the private party. She was my older sister, and all my life I thought of her as someone who could handle herself in any situation. I wasn't worried, and I didn't want to be a pest if she was having a good time. So I just planted myself at the bar and listened to music, talked with a few guys. Finally, it was like three-something in the morning, and she calls me on my cell phone."

"What did she say?"

"She was headed home already in a cab. She said she came looking for me in the club and couldn't find me. Which—if it was true—means that she didn't look very hard."

"Did she tell you she'd been raped?"

"No. She sounded pretty shook up, though. And then I was worried. Because it's not normal for Teresa to sound scared. Wasn't normal, I mean."

She looked away, and Jack saw in her expression how difficult this must have been for Cassie—the confusion as to whether she should talk about her sister in the past or present tense. Jack said, "Did you speak to her the next day?"

"She wouldn't talk to anyone for about two days. Missed work on the following Monday, too. I was getting really concerned. Then, like three days later—it was a Wednesday morning—she called and told me she went down to the police station."

"That's when she told you about the rape?"

Cassie lowered her eyes, her mouth tightening. "Yeah. It was awful. I felt terrible, you know, because I was the one who encouraged her to go to the party."

"I'm sure she didn't blame you."

"I'm not so sure," she said in a voice that faded.

"What happened next?"

"Okay, this is where my information gets sketchy. I'm not trying to withhold details, but the fact is, I was lying low once the police investigation started. My visa was expired, and I was in this country illegally at the time. Teresa made me promise not to get involved as a witness. She was afraid I'd be deported."

"You're legal now?"

"Yes. I married a U.S. citizen."

"Do you know if your sister decided to prosecute?"

"Yes, of course. It went to a preliminary hearing. The judge found Montalvo guilty."

"Actually, the preliminary hearing is not a determination of guilt or innocence," said Jack. "It's just a hearing at which the judge decides whether there is probable cause to believe that a crime has been committed. In a rape case, it would be more than enough if the prosecution presents evidence of some penetration and testimony from the victim that it was nonconsensual. At trial, things would get much more contentious."

"Well, that doesn't really matter. Before the trial even started, Teresa vanished."

"How do you mean, 'vanished'?"

"The day after the hearing was over, she was gone. So was Montalvo. The police went looking for both of them. Never found a thing."

"When you say the police never found a thing, did they find evidence to suggest that Teresa was the victim of foul play?"

"You mean beside the fact that she was missing and so was the man she'd accused of raping her?"

"Yes," said Jack. "I mean physical evidence."

"Nothing that I know of. She was just gone."

"Which is probably what's feeding the FBI's theory now that she's still alive—that Mia is Teresa."

"The FBI asked me if I had anything with Teresa's DNA. I guess they want to compare it to Mia Salazar. Unfortunately, I couldn't help them. But they seem pretty convinced even without the scientific testing."

"I'm sure their forensic people have already weighed in on this. They're good, but that doesn't mean they're always right."

The waitress came by to freshen Jack's cup of coffee. When she was gone, Cassie said, "I told the FBI that I didn't think Mia was my sister. After sleeping on it, maybe I overreacted."

"How do you mean?"

"It's not that their theory is flat-out crazy. I just don't want to entertain the possibility that Teresa could be alive until they show me some real proof. It was a nightmare losing my sister. I don't need false hopes."

"That's understandable," said Jack. "I'm sort of looking at it the same way, playing devil's advocate, trying not to jump to any conclusions that would give you false hope."

Her hand shook as she dug into her purse. "I have these photos I wanted to show you." She removed two from her bag and laid them flat on the table. One was an old photograph of Teresa. The other was the more recent shot of Mia that Agent Henning had given to her.

Jack leaned forward, elbows on the table, studying them closely. Teresa's hair was longer and wavier than Mia's, but it was the same dark brown in color. Her eyebrows were much heavier, and, to be brutally honest, Teresa's nose was more prominent—more like Cassandra's than Mia's. Mia had fuller lips, and her cheekbones seemed more angular.

"How old was Teresa when she went missing?" asked Jack.

"Twenty-six."

"So she'd be thirty-three now. Mia just turned thirty."

"Agent Henning mentioned that. Basically, her position was that if you were going to start a new life and take on a new identity, wouldn't you shave a few years off your age?"

Jack couldn't disagree. "I'm more troubled by the facial features. I see definite similarities. But before going so far as to tell you, yeah, I think your sister's alive, I'd want the obvious differences explained."

"Agent Henning suggested plastic surgery."

"Possibly. By any chance, did your sister have a scar on the inside of her left thigh?"

"Not to my knowledge. The FBI asked me the same thing."

"That's because I told Henning that Mia had one. I saw it myself."

Cassie finished the last of her bagel and pushed the plate aside. "It could have resulted from an injury after Teresa became Mia."

"Or it could have been from the rape itself," said Jack. "Do you know anything about the injuries your sister sustained?"

"I don't remember anything about a leg wound. But not everything about the assault was made public, since the case never got to trial. And I never saw the medical report."

Jack's gaze returned to the photographs, and he shook his head. "It doesn't make sense. If these two woman are the same person, then your sister had no fear of plastic surgery. She did some serious work to change her appearance."

"So?"

"So . . . if she wasn't afraid of plastic surgery, why would she leave an ugly scar on the inside of her thigh? Any doctor who was capable of doing this kind of work to her face could easily have taken care of that scar."

Cassie considered it, then said, "You're right. That doesn't make any sense."

"I'm not trying to discourage you, but like you say, it never does any good to encourage false hope, either. We could be dealing with a serial rapist who's drawn to a certain type of woman. Attractive Latin women who look like Mia and Teresa. Similar height, similar build. That doesn't necessarily mean that Teresa *is* Mia."

"Either way, what you're saying is that Gerard Montalvo is back. Which means that no one on this earth wants to nail this guy more than I do."

"I suppose I'm a close second," said Jack.

"Right. You mean if Mia is Teresa."

"It's actually simpler than that. I know what this guy did to Ashley

Thornton. I watched the video of Mia screaming in pain. Whether Mia is or isn't Teresa, somebody has to stop this monster."

"You're right. I didn't mean to minimize your feelings. Agent Henning did tell me that you were in love with Mia."

"What else did she tell you?"

"That she married a rich guy, Ernesto Salazar. Which is another thing that bothers me about the FBI's theory. Teresa was not the type to marry for money."

"Strict personality comparisons probably won't get you very far in this situation. Being raped can change a woman. Psychologically speaking, you may not be looking for the same person."

"I suppose that's true. Whichever way you look at it, the Teresa I knew is gone."

Jack felt as though he should say something to console her, but he could only manage to move the conversation along. "Anyway, it's not really fair to say that Mia married for money. Her best friend told me that she was looking for protection, which fits with the FBI's theory."

"Yes, it does. Naturally, Teresa was terrified of her attacker. That's why it took her three days to go to the police. The last time I talked to her, the possibility of retaliation from Montalvo was clearly on her mind. It freaked her out when he got out on bail. She begged the police for protection."

"Did they give it to her?"

"Obviously not. Which is why one of two things happened. Either she ended up dead. Or she ran away and created a whole new life."

"And she married Salazar to get the protection the police wouldn't give her."

"That's why I don't trust the FBI with this. I don't think they'll ever tell me the whole story. They even told me not to talk to you."

"That doesn't surprise me. They're afraid I might screw up the investigation if I try to hunt down Gerard Montalvo on my own."

"Well, I don't trust the cops to hunt him down. They let him get away the first time. Definitely let him get away with rape. Maybe even murder."

Jack brought his cup to his lips, speaking over his coffee. "Is there something you'd like to propose?"

She tucked the photographs back into her purse. "We should be helping each other. Henning told me that you're the one who will be talking directly with the kidnapper. You have to pay the ransom. Is that true?"

"Yes."

"Then I'm sure you want to know as much as possible about the woman you're trying to save."

"That's a fair statement."

"Then it should be a no-brainer. Going forward, I'm the best person to know if your girlfriend Mia is actually my sister Teresa. So here's the deal. If you're honest with me about everything you do, everything that happens, I'll be honest with you. You'll know everything I tell the FBI and more. If we stay together on this, neither one of us will be at the mercy of Andie Henning and the FBI for answers."

"That sounds good to me. Except we're already behind the eight ball. Obviously the FBI knows something that you and I have yet to figure out."

"What?"

"Think about it," said Jack. "I doubt that Agent Henning zeroed in on your sister's rape solely because of her physical similarities to Mia. That probably wasn't even their principal search criterion, given the fact that Ashley Thornton, the kidnapper's first victim, looked nothing like Mia. I suspect that Montalvo popped up on the FBI's radar screen because, number one, he was a sex offender. Two, he was a scuba diver. And most important, the modus operandi of the Got the Look Rapist was similar to that of the Wrong Number Kidnapper."

Cassie seemed to be searching for an answer, then shrugged. "Nothing I ever saw or heard about the Got the Look Rapist ever made mention of ransom demands or families being forced to pay what the victim was worth."

"I'm not saying it has to be an exact match. Just something similar."

Again, she struggled. "That's hard for me to say, since I didn't attend the hearing. Like I told you before, Teresa didn't want me anywhere near the courthouse, because I was illegal at the time."

"That's all right. You're going to be more helpful to me than you can even imagine. I'm sure we'll find the common operational thread."

"Right. Got any ideas on where to start?"

Jack leaned back in the booth, the wheels turning in his head. "Yeah. Now that I have the name of the FBI's chief suspect, I certainly do."

37

___
.

Her days were beginning to bleed together.

Mia had struggled desperately to keep track of time. It was a huge challenge, especially since her captor had moved her to this new room. She was no longer blindfolded twenty-four hours a day, but there were no windows, and he allowed the light on for only short periods of time. Perhaps most disorienting of all—and the reason, she surmised, that she'd been moved to another room—was the complete absence of external sounds. Even when she pressed her ear to the floor or wall, she heard nothing to distinguish night from day. It was like living in a soundproof cocoon, no traffic noises outside the building, no television newscasts playing in the next room, not even the sound of water passing through pipes. In the old room, at least, she'd been able to discern *something* beyond her own four walls, even if it was just a dull, throbbing sound in the background. It was impossible to know what those faint, distant noises might have been, but she'd settled on a construction crew working on a road or a building, which at least let her conjure up images of daylight and civilization. Without those sounds, the best gauge of time was the number of meals her captor served and the number of bathroom breaks. That worked for a while, but he seemed wise to her counting. Meals started to come irregularly, sometimes not until she was famished, other times when she wasn't hungry at all. She would be forced to endure a long stretch without a bathroom break, and then he'd give her two in a row, almost back to back. If his intention had been to thwart her efforts to keep track of time, it worked. She was now officially clueless as to how long it had been since her abduction.

This guy has kidnapped before, she realized.

She checked her injured toe. A scab was just beginning to form, which told her that it had probably been a few short days since he'd moved her from the old room—since he'd crushed her toe and video-taped her screams. It seemed like weeks.

Can this go on for months? Or even years? She wondered if she would eventually come to measure the passage of time by the hours or days between his sadistic urges, if someday her only frame of reference between attacks might be how long the bruising took to subside. The very idea made her nauseous, and she forced herself not to think such dark thoughts. In a way, she'd been lucky so far. Horrible as it had been, the mangled big toe was her only physical wound. Apart from that one violent episode, her captor seemed content to videotape her sponge-bathing or defecating in a plastic bucket, all exercises in breaking her spirit, total humiliation. She feared, however, that it was only a matter of time before he became bored with the voyeurism and psychological games. He would want something more.

Money, she prayed silently. *Lord, let it be money he wants.*

But who would pay it?

The doorknob turned, which gave her a start. The door opened a crack, and his voice filled the room. "Get down, turn around, and face the wall."

On her knees, she slid across the floor and stared into the corner, her back to the door. This was their routine, and it marked the end of her "reward session," a period of an hour or so during which he allowed her to keep the blindfold off and the light on. The sessions followed a familiar pattern. He would enter the dark room with a flashlight. The beam of light in her eyes and a mask or nylon stocking over his head prevented her from seeing his face. He'd bring her a bottled water and a sandwich, turkey this time, other times roast beef. He'd unfasten the bindings on her legs and wrists, tell her to face the wall, and then remove

her blindfold. On his way out, he'd switch on the ceiling light. The fixture had three sockets but only one bulb, maybe forty watts, at most
sixty. Alone, she'd have time to eat and move around inside her dimly
lit room. Three paces wide, four paces long. She'd walk in circles, run in
place, do yoga stretches—anything to distract herself and get the heart
pumping from something other than fear. It was the kidnap victim's
version of recess.

It always ended too soon.

"Do you need to go to the bathroom?" he asked.

She did, but it wasn't urgent, and she was certain that he had that
damn camera with him again. "No," she said. Then she waited. The
next step in their routine was the return of the bindings and the blindfold, but the familiar sound of his footfalls across the room didn't come.

"I'll leave this right here for you," he said. "Don't turn around until
I'm gone."

The door closed, and it took her a moment to absorb the break in
the usual pattern. She'd dreaded the return to "lights out" and sensory
deprivation. But those fears had not been realized. The light remained
on. Mia was still free to move about, free to take in her dank surroundings. Slowly, she turned and spotted a red plastic bucket on the floor
near the door. Her bladder was fuller than she'd led her captor to believe. It wasn't her usual bathroom bucket, but for once she had privacy,
and it would certainly do the trick.

She rose and started to unbutton her pants as she crossed the room,
then stopped short as she reached for the bucket. Something was already in it.

A lightbulb.

She stood motionless, staring into the bucket. It appeared to be an
ordinary incandescent bulb, but Mia couldn't tear her eyes away from
it. Her imagination was working overtime, and in her mind's eye she
could see the lightbulb smashing against the wall. She could hear the
familiar pop, the explosion of glass into hundreds of shards that would
fall to the floor like lethal snowflakes. They would be sharp, razor sharp,
and she would select one large enough to do the job. It was more of an

impulse than a plan. Either way, she didn't act on it. The bulb was right there inside the bucket, well within reach, almost beckoning to her. But it was as if her hands were glued to her side.

Why a lightbulb? she wondered. Why had he left it for her? Only one answer came to mind. This was no coincidence. She wasn't being paranoid. Mia had yet to see her captor's face, but the lightbulb—the image of the *broken* lightbulb—was the breakthrough she'd never really wanted.

She suspected that they'd met before, and she assumed that the lightbulb was a pointed reminder—a reminder of how she'd ended up with that scar on her inner thigh.

38

Jack was driving from the LeJeune Diner to his office when he took the phone call from Andie Henning. She wanted to know if Mia had kept a toothbrush or hairbrush at Jack's house. Or maybe a tube of lipstick. She did, Jack told her. "But I got rid of all that stuff when I found out she was married. It was sort of therapeutic spring-cleaning for me."

"Damn," was all she said.

The traffic light changed, and Jack braked, even though it was the leading cause of death in south Florida—putting yourself at the mercy of some joker behind you who, red light be damned, is determined to race through any intersection that isn't blocked by at least six squad cars, a jackknifed tractor trailer, and several fallen trees.

"Why do you need a DNA sample?" Jack was playing dumb, but it seemed okay to ask about DNA even though Andie hadn't explicitly mentioned it.

"I can't tell you why."

"What a shock. Hold on a second, I need a jolt from my defibrillator. *Clear!*"

"Very funny. Would you mind meeting me at your house, please? I'd like to bring a forensic guy with me. If you're like most single men, you probably haven't washed your linens since the first Gulf War. Maybe we can find a hair on a pillowcase or something."

Ordinarily, Jack would have resisted until he got a satisfactory answer, but he was just as eager as the FBI was to find out if Mia was Teresa. He agreed to meet her at eleven o'clock.

Jack arrived home a little early. He took the extra time to drift through the house, searching for traces of Mia—not the faded photographs and tickets torn in half that someone whose name Jack couldn't remember had sung about in the sixties, but trace evidence that the FBI might find useful. He started in the bathroom, and ooh, baby, was it ever a mess again. Mia had forced him to keep it reasonably clean while they were dating, but it had since reverted to the kind of hellhole that only Theo could be proud of. Hopefully the FBI forensic expert had handled a few mass murders or natural disaster sites—something that would give him the stomach to enter Jack's bathroom.

Jack walked to the kitchen and grabbed a soda from the refrigerator. Alone in the house, he finally had some quiet time to digest his conversation with Cassandra. The possibility that her sister Teresa had turned herself into Mia started to play on his mind. A week earlier, he would have told anyone that Mia deserved an Academy Award, the way she'd fooled him into thinking she was unmarried. That gig, however, was nothing compared to assuming an entirely new life and a new identity. Then again, maybe it was easier to become someone else entirely and forget that the other "you" had ever lived. There was no switching back and forth between roles, no two sets of friends, no stress over having to be in two places at the same time. At some point, didn't everyone want to chuck it all, wipe the slate clean, and start over? In some ways, it could be fun. It depended on what you were running from—and whether you could ever really leave it all behind.

His cell phone rang, and he figured Henning was calling to tell him she was running late. Of course, she wouldn't be able to tell him *why.*

Jack opened the flip phone and checked the display, but it wasn't

Henning. It was another "Out of Area" call from an undisclosed number. His pulse quickened, and his suspicions were confirmed just as soon as he said hello.

"You got my money, Swyteck?" The voice was deeper than before, slower and less robotic sounding. Mia's kidnapper had apparently found himself a new toy in the voice-alteration department of the local spy shop.

"Only if you're willing to let her go," said Jack.

"Anything's possible."

Jack started to pace, slowly circling the center island in his kitchen. "Like I said before, I don't like to deal in possibilities. I need some certainties."

He snorted. "Sorry, dude. This kidnapping doesn't come with a money-back guarantee."

"I'm not asking for that. I just want to take some of the guesswork out of the ransom payment."

"Then pay me what she's worth, and you've got nothing to worry about."

Jack stopped at the sink and opened the window. The kitchen hadn't seemed hot prior to the phone call, but he suddenly could use the breeze. "Here's what I'll do for you. When I got divorced, I was required to file a net worth statement with the court. That was a couple years ago, and some things are outdated. My Mustang, for example, got torched last year, so that's out. On the other hand, I'm doing a little better in the law practice than I was back then. Anyway, I updated it, and it's all there in black and white. Total disclosure."

"What kind of crap is this?"

"Please, just listen. To show you that I'm dealing in good faith, I'll post my current net worth statement on my home page on the Internet, www-dot-jackswyteck-dot-com. Go there, check it out, then let's talk again. Ask me anything you want."

"Fine. Here's a question for you: Are you trying to get your girlfriend killed?"

"I just want to see if we can agree on a number. Something every-one can live with." The pun was completely unintentional.

"We're going to do this my way, not yours. I told you yesterday that you bought yourself another twenty-four hours. Time's up."

"I'm not looking for a major delay."

"No delays. Period. Do you understand me?"

Jack couldn't put the thought of Ashley Thornton and her hus-band's million-dollar ransom out of his mind. He had to push this guy to cut a deal, but to do that, he needed to take control. He had to do something to let this loser know that he wasn't as clever as he thought he was, that Jack wasn't going to fall into the same trap as Mr. Thorn-ton. Then, maybe, he would have some power to negotiate. "Let me ask you a question, pal."

"I'm through with the questions."

"Would you—"

"I'll hang up."

"Would you say—"

"Don't push me, asshole."

"Would you say Mia's got the look?"

There was silence on the line. Jack was leaning against the kitchen counter, his hand shaking, but he was certain that the caller was still there.

"That's a very good question, Jack. Can I call you Jack?" The voice was calm and steady, no sign of distress.

"Sure. Got one more for ya, though."

"What's that?"

"Should I tell the FBI about these questions that keep percolating around in my mind? Or do you think maybe this is something you and I would rather keep to ourselves?" It was a bluff, of course, since the FBI probably knew at least as much as he did. But Jack alone was in direct communication with the kidnapper, the only person in a position to play the bluff.

"Nothing like secrets between friends, is there, Jack?"

"Nothing like it."

"I'll look at your Web site."

"Good. One other thing."

"Name it."

"You didn't answer my question."

There was another pause, then an empty chuckle. "Yeah. Even after the plastic surgery. I'd say your girlfriend's still got the look."

The caller disconnected, and Jack stood alone in his kitchen.

39

•

Andie and her forensic specialist showed up at Jack's house just a few minutes after the call from the kidnapper. The logical starting point for forensics was the closet where Mia kept her clothes whenever she spent the night. Jack pointed the specialist in the right direction. As soon as he disappeared into the bedroom down the hall, Andie looked at Jack and said, "Tell me."

The color had not yet returned to Jack's face, which apparently telegraphed the fact that something important had happened. Jack felt the need to sit down if they were going to talk about it. They went to the living room, Andie on the couch and Jack in the armchair. He didn't come right out and tell her that he'd spoken to Cassandra, but he told her everything else, which made it easy enough for Andie to deduce that he and Cassandra had formed an alliance of some sort.

"This concerns me," said Andie.

"Why? Because you told Cassandra not to talk to me, and she did?"

"Frankly, that's part of it."

"What do you expect when the FBI's pat answer to every question is 'Sorry, I can't answer that.'"

"I use that response only when protocol dictates it."

"Why would protocol dictate that you tell me nothing about Teresa and Gerard Montalvo? And don't tell me that you're sorry, you can't answer that."

"Lots of reasons. Not the least of which is the way you haul off and make important strategy decisions without consulting me. Like letting the kidnapper know that we're pursuing the Got the Look Rapist."

"He doesn't know you're onto him. Right now, he thinks the only way the FBI discovers his past connection to Mia—or Teresa—is if he doesn't play ball with me. You don't see that as a strategic advantage?"

"No, damn it. We're issuing a BOLO for Gerard Montalvo by the end of the day."

"You can't do that. It will look like I broke our agreement. He'll think the BOLO issued because I told the FBI that he was the Got the Look Rapist."

She massaged between her eyes, as if a massive headache were coming on. "You're making me crazy."

"Sorry, but it's you and your tight-lipped rules that got us into this mess. If my life's on the line, I need to know everything you know."

She thought for a moment, as if fighting the urge to tell him that it was out of the question. "All right, look. You and I don't have to like each other, we just have to get along."

She was starting to sound like his ex-wife, but he let it go. "What are you proposing?"

"I'll go to my ASAC this afternoon. I'll see if I can get you approved for a higher level of clearance."

"That's a start."

"But I'm not pulling the BOLO. It's going out by the end of today."

"Then what do I tell psycho boy?"

"Tell him that it wasn't you who figured out that he was the Got the Look Rapist, it was the FBI. You were actually doing him a favor by tipping the FBI's hand more than twenty-four hours before the BOLO issued."

"That's not going to placate him."

"Do you have a better idea?"

Jack slowed down, trying to sound as calm and collected as he could. "I think this little misunderstanding points out one thing. You and I need to settle on an overall strategy, and we need to stick to it."

"I agree with that."

"Good. Here's how I see it, and you tell me if you disagree. Every time I talk to this guy, he tells me no cops. So, step one is for me to talk the talk and walk the walk as if I'm going at this alone, no police, no FBI."

"I don't recommend that you go it alone."

"Granted. But I have to create that impression. Which means that I do the negotiations, I deliver the ransom. You guys are never far behind me, but you're out of sight. Agreed?"

"In concept, yes. But I want you to think twice about paying a ransom. Mr. Thornton paid a million dollars, and it didn't help."

"Yeah, but that first kidnapping was different, the one with the auto mechanic in Georgia. He paid how much ransom?"

"Nineteen thousand dollars."

"And his wife was released unharmed. So the way I see it, I'm not married to Mia, and we didn't even date that long. But I have a little more money than that auto mechanic. So our magic number may be somewhere between nineteen thousand and a million. Hopefully closer to nineteen thousand."

"But if you pick the wrong number with this guy it's game over. He kills Mia. My recommendation is that you string out negotiations as long as possible, never agree on a number. Your dialogue should be structured so that you elicit clues about his whereabouts. We slowly build one piece of information on top of another until we can either box him in and force a surrender or move in with Hostage Rescue and take him out. I can coach you on what to say and how to get him talking."

"That sounds great in theory, but you're trying to buy more time than he's willing to sell. I say I pay a ransom, but I insist on a simultaneous exchange—I hand over the money and he releases Mia at a specific time and place. That's your opportunity to take him out."

"That's an option, but I have to warn you: A simultaneous exchange is a volatile and dangerous scenario."

"The only other option is to drag this out indefinitely and see more home movies of Mia being tortured. I don't want that."

"Nobody wants that. But please consider what I'm saying. I know what works and what doesn't."

Jack paused. He was suddenly reminding himself of the clients who came to him for his expertise as a trial lawyer and then proceeded to tell him how to try their case. "I will consider it," he said, "but we still have to be prepared to pay a ransom. Even under your plan, it may ultimately come down to a matter of how much money we can pony up."

"If you want to pay a ransom, I can't stop you."

"I'm looking for more than the FBI's passive acquiescence. What I want to know is, are you willing to put any money on the table to obtain Mia's release?"

"You know the FBI would never do that. Payment of a ransom is the responsibility of the victim's family—or in Mia's case, her boyfriend's responsibility."

"This is different. I'm helping the FBI to catch a serial kidnapper. He murdered his second victim and tortured his third."

"I can't put in a funding requisition for ransom money. I'll be laughed out of the bureau."

"Then call it something else. It's more like a funding request for an undercover operation, don't you think?"

"If I were using an agent to deliver a ransom as bait, I'd say yes, arguably. But I can't put federal dollars in your hands to pay over to some lunatic as ransom. It's not the same thing."

"What if I agree to use the money only as bait, like the proof-of-life payment I was supposed to deliver in downtown Miami? Would that fly?"

"Not in a simultaneous exchange where you deliver the ransom. That's all I need for the kidnapper to figure out that you're toting marked bills. Then I'll have two dead civilians on my hands."

"Can you at least focus on trying to get some money? We can talk delivery logistics once we know what your number is."

She paused, then said, "I'll see what I can do."

"How much do you think you can get?"

"I have to be honest. Budget is tight these days. Since nine-eleven, every spare nickel seems earmarked for Homeland Security."

"How much?" said Jack.

She seemed almost embarrassed to say it. "I could probably get approval for twenty thousand dollars."

"Twenty thousand?" said Jack, scoffing. "He killed Ashley Thornton because a million wasn't enough."

"Her husband was extremely wealthy. You're not her husband, and you're not wealthy."

"He already rejected ten thousand dollars as proof-of-life money. We have to put serious money on the table."

"I can't promise anything. When I put in a request to grant you higher security clearance, I'll try for more funding. But you have to give me something in return."

"That's fair. What?"

"I want you to promise not to pursue Gerard Montalvo. That's my job, not yours."

He thought about it, then chose his words carefully. "I promise I won't interfere."

She didn't push, but it didn't take a genius to realize that a promise not to interfere wasn't exactly a promise to stay out of the hunt. She flashed a hint of skepticism and said, "Do you remember the first time the kidnapper talked to you? He warned that if you crossed him, the person who pays is the one you care about more than anyone else."

"Yeah. At that point in the game, I wondered how he even knew that Mia and I had been seeing each other, let alone that I cared that much about her. I guess she told him right off the bat."

"I'm not so sure he was talking about Mia. I think he meant you."

"What?"

"To a self-centered sociopath, the person you care about more than anyone else is yourself. In other words, if you screw up, *you* will be the one who pays. And he didn't mean in dollars."

Jack wasn't sure if she was right or if she was trying to scare him into being more cautious. Either way, he got the point.

Andie continued, "In all the kidnappings I've handled, I've never lost a messenger. Don't be my first."

"Don't worry about me," he said. "I'm worried about what's going to happen to Mia when you issue that BOLO for Gerard Montalvo and he thinks I reneged on my promise."

"I'm worried about that, too."

"Well there you go," said Jack. "We finally agree on something."

40

•

That night, Jack and Theo paid a visit to Miami's hottest new dance club. It was work, not play. They were following the next logical lead along the thread that connected Mia to Teresa, notwithstanding Jack's promise to Agent Henning. He'd agreed not to interfere, not to crawl under a rock.

Jack wasn't the clubbing type, so the trip required a little advance preparation.

"South Beach is yesterday's news," Theo told him.

What? You can't mean the South Beach? As in Ocean Drive, art deco, Gucci-clad bimbos, hard-bodied hotties with pocketfuls of ecstasy and their adjusted gross income draped around their necks in the form of fourteen-karat gold? You mean that South Beach?

"No way," said Jack.

"Seriously, dude. It ain't happenin' there no more."

That kind of exaggeration was heresy on Miami Beach, but it was music to the ears of the Miami Design District. Nestled in the heart of Little Haiti—Miami topped even Port-au-Prince in HONK IF YOU LOVE HAITI bumper stickers—the Design District was conceived in the nineties as a collection of furniture showrooms and boutiques that catered to cutting-edge designers and architects. Naturally, certain city planners scoffed at the idea of supermom dropping off her kids at private school on her way to a tennis lesson, picking up her girlfriend from the spa, and then heading up to Little Haiti for some shopping. After all, they didn't call it Little Haiti because it was filled with wealthy white folks. But the designers came, and some big names, too. Art galleries, antique shops, and trendy little restaurants popped up. Soon, word got out—*Like seriously, girlfriend, I found a Roche Bobois leather sofa for just nineteen thousand dollars*—and the Design District was the In Place.

Then came the velvet ropes. Actually, the district had just one velvet-rope club, but Miami was the kind of place where one of anything could constitute a trend.

Club L'fant was arguably hotter than any nightspot on South Beach. Like everything else in the Design District, it had been converted from an old warehouse, but it was the only place in the neighborhood still hopping at 1 a.m. Two bouncers stood outside the main entrance, each with a hand on the velvet rope. Their names were Lionel and Richie, for real, and any joker who linked their names together and started humming "Three Times a Lady" was immediately bounced as *way* too old to be there. Lionel was French, six five, conversant enough in English to keep out the losers and have his way with the ladies. Richie was six feet three, a Miami High dropout, an ex-con.

And he was a friend of Theo's.

"How you doin,' my man?" said Richie. Jack watched as he and Theo shook hands eleven different ways, finishing with a smile and an exchange of punches to their rock-hard biceps—the standard prison-yard ritual.

"This here's my buddy Jack."

"Your buddy?" said Richie. "Looks more like your accountant."

Jack had expected him to say "lawyer," but he was somehow even more offended. Theo laughed and said, "Nah, he's cool. But this visit is business." *Bizzniss.*

"What kinda business?"

"Need to speak to the owner. You think you can arrange it?"

"Tony's upstairs in his private club. No way I can get both you *and* Mr. Stiff in there. Maybe he'll come down and meet you at the bar, if you want to call in some old markers."

Theo's expression turned serious. "I'm calling them in."

"No problem, bro."

Theo gave him a friendly slap on the arm, his way of saying thank you. The red velvet ropes parted, Richie stepped aside, and Jack and Theo entered, much to the envy of the block-long line of beautiful people waiting to get inside.

Club L'fant was in a serious party mode, with every table full, the dance floor packed, and the waiting line three deep at the bar. Designer clothes and flashy jewelry were everywhere, people outfitted to show off their money, their buff body, their collagen lips, their Botoxed brows, and in many cases, their utter lack of taste. It was a fashion paradox, the way a quest to be different could make everyone look the same. One trend was especially obvious. Some women seemed to think it stylish to rip the designer label from their jeans—and about half of the backside of their pants right along with it, so that their bare skin brushed up against the guys whenever they squeezed through the crowd. As Jack made his way to the bar, he learned how to say "nice ass" in five different languages.

Theo managed to find two open stools right beside the large glass-encased colony of leaf-cutting ants. The South American insect was the club's signature insect. (L'fant was short for leaf-cutting ant, and it hardly seemed coincidental that this particular species was also known as "the big butt ant"). Jack watched as the bartender reached inside the glass container, plucked out a live ant, and dropped it into a vodka martini.

"Has a walnut taste," said Theo. "And they say it's an aphrodisiac."

Jack glanced at the couple sucking face beside him, while a third guy was feeling his way through the gaping hole in the backside of the woman's jeans. As if they needed the ants, thought Jack.

The crowd was getting drunker and louder with each passing minute, and Jack was beginning to question whether this was the best way to track down Gerard Montalvo. A distracting dance-enhanced version of his favorite Matchbox Twenty song started to play loudly over the sound system. Theo was trying to sing along but obviously didn't know the words, twisting the lyrics into "I'm not crazy, I'm just a British au pair."

Finally, as Theo's friend had promised, Tony Fontino, the club owner, arrived with a bodyguard bigger than Theo. After the introductions, Fontino said, "Richie said you wanted to talk business. Come on over to my table."

Fontino and his bodyguard led them around the ant tank to a small round table beside the stage. The little sign on top said RESERVED, which struck Jack as slightly ironic, since Fontino struck him as anything but "reserved." He was wearing a shiny silk suit, and the matching diamond ring and earrings would have made Paris Hilton jealous. Jack and Theo sat with their backs to the stage, opposite Tony and his bodyguard. A waitress brought refresher drinks for Jack and Theo, a signature ant martini for Tony.

"So what kind of business you wanna talk about?" asked Tony.

Theo said, "I'm thinking of opening a club here in the Design District."

Jack sat back and listened. It was a ruse, but Theo could smoke a con man if he had to.

"So?" said Fontino.

"Call it professional courtesy," Theo said with a shrug. "Don't want to step on nobody's toes."

Tony offered a condescending laugh. "No worries, man. You can have the losers we turn away at the door."

"Your partner feel the same way?" said Jack.

"Partner?"

Jack did a little gut check before posing the next question. It was, after all, the whole reason they'd come to this place. "It's our understanding that Gerard Montalvo is your partner."

"*Was* my partner," said Tony. "I haven't seen or heard from Gerard in seven years."

"That so?" said Jack. "Hope he didn't leave owing you money."

"That's none of your concern," Tony said in a voice so serious that it sounded almost like a threat.

"Easy," said Theo. "No reason to get stressed about it. You tell us you got no more connections to the Montalvos, we believe you. That's it."

"What's with all the questions about Gerard? You guys cops or something?"

"Just a couple of careful businessmen who've done their homework. We know you and Gerard was co-owners of Club Vertigo on South Beach and Club Vertigo two in Atlanta."

"So what?"

"So, we wanted to make sure that if we open up a new club here in the Design District, we don't end up pissing off Gerard and the whole Montalvo family."

Tony glared from across the table, then shifted his gaze toward Jack. "You two shits can't cut it in this business, Gerard or no Gerard." He rose, and his bodyguard popped from his seat. "Keep the table if you like, boys. It's as close as you'll ever get to owning a successful nightclub."

Tony turned and disappeared into the crowd, his bodyguard right behind him.

Jack said, "That didn't go exactly as planned, did it?"

Theo downed the rest of his beer. "Let me go talk to him. I can get more out of him one on one. And at the very least, I gotta kick his ass for calling me a shit." He was out of his seat and tailing Tony before Jack could tell him not to bother.

Jack just shook his head, alone with his thoughts. Going to Montalvo's old business partner had been a low-percentage plan to begin with, and Jack was now wishing that he hadn't let Theo talk him into it. If Jack's theory about what had happened seven years ago was correct, Montalvo skipped town after he threatened—or maybe even tried—to kill Teresa. That was the price she paid for bringing the rape charge. Rather than stand and fight, Teresa panicked and ran, fearing that Montalvo would come get her. All these years later, it looked as though he'd finally found her. But the idea that Montalvo's business partner would confirm any of that seemed remote, at best.

Jack heard noises from behind as the band was setting up onstage.

The chair beside him scraped against the floor, and he turned the other way to see a woman joining him at the table.

"Don't mind Tony," she said. "He's a certified asshole."

"You know him?" said Jack.

"Yeah. Terri's my name." She offered her hand, and Jack noticed that her nails and lips were the same dramatic red. The hair was blond, and she had lots of it. A perfect tan covered a body that was definitely no stranger to the gym. She looked to be in her midtwenties, but taking the kindness of dim lighting into account, Jack guessed she was a little older—still pretty, but with an edge. She leaned forward as she spoke, cutting him a look which only confirmed that her strong suit was not class but raw sex appeal.

"I'm Jack. How do you know Tony?"

"He's my producer."

"Movie producer?"

"Yeah. Adult films."

"So you would be a . . ."

"A porn star, yeah." She copped a little attitude, then added, "Do you have to say it like you're my father?"

"Sorry."

"It's okay. I didn't mean to snap at you. I'm just really nervous tonight. My husband, he's in the business, too. They're filming right now."

Jack nodded, as if he understood, but this conversation was headed in a direction that was way beyond his comprehension. "That must be tough, knowing he's with someone else."

"Nah, please. He has his films, I got mine. We got an understanding."

"I guess it would be hard to have a conventional marriage in your situation."

"Who the hell wants one anyway? There's your conventional marriage, right over there." She was pointing at the ant colony on the bar.

"Leaf-cutter ants marry?"

"No. But here's something interesting. Queens and drones are the only ants in the colony that can fly. Guess what happens to the queen when she mates."

"She dies?"

"No, worse. She loses her wings. Can't fly no more. She has to stay home with the drone, who of course is such a lazy son of a bitch that he doesn't do anything but mate. He doesn't gather food, doesn't build shelter, doesn't fight off predators. Just fucks the queen and takes her wings. Sort of symbolic, don't you think?"

"So you still have your wings?"

"Yeah," she said with a suggestive smile.

Jack figured that someday, perhaps in his eighties, he might look back on tonight as one of those moments in life when he should have stood up and shouted, "Thank God I'm not married!" But a quick reality check told him that she was probably coming on to his wallet, not him. He took the safer route, steering her back to her husband. "If you and your husband have this understanding, then why are you so nervous?"

She leaned closer, lowering her voice, as if sharing a secret. "Because tonight he's doing anal sex. It never fails, whenever he comes home from an anal scene, he's in the mood for a blow job. Always. I swear, sometimes it seems like he does that just to gross me out. It's a power thing, I'm sure. You think I should say something, or am I being a prude?"

It was a mood killer of monumental proportions, and Jack was doing his best to be polite. She had genuinely bared her soul to him—which was undoubtedly much more difficult than taking off her clothes—but damned if Jack could come up with an intelligent response. "Terri, I'm the last guy on earth you should ask for marriage advice. I'm sure you'll work it out."

"But—"

"Look, I gotta get going. It was nice talking to you."

She grabbed his forearm. "Please, don't go. I heard you asking Tony about Gerard Montalvo. That's why I came over. We should talk."

Jack settled back into his chair. "You know Montalvo?"

She nodded. "Intimately."

It was as if someone had turned off all the bar noises, the laughing, the chatting, the music. Terri had his complete attention. "He was your boyfriend?"

"Nothing like that. He just always took an interest in my films."

"Like Tony? Your producer?"

"No. Tony is strictly a money guy. He doesn't get involved in the actual production. Gerard was different. He'd come watch."

"So he was more like a director?"

"No. More like a pervert."

Jack thought for a moment, then figured he'd take his shot. "Terri, if I were to say you've got the look, would that mean anything to you?"

She laughed, then took a long drink. "You *do* know Gerard, don't you?"

"So you know about the rape case?"

"Sure. We all knew about it. Gerard denied it, of course. Said that girl made it all up. And we all pretended to believe him. Until he split. Why does a guy run if he's innocent?"

"Do you have any idea where he went?"

"Nobody does. Guy just vanished, gave up everything. Like I say, kind of tells you he was guilty, doesn't it?"

"Did you know the girl he attacked? Teresa?"

"No. But I saw her picture once. She's definitely got the look."

"What do you mean by that?"

"You don't know what 'got the look' means?"

"In a general sense, yeah. But what does it mean to Gerard?"

She sucked the olive from her martini glass, then popped it back. "You ask really smart questions, you know that?"

"Thanks. It's what I do. But tell me. What does 'got the look' mean to Gerard?"

"Okay, here's the thing. This is going back seven years, and I was really young. Gerard wanted me to do this movie for him. It's about a guy who pays women to have sex with him."

"How original. He wanted you to play a prostitute?"

"No. Not at all. See, that's what the movie was all about. This guy would approach women who were married, or who sang in the church choir, that kind of thing. These are women who would never take money for sex in their life—until someone came along and offered them enough cash."

"So he'd look for women who . . . what? Looked like prostitutes?"

"No, no. You're totally missing the point. There's a ton of women out there who won't admit what they are. These are women who act like they're above it, but the honest truth is they'd sell their body in a minute if the price was right. That's the woman he's looking for."

"And he's able to find this type of woman because . . ."

She shrugged and said, "She's got the look."

Jack's gaze drifted toward the crowded dance floor. It was a subconscious thought, but he found himself making snap judgments on a case-by-case basis. *She's got the look. She doesn't. Does. Doesn't.* He was forcing himself to think like Gerard, and it was as if someone had finally switched on the lights.

"You okay?" said Terri.

"I'm good," he said with a thin smile. "You have no idea how good."

41

.

The FBI issued a BOLO for Gerard Montalvo at 8 a.m. the following morning. Andie stood to the left of the assistant special agent in charge as Paul Martinez, special agent in charge of the Miami office, made the televised announcement. The press conference had originally been scheduled for 5 p.m. Wednesday, but Andie had persuaded Martinez to postpone it for an additional fifteen hours. Her hope was that the kidnapper would call before his picture was on every television screen across the country. That way, Jack could explain his apparent breach of silence and hopefully stem any retaliation against Mia. The kidnapper didn't call, and the FBI couldn't wait any longer.

Montalvo's face was on every morning news show, albeit a seven-year-old photograph.

Jack caught an early flight from Miami to Atlanta. It wasn't exactly a trip back to the scene of the crime, but close. Jack wanted to talk to the assistant district attorney who'd prosecuted the Got the Look Rapist.

Charlene Wright was in her third year of private practice after a fifteen-year career as a Fulton County prosecutor, the last eleven in the Crimes against Women and Children Unit. Before that, she was director of the rape crisis program at Grady Memorial Hospital. Her legacy at the DA's office was a victim/witness assistance program that earned her a special commendation from the governor, but she was no less proud of her string of convictions that added up to several thousand years of prison time for Atlanta's worst sex offenders.

Jack was curious to know how Gerard Montalvo had slipped through her fingers.

He called ahead from the airport, and Charlene agreed to meet with him at her midtown office before lunch. It turned out to be one of those rare instances where the actual person was nearly an exact match for the image Jack had attached to the voice on the other end of the telephone line. Charlene was a forty-something African American, not a centimeter of extra hair on her head. She was thin as a steel rod and tough as one, too. Her demeanor was pleasant enough, but her tight handshake was a subtle reminder that she could crush you like a bear trap at any moment. She offered Jack a seat on the couch, and she took the striped armchair, her back to the window.

"Thanks for meeting me on such short notice," said Jack.

Charlene was squeezing a little orange stress-relief ball as she spoke. "Agent Henning told me you'd probably be coming to see me. I figure if you're going to pay Teresa's ransom, you're entitled to know what she's been through."

"So, you're convinced that Mia used to be Teresa?"

"No doubt in my mind."

"Are you equally convinced that the kidnapper is Gerard Montalvo?"

"Montalvo and his 'Got the Look' proposition forced women to put a value on their own body. It's not that much of a psychological stretch to infer that the same sociopath would force a husband to put a value on his kidnapped wife."

"Is that a yes—Montalvo is the kidnapper?"

"I do agreed that the psychology behind the MO is similar in the two crimes. Beyond that, Henning didn't tell me much about her suspect. Basically, nothing more than what was said at this morning's press conference."

"Welcome to the club," said Jack. "Which is why I'd really like to learn more about Montalvo and that first crime against Teresa."

She hesitated just long enough for Jack to sense that a disclaimer was coming. "The case against Montalvo was technically still an open file when I left the DA's office. I can tell you what you want to know, so long as it was public information."

"I'll take whatever I can get. It was obviously public information that Montalvo fled at the end of the preliminary hearing. Tell me about that."

"Not much to tell. The judge ruled that there was sufficient evidence to bind him over for trial. Next morning, he was gone, and so was Teresa. That was the last anyone heard of them."

"What was your initial thought? That he killed Teresa and took off?"

"We had to consider that, yes. But it seemed equally plausible that Montalvo threatened her before he fled, or that he tried to harm her and she escaped. Since her car was missing, we didn't rule out the possibility that she went into hiding, maybe even left the country."

"Interesting. You held out hope that she was alive, but her sister was convinced that she was dead."

"I didn't say we held out *a lot* of hope," said Charlene. "We never found her car, and she left everything behind. Passport. Money in her checking account. Her credit-card spending trail ended the day before she disappeared. The way she left, you'd think she was dead."

Jack considered it. "Or, more important, Montalvo would think she was dead. If she thought he might come back to get her, it behooved her to create the impression that she succumbed to her own fears and drove her car into a canal or a lake somewhere."

"Yes. Or as you say, she could have been so afraid that Montalvo was out to get her that she didn't have time to pack a bag and take care of her affairs."

Jack took a moment to collect his thoughts. Charlene passed the stress ball back and forth, left hand to right. It was obvious that the Montalvo case nagged at her—the one that got away.

Jack said, "Why do *you* think Montalvo jumped bond, Charlene?"

"I thought we'd already covered that."

"Not entirely. Was it because you had such a strong case against him?"

"Like I said, I can't comment on that. The file was still open when I left the DA's office."

"I can't imagine that you made a habit of bringing weak cases."

"No. But some cases are more difficult than others."

"Yes. But if this was such a difficult case for the prosecution, I'm sure Montalvo's lawyer would have told him that. Why would he have run?"

"I'd say he overreacted to the ruling at the preliminary hearing. He went home, and poor little rich boy finally came to terms with the fact that he might do serious jail time. You get convicted of rape in Georgia, it means ten years, minimum, even if it's a first offense."

"Probably more like ten to twenty in his case."

"How would you know that?"

"I saw the scar on Mia's leg. She never told me how she got it, but if she got it when she was Teresa, that's a nasty aggravating circumstance."

Charlene's expression hardened. "She was cut pretty bad. That's why it burned me up so much, the way the family came after her."

"The family?"

"The Montalvos. They threw everything they had at her, trying to make it look like she made it all up so she could file a civil lawsuit. Like it was a shakedown for the family's money."

"How rich were they?"

"Filthy. Gerard owned five or six nightclubs that hemorrhaged hundreds of thousands of dollars every year. Family didn't care. It was just chump change."

"Did their strategy work? Going after Teresa, I mean."

"It definitely got to her. I prepared her for the usual assortment of idiotic statements that rape victims face. Cracks like, 'If you go walking in the rain, you're bound to get wet.' But even I was surprised by the lengths the family went to in their efforts to paint her as someone who falsely cried rape so that she could sue for millions civilly."

"What kind of things did they say about her?"

"Well, the first thing they had to deal with was that cut on her thigh. That son of a bitch sliced open her leg with a broken lightbulb. Then he had the audacity to claim that she cut herself, just to bolster her rape charge. And that was only the beginning."

"Tell me," said Jack. "It will help me understand him better."

She drew a breath, thinking. "Let me see if I can even recall every-thing. They doctored some photographs showing her with naked men. Digital stuff, you know. She did some modeling in her early twenties, and they somehow got hold of the photos."

"Nude, you mean?"

"No. These were totally innocent. Just close-ups of her face. But it doesn't take a digital-photography genius to paste a girl's smiling face between two gigantic erections, make it look like she's about to take on both of them. This was plastered all over the Internet two days before the preliminary hearing."

"Scumbags."

"Then there was the poem."

"A poem?"

"Yeah. They leaked it to the press and said it was a poem she'd writ-ten in her diary. Then somebody recognized it as song lyrics, so they changed their tune and said it was a song on one of her favorite CDs."

"What song was it?"

Charlene made a face, as if she were trying to divide 694 by 17. She rose and went to her computer. "I remember some of the lyrics. Let me search and see what happens." She typed a few words, then got her re-sults. "Here we go." She stepped aside, and Jack checked out the lyrics to "Nasty Girl" by Bronx Bitches.

"It's a group of female rappers," said Charlene.

Reading the lyrics, Jack would have guessed as much:

I make it nice and E-Z, then I say raped me, boy you gonna pay me.
Cuz I'm lookin' for the big bucks, careful who the star fucks.
Think you got some big balls?
I want 'em. I got 'em. I cut dem off.

Jack stepped away from the screen. "Doesn't sound like something Mia would like."

"Of course she didn't. It's just one more stunt that Montalvo and his club goons pulled to discredit her. I'm sure there were others, but that's all I remember now. They put this girl though living hell."

"Did the defense put on any evidence at the preliminary hearing?"

"They had one witness. A bouncer from Gerard's nightclub. He testified that Teresa knew she was going up to the room for money."

"Wait a second," said Jack. "You mean the defense, on its own initiative, revealed the meaning of 'Got the Look'?"

"Yeah. It was the main thrust of the bouncer's testimony."

"So, their defense was based on an actual admission that Gerard liked to hire women for sex who were—"

"Hooker virgins," said Charlene. "Hookers who never hooked before. I think those were the witness's exact words."

Jack mulled it over. "Not a bad strategy, actually. You tell the honest truth about something totally embarrassing, and that gives the world all the more reason to believe your story that Teresa had consensual sex for money."

"It definitely gave us fits outside the courtroom. Local talk radio had a field day. One of my well-meaning friends from the rape crisis center was even quoted on the front page of the *Journal-Constitution* saying that a prostitute deserves the same protection from rape as anyone else. That's true, of course. But imagine how that made Teresa feel, to be lumped together with prostitutes who need protection."

"How did you plan to counter that?"

"That's when we brought in our surprise rebuttal witness."

"Who?"

Her expression changed, and it was the closest thing to a real smile Jack had seen on Charlene's face all morning. She walked around her desk and removed a videocassette from the side drawer. "I dug this out just yesterday for the FBI, overnighted a copy to Agent Henning."

"Is that the whole preliminary hearing?"

"Just the state's rebuttal. Local television covered our final witness, live, once they got wind of what was afoot. One of my more clever moves as a prosecutor, if I do say so myself."

"I'll watch with interest," he said, taking it.

"Do that," she said, her tone very serious. "And I'll bet you come away with a much better understanding of why Mr. Montalvo ran for the hills."

42
.

The videotaped broadcast of Gerard Montalvo's preliminary hearing arrived in the FBI's Miami field office the following morning, direct from Charlene Wright.

Andie found a quiet room on the second floor with a television and a VCR. Paul Martinez sat beside her at the conference table. The lights were off, and the two agents were bathed in the bright blue glow of an idle television screen.

"Will this take long?" asked Martinez.

"A few minutes. This Charlene Wright works very efficiently. Supposedly, it's a complete refutation of Montalvo's claim that the victim cried rape just so she could tag him with a multimillion-dollar civil suit."

"Let it roll," said Martinez.

Andie hit the Play button, and the screen came to life. First a test pattern, then the WXIA logo, and finally the date and the case name—*State of Georgia v. Gerard Montalvo*—which carried them back to Georgia Superior Court, some seven years earlier. The camera focused on the witness, a slightly balding but handsome man wearing a dark blue suit and a bright red tie. There were some background noises in the courtroom, the shuffling of feet, a few coughs from the gallery. Then the camera angle widened, and Andie watched the screen as Charlene Wright approached her final witness for the prosecution.

"Please state your name and occupation," said the prosecutor.

The witness leaned toward the microphone. He didn't appear nervous, but something about his body language suggested that the witness stand was an odd place for him to find himself. "My name's Henry Talbridge. I'm a licensed attorney in the state of Georgia."

"What kind of law do you practice?"

"I'm a trial lawyer."

"Are you familiar with this case, State versus Montalvo?"

"Yes, I am."

"Do you know the alleged victim?" Wright turned to the judge before the witness could answer and said, "Your Honor, I'll maintain the protocol of not mentioning the victim by name, despite the fact that the defense has done its best to make her the most recognizable figure in Atlanta since Hank Aaron."

"Objection." The voice came across loudly over the videotape, but the defense counsel remained off camera.

"Sustained," said the judge, "but the government's point is well taken. The witness may answer."

"I do know the alleged victim," said Talbridge. "In fact, I'm her attorney."

"When did you become her attorney?"

"I believe it was one week after she reported her assault to the police."

A chorus of rumbles emerged from the gallery.

Off-screen, back in the FBI conference room, Martinez grabbed the remote control and hit the Pause button. "She hired a civil attorney before the criminal case was even held over for trial?"

"Apparently so," said Andie.

"How does that refute the argument of the defense that she was gunning for a lawsuit and a big payoff?"

Andie shrugged. "I guess we can watch and find out."

Martinez hit Play, and the action continued on-screen.

The prosecutor said, "Now, Mr. Talbridge, I'm sure you're aware of the various questions that the defense has raised about the bona fides of the accusations against Mr. Montalvo."

The witness scoffed and said, "That's putting it mildly. It's a daily deluge of charges that my client is nothing but a gold-digging liar."

"*How is your client coping with those accusations?*"

"*Objection. How is she coping? Is this witness her lawyer or her psychiatrist?*"

"*I'll rephrase,*" the prosecutor said. "*Mr. Talbridge, in the past two weeks, how many times have you, personally, been asked if your client intends to file a civil lawsuit against the accused if he is convicted of raping your client?*"

"*Oh, my word. Hundreds of times.*"

"*And your answer has been—what?*"

"*My client and I will make that decision at the appropriate time.*"

"*And when is the appropriate time?*" asked the prosecutor.

"*Well, originally we thought it would be after the criminal trial was over and all the facts came out. But in light of the vicious attacks on her credibility, my client decided that the appropriate time to make that decision is right now.*"

"*All right, sir,*" said the prosecutor. "*If you'll indulge my asking the question one more time: Does your client intend to file a civil lawsuit against the accused if he is convicted of raping her?*"

Defense counsel was on his feet. "*Objection, Your Honor. This is all hearsay.*"

Wright said, "*Hearsay is allowed in a preliminary hearing, Judge.*"

The judge furrowed his brow, then answered in heavy southern drawl. "*Hearsay is allowable, Ms. Wright. But I feel most compelled to info'm the witness that by answering this question, it would appear that the attorney-client privilege is waived. The defense would then be free to question Mr. Talbridge as to all communications between himself and his client.*"

Talbridge answered, "*We're aware of that, Your Honor. We're waiving.*"

The defense counsel almost smiled. "*Objection withdrawn, Your Honor.*"

The prosecutor returned to the witness and said, "*Please answer the question, sir: Does your client intend to file a civil lawsuit?*"

"*She has decided that she will not under any circumstances file a civil suit against Mr. Montalvo.*"

"*Even if he is convicted?*"

"*Yes. Even if he is convicted.*"

"*Did she tell you why she came to this decision?*"

"*She is tired of being called a liar. She doesn't care about the money. She wants the man who raped her in jail. And she wants the world to know that."*

"Thank you, Mr. Talbridge. No further questions."

There was silence on the television screen. It was a bold move to put the victim's lawyer on the witness stand, but Andie hardly saw it as the stroke of genius that Charlene Wright had promised her. She was about to rewind the videotape, thinking that perhaps she had missed something. She held off, however, as the judge called for cross-examination by the defense.

"Bravo, Mr. Talbridge," Montalvo's attorney said as he approached the witness. "That was a gallant effort. But let me ask you something. In all the lawsuits you've filed in your distinguished career, have you ever sued anyone more wealthy than Gerard Montalvo?"

"I've sued many wealthy people."

"I'll bet you have. That's exactly why your client hired you, isn't it? Because you get the big bucks?"

"She hired me because I'm an experienced trial lawyer."

"How many times have you met with your client, Mr. Talbridge?"

"Just twice, actually."

"Twice?" the defense counsel said, sounding somewhat surprised. "Okay. What did you discuss the first time you met?"

"She wanted to know her rights as the victim of a violent crime. She was concerned about whether Mr. Montalvo would be entitled to bail, what hearings she as the victim would be allowed to attend, and whether she would have any input into the DA's decision to plea-bargain the case."

"Did you also advise her of her right to sue Mr. Montalvo for money damages if he was convicted?"

"Yes, I did."

"So from your very first meeting, that subject was discussed."

"Yes, it was."

The lawyer's chest swelled with satisfaction. "Thank you, sir. How about your second meeting with the alleged victim. When was that?"

"Last night."

"And did you discuss the possibility of suing the defendant at that meeting?"

"Not exactly. We discussed the possibility of a settlement offer."

"Oh, I see. So, throughout this preliminary hearing, you and your client have been angling toward a settlement strategy that would allow her to get her hands on some quick cash. Is that a fair statement?"

"No, I wouldn't say that's fair."

"Well, sir. How many millions did you intend to demand from Mr. Montalvo in this settlement offer you and your client discussed last night?"

"Actually, the demand is just one dollar."

The smugness drained from the lawyer's face. It was as if he'd just swallowed his tongue. "Excuse me? Did I hear you say one million dollars?"

"No, sir. My client will agree to settle all civil claims she may have against Mr. Montalvo for the grand sum of one American dollar. No admission of liability on his part is required. In exchange, she'll sign a general release that forever discharges Mr. Montalvo from any and all civil liability. It's her way of putting this money sideshow behind us once and for all. She's sick and tired of the smear campaign that your client has conducted."

"Objection, Your Honor!"

"She is fed up with Mr. Montalvo's accusations that she is in this for the money."

"Judge, I object to—"

"And she wants to show the world that all she desires is for the man who raped her to spend the rest of his life in jail."

"Judge, I strenuously object to this grandstand stunt."

"It's no stunt, Your Honor. I have the signed release with me today, and I'm prepared to deliver it just as soon as Mr. Montalvo opens his wallet and hands me a crisp one-dollar bill."

"I move for a mistrial!"

"This isn't a trial," said the judge.

"You know what I mean, Judge. This proceeding is an outrage."

"I don't know about that," said the judge. "But I would like to see counsel in my chambers. Right now."

The screen went black, and the speakers hissed with static. Andie hit the Off button on the remote control, then rose from her chair and switched on the lights.

"Well," said Martinez, "that was unlike any preliminary hearing

I've ever seen before. Beautiful, really. They completely gutted Montalvo's claim that she was lying out of greed."

"They did much more than that," said Andie.

"How do you mean?"

"We're dealing with a kidnapper who drowned a completely innocent woman in an underwater cave because a million-dollar ransom wasn't the right number. Kind of makes you wonder, doesn't it?"

"What?"

She looked away, as if afraid to answer her own question. "What's he got in store for the woman who lowballed him in a televised court proceeding?"

Martinez drummed his fingers on the tabletop, thinking. "There's only one way to answer that, Henning."

"What's that?"

"Find this guy. Fast."

43

.

The one-eyed monster was staring at her again.

Mia's mangled toe was no longer a source of constant pain, but the throbbing returned upon the mere sight of the video camera. Clearly there was a Pavlovian association imbedded in her subconscious; her captor wouldn't go to all the trouble of setting up the camera unless he intended to hurt her.

She waited in silence, seated on the hard floor with her legs extended straight out in front of her. As usual, her hands and ankles were bound with plastic handcuffs. The room was completely dark, save for the narrow tunnel of brightness that shot like a laser from the tripod. It was a tightly focused beam, a rope of light that seemingly tethered her to the video camera. Her kidnapper had used the same lighting system before. That first time, however, the beam of light had been directed straight at her face with blinding intensity. This time, the focus was different, and the difference was troubling.

The spotlight was aimed below the waist.

Mia could feel her body temperature rising, the combined effect of frayed nerves and the halogen bulb. Her captor was a silhouette in the shadows, lurking behind the glowing spotlight. She couldn't really see him, but somehow she felt his stare. Then she heard his footsteps. Finally, she saw the knife.

He was towering over her, the steel blade glimmering in the bright light. She didn't dare make eye contact. She stared down into her lap, which only heightened her anxiety, as the spotlight was aimed at her most private zone.

He got down on one knee, his face contorted and unrecognizable behind the tight nylon stocking. A wad of cotton or something similar in his mouth distorted his voice. "Don't make a move," he said, brandishing the knife just inches from her cheek. She was terrified, but she complied to the letter, barely even allowing her chest to swell with each shallow breath. She knew the price of disobedience.

With a flick of the knife, her hands were free. Another quick swipe, and the ankle binders were broken. He rose and stepped back behind the camera. Mia remained motionless, still heeding his order not to move.

"Take off your pants," he said.

Not very long ago, a command such as that would have met with defiance, or at least indignation. Those days were over. Without a moment's hesitation, she unbuttoned her jeans and unzipped the fly. She worked her pants down steadily, around the hips and past the knees—fast enough to satisfy him, but not so fast as to arouse suspicion. She pulled them off one leg at a time and then laid them aside. He'd said nothing about removing her underwear, so she left it alone.

"Sit yoga style for me."

She was afraid to ask for clarification, so she guessed that he wanted her to sit *baddha konasana*, a position she'd learned in a stretching class at her health club. She sat upright, her knees bent and flaring outward, the souls of her bare feet touching and the heels drawn inward toward her groin. She felt somewhat vulnerable, but it was better than spread-eagled.

"Good," he said. "Now move your feet forward a little—away from your body."

So much time in captivity had stiffened her joints, and she found it impossible to move her feet without a helping hand. She pushed gently against her heels, sliding the feet away from her, all the while remaining in the yoga position.

"Very good." He adjusted the spotlight. It was aimed straight at her crotch, but she felt no embarrassment. Only fear.

"Hold it right there, bitch."

Mia didn't move. She wanted to close her eyes and begin her mental escape, but she remembered how furious that had made him the last time, how he had mashed her toe even harder whenever she looked away from the camera. She kept her eyes wide open this time, staring straight into the blinding spotlight, as if seeking the refuge of darkness in the brightest point of light. She wanted to find her safety zone, that trancelike state of numbness that carried her through the worst of times. She was unable to concentrate, however. Try as she might to detach herself from the moment, she could still sense his unnerving presence, almost feel him moving about the room. She heard him coming toward her, and she started at the sudden clamor beside her. It was the sound of the bucket hitting the floor, the same bucket that he had left with her earlier. She peered cautiously over the rim, just like the last time. The only thing inside was the lightbulb. In a sudden blur he smashed it with his heel, and the loud pop made her heart skip a beat.

"Take it," he said.

She glanced toward the camera, but otherwise she didn't move.

"Do it!" he shouted.

She trembled as her gaze drifted back to the broken lightbulb, the twisted filament, the razor-sharp shards of thin glass.

"I said do it!"

"Do what?" she asked, barely audible.

"Don't talk back to me. Just do it. Show him."

"What are you talking about?"

"You know exactly what I'm talking about. Show him, damn it."

"Show who? Show what?"

She could hear the anger in his heavy footsteps as he hurried to her side, grabbed her by the hair, and jerked her head back. He pressed the broken lightbulb into her palm, curled her hand into a fist, and squeezed until the sharpness sliced her skin. Blood oozed from her clenched fist like water from a sponge, but she contained her scream, denying him that satisfaction.

"What do you want me to do?" she said, her voice quaking.

"I want you to show him," he said as he grabbed between her legs. He was squeezing hard, bringing tears to her eyes, nearly ripping the old scar tissue from the inside of her thigh. "Show Jack Swyteck how you cut yourself. *Teresa*."

44

·

Even at three o'clock in the afternoon, it seemed only fitting to hold the most important meeting of the trip over the most important meal of the day. So Jack chose the Five Points Diner, where breakfast was served 24/7. The sign out front would lead you to believe that "five points" meant the tines of a fork, but it actually referred to downtown Atlanta's best-known intersection, where Peachtree connects several major thoroughfares. The old diner wasn't exactly the area's shining jewel, but it was convenient, just a few MARTA stops south of Charlene Wright's midtown office, not far from the courthouse and the glimmering gold-leaf dome of the capitol building. Most important, it was directly across the street from Bud's Bail Bonds.

Jack wasn't sure if there actually was a Bud or if it was just a catchy trade name for a guy named Wilbur or Maurice. A little checking around with local attorneys confirmed that there was indeed a Bud, better known as Ball-Bustin' Bud. It required no imagination on Jack's part to discern how a bail bondsman earned a name like that. Bud operated much like any other bondsman. If a judge set your bail at one hundred thousand dollars, you gave Bud ten grand, and he posted bail. The ten thousand was nonrefundable. If you skipped, Bud was out ninety Gs. At least until he found you. That was where the ball bustin' kicked in. And rest assured, Bud would find you. Eventually.

Word on the street was that he was still looking for Gerard Montalvo, even after seven years.

Jack's initial inclination was to handle Bud by himself, but the more he learned about his reputation, the more he realized that he needed a little extra something to even the playing field. When it came to dealing with thugs, Jack had one great equalizer at his disposal. All it took was a phone call. Theo caught a midmorning flight from Miami and met him on the sidewalk right outside the Five Points Diner.

"Pancakes," said Theo. He was staring at the steaming stack of hotcakes painted on the diner's plate-glass window. "Blueberry pancakes is what I want. With butter and lots of syrup."

"Pardon the reminder, but your only job here is to convince Ball-Bustin' Bud that you can be an even worse badass than he is. Can't you order something a little more . . . tough guy?"

"I want pancakes."

"All right, fine. Just, I don't know, order a side of raw bacon or something."

Jack entered the restaurant and Theo followed. The old man at the counter never looked up from his plate of runny eggs over easy. The short-order cook was scraping grease from the griddle with a pumice stone, like nails on a chalkboard. A big guy with a crew cut and a neck as wide as a sequoia was seated in the booth by the window, drinking coffee. He was wearing a black leather jacket, blue jeans, and a plain white T-shirt. His eyes were like a night watchman's, narrow and discerning. He had the nose of an ex-boxer, which was to say that it had apparently been rearranged several times before finally retiring to a place just left of center on his face. A toothpick dangled from his lips, and it moved to one side when he sipped his coffee, never leaving his mouth. His huge hands were covered with the tattoo of a spiderweb, as if to tell the world that no one ever escaped his grasp.

Theo and his pancakes, thought Jack. *Now this guy is a real badass.*

Bud rose and introduced himself, the toothpick wagging as he spoke. They slid into the booth, Jack and Theo on one side, Bud on the other. Bud was less than subtle in sizing up Theo, probably trying to decide if he was armed, dangerous, or both of the above. Jack heard a toilet flush somewhere toward the end of the back hallway. A waitress emerged from the bathroom, wiping her hands on her coffee-stained apron. She grabbed a pot of coffee on her way to their table and refilled Bud's half-empty mug, saying nothing, displaying all the warmth and personality of a walking cadaver. She pulled a dog-eared notepad from her back pocket, yanked a pencil from behind her ear, and took their orders. Just black coffee for Jack, a double stack of blueberry pancakes for Theo.

"Hold the whipped cream," said Theo. "Cuz I'm a badass."

Jack could have killed him on the spot, but he decided to wait for another day, hopefully in the not too distant future, when they were traveling together in a state without capital punishment.

Bud looked confused, as if not quite sure what to make of Jack's sidekick. "So, what's the deal, gents? How much is the bail?"

"There is no bail," said Jack.

"Then what the hell is so urgent?"

"We're here to talk about a guy named Gerard Montalvo. I'm sure you've heard of him."

"Everyone's heard of him now. I saw the BOLO the FBI issued this morning. Said he's wanted for kidnapping."

"I would imagine that you remember him better than most people."

"Course I do," he said, scoffing. "Son of a bitch skipped bail and cost me almost half a million."

"He didn't put up any collateral?" said Jack.

"Shit yeah. I always get collateral. But you ever tried litigating against the Montalvo family? I swear, the richer these sons of bitches are, the harder it is to squeeze a dime out of them. Their lawyers got me tied up in knots. Only way I'm gonna see that money is to put a gun to Gerard's head. Not that I would do that, of course."

"Of course," said Theo. "Gotta find him before you can put a gun to his head."

The remark seemed to intrigue Bud. "Are you saying you can find Gerard Montalvo?"

Jack leaned closer, lowering his voice for effect. "I'm saying we have found him."

A wave of interest washed over Bud's face. "If that's true, you guys are my new best friends."

Jack laid his hands atop the table. "Here's how I see it. You'd like nothing better than to get your half million dollars back from Montalvo. For my own reasons, I'd like to get my hands on just half that much."

"So what are you proposing?"

"Here's the deal," said Jack. "I'll pay your usual fee, ten percent. In other words, I'll put up twenty-five thousand dollars for a thirty-day loan of a quarter million dollars. After the thirty days, I give you back your quarter million, *and* Gerard Montalvo is back in police custody."

"What good does that do me?"

Theo said, "I been in prison. I know what kind of pressure you can bring on someone inside the box to make his family pay off a debt."

Bud nodded, as if he liked the way Theo's mind worked. "That would make me a very happy man. But how are you in any kind of position to deliver on a promise to have Montalvo back in police custody within thirty days?"

"We'll deliver," said Jack.

"But what if you *don't?*"

The waitress returned, and all conversation ceased. She slid a double order of pancakes in front of Theo. He looked quizzically at his plate of food, his expression turning sour.

"What the hell is this?" he said.

"Blueberry pancakes," she said in her gum-cracking monotone.

"These ain't blueberry pancakes."

"Yeah, they is."

"What's this stuff on top?"

"Blueberry compote."

"That's not blueberry pancakes. Blueberry pancakes are pancakes with blueberries inside."

"Ours come with blueberry compote on top."

"Then you shouldn't call them blueberry pancakes. Cuz I can't eat this."

"It tastes the same, trust me."

"I trust you, darlin'. But when I sees this stack of pancakes covered in blue goop, it don't make me think, *Mmm, dig in.* It makes me think, *Who let the Blue Man Group shit all over my breakfast?*"

"Then eat around it."

Theo shot her one of his patented looks, the kind that could tie even an ex-con's intestines in knots. "No, I'm not gonna eat around it. Cuz here's what's gonna happen, babe. You're gonna take this plate to the bathroom, you're gonna drop this compote in the crapper, and you're gonna flush. And you're gonna keep right on flushin' till a big blue load of blueberry shit comes floating out somewhere in the middle of Lake Lanier. Then you're gonna go back in the kitchen and bring me some real blueberry pancakes. Got it?"

His glare intensified. The waitress was so speechless that she'd even stopped chomping on her chewing gum. Jack felt a little sorry for her, even though he knew that Theo was just putting on a show for Bud's benefit. She took the pancakes and slithered away.

Bud chuckled, toothpick wagging faster than ever. "I like your style, pal."

Theo was stone-cold serious. "Like Jack said: We'll have Montalvo back in jail in thirty days."

"But you still haven't answered my question. What if you don't?"

Jack said, "Then you keep my twenty-five grand, and I pay you back the quarter million. You made twenty-five thousand dollars in one month."

"Pay me back out of what?"

"Three-year promissory note. Ten percent interest."

"Twenty," said Bud. "And before I deliver one red cent, I need proof that you know where Montalvo is. I don't care if you are the son of a former governor. I'm not laying out this kind of money on blind faith."

Jack didn't want to play this final card, but a guy like Bud was his only chance of raising this much cash in a matter of days. He pulled his

Dictaphone from his coat pocket and gave it to Bud, along with an earpiece. Jack said, "Montalvo kidnapped my girlfriend. This is his last phone call to me. His voice is disguised, but he gives himself away at the end. He's the Got the Look Rapist."

Bud seemed more than a little skeptical, but Jack definitely didn't want to get into the whole story of how Mia was Teresa. "Go ahead," said Jack. "Listen to it. I haven't shared this with anyone but the FBI."

Bud inserted the earpiece, hit Play, and listened in silence for about two minutes as the conversation unfolded. The tape ended with the kidnapper's response to Jack's pointed question—whether he would still say the Mia's "got the look." Some of the skepticism had drained from Bud's face, but he still didn't look convinced. "Okay, he seems to acknowledge that he's the Got the Look Rapist. But the caller's voice is disguised. How do I know this isn't you and Theo cooking up some scam?"

"Didn't you hear Jack's voice?" said Theo. "If he was faking it, he should get an Academy Award."

Bud drew a deep breath, as if he were almost willing to concede that Theo had a point. "You geniuses got a plan?"

"Does Miami *habla español?*" said Theo.

"Huh?"

"He means yes," said Jack.

"What is it?"

Jack couldn't spell out everything to a stranger, but any lender had a right to know his money wasn't being squandered. "It's a few simple steps. One, I continue dealing with him in a way that will convince him that I'm following his order to keep the cops out of it."

"You gonna arrest him yourself?"

"No. The FBI has to be involved. But it's my job to make him believe he's dealing only with me. And it's up to me to negotiate a simultaneous exchange. He gets the money when he gives me Mia. That's the only way I can lure him out into the open to let the FBI do its job."

"How do you get him to agree to your simultaneous exchange?"

"That's where your loan comes in," said Jack. "I have to assure him that the payoff at the end of the day is big enough to justify the risk. So far, the FBI is only willing to put up twenty thousand as bait. I need a lot more than that to lure Montalvo out into the open."

Bud seemed nearly sold, but not quite. "Quarter million bucks is a lot of money. Even if you just plan to use it as bait, there's no guarantee you won't lose it. I'm gonna need some collateral."

"If I had that much collateral, I'd be talking to a bank," said Jack.

"I didn't say full collateral. Just something to show me you're serious."

Theo pulled an envelope from inside his jacket and slid it across the table. Bud opened the envelope and gave the contents a quick once-over. "What's this?"

"Property deed and liquor license," said Theo.

Jack couldn't believe his eyes. "Theo, what are you doing, man?"

"Quiet, Jack." He looked straight at Bud and said, "It's from my bar—Sparky's. Hole-in-the-wall joint that ain't worth a shit, really. But the real estate and liquor license are good for about two hundred grand."

Jack wanted to snatch it away, tell him no way. Before he could react, however, Bud folded it up and tucked it into his coat pocket. "How soon you need the money?"

"Two days," said Theo.

"That's fast."

"If we weren't in a hurry, you'd be losin' this loan to Ditech. Can you do it?"

"Yeah. I can do it. But just so we're clear on this. Your twenty-five grand is nonrefundable. If Montalvo isn't under arrest in thirty days, then Sparky's is under new ownership. As for the rest of the money, I'll find you guys." He balled his hands into one big fist, the two halves of the tattooed spiderweb coming together. "Montalvo got away from me. But you won't."

"No problem," said Theo.

Bud downed the rest of his coffee, rose, and shook hands. "I'll call you in the morning with wire instructions. Pleasure doing business with you boys."

"Likewise."

He turned and left the restaurant. When the door closed behind him, Jack was right in Theo's face, incredulous. "What in the hell made you bring your bar into this?"

"Bondsmen don't work without collateral, Jack. You think I didn't know that before I got on the plane and came here?"

"I was hoping he'd loan me the money if I could just convince him that Montalvo would be in his grasp."

"Then you was dreamin'. He may be Ball-Bustin' Bud, but he's still a businessman."

"And so are you, damn it," said Jack, his voice straining. "I can't believe you did that."

"I wouldn't have a bar if you hadn't got me off death row and got me that nice chunk of change from the state of Florida for violation of my civil rights."

"They took away four years of *your* life, not mine. That settlement money is yours, Theo."

"Exactly. And I can do whatever I want with it."

"We're talking about your bar, man. Your dream. You can't put all that at risk."

Theo was completely serious. "Do you love her or don't you?"

Jack didn't answer.

"I thought so," said Theo.

Jack still couldn't speak. Without being asked, Theo had done something that Jack could never have asked him to do. He wasn't sure what he was feeling, but he could feel it all the way to his core, that combined sense of fulfillment and embarrassment that comes when you finally realize that your best friend is a better person than you are.

"Just do me one favor," said Theo.

"Name it."

"Don't fuck this up."

Jack didn't know if he meant the delivery of the ransom or whatever the future might hold for him and Mia. Either way, the answer was the same. "I won't, man. I promise."

45

.

Jack caught up with Mia's old lawyer in the library at the federal court of appeals building. Henry Talbridge had aged quite a bit since the videotape of the preliminary hearing, seemingly more than seven years, suggesting that perhaps his late sixties had brought some health problems. They stepped out to talk in private at the end of a long marble corridor, beneath an impressive oil-on-canvas portrait of the Honorable Thomas A. Clark, a true gentleman of a judge whom Jack remembered from his early days with the Freedom Institute. Back then, Jack would routinely file eleventh-hour requests for stays of execution, most of which were speedily (and quite correctly) denied, but there was always a glimmer of hope if Clark was on the appellate panel. Unfortunately, Jack wasn't finding Talbridge anywhere near as receptive.

"Sorry, young man. I just can't talk to you about Teresa's case."

"It's extremely important."

"Yeah, I heard the same thing from about two dozen reporters who called my office this morning. The press has been all over me ever since the FBI issued that BOLO for Gerard Montalvo. I had to hide out here in the courthouse library to get any work done. How the heck did you find me here, anyway?"

"Your secretary tipped me off."

"Virginia? That's a shocker. She's usually a better secret keeper than the CIA."

"I'm a sole practitioner, too. And I came all the way from Miami to talk to you."

"Ah, that explains it. Virginia has a soft spot for any lawyer who isn't too self-important to lick his own stamps and answer his own telephone."

"So, can you answer a few questions for me? It'll just take a minute."

He seemed sympathetic, but he didn't budge. "Even if I wanted to talk to you, everything she told me is protected by the attorney-client privilege."

"Tell you what. It's bumping up on dinnertime. Can we sit down and talk somewhere? If I can't change your mind in less than five minutes, dinner's on me at Bone's." Jack didn't know many Atlanta restaurants, but anyone who ate steak knew Bone's.

"You're on, pardner."

They drove in separate cars, and twenty minutes later they were seated at a table with Mia's sister, Cassandra. Jack had called ahead and told her to be there. Cassandra had never met her sister's lawyer before, but there was a look of recognition on the old man's face as soon as Jack made the introduction.

"Goodness gracious, you sure do look like your sister."

"Thank you," she said. "I guess I'm pretty close to the age she was when she hired you."

They were three at a square table for four, and Jack had to shift the mixed-flower centerpiece toward the empty place setting in order to see Talbridge's face. "The family resemblance is no longer quite as strong," said Jack.

"I noticed."

"You've seen Mia's photograph?"

"Yeah. The FBI showed it to me before they issued their BOLO this morning. Asked me if I thought she was Teresa."

"What did you say?"

"Possible. Honestly, I see more resemblance between Cassandra and Teresa than between Mia and Teresa."

"It doesn't matter," said Cassandra. "The FBI called me this morning with the results of a DNA analysis. Teresa is definitely Mia Salazar."

The test results were news to Jack, but that explained the FBI's eagerness to issue the BOLO for Montalvo.

"That's amazing," said Talbridge. "All these years, I thought I'd gotten her killed with my testimony at that preliminary hearing. We were just trying to refute Montalvo's argument that she was crying rape for the money. Next thing we knew, the two of them had gone missing and—well, I don't have to tell you the story. The police never found her body, but it seemed pretty obvious what Montalvo had done."

"Unfortunately, it appears that Montalvo has finally caught up with her."

"Yeah, that's what I gathered from the FBI's press conference. Poor girl. Can't believe this nightmare won't end for her."

"That's why we need your help."

"Now, explain something for me," said Talbridge. "Exactly how is it that you're involved in this, Jack?"

Jack fumbled for a response. "It's a little complicated."

"Actually, it's quite simple," said Cassandra. "Teresa made a new life for herself as Mia. She and Jack are in love, and he's doing everything he can to get her back. That includes paying her ransom."

It wasn't the whole truth—she'd left out a few little things like Mia's marriage—but Jack found her selectivity soothing. Maybe it really was that simple. Maybe that was what kept him going.

"Is that true?" said Talbridge. "You're paying the ransom?"

Jack nodded. "I lined up the money today."

"But isn't she married to some wealthy guy from Palm Beach?"

"I didn't break up the marriage," said Jack.

"I wasn't accusing you, pardner. But isn't he paying a ransom?"

"He claims he did, but I have my doubts. In any event, it wasn't enough to get her released. I'm her last shot. I've lined up a quarter million dollars, and I'm angling for a simultaneous exchange. No Mia, no money."

Cassandra reached across the table and touched the back of the old man's hand. "He's putting a lot on the line, Mr. Talbridge."

Talbridge retreated into thought, bringing his fingertips together to form a steeple. Then he checked his watch. "I'm not sure you made it under your five-minute time limit, but I guess you won't be picking up the check tonight after all."

It took Jack a moment, but then he recalled their agreement—dinner was on Jack if he couldn't convince Talbridge to talk about Teresa's case in less than five minutes. "So we can speak freely now?"

"Let me put it this way," said Talbridge. "There's still a little matter of the attorney-client privilege, but I've just named you my co-counsel in the civil case of *Teresa Bussori versus Gerard Montalvo*."

"The case that never was," said Jack.

"And that never will be. But if you're putting out a ransom, I think it's time I brought you up to speed on the facts."

"I'm eager to hear them," said Jack. "All of them."

•

46

After dinner, Jack said good-bye to Cassandra and followed Talbridge back downtown to his office. The old building was a smaller version of the famous Flatiron Building in New York, a triangular footprint situated on the south side of an X-shaped intersection. The Law Office of Henry Talbridge was on the third floor, and if you thought of the suite as pie-shaped, it was probably fair to describe the ingredients as mincemeat. There were chairs, but no place to sit, as every available surface was covered with expandable files, loose notepads, and law books. There were filing cabinets, but they were almost completely hidden behind floor-to-ceiling stacks of dusty banker's boxes, some even blocking the windows. Many appeared to have been there for years, the labels yellowed with age and the cardboard sagging beneath the weight. It was as if the box tops had curled into columns of smiles, the happiest blokes on the bottom.

"I'm sure Teresa's file is here somewhere," said Talbridge. "It's only seven years old."

"Only?" said Jack.

"Yeah, I clear the place out about once a decade, whether it needs it or not."

Jack now fully understood why Talbridge had never taken on a partner in over forty years of private practice. He was an Oscar Madison who made Theo Knight look like Felix Unger. "Any suggestions on where to look?"

"Not a clue. I'll call my secretary. Not sure how she does it, but she knows where everything is."

Talbridge scanned the room for a telephone, as if he knew it had to be somewhere in all the mess of files and papers. He gave up and dialed on his cell. It was a short conversation, punctuated by a few grunts from Talbridge's end, followed by an "I'm truly sorry, Virginia." He tucked the phone away, then spoke to Jack. "Virginia and I have been together forever, and it's always the same routine. Bitches me out for bothering her at home, then she calls back in five minutes with the answer. We'll just have to cool our heels for a while. You like a good cigar?"

"Actually, I'm not big on them." *Yet another source of cultural embarrassment for this half-Cuban boy's abuela.*

Talbridge lit one for himself, going through several stick matches. "Don't tell my doctor."

A cloud of smoke soon filled the room, as there was no after-hours A/C to clear the air. If Talbridge's secretary didn't call back soon, it would take a good month for Jack to stop smelling like a walking Monte Cristo. "So, tell me something," said Jack. "Whose idea was it to make the one-dollar settlement offer at the preliminary hearing? Yours or Charlene Wright's?"

He inhaled deeply, his face aglow with a cigar lover's satisfaction. "Actually, it was Teresa's."

"Was it ever really her intention to file a lawsuit?"

"She came to me because she wanted to know all her rights as a victim. Honestly, her focus was on the criminal process, mostly staying informed about the progress of the case and making sure that the DA didn't cut some sweetheart deal with the Montalvo family that ended with a slap on Gerard's wrist."

"But you did talk about a civil lawsuit?"

"Sure we did. And there's not a damn thing wrong with a victim exercising her right to seek compensation from a rapist. If I walked up and hit you over the head with a hockey stick, you'd probably sue me, right? This isn't some joker who wants a million dollars for the emotional distress of finding no prize in his box of Cracker Jack."

"But obviously she was willing to forfeit that right."

"I thought it was beyond reproach when she put the one-dollar settlement offer on the table. She wanted to make it a nonissue. But Montalvo's lawyers started spinning the media just as soon as we walked out of the courthouse."

"How do you mean?"

"Well, they tried to characterize it as purely a publicity stunt. They said the only reason we made the offer was because we knew it would never be accepted in open court. That kind of thing."

"What was your response?"

Talbridge examined the uneven burn on the tip of his cigar, struck another match. "Nothing at first. I felt like they were just digging a deeper hole for themselves. But I was pretty quick to realize that these guys were no public relations dummies."

"They had a counterattack planned, I presume."

"Oh, you bet they did. But the old he-coon walks just before the light of day."

"Excuse me?"

Talbridge smiled, the smoldering cigar clenched between his teeth. "Sorry, we southerners are full of our expressions, which of course goes hand in hand with our God-given ability to just keep on talking till we think of something to say. What I mean is that Henry Talbridge ain't no fool. I was on to Montalvo and his high-priced spinmasters. I got wind that they had a plan of their own."

"A counteroffer?"

"Nah. The settlement was a dead letter. They was gonna have Gerard sit for a polygraph. You know, have it administered by some flunky who would give them the best results that money could buy. Then they'd run to the press and say Gerard passed a lie detector test. But I decided to beat them to the punch."

"How?"

"I went to Charlene Wright and said let's give Teresa a polygraph."

The phone rang before Jack could follow up. Talbridge answered with an obsequious "Yes, Virginia, darling." He thanked her several times, promised never to bother her again at home before hanging up. Then he said to Jack, "Told you she'd call back. Help me out here, would you, pardner? Looks like we'll be digging straight to the bottom of stack D."

Talbridge led him to the conference room, which was filled with stacks of banker's boxes that looked even older than those in the reception area. "Your back's gotta be stronger than mine, young man. It's that one—D-eleven—second from the bottom."

Jack unloaded two boxes at a time until they reached the right one. "So, did you end up giving her a polygraph?" asked Jack.

Talbridge flipped off the box top and thumbed through the files. "Oh, yeah. That's what I wanted to show you." He yanked out a file, announcing, "Here it is."

"What's that?"

"Report from Teresa's polygraph examiner. Charlene and I agreed that we should use the best in the business, and we found him. Former FBI, list of references you wouldn't believe. No monkey business in his examinations. Not everyone believes in polygraphs, but even the skeptics give this guy credit."

Jack thumbed through the report, skipping the standard introductory pages about how the test was administered, where, over what period of time. He went straight to the final page—the results—and stopped cold.

"She failed," Jack said in quiet disbelief.

"Yup. She failed. Interesting, ain't it?"

Jack was gazing in the general direction of Mia's old lawyer, but suddenly the room was a blur, a big cloud of cigar smoke. "Yeah. I'd say that's interesting, all right."

47

·

J ack flew back to Miami early the next morning, and Theo picked him up at the airport. Jack almost didn't recognize his friend's VW. A strange contraption was mounted on the forward section of the roof, extending out above the windshield. It appeared to be sculpted fiber-glass, spanning the width of the car, about two feet high and two feet long. The design was somewhat aerodynamic, like one of those roof-mounted luggage boxes—not the whole box, however, just the nose. Jack couldn't imagine how it could enhance the looks or performance of Theo's low-riding Jetta.

"What's up with that thing on your roof?" Jack said as he climbed into the passenger seat.

"You saw it, huh?"

It was like asking if he'd noticed the third eye in the middle of his forehead. "Yeah. What is it?"

"Keep an open mind now, all right?" Theo said as he drove them away from the curb. "The idea came to me last night. I saw a guy driv-ing down the expressway with a mattress on the roof of his Chevy. And he must think he's Superman or something, cuz he's cruising along at fifty-five miles per hour and he's got one skinny arm out the window try-ing to keep a queen-sized mattress from flying off. I'm sure you've seen these idiots before."

"Uh . . . yeah," Jack said warily.

"So I sees this and figure, hey, there's gotta be a better way, right? And that's when it hit me: a mattress spoiler."

"A what?"

"Think about it, man. We got a quarter million dollars coming from Ball-Bustin' Bud in Atlanta. Let's say we take just ten grand and develop a prototype of this thing. Put another twenty toward an infomercial. You can sell meatballs to vegetarians if you got a fucking infomercial. This could be a gold mine."

"Theo, what have you been smoking?"

"Okay. How about five grand?"

"I'm not putting five *cents* into mattress spoilers."

Theo groaned, then turned his attention back to traffic. "Damn, Swyteck. This is why you'll never be rich."

They rode in silence for several miles, and by the time Theo had cursed out every incompetent driver between the airport and Coral Gables, he seemed to have put the mattress spoiler to bed, so to speak. "How'd it go with Henry Talbridge?"

"Fine," said Jack. "Until he showed me the polygraph that Mia failed. That Teresa failed, I should say."

"You mean they gave her a lie detector test on the rape?"

Jack pulled the report from his briefcase, as if he needed to see it again to believe it. "She was asked three key questions. One: 'Were you raped by Gerard Montalvo?' She answered yes."

"And that was a lie?"

"In the examiner's opinion, her response showed signs of deception."

"Whoa, dude. What was the next question?"

" 'Did Gerard Montalvo force you to have sex with him against your will?' Again, her answer was yes."

"Another lie?"

"Same interpretation by the examiner. Shows signs of deception."

"That's not good, buddy. What was the third question?"

"This has to do with the scar on the inside of her thigh that I told you about. She was asked: 'Is Gerard Montalvo responsible for the injury to your leg?' Her response was yes."

"What did the examiner have to say about that?"

"He didn't say she was lying, but he didn't bless it, either. He characterized the result as 'inconclusive.'"

"What kind of lame-ass finding is that?"

"Basically he can't tell if she was lying or telling the truth. It happens more than you'd think in polygraph examinations."

Theo stopped at the red light and started tapping a little drumroll on the steering wheel, as if rhythm of any kind helped his brain to process all this information. "Why didn't that prosecutor tell you about the polygraph? What's her name, Charlene?"

"Charlene Wright. I called her at home late last night and asked her the same thing."

"What'd she say?"

"First off, she seemed very surprised that Henry Talbridge shared the polygraph with me. The conversation didn't go much beyond that, except for one important point. Charlene never stopped believing in Teresa."

"How does she explain a failed polygraph?"

"She thinks that with all the stress, the threats that Teresa was getting from Montalvo and his cronies, it was no surprise that she failed. No one would have passed under those conditions."

"What does Talbridge think?"

"He wants to agree with Charlene, but he did point out that the polygraph is a real sore spot for her. It was the end of her at the DA's office. She lost all credibility with her supervisors because she believed so much in the case."

"That's pretty harsh. I mean, it's not a good thing that Mia flunked a polygraph, but those things aren't a hundred percent reliable."

"No, but if I had to make a generalization, prosecutors attach more weight to them than defense lawyers do. And you have to remember, Mia took over three days to report the rape to the police. That means she showered, changed clothes, ate, went to the bathroom. Beyond seventy-two hours, a forensic exam isn't going to turn up much in the way of physical evidence. This was a he-said, she-said case, except for the cut on her leg. And the polygraph was inconclusive as to whether she got that from Montalvo."

"So, what does that mean in this situation? Was the DA's office still going after Montalvo, or were they gonna drop the whole thing?"

"That's what I was hoping to find out from Charlene. But she's not talking."

"Maybe we can figure it out for ourselves. What's the exact sequence of events here?"

The traffic light changed, and Jack tucked the polygraph report back into his briefcase as the car started forward. "Talbridge testified on the last day of the preliminary hearing. Right after that, he found out that Montalvo was going to take a polygraph and leak the results to the press, so he and Charlene arranged for Teresa to take one the next morning. She failed, much to their surprise. About two hours later, the judge issued his ruling that there was sufficient evidence to bind the case over for trial."

"Obviously the judge didn't know that the alleged victim flunked a polygraph."

"It wouldn't be admissible anyway, but you're right. The only people who knew about it were Mia, the examiner, Henry Talbridge, and Charlene Wright."

Theo changed lanes as they neared Jack's office. "So the judge made his ruling, and the prosecutor is sitting on a polygraph that says the victim is lying. What does the DA do then? Drop the charges, or ignore the polygraph and go full speed ahead?"

"The very least any decent prosecutor would do is sit down and have a candid conversation with the accuser. But the fact is, we'll never know how Charlene and her supervisors were going to handle the dilemma. Both Mia and Montalvo went missing less than twenty-four hours after the judge ruled that the case should proceed to trial."

"Which makes you wonder: What the hell made both the accused and the accuser give up everything they owned, turn their backs on everybody they knew, and become someone else?"

"Whether Mia was telling the truth or outright lying, it's conceivable that she would flee out of fear that Montalvo would retaliate against her. It's even more believable if she was lying, since she wouldn't be motivated to stand up to Montalvo's threats in order to see that justice was done."

"I'll buy that. The harder question is, why would Montalvo run?"

"Because he was guilty?" Jack suggested.

"That's one reason. But that's now debatable."

"Because he thought he would be found guilty even though he was innocent?"

"How many innocent men cut and run after a stupid preliminary hearing?"

It was a valid point, one that made Jack think for a moment. "Maybe we need to ask a more basic question. As in, guilty of *what*?"

"I'm not following you."

"Maybe Montalvo wasn't afraid of being found guilty of rape. Maybe his real fear was that he'd be held accountable for Mia's sudden disappearance after the judge ordered the case held over for trial."

"Still, you gotta ask: How did he get so afraid that he took off and ran?"

The car came to a stop outside Jack's office. He reached for the door handle and said, "Theo, my friend. *That* is exactly what we need to find out."

48

.

Jack got out of the car, and Theo followed him into the office to raid the candy dish. Dani, Jack's temporary secretary, was seated behind the reception desk, but she wasn't her usual cheery self. She was downright glum.

"What's wrong?" said Jack.

"Oh, nothing."

Jack was a man, and he had plenty on his mind—two strikes against him—but even he could tell that it was *not* "nothing." He pretended to sift through the stack of mail on the counter, but he kept a concerned eye on Dani. She was definitely not herself. "You want to talk about it?"

She shrugged and said, "It's my boyfriend. He got accepted to med school at Stanford."

"Wow. That's a long way away. So . . . I'm guessing that he called to break things off."

"No. He asked me to go with him."

"Whoa. That's a big decision. Are you actually considering it?"

"Do you think I shouldn't?"

"I think—" He stopped himself. "I think you should talk to your parents."

"You're such a lawyer," she said, smiling. "Don't worry. I'm not going. But I would go in a heartbeat if I thought he was the one."

Jack was intrigued, the way she seemed so sure. "You would?"

"Absolutely. Like my grandmother used to say. You can't just grab the next bus that comes along. Love doesn't work that way."

"Ah, the old love-means-never-having-to-ask-for-a-transfer theory," said Theo through a mouthful of peppermints.

Dani wrinkled her nose; *Love Story* was long before her time. Jack just shook his head and started back to his office. Dani would be fine, he knew. He wished he had that same self-assurance, the innate ability to know if it was worth moving across the country to be with that certain someone.

Maybe Dani could tell him how much Mia was worth.

Jack switched on the lights and went to his desk. Theo had completely emptied out the dish of peppermints, and he was now rummaging through the minirefrigerator beside Jack's credenza in search of something to drink. Jack's computer was running, so he quickly checked his e-mails. He scrolled past the ones from recognizable senders. It was the ones from unknown sources that concerned him—the ones that could be from the kidnapper.

A subject line that read "Check this out" got his attention, but it was for diet pills. A few others made his pulse quicken, but, collectively, they were for fat people with small penises who needed to borrow money fast.

"You think Mia lied about the rape?" said Theo.

Jack looked up from the computer screen. "I don't know what to think at this point."

"One other thing about that polygraph exam. I didn't say nothing before, but I guess I don't have to remind you. I flunked one, too. Remember?"

"Of course I remember."

"Sometimes you try too hard to pass, not because you're lying, but because there's so much at stake. I think that can make you flunk."

"I know. Thanks."

Jack turned his attention back to his list of unread e-mails, then found one that looked promising. The subject line read "Our little secret". He opened the e-mail with a click of the mouse, but the message had no text. A digital photograph filled Jack's display screen. At first, he couldn't figure out what it was. He narrowed his eyes, gaining a little different perspective. And then it hit him.

The photo was an extreme close-up of the scar on Mia's inner thigh.

"Oh, shit," said Jack.

"What?" said Theo.

Jack was staring at the image on the screen, unable to move, barely able to speak. He quickly deduced that the photograph was a teaser of sorts for the attachment to the e-mail.

The kidnapper had another video for him.

Jack drew a breath and said, "This can't be good."

49

•

J
ack downloaded the video attachment to the e-mail and took it straight to the FBI. Watching it once had been bad enough. Watching it again with Andie Henning was practically unbearable. The idea of seeing it a third time with a trained criminal psychiatrist was nearly enough to push him over the edge.

"Jack, you don't have to stay for this if you don't want to," said Andie.

He considered it, but walking out somehow felt like the wrong thing to do, like an act of abandonment. "I'll stay," he said.

They each pulled up a chair to the computer station, and Andie adjusted the flat-screen monitor so that all three could see. The opening frame was painfully familiar to Jack by now. The camera never showed Mia's face, never turned away from the scar on the inner thigh. It was impressive not in length but in the sheer density of scar tissue. Naturally, the camera's tight focus exacerbated things, the way nighttime seems to exaggerate every fear and anxiety. Perhaps it seemed even worse to Jack because he knew the softness, the smoothness, the perfection of her unmarred skin. But this one flaw, this hideous scar, seemed to have bubbled up from the skin like lava from the earth.

Andie hit the Play button. The video began to roll, and the audio kicked in.

"Show him." His voice sounded thick, as if disguised by a wad of cotton or something in his mouth.

"What are you talking about?" said Mia.

"You know exactly what I'm talking about. Show him, damn it!"

There was a short blip in the video, a momentary blackness, as if something had been edited out. It pained Jack to imagine what might have transpired off camera. The image returned to the screen, the same tight shot of the scar on her leg. It was impossible to determine the length of the apparent break in filming, but it had been long enough for Mia's captor to release some of his rage. His voice sounded calmer in the next segment.

"Now are you ready, Teresa?"

She gave no audible response. Jack had no way to gauge Mia's readiness, but her compliance was evident. Her right hand came into view, grasping a broken lightbulb by the base. The jagged glass was crystal clear and razor thin. She turned it one way, then the other, as if trying to decide which edge would be the more efficient scalpel.

"Do it," he said.

Her scarred leg heaved up and then down, ever so slightly. Jack could almost feel her lungs expand and contract with a deep, calming breath. Perhaps he was imagining it, but he thought he noticed the muscles tightening beneath her skin. Then, with surprising steadiness of hand, she brought the long, jagged shard of glass to the top of the scar. It was so sharp that the first drop of blood came with hardly any pressure at all. Slowly, however, she applied more pressure, and the very tip of broken glass disappeared beneath her skin. Deeper it went, until a rivulet of blood trickled onto the glass and ran down to her thumb. The pressure ceased, and she pulled the glass from her thigh. The bleeding continued, so much blood for such a small wound, like a nasty razor cut that just wouldn't quit. The camera remained steady, focused on the newly opened wound.

"All of it," he told her. *"Show him the whole thing."*

Somewhere beneath the blood was a puncture wound. She brought the crimson-coated tip of glass toward her scar and slowly reinserted it.

For a moment, the video streaming across the screen was like a still photograph, no sound, no bodily movement whatsoever. Finally, her hand began a slow journey downward, the shard of glass opening the old scar from top to bottom. The bleeding intensified, but the job wasn't finished. With a surgeon's care, she retraced the cut from bottom to top, then top to bottom, then back up again. With each pass of the hand, the wound grew wider, the glass dug deeper, the blood flowed more freely. Then she dropped the broken bulb between her legs, and the screen went black.

Jack took a breath. Andie switched off the monitor, as if to erase all trace of the disturbing image. Neither of them said a word, waiting instead for the reaction of the criminal psychiatrist.

Eve Stapleton had twenty years of experience with law enforcement, ten with the bureau's Investigative Services Unit in Quantico, Virginia, where she'd seen the worst of the worst. It wasn't that she had any less empathy for victims, but her training enabled her to maintain an almost academic air about herself, even when viewing something like this.

Stapleton took a moment to frame her thoughts. "Let's start with the e-mail you received. The subject line, in particular."

Jack said, "It came to me with a three-word description: 'Our little secret.' Which made me immediately suspicious."

"Sounds to me like just another tagline for spam. What made you so suspicious?"

"In my last conversation with the kidnapper, I in effect told him that I was well aware of his past as the Got the Look Rapist. We came to an understanding of sorts that I would keep my discovery between us. I wouldn't tell the police."

Andie slid her chair away from the computer table, putting a little more distance between herself and the others. "The fact that the e-mail was labeled 'Our little secret' is obviously sarcasm. We issued the BOLO yesterday morning. The whole world is looking for Montalvo."

"Looks like Mia paid the price for that one," said Jack.

"It seems like more than payback," said Stapleton. "The obvious point the kidnapper is trying to make is that Mia—Teresa—cut herself seven years ago to fabricate a rape claim."

"Well, wait just a second," said Jack. "Just because some lunatic points a camera at his prisoner and tells her to cut herself doesn't mean that the original wound was self-inflicted."

"Obviously this was compelled. I presume he edited out her screams to create the false impression that she was comfortable with cutting herself."

"I can have our AV people check for that," said Andie. "They'll be checking for background noises again anyway, just like the last video."

Stapleton nodded. "Nonetheless, I understand that her polygraph examination did raise some question about the cause of the original injury. She answered yes when asked if Gerard Montalvo was responsible for the wound to her thigh. The examiner couldn't tell if her response was the truth or a lie."

"Polygraphs aren't infallible," said Jack. "Especially when you're testing a woman who has been threatened and harassed for weeks because she went to the police and reported the most harrowing physical and emotional trauma of her life."

"True," said Stapleton. "But that doesn't change the psychological motivation behind the making of this video. At the very least, the circumstances of the sexual assault were such that he views it as her fault. That she deserved it, or that she brought it on herself. Which is not an uncommon rationalization for a rapist."

Jack said, "A twisted mind can create a pretty distorted picture of something that happened seven years ago. There's no doubt in my mind that he was applying some form of coercion behind the scenes while making that video. This wasn't simply a demonstration of what she did to herself seven years ago. It was self-mutilation with a gun to her head."

"I agree with Jack," said Andie. "As I see it, the real question raised by the video is *why* does the kidnapper find it so important to convince Jack that the original wound was self-inflicted?"

Jack had his own theory, but he waited for Stapleton's take on it.

She said, "My impression is that he thinks it's relevant to Jack's determination of how much Mia is worth. He's demanding a ransom that not only covers what she's worth to Jack, but also pays him back for the damage she did to him when she—as Teresa—accused him of a rape that, in his own twisted mind, was her own fault."

Andie gave Jack an assessing look. "Are you sure you want to take money out of your own pocket and pay a ransom to someone with that kind of mind-set?"

"What choice do I have?"

"You could choose not to pay a ransom."

"That would make me no better than her scumbag husband. She'd be dead in an hour. I'm sure of it. You and I have been over that before. You promised to try for more money to use as bait."

"I got more."

Jack's interest was piqued. "You did?"

"Yes, but it's to be used only as bait. I made it clear before that the FBI would never give you money to pay an actual ransom. You could show him the money. You might even allow him to take a small amount of cash, with the hope that the FBI could trace the marked bills. But this is not a loan or gift for you to use as you see fit."

"So the FBI puts up the bait, but you don't put it at risk," said Jack.

"We operate within strict constraints is what I'm saying."

"How much are you willing to pony up?"

"I got approval for fifty thousand dollars."

"That's not enough."

"It's all I can get. And even at this level, I'm going to need certain concessions from you."

"Ah, the fine print," said Jack. "Talk to me."

"The FBI would need greater control over your dealings with the kidnapper."

"Are you still hacked off about the fact that I mentioned the Got the Look Rapist to him?"

"That's one example," said Andie. "But I'm talking about more comprehensive control. The decision to pay a ransom, how much to pay, where to pay it, how to pay it, when to pay it—all that has to be under my direction. Your communications would have to be more scripted, your movements and day-to-day actions more choreographed."

"What if I disagree with your recommendations?"

She hesitated, seeming to search for the right spin. "I think you should recognize that this is our job, and that you can't be objective about these kinds of decisions."

"In other words, if I take your money, I give up my right to disagree."

"I'm not going to shove anything down your throat, Jack. The only thing you definitely give up is the ability to tell the FBI to get lost. You've decided to handle this on your own."

Jack didn't want to insult her, but he was thinking about Ashley Thornton. The FBI hadn't done her much good. "Let me ask you something," said Jack. "That first Wrong Number kidnapping that you discovered through VICAP. The one with the young auto mechanic up in Georgia who paid nineteen thousand dollars—everything he had—to get his wife back."

"What about it?" asked Andie.

"Was the FBI involved in that?"

"No. The kidnapper warned him not to call the cops, so he didn't. He reported the crime after he got his wife back."

"Did the kidnapper also warn Drew Thornton not to call the cops?"

"Yes," she said quietly.

Jack's response didn't come quickly. It was more like a slow-moving freight train, impossible to stop. "I'm not saying I don't trust you. I'm not even suggesting that I don't want the FBI involved. But I'm keeping my options open."

"You don't want our money?" said Andie.

"Not on your terms. Look, I agree that under the best of circumstances, the safer approach would be for me to engage this guy in a dialogue and draw out information that hopefully would enable the FBI to pinpoint his location. But this video makes it crystal clear that we don't have time for that. Hell, he's too smart to even *talk* to me. He's sending tapes, no negotiation. We need to force his hand, force him into making a mistake."

Andie didn't answer, but she didn't disagree, either.

"I say it's time to angle for a simultaneous exchange," said Jack. "If I have to use my own money to lure him into the open, then that's the way it's going to be."

50

.

Andie ate lunch at her desk. Stacked beside her cup of microwaved minestrone were leftover copies of the FBI's original psychological profile for the Wrong Number Kidnapper. She dabbed away a drop of soup from the margin and gave the top page a quick once-over. "Angry white male, probably midthirties. Possibly a former high roller, a once-successful businessman who lost everything—money, family, friends. May even be homeless."

What a rabbit hole that had turned out to be. A team of agents wasted a solid week in Miami's cardboard cities looking for the bankrupt CEO of Never_Turned_A_Profit.com.

Andie laid the old profile aside and took one last swallow from her bottle of noni juice. She didn't care for the taste, but in her mind it was the tropical equivalent of cod-liver oil. Aggressive snow skiing had taken a toll on her right knee, and the juice of the noni, an exotic fruit from the Cook Islands, seemed to combat the added pains of rainy days. A doctor had once warned that the joint could become arthritic, though the future was difficult to predict in Andie's case. As an adopted child, she had only limited knowledge of her biological parents' medical histories. Nonetheless, "potentially crippling arthritis" was yet another theory that friends and colleagues had posited to explain her decision to leave Seattle and its cold, damp winters. Wrong again, of course. Her sudden beeline to Miami had had nothing to do with health.

Unless you were talking about mental health.

The intercom buzzed, and the receptionist told her that Cassandra Nuñez was in the lobby.

"I'll be right out," she said. Since the trip to Atlanta, Andie had remained in phone contact with Mia's sister, so she was well aware that Cassandra had come to Miami. The latest videotape warranted another face-to-face discussion. Andie greeted her in the lobby and escorted her back to her office, where they spoke behind a closed door.

"Thanks for coming in," said Andie as she took the seat behind her desk. "I thought I might as well take advantage of the fact that you're in town, do this in person."

"Of course, that's why I stayed down here instead of going back to Atlanta. Even if I can't help, it makes me feel better just to be here. I need to be close. That's the way my sister and I always were. Close."

"I can relate to that."

"Do you have a sister?"

"Uh . . . that's a complicated situation."

Cassandra scoffed. "It can't be more complicated than me and Teresa. For the past seven years, I thought my sister was dead."

"No, but it's still pretty screwy. I hadn't thought about it until just now, but I had sort of the opposite situation with my sister. I never knew she existed until I was a teenager."

"How could that be?"

Andie paused, not sure that it was advisable to share too much of her personal life. But there were things she wanted to know about Cassandra and her sister, and revealing a little something about herself might open up a dialogue. "I grew up in foster care until I was adopted at age nine," said Andie. "I didn't get interested in my biological family till I was in high school, and my adoptive parents helped me piece some things together. That's when we found out about my twin sister."

"Wow. Did you become close after that?"

"It took some time—years, actually. But we did become very close."

Cassandra turned quiet, though she seemed to be thinking more about her own situation than Andie's. That was a good thing, as it was Andie's intention to steer the conversation in that direction. "Tell me something about your sister, would you?"

"What would you like to know?"

"What was she like when you were younger?"

"I'm not sure what you want to hear. She was the pretty one, the athletic one, the popular one in school. She was the girl every other girl wanted to be, including me."

"Was she truthful? Or was she the type to make things up?"

"Teresa was very truthful."

"What about anger?" asked Andie. "Would you say she was the type to keep things bottled up inside? Or did she express herself?"

"She got angry, sure, but I wouldn't say she had a temper or that she was a complainer. In fact, the only times I remember her getting really angry were when people were mean to her friends or to me. That's the kind of person she was."

Andie nodded, accepting the response. She turned her chair to face the computer. "I would never force this on anyone, but are you prepared to see the latest video of your sister?"

"I've seen it already," said Cassandra.

"You have?"

"Jack Swyteck e-mailed the file to me. I watched it this morning." Her expression tightened, and her voice weakened. "I don't need to see it again."

"No, of course you don't. I wouldn't have suggested it had I known." Andie swiveled her chair away from the computer, then leaned into her desk, a little closer to Cassandra. "I did want to talk to you about a specific aspect of the video, however. This is something that was raised by one of our criminal psychiatrists."

"Sure. Anything to help."

"It appears that we're dealing with a rapist who has managed to convince himself that the rape was your sister's fault. He may be delusional, or something else may be going on."

"What do you mean by 'something else'?"

"I want you to think back to that night you and your sister went to the bar in Atlanta, Club Vertigo. Was there anything—anything at all—to suggest that there might have been a past history between your sister and Gerard Montalvo?"

"You mean did they know each other?"

"Know each other, date each other."

"No way. I had to tell her who Gerard Montalvo was. She couldn't have cared less about the invitation to his party. *I* was the one who insisted that she go up to his suite and check it out."

"You're sure of that?"

"Yes, of course I'm sure," Cassandra said, her voice taking on a defensive edge. "What on earth is wrong with you people? My sister was raped. Why is it so hard for everyone to understand that?"

"I do understand. Trust me, I wouldn't even be asking these questions if your sister hadn't failed a polygraph examination."

"She was raped. I know it."

"How do you know it?"

"Because . . . because I'm her sister. She told me what happened."

"She told you three days after the fact. Why did she wait?"

"It took her three days because she needed three days. It might have taken another woman three weeks or three years to finally be able to talk about it. All that matters is that she finally spoke out. And I know she wouldn't have lied to me."

"Don't take this the wrong way, but how do you know that she wouldn't have lied to you?"

Cassandra scoffed, as if the question were ridiculous. "She had no reason to lie to me. I told you. We're sisters."

"Okay," said Andie. "For the moment, I'll take that answer at face value: Your sister wouldn't lie to you. You're sure of that."

"That's right."

"Here's my trouble," said Andie. "Let's go back to the first time you and I talked. You said you were certain that your sister was dead. And the reason you gave is that your sister would not have been able to cut you out of her life, even if she had fled to some far corner of the earth for her own safety. Somehow, someway, she would have made contact with you."

"Yes. I believe that's true."

"So, for seven years, you truly believed that your sister was dead."

"Correct."

"Not only did you think she was dead, but you thought Gerard Montalvo had killed her."

"That's right."

"You thought he had killed your sister and run off, escaped. In other words, that he'd gotten away with murder."

"That's exactly right."

"Then let me ask you this: Why didn't you ever ask the district attorney to bring murder charges against Gerard Montalvo?"

"I . . . I don't know. Maybe I did ask."

"No. I talked to the DA about this. You never asked."

"Okay, then maybe I didn't. But don't they have to catch him before they can charge him?"

"Not at all. Every day of the week, people are indicted in absentia."

"Well, I suppose if I had known that, I would have asked them to do it."

"So that's your answer? You were convinced that Gerard Montalvo had brutally raped and then murdered your sister. But in the seven long years that followed your sister's disappearance, you never once asked the DA to indict him for murder because you thought the police had to catch him first?"

"I think that's right," she said quietly.

"Are you sure that's your answer?"

Cassandra fell silent, as if uncomfortable with Andie's apparent skepticism. "Maybe there was a part of me that never gave up hope that she would turn up alive. Maybe that's why I never pushed for murder charges to be brought against Gerard in absentia."

"So you were sure she was dead, but you weren't sure she was dead."

"You don't have to make it sound ridiculous. My answer is my answer."

Andie studied her expression, allowing the pall of momentary silence to do its powerful work. "All right," she said finally. "Then that's your answer."

"Is there something wrong with it?" asked Cassandra.

"No. Nothing wrong with it at all. It's a perfectly fine answer."

For a liar, thought Andie.

51

•

Around one o'clock Jack arrived at a dusty construction site, a one-acre tract of land on Hammock Lake. It was covered with beautiful old oaks that the owner of a very modest home had planted in another era, back when "cracker" still meant an old Florida redneck moving cows across the prairie at the crack of a whip, not a dopehead smoking crack in the alley. A bulldozer was in the process of reducing an old ranch-style house to rubble, making room for another new mega-home from Salazar Properties. Jack parked on the street, then caught up with Ernesto Salazar at the end of the old asphalt driveway. He was reviewing final drawings with his architect. Salazar excused himself, and he and Jack walked toward the lake, away from the architect and noisy bulldozer.

"I received another video of Mia," said Jack.

They were standing at the water's edge, looking not at each other but out across the lake. The croaking bullfrogs in the weeds were actually louder than the bulldozer behind them. "I know," said Salazar. "Agent Henning told me."

"Did she show it to you?"

"I didn't want to watch. Didn't see the point."

"I'm not pushing it," said Jack. "But I brought you a copy."

"What for?"

"On the outside chance that you might see the trouble she's in and help her."

"I've done my part," said Salazar.

"You gave the kidnapper a twenty-dollar bill and some audiotapes of me and Mia. That hardly helped her cause."

"Twenty dollars? I told you it was a half million."

"The kidnapper said it was twenty."

"Well the kidnapper is full of shit. He's just trying to con more money out of you."

Jack studied his expression, searching for the truth. "Why should I believe you?"

Salazar let out a mirthless chuckle. "Why? Why should I give a damn what you think? Why should I—"

Jack waited for him to finish, but Salazar went silent. It wasn't so much that he'd lost his train of thought. He seemed to have abandoned it. He drew a breath, and his voice lost its edge. "You should believe me for one reason. You, of all people, should know that any man would want her back."

"Are you saying that you still love her?"

"Hell, I never stopped. Don't misunderstand me. When it comes to being a husband, I was about as shitty as they get. Monogamy's not for me, but that doesn't mean I stopped loving her. I started cheating on her three months after we were married, and I've honestly lost count of all the mistresses since then. She tried to make me stop. Two years ago she said she wouldn't sleep with me again until I stopped sleeping around. Not once did she take a lover of her own. Until she met you. Which, of course, is the reason I hated your guts."

"I didn't know she was married."

"Of course you didn't. She would never have told you that. The risk was too great."

"What risk? Sounds like she wanted out of the marriage anyway."

Salazar shook his head, not disagreeing with what Jack was saying, but as if to convey how little Jack understood. "I had her boxed in," said Salazar.

"How do you mean?"

"Like I told you before: I was her protector."

"Protector from what?"

"That scar on her leg. I knew how she got it. She told me about the rape, why she'd changed her name. I even knew her old name, Teresa Bussori. She gave me too much knowledge, which turned out to be her Achilles' heel."

"What do you mean?"

"Let me put it this way. Mia was in no position to tell you about me, or to tell me about you. Unless she was ready to tell the world that she was Teresa Bussori."

"Are you saying that you threatened to blow her cover if she left you for someone else?"

"I'm not proud of it. But without a prenuptial agreement, it was the only leverage I had."

Jack wondered why Salazar had finally opened up like this, but he'd been on the listening end of conversations like this before, mostly with clients who'd finally unloaded secrets they'd held for far too long. Truth be told, precious few secrets went to the grave with anyone.

The bulldozer behind them revved its engine. It was struggling with the carport. Jack said, "Why didn't you tell the FBI this two weeks ago?"

"My attorney told me to stop talking to them. He's convinced that I'm still a suspect in Mia's disappearance."

"Fortunately, they seem to have figured out the Montalvo connection on their own."

"It's not that I was trying to sandbag their investigation. Honestly, I didn't see how her kidnapping could have anything to do with the rape charges against Montalvo. If this is all about his revenge against Mia, then why the previous kidnappings?"

"The FBI doesn't have any problem with that."

"They don't?" said Salazar.

"Nah. The other kidnappings could have been practice for the big one, the only one that mattered. Or maybe he wasn't able to find Mia, so he used the other women as psychological substitutes for his rage. Or maybe he just wanted to divert the focus of the police away from the Got the Look Rapist, make it look like Mia was just another random target."

"You buy any of that?"

"It doesn't matter what I think," said Jack.

"Yes it does. You're the man in the middle now. You're the one who needs to ask himself, *Why now?* Why after seven years does Montalvo finally focus on Mia?"

"Maybe it took him that long to find her."

Salazar shook his head. "That's the kind of rationalization that Mia would expect from me, not you. The total avoidance of personal responsibility."

"What are you talking about?"

"I have my own theory as to why Montalvo came back now, as opposed to some earlier time in our marriage." He paused for a moment, his voice taking on an accusatory edge. "I think it's because she started cheating."

"What does that have to do with anything?"

"Once Mia started sleeping with you, Montalvo could safely assume that her husband wouldn't go the extra mile to save her. In other words, he'd much rather deal with you than with me, Swyteck. And you know why?"

Jack didn't answer.

He took a half step closer to Jack and said, "Because even a kidnapper knows better than to take something of value from Ernesto Salazar. *That's* why."

It was a threat, to be sure, Salazar's way of conveying that the score had yet to be evened for sleeping with Mia. Jack had more important things on his mind than a smaller man's ego. But now more than ever, locked in this stare-down with Mia's estranged husband, Jack sensed that if Salazar had indeed delivered anywhere near the half million dollars he claimed to have paid, it was not out of love for his wife. It was all about maintaining control over her.

"You're a rich man, Ernesto. But you're still a punk. Mia deserves better than that. Way better."

"And you're just the man to find it for her, aren't you?" Salazar said with heavy sarcasm.

Salazar was still talking as Jack turned and walked away, but Jack didn't hear it. Behind them was a deafening rumble, the sound of the roof collapsing on the bulldozed structure.

You're damn right I am, thought Jack.

52

·

Mia was tending to her wound. She first applied pressure to stop the bleeding. He brought her a tube of liquid stitches, a substance that bonded with the skin like Krazy Glue to close an open wound. She applied it and pinched the gash closed for a minute. It held. She felt a sudden warmth on her face, and she realized that she was crying. That was normal, she supposed—if any part of a ritual that involved slicing your own flesh could be considered "normal."

The lightbulb had come as no surprise to her. It was the cornerstone of her worst fears, which began that night in Montalvo's suite at Club Vertigo II. She went to the after-hours party with low expectations, fully intending to do nothing more than her best "hi and bye" routine. About a dozen people were already inside when she presented her "Got the Look" pass to the bouncer at the door. Maybe it was because she was new to the group, or maybe she really did have "the look." For whatever reason, Montalvo took an immediate interest. He spoke only to her, ignoring the other guests who came and went. Each time the door opened, a cloud of cigarette smoke and a blast of loud music from the dance club would fill the room. Through it all, Montalvo kept talking, obviously trying to impress her. He seemed harmless enough at first, even charming and engaging at times, so Mia wasn't worried. Then someone popped a videotape into the VCR. Mia didn't pay any attention to it, but slowly the crowd started to thin. She, too, was ready to leave, but before she knew it, the bodyguard was whisking the last few stragglers out the door. She and Montalvo were the only ones left in the suite.

"Stay awhile," he said.

"No. I really have to go."

The video continued to play, and Mia followed his gaze as it drifted toward the television screen. It didn't take long to figure out what kind of movie was playing. A steamy shower stall filled the screen. The glass was fogged, but the shower door was open. The camera then cut to the bathroom mirror, which was angled just perfectly to capture the action inside the shower. A young woman was completely naked, seated on the marble bench beneath the showerhead. Her hair was in pigtails to make her look even younger than she was, a turn-on in this industry. Her legs parted, and slowly she began to rock back and forth, hands working between her smooth thighs.

"I'm leaving," said Mia.

He took her by the wrist, gentle but firm. He had that cheesy play-boy smile. "Just stay another minute."

She tried not to look worried, but her instincts were on high alert. She could hear the sound track from the film, the moaning and groaning. The woman in the shower appeared to be masturbating.

"Let go of me right now," she said.

"Just stay five more minutes," he said.

She was frozen for a moment, praying that he would just let go, making her plan of action if he didn't. Should she run for it? Dial 911 on her cell phone? She considered the can of Mace in her purse, then silently cursed herself for having given it to her naive little sister, who never thought of such things. She avoided eye contact with Montalvo. As her gaze swept the room in search of all possible exits, she caught another glimpse of the television screen, and this time she saw what the movie was really about. The woman wasn't masturbating. She was holding a broken lightbulb. The camera angle widened, as if to pose the symbolic question *Is there anything more red than blood on white marble?* It was on her hands and thighs, running down her legs in long, thin rivulets of crimson that gathered on the white tile.

Montalvo leaned closer, his grip tightening on her wrist. "Do that for me," he said, his voice somewhere between a groan and a whisper, "and I'll pay you ten thousand dollars."

She broke free and slugged him across the side of the head, screaming as she ran for the door.

The doorknob turned, a creaking sound that jarred her from her seven-year-old memories and drew her back to the present nightmare. The creaking noise stopped, but the door did not open. Had he changed his mind? Or was he toying with her yet again, twisting the proverbial knife in her gut, making her sit and wonder . . . was he coming or wasn't he? He was constantly playing mental games, and Mia did her best to combat the effects. She remembered growing up, when things weren't going her way, how her father had always told her to think of all the people who were worse off than she was. The burn victim. The quadriplegic. The young child who had never even heard the words "heart attack" but was suddenly fatherless. It was a flawed psychological tool, as if the guy with no shoes was supposed to be happy because he wasn't the guy with no feet. In Mia's case, its application was downright ridiculous. She *was* the guy with no feet. She was days or hours or perhaps even minutes away from becoming the poster child for people in misery, the unlucky young woman whose unspeakable suffering at the hands of her kidnapper would ease the pains of others for years to come.

Remember Ernesto Salazar's wife, that woman who was kidnapped? Well, just be glad you're not her.

The door opened. He was back.

"Don't move," he said as he entered the dimly lit room.

She wondered why he still bothered to disguise his voice and cover his face with a mask. It was as if he'd somehow forgotten what he'd forced her to do, the things he'd said to her in the making of the last video. She wondered what he'd done with it, whether he'd shared the video with Ernesto or Jack or whoever was bidding for her freedom. Would they or the police be able to piece enough of her past together to determine his identity? Was he *trying* to reveal himself?

He crossed the room, stopping just a few feet away from her. She didn't look up, didn't want to make eye contact. But she did notice his camera. It was time for another movie, the thought of which was enough to make the gash on her leg throb with pain.

"Here," he said as he handed her a single sheet of paper. It was typewritten, like a script. "Read it once to yourself," he said, "just to be familiar with it. Then you're gonna read it out loud, with the camera rolling."

Reading in such poor lighting wasn't easy, but her eyes were accustomed to it, so she managed just fine. There were only three paragraphs. She tried to show no reaction, but as she reached the final sentences, he must have read the expression on her face.

"That's right," he said. "Your boyfriend is paying a ransom."

She looked up. "Then we'll be square, right? After he pays what you want?"

The response was slow in coming, and it wasn't what she wanted to hear. "Just read the fucking script." He turned away to set up the camera, the lighting.

Again she tried to show no reaction, but it was as if the one-page script were vibrating in her hands. Nerves were getting the best of her. He was making false promises, exactly as she'd feared. It came as no surprise at all, really, given the way he'd treated her so far, the ugly history between them. This wasn't the stuff that deals were made of.

I have to escape, she told herself. *It's the only way out.*

"On the count of three we're rolling," he said.

She gripped the paper with both hands, struggling to hold it steady.

One way or another, she knew, this would be the final video.

53

After her conversation with Mia's sister, Andie took a short walk down the hall to the SAC's office. She couldn't prove it, but she was willing to bet the farm that Cassandra had known for quite some time that her sister was alive. Had Andie's own sister been raped and murdered, Andie would have been all over the police and prosecutor to bring the killer to justice. According to the Atlanta authorities, however, Cassandra had never followed up.

"Maybe that's because Cassandra was an illegal alien," said Martinez. He was behind his desk, seated in an oxblood leather chair, hands clasped behind his head. "If she came forward, she risked deportation, right?"

"That doesn't wash," said Andie. "She married an American and got her citizenship four years ago. I can buy into the illegal alien and fear of deportation before that. But why no follow-up in the last four years?"

"That's a good point. What does Cassandra say about that?"

"I haven't pushed it yet. I don't want her to shut down, stop taking my phone calls. What would you do?"

"That's a strategy call," he said. "All I can say is follow your instincts. So far, they've served you very well in this case."

A little more guidance would have been nice, but she had to settle for a show of approval and support from her SAC. She thanked him and returned to her office.

No doubt about it, she was making a name for herself in Miami with the Wrong Number Kidnapper. Her supervisor was happy. She was getting positive feedback from the Critical Incident Response Group in Quantico. Even her in-office nemesis, Pete Crenshaw, had toned down the backbiting. She had thrown herself into this case and made it the center of her universe. The bureau respected that kind of dedication. Had anyone bothered to ask why she was so committed, however, Andie wasn't sure how she would have responded. Because she approached every case this way? Because she was new to Miami and had no life outside her work? Those were certainly plausible explanations. Too bad they weren't true.

Andie went to the window and looked out toward the parking lot. There was a field beyond, and a nine-foot-high chain-link fence defined the perimeter. Security concerns had given many a government building a prisonlike quality, though Andie knew exactly why that comparison crossed her mind. She'd been thinking about prison ever since Cassandra had asked about her sister. Andie hadn't revealed much about herself, but it was impossible to scratch the surface when it came to her Native American family. Going there, even for just a moment, was like opening the floodgates. Not that she'd lied to Cassandra. Andie had grown up in foster care till she was adopted at age nine, and it was also true that she'd known nothing about a sister until many years later. The demons lay in what she hadn't told, though the heart of the story was in plain view for the world to see. It was in Andie's eyes. Those exotic, beautiful, *green* eyes. Andie's mother was a Native American woman married to a Native American man. And then along came Andie—the baby with the telltale eyes of an Anglo. Andie and her twin sister never made it home from the hospital. Neither did their mother. Her husband shot her dead in the maternity ward. The killer went to jail. Andie and her sister went into foster care.

Andie continued to stare out her office window toward the chain-link fence. It wasn't helpful to think about the past, but she couldn't help herself. That was the problem with keeping secrets; you couldn't keep them from yourself. She hadn't planned on leaving Seattle. Somehow, deep inside, however, Andie knew that if she visited that man, she would end up running away from the city, the job, and the people she loved. She would have to find someplace new. She went to see him anyway. It was that important.

And it was worse than she'd expected. Far worse.

Washington State Penitentiary was no place for the superstitious. The address alone was a dark omen: 1313 North Thirteenth Street. The only way to feel worse was to arrive on Friday the thirteenth.

Andie arrived on a Saturday during regular visitation hours. This was personal, not FBI business, and she pulled no favors or special treatment through the warden or the bureau of prisons. In fact, she preferred not to call attention to herself. She'd jumped through the same hoops as anyone else who was not on an inmate's approved list of regular visitors. It had taken two weeks to obtain clearance, plenty of time for her to reconsider her decision. At several points along the five-hour drive from Seattle, she was again tempted to turn back. She stayed the course, however, determined to see this through.

The penitentiary was on 540 acres of farmland in southeast Washington, a veritable fortress in an otherwise scenic valley framed by the Blue Mountains. The town of Walla Walla (the name was from a Native American word meaning "many waters") could only be described as charming, having earned the Great American Main Street Award from the National Trust for Historic Preservation. Under different circumstances, Andie might have been tempted to visit one of forty nearby wineries, but on this trip her only destination was the state's largest correctional facility, which housed more than two thousand offenders. There were four separate facilities within the institution, each equipped to handle different levels of custody. Andie went to the Main Institution, a closed custody building that was second only to death row in terms of security.

"This way, please," said the corrections officer at the entrance to Building One.

Upon entering, Andie didn't flash her badge or do anything else to distinguish herself from the other visitors. She simply presented herself at the check-in station in accordance with the visitation policy. A female corrections officer conducted a quick inspection to make sure she met the dress code. No transparent or translucent clothing. No bare chest or midriff. Blue jeans were fine, so long as the waistline was not more than three inches below the navel. And, of course, undergarments were mandatory.

"You're clear," said the guard.

Most of the visitors broke off toward the activity center, where inmates in the general population were allowed face-to-face visitation. Andie, however, was routed in another direction.

"Inmate Wicasa has been reassigned to Segregation Unit One," said the guard. "Personal-contact visits have been denied."

Only after a moment did it register that Andie was there to see a man named Wicasa. "You mean I drove all the way from Seattle for nothing?" she said.

"He can still have visitors, just no personal contact. You'll be separated by a glass partition."

Andie tried not to show how little she cared. It wasn't as if she'd planned a big hug and kiss for the man who'd shot and killed her biological mother. "That's fine," she said.

The corrections officer led her down the hall to the visitation area. Another guard showed her to station number 3, which, as the numbering system implied, was the third of five stations on the visitors side of the glass partition. The other side was for prisoners, a narrow room about five feet deep and twenty feet long with a solid metal door in the rear. Down to Andie's right, at station 5, a woman was staring at an older inmate through the glass, neither of them saying a word, as if they'd run out of things to talk about after so many years on the opposite sides of prison walls. Andie looked away, not wanting to be caught staring at another's misfortune. She scooted her chair closer to the glass, closer to the phone box on the counter. She waited.

A buzzer sounded, which gave her a start. On the other side of the glass, the metal door slid open. A gray-haired man dressed in an orange prison jumpsuit entered the room. The door closed behind him. He walked slowly toward the glass and sat in the chair facing Andie. For a moment, they just studied one another from opposite sides of the glass. The name on his breast pocket—WICASA—was stenciled in black letters, and it was the only way for Andie to know that she'd found the right man. He was a total stranger, except for the way in which he had so profoundly impacted her life.

Three feet away, was all she could think. She was sitting three feet away from the man who had killed her mother.

He was by no means fat, but he was a large man, and Andie surmised that he'd spent countless hours in the prison gym as a younger inmate. The muscles had softened with age, but his expression had hardened into a perpetual scowl. His skin, though brown, had an unhealthy ashen quality that was the prison pallor. It was surprisingly smooth, however, with relatively few wrinkles for his age. A man sentenced to life without parole apparently didn't spend much time worrying about his release. What captivated her most, however, were his black, piercing eyes. They seemed to smolder with anger as he locked like radar onto Andie's pools of green. It was as if he were looking into someone else's eyes, dredging up the past. She could almost feel the hatred coming through the glass.

He pressed the phone to his ear. Andie picked up on her side. Again, there was silence, as if neither one knew where to start. Finally he said, "Those eyes don't lie."

Andie didn't disagree.

He breathed into the phone, something between a scoff and a grunt. "After all these years. You finally want to know about the man who was married to your mother?"

Truthfully, she couldn't have cared less about him, but she opted for a more conciliatory response. "I'm actually more interested in my biological father."

"What about him?" Even after all these years, there was bitterness in his voice.

"Whatever you can tell me."

"Why do you want to know?"

"I need to find him, but I don't even know his name."

"And you think I can help you?"

"I hope so. No one I've talked to knows anything about him. You're my last shot."

He smiled sardonically. "What are you looking for, a nice little Anglo family reunion? You think they want to make you a part of their family, the little multiethnic bastard that came along when Johnny Green Eyes knocked up some Indian bitch?"

Andie took a breath, refusing to let him get under her skin. "I want information, that's all. Do you know his name?"

"Of course I know his name. Your mother thought she was so clever, sneaking off the way she did. This went on for months. I knew what was going on, and I told her I wasn't gonna put up with it. For a while there, I believed her when she said it was over. Then you popped out, and . . ."

She looked away, as if to hide those green eyes. "And you lost control."

"I didn't lose nothin'. I gave her what she deserved."

Andie could have argued about the punishment fitting the crime, but she wasn't there to defend an adulteress. "So you can help me? You can tell me his name?"

"I could. But why should I?"

"Because it's not my fault that my mother cheated on you. This is important. I wouldn't come here if it weren't really important."

He fell silent again, but Andie could almost see the wheels turning in his head. "All right," he said. "I can give you his name."

"Thank you." Andie pulled a pen and a notepad from her purse. "What is it?"

"Not so fast." He leaned closer to the glass, as if sharing a secret. "First, I need to know what it's worth to you."

"You want me to pay you?"

"I have something you want. All I'm saying is that it's negotiable."

Andie wasn't surprised, but she wasn't pleased, either. "What do you have in mind?"

"Do you know how long I've been in here?"

"Yes." She'd done her homework. He'd committed his first felony, aggravated assault, long before Andie's birth. After shooting Andie's mother, he copped a plea and served twelve years for second-degree murder. He kept out of trouble—or at least he didn't get caught—for nearly a decade after his release. In 1994 he was convicted of armed robbery, his third violent felony, resulting in a life sentence under Washington's three-strike law.

"Twenty-one of the last thirty-three years," he said. "This is where I been."

It hardly seemed helpful to point out that it was his own damn fault. "That has to be tough," she said.

"Yeah," he said, chuckling with disgust, "it's tough all right. So here's what we're gonna do. You come back in two weeks. By that time, I should be out of segregation, and I'll have my full visitation rights."

"I can't wait two weeks."

"You're gonna have to. Because I can't get what I want so long as we're sitting on opposite sides of a glass wall."

Andie hesitated, then said, "I'm not smuggling anything in here, if that's what you're suggesting."

"You don't have to bring me nothing. Just show up."

Suddenly, the idea of smuggling contraband didn't sound so bad. "What are you asking me to do?"

A thin smile creased his lips. "I'm not asking for nothing that doesn't happen here every Saturday morning during general visitation hours."

"Forget it."

"You want to know your father's name or don't you?"

"Name another price."

"There is no other price."

"Then there's no deal."

He shrugged and said, "You'll come around. I can wait. I got nothing but time on my hands."

"I'm not coming back."

"Sure you will. If you're anything like your mother, you'll be back."

"You're disgusting."

"So shoot me. It's not like you and I are blood."

"I'm not doing you any sexual favors."

"Aw, come on, girl. Be reasonable. Look here. I won't even make you swallow."

She was about to hang up, but he caught her just in time. "George," he said.

Andie looked at him quizzically through the glass.

"Your father's first name is George," he said. "If you want to know the last name, be back in two weeks. Come back with a smile and I'll even wear a condom."

He seemed pleased with himself, but there was nothing Andie could do. He hung up the phone and signaled for the guard. The buzzer sounded. The door opened. Andie watched in silence as the key to her past disappeared behind prison walls.

54

·

The engine growled as Theo found fifth gear. Jack was calling out directions from the passenger seat, the floorboard vibrating beneath his feet. They were headed south on the turnpike, and the speedometer was bumping up against ninety. Jack's body jerked to the left, then right, as Theo threaded his way through multiple lanes of slower-moving traffic.

"Take the next exit," said Jack.

"This one?"

"No, next one."

"This one is the next one."

"No, the next one is the one after this one."

"Bullshit. The one after this one is the second one, and the next one comes right before that."

Jack shot him an incredulous look, though as usual he sensed that wisdom lay somewhere in the doublespeak. "Take exit eleven."

"Now you're talking, boss."

Theo downshifted and cut his cruising speed in half as the car curled around the off-ramp. They blew through the traffic light and headed west. The sun had just set, and a fading orange ribbon hovered over the horizon.

Jack checked his notes. "Stay on this road for eight miles."

"Eight miles? We'll be up to our eyeballs in alligators. Literally."

"That's what Mia said. Eight miles west off exit eleven."

"Let's see if we can make it in four minutes."

Jack assumed he was kidding, but there was no telling with Theo. Time, of course, was of the essence. The video file had come by e-mail, and Jack had braced himself for the worst upon opening it. Compared to the self-injury demonstration in the previous video, however, this one was tame. Mia was reading from a script. Her voice quaked in spots, but she seemed relatively composed as she delivered the message. It was basically a map—to *what* was the big question. Would it lead them to Mia? Or was it a trial run, another teaser that was a prelude to the big exchange?

Jack grabbed his cell phone and speed-dialed Agent Henning. The videotaped message had stressed that Jack was to come alone, no cops, but that wasn't part of Jack's plan.

"You on us?" Jack asked her.

"Yes, but tell Jeff Gordon to slow down. We're hanging back far enough to give the illusion of no law enforcement coverage, but I can't get the state troopers to stand aside if you're a danger on the highway."

Jack glanced at Theo and said, "Take it down a notch."

Theo dropped his speed to seventy-five mph, Sunday driving by Miami standards.

Henning said, "Are you wearing the Kevlar jacket we gave you?"

"Never leave home without it."

"Good. I know you may be tempted to pack a weapon, but just don't. A SWAT team is on the way. You won't even know they're there unless and until you need them. If you're armed, you might shoot one of them."

"Agreed."

"Remember, when he calls you, keep him talking as long as possible. Our techies are good, but tri-angulating cell phones takes time. Do you want to review the questions I gave you?"

Her handwritten script was in his breast pocket. It reminded him of his first trial, the way he'd stayed up the night before and written down every question he planned to ask his witnesses. It never worked that way. "I have your list. I'll do my best to buy your techies some time, but my goal is to make him commit to a simultaneous exchange. That's the plan."

She paused, as if the pit bull inside her wanted to keep arguing about their different strategies. "Are you carrying ransom money with you now?"

"No. My money doesn't come in until tomorrow morning. All I want now is for him to name his price for a simultaneous exchange. Then we take it from there."

Jack bristled at the thought of another lecture on his chosen strategy, but finally, he sensed a wave of reluctant acquiescence over the line.

"Good luck," she said. It came across as genuine, not sarcastic.

"Thanks," said Jack.

"Oh, one other thing. Just remember: If he wanted to kill you, Swyteck, he would have done it a long time ago. He doesn't need to drag you out into the middle of nowhere to take a shot at you. He's just making you jump through hoops. It's all about control."

"Funny. That's exactly what I intend to take from him."

"What?"

"Control."

Jack ended the call. The numbers on the odometer continued to roll quickly. They were well beyond the suburban sprawl, deep into Miami-Dade County's western farmlands. It wasn't as far as the Everglades, as Theo had predicted, but it was just as isolated. Tomato and pepper fields were to the south. To the north were hundreds of acres of alms and ornamental plants, all of which were rapidly disappearing in the encroaching darkness. The lighted sign at the entrance read WHITMORE NURSERY.

"Turn here," said Jack.

Theo steered onto the dusty road, and the popping sound of loose gravel replaced the steady whine of the paved highway. Jack again reviewed his notes, but this time he had to switch on the dome light to see. The instructions became more precise as they neared their destination.

"Two point two miles north," said Jack.

Theo didn't answer. He was shifting into his serious mode. "Hope they're out there."

"You mean the FBI?" said Jack.

"I don't mean palmetto bugs."

Theo stopped the car precisely at the 2.2 mile mark and killed the headlights. Jack stepped out and surveyed the vast fields of royal palms. They were mature trees, some forty feet tall, their fronds rustling in the breeze against a darkening blue backdrop. It was like standing at the entrance to a tropical forest, except that the trees were perfectly aligned in croplike rows. As the last remaining colors of sunset vanished, the stillness of night only heightened Jack's sense of foreboding. He pulled a flashlight from his pocket, though he hardly needed another look at his notes. He had committed Mia's directions to memory.

"You want me to go with you?" asked Theo.

Jack would have liked the backup, but the instructions were to come alone. "Wait here. Leave your cell phone on."

In a matter of minutes, the nursery had shed the comfortable glow of dusk and cloaked itself in inky black impenetrability. A distant part of Jack's brain was telling him to move, but his city-conditioned ears forced him to pause long enough to assimilate the symphony of strange new sounds. He heard birds returning to roost, swarms of insects buzzing, bullfrogs croaking in the distance, raccoons foraging for a meal. He could smell the ammonia from fertilizers and almost taste the windswept pollen. The warm, humid air wrapped him like a damp bedsheet. The Kevlar jacket made him even more uncomfortable. It was as if all of his senses were on heightened alert, including a sixth sense that told him his every move was being watched. He hoped it was the FBI.

He feared it was someone else.

Jack's gaze swept the field. Each row of palm trees was marked by a letter and number. He found the hand-painted sign for row R-17 and started toward it. His gait was short at first, then longer. It shortened again as he came to the end of the dirt road and reached the start of row R-17. The rows were planted ten feet apart, each towering tree trunk almost a foot in diameter. The canopy of fronds blocked out the moonlight, turning the space between each row into a dark tunnel. Jack stared down tunnel R-17, but the end was so far away that there was no sign of light. It was like the entrance to an underground labyrinth.

Go to the twelfth tree in row R-17. Those were Mia's instructions. In the darkness, Jack couldn't see beyond the fourth tree. He switched on his flashlight, which created an entirely different problem.

Why not just draw a big target on your back, Swyteck?

He cut off the flashlight and waited for his pupils to readjust to the darkness. It took only a few seconds. Before he could take a step, however, lingering doubts were again nibbling away at him. He didn't have to do this. Or did he? Agent Henning had given him an out when he'd called to tell her about the new video. She'd offered to send an undercover agent in his stead. Like the last time, however, they both knew that a substitute wasn't workable. That kind of game playing could easily get Mia killed.

Jack collected his thoughts, and Henning's words of encouragement replayed in his mind. *If he wanted to kill you, Swyteck, he would have done it by now.* That kind of logic had gotten many a hero killed, but it was the best Jack could do at the moment. He stepped into the grove, the earth soft beneath the soles of his shoes. He stopped and listened. Beyond the sounds of nature, he heard only his own breathing. Goose bumps tingled on the back of his neck, but it was a warm night, and he knew it was just nerves. This was risky, to be sure, but he'd taken bigger risks for reasons far less important.

A sudden swishing sound startled him. The next thing he knew, sheets of water pelted his face. It was as if someone had turned a water hose on him, but he quickly realized that it was the sprinklers. They were the high-powered commercial kind that could shoot water a hundred feet or more. Jack was getting hit from at least two different directions. The grove of palm trees was transformed into a rain forest, with the emphasis on rain. The water felt cool, like a refreshing spring shower, but it smelled of sulfur and fertilizer runoff, typical of shallow wells in the area. Jack stopped for only a moment, which was long enough for his clothing to be fully soaked. His Kevlar jacket had a built-in GPS tracking chip, but Jack wondered if the effectiveness of such gadgets was impaired by wet conditions. Then he wondered if the activation of the sprinklers had been purely a coincidence, or if it was by someone's design.

There wasn't time to worry about it.

He continued pushing forward, through the man-made equivalent of a driving rainstorm. He passed the third palm tree in row R-17, then the fourth, some forty feet deep into the dark grove. Each time he approached another tree, he slowed his pace, bracing himself for the possibility that someone was hiding behind the thick trunk or lurking in the darkness.

The water was coming down in buckets now, the sprinklers having reached peak performance. His pace quickened, as if the wet conditions had added another element of urgency. The deeper he went into the grove, the darker it got, and the falling water wasn't helping the visibility. His wet clothes were pasted to his body, and the ground beneath his feet was like a moist sponge. He passed tree number nine and then ten. Another twenty feet to go, but his visibility was down to about five. He stopped. His better judgment simply wouldn't allow him to stumble blindly into a potential trap. Perhaps a lighted flashlight *was* like strapping a big target onto his back, but he had to see where he was going. With a flick of the switch, a beam of yellow light stretched out before him, pointing the way.

He continued walking past the tenth tree. He stopped at the eleventh. The flashlight was just powerful enough to illuminate tree number twelve. He studied it from ten feet away, but saw nothing unusual about it from that distance. Cautiously, he stepped closer. Mia's video had told him simply to go to the twelfth tree, but it hadn't said what to look for once he got there. He inched closer, stopping only when he was close enough to touch the tree's smooth gray bark. He inspected it closely, searching for any message that may have been tacked to the trunk or perhaps carved into the bark. He saw nothing—until he looked several feet beyond the tree. Something was sticking straight up from the ground. It was straight and narrow, like a post, but it was skinnier. He wiped the water from his eyes and noticed the metal base.

It was a shovel.

Jack went to it immediately. The ground was saturated, but the earth around the shovel appeared loose, as if recently dug. Not for a moment did he think about buried treasure, but *something* was buried here. His heart pounded, and suddenly the only thought in his mind was that of Ashley Thornton trapped in a cave beneath the Santa Fe River—*alive*.

He laid the flashlight on the ground and started digging furiously, pitching shovelfuls of dirt to the side. It was easy work, and he was clearly unearthing the same hole someone else had dug not long before him. He kept digging until his shovel bumped up against a bag of some kind. The pointed tip of the spade didn't pierce the material, but he stopped nonetheless, fearing that it may have damaged the contents. He tossed the tool aside, dropped to his knees, and started clearing away the loose dirt with his hands. The bag was made of thick plastic, but it was still partially buried, which made it difficult to tell how large it was. He dug faster, and in just a few seconds he'd pushed aside enough dirt to find a handle. He grabbed it with both hands and pulled with all his might. On the third strong tug, the bag popped from the grip of the earth. He fell backward, and the bag came with him.

It was a large bag with a drawstring opening. It had no telltale shape, and Jack jostled it with his foot to see if he could get a clue as to its contents. It seemed to contain not one large object but several smaller ones—like pieces or parts. He didn't dare speculate on what kind of parts. He tore open the drawstring, aimed his flashlight inside, and froze.

"Theo!" he shouted—not with any clear thought in mind, just the growing sense that he was in need of help.

Suddenly an entire team of FBI SWAT was upon him, dressed in night-camouflage fatigues, automatic rifles at the ready. Theo came up quickly behind them, soaked from the sprinkler spray.

"Don't shoot him!" Jack shouted.

"What is it, man?" Theo asked, nearly breathless from the run.

The sprinkler water was still falling in sheets, and even with the flashlight, it was hard to tell exactly what was inside. Jack was too savvy to sift through it and destroy potential evidence. But right on top, in plain view, the skull was a dead giveaway.

The remains were indisputably human.

Theo approached, then stopped, as if sensing that the news wasn't good. Jack didn't say anything, didn't even look in his friend's direction. He closed the bag and let it fall to the ground, then pulled his cell phone from his pocket and speed-dialed Andie Henning.

55

·

Jack watched from the rubbernecker's side of yellow police tape. He couldn't see much, just the distant glow of portable vapor lights and the occasional sweep of flashlights from the darkest reaches of Whitmore Nursery. Rural crime scenes tended to be large, and the FBI had marked off R-17 and several adjacent rows of palm trees. Jack and Theo were relegated to the dusty access road nearly a quarter mile away from the remains Jack had uncovered.

For more than two hours, a steady stream of crime scene investigators disappeared into the grove. Agent Henning had urged Jack to go home, promising to notify him just as soon as the forensic team knew anything. Jack stayed put, but he fully intended to hold her to her promise. He and Theo seated themselves on the hood of Andie's car, feet on the front bumper, to make sure she didn't leave without speaking to them. Jack checked his watch every few minutes. Strangely, the night seemed to be getting warmer as time wore on—or perhaps the gathering beads of sweat on his forehead were simply a sign of frayed nerves. He knew that sooner or later, Andie would emerge with good news. Or bad.

"It can't be Mia," said Jack.

Theo listened in silence as Jack verbalized his thoughts for the tenth time in two hours.

"There was virtually no flesh or soft tissue of any kind left on those bones," said Jack. "And no odor. None. A body can't decompose that fast. It just can't be her." Jack breathed a heavy sigh, unable to accept his own analysis of the situation. "Then again, there was Jorge Cantera and his dead mother."

"Who?" said Theo.

"Cantera was another death row inmate I represented before I defended you. He stabbed his mother to death and dumped her body in the Everglades. I saw what the cops fished out two weeks later. Wasn't much left."

"This isn't the Everglades."

"It's still Florida. We live in our air-conditioned, pest-controlled world and forget what this land-filled swamp is really like. One of my father's favorite old stories on the campaign trail was something his grandmother shared with him. When she was growing up, they had to rest each leg of the kitchen table in an open can of kerosene to keep the bugs from crawling up and walking away with dinner."

"When I was growing up, bugs *was* my dinner," said Theo.

"My point is, with the insects down here, the dampness, the hot weather—it all hastens decomposition."

"You should just forget about that lunatic client of yours and his poor mama. Like I said, we ain't in the Everglades. Second of all, Mia hasn't even been gone two weeks, let alone dead that long. Take the worst-case scenario, all right? Let's say all those videotapes you been watching were filmed on day one, and let's also say Mia got killed right after making them. How long would she be dead?"

Jack had to think about that one. "Twelve days."

"See, what did I tell you? Not even two weeks."

Jack appreciated Theo's effort, but two days' difference was hardly cause for optimism.

Theo climbed down from the hood of Andie's car, walked down the dirt road to the police barricade, and then tried without success to bum a cigarette from the uniformed police officers guarding the entrance to the nursery. Jack watched his friend for a while, then lost interest. He turned his attention to the stars, to the heavens, to God out there, if He was listening. Jack started to say a prayer, then stopped. It seemed pointless to pray that it wasn't Mia in that canvas bag. Those were either her remains or they weren't; if they were, it was asking way too much to expect God to somehow transform them into someone else's at this stage. The most Jack could ask for was the strength to deal with the unthinkable. He wasn't ready to make that request. Not yet.

A beam of light shot like a lance from the grove. It bounced slightly from side to side, then up and down, like the leading end of a flashlight. Jack had a feeling about this one, and his instincts proved correct. Seconds later, Andie Henning and one of her investigators emerged from the dark, tunnel-like entrance to row R-17, flashlights in hand. Jack jumped down from the hood of Andie's car and hurried to the edge of the taped-off crime scene, where he signaled and caught her attention. Andie turned and said something to the investigator—Jack was too far away to hear—and the two of them started toward him. Jack struggled to see their faces, trying to get an advance read on the impending news. It was too dark to tell anything, so Jack blurted out his question as they approached.

"Is it her?"

Andie and the investigator ducked under the police tape and crossed over to Jack's side. Andie didn't answer right away, and Jack had the sickening sensation that she was about to feed him the same old party line: *Sorry, but I can't tell you, Jack.* It was possible that he'd misread her body language, or perhaps the raw emotion on his own face caused her to change her mind. Whatever the reason, she looked at him and said, "It's not her."

A wave of relief washed over him, but it was quickly followed by healthy skepticism. "How can you determine that so fast in the field?"

Andie gestured toward the man standing beside her. "This is Dr. Ruben Calhoun. He's a forensic anthropologist, and we're fortunate to have him here in Miami. He studied at the University of Tennessee Forensic Anthropology Facility in Knoxville."

Jack had never been there, but he'd heard about the picturesque tract of land near the UT Medical Center that was surrounded by razor

Got the Look   301

wire and dedicated to the study of postmortem decomposition. At any given time, about forty cadavers lay about the property under a variety of conditions: in sun or shade, clothed and unclothed, buried in shallow graves, stuffed into the trunks of cars, or submerged in water. It was the longest-running and most comprehensive undertaking of its kind in the world. "You mean the body farm?" asked Jack.

"We don't really call it that—kind of makes you think of cadavers lined up like peas or carrots—but yes, that's the place."

"So if it's not Mia, who did I dig up in row R-seventeen?"

Calhoun cleared his throat, as if ready to deliver an address. "First off, I can say with confidence that the remains you uncovered are human."

"No offense, Doctor, but anyone who can distinguish a human skull from a soccer ball could probably speak with equal confidence."

"Um, yes, that may be so."

Jack glanced toward the grove. "Pretty good place to dump a body, I suppose. These trees take a generation to mature. Nobody's going to dig around in there for a good twenty-five years. Plus you have years and years' worth of pesticides and fertilizers leaching into the soil and destroying physical evidence."

"Assuming the body has been there that long," said Calhoun.

"How old do you think these remains are?"

Calhoun started to say something, but Andie interjected. "We're not prepared to speculate on that matter just yet."

"They looked a hundred years old to me," said Jack.

"Looks can be deceiving," said Calhoun, "especially in this environment."

Andie interrupted, reiterating the point more forcefully. "Jack, we've gone around and around like this before. You're not part of the investigative team. There are things we can't share with outsiders."

Jack wondered what theory or information the FBI was hiding from him, but Agent Henning always seemed to have her reasons—or at least her orders from above. "Then let me ask a slightly different question," he said. "How long do you think those remains have been here?"

"I don't know yet," said Calhoun.

"Days? Weeks?"

"He said he didn't know," said Andie.

"The reason I ask is that the earth around the bag was loose, which suggests to me that this shallow grave was dug recently."

"Yes, it does appear that way," said Calhoun.

"How long would you say—hours, days, weeks?"

"I need to run a few tests. I've collected soil, vegetation, and insect samples that will help narrow that down."

Jack glanced at Andie. "What's the FBI's bet?"

Andie was silent, though Jack sensed that she wanted to tell him as much as she could without running afoul of strict orders from her superiors. He pushed a little. "So, the three known kidnap victims are from Georgia, central Florida, and now south Florida. And depending on what the tests show, we may have another victim from south Florida."

"Who said anything about another victim?" said Andie.

"Why else would he lead us to a shallow grave? It seems obvious that he's taunting us, showing us that he means business when he says he's going to kill Mia. Perhaps he wants us to know that Ashley Thornton isn't the only woman whose husband miscalculated her worth—with disastrous consequences."

"I can't even begin to comment on that," said Andie.

"I'll bet this body has been here for months, probably a kidnapping gone bad that was never reported to the authorities. Or one that was reported but that, for some reason, simply didn't show up in your VICAP search for kidnappings similar to the Thornton case."

"If the body was here for months, then why would the dirt be freshly dug?" said Andie.

Dr. Calhoun raised an index finger, as if to underscore his point. "There's a better reason why your theory doesn't wash, Mr. Swyteck. It's the very same reason that I'm able to look you in the eye and tell you with one hundred percent confidence that these remains do not belong to Mia Salazar."

"I'm all ears," said Jack.

The doctor glanced at Andie, as if seeking approval to share his findings with Jack. Andie considered it, then gave a nod. Calhoun said, "The bag you found contains a pubis bone."

"Meaning?"

Again, the doctor checked with Andie, but she did nothing to silence him. "A *man's* pubis bone," he said. "Not a woman's."

It took a moment for his words to register. Jack's gaze shifted toward the dark grove of palm trees in the distance, his voice trailing off, as if it didn't matter if anyone heard him. "Now there's a confusing turn of events, Doctor."

"Amen to that," said Andie.

56

•

The money hit on Saturday morning, right on schedule. Theo's deed and liquor license were the only collateral for the loan, so Bud the bondsman wired the funds from Atlanta to Theo's bank account in Miami. Just after ten o'clock, Theo arrived at Jack's house with the cash and the bad news.

"Now I know why they call him the ball buster," said Theo as he breezed into the kitchen and set the metal suitcase on the countertop. "He gave us only two hundred thousand."

Jack nearly choked on his coffee. "What?"

"He changed his mind about a quarter-million-dollar loan with only partial collateral from me and a personal guaranty from you. My bar is worth two hundred grand, so that's all he's willing to loan us."

"That wasn't our deal."

"No shit. His wiring instructions said to send the money back if we don't like the new terms."

"You should have sent it back."

"And then what? Give the kidnapper an IOU?"

Jack reached for the telephone, but Theo stopped him. "Don't bother. I already talked to him. He won't budge."

Jack settled back into his chair. Nearly ten hours had passed since he and Theo left Whitmore Nursery, and Jack had hardly slept. He'd been relieved to hear the ME say that the body in the bag couldn't possibly be Mia's, but speculation over whose it might be kept his brain in high gear. He was wide awake and waiting on the pivotal phone call from Andie Henning—the definitive ID of the victim—which he needed in order to plan his next move. At this point, a curveball from Ball-Bustin' Bud was the last thing he needed. "Now what are we supposed to do?"

"How much more cash can you scrape together?"

"I liquidated whatever I could yesterday, about seventy-five thousand. But twenty-five of that was wired to Bud for his fee."

"So that leaves fifty. That's cool. We got a quarter million altogether."

Jack shook his head. "I have to put enough cash on the table to make him want to take the risk of a simultaneous exchange. I don't think we're there."

"We have to be more creative."

"How? Find someone who prints money?"

Theo said nothing. He simply arched an eyebrow.

Jack shot him a look of reproval. "I was kidding."

Theo remained silent, but the expression on his face spoke volumes.

"No. No way. Uh-uh." Jack was shaking his head and waving his hands as he spoke, lest Theo think it was actually open for discussion.

"Why not? I know this Romanian guy up in Fort Liquordale who—"

"Stop right there," said Jack. "Do you remember what happened the last time I heard you start a sentence with 'I know this guy who . . .'?"

"Not really."

"All I wanted was a quick flight out of the Ivory Coast. You hooked up with a guy who just barely made that stolen prop plane fly faster than the bullets that were chasing us."

"The plane wasn't stolen. He was repossessing it."

"A finer distinction that was apparently lost on the guards with the AK-forty-sevens."

"If you want to argue with results, then why don't *you* find someone who can fork over seven figures before lunchtime?"

He had a point, but Jack was still skeptical. "All right. Just for the sake of amusement, how does it work?"

"We take the two hundred thousand from Bud. That should buy us two million in convincing counterfeits."

"And about ten years in a federal penitentiary."

"What's your alternative? We got a quarter million in our hands. Even a million wasn't enough for Ashley Thornton. Two million would tempt anyone enough to make a simultaneous exchange. And then you let the FBI snipers take him out."

Jack looked out the kitchen window, thinking. "This is crazy. I'm a lawyer. I can't buy counterfeit bills."

"You got a better idea?"

Jack walked to the kitchen counter and popped open the metal suitcase. Bundles of crisp hundred-dollar bills lay side by side. He reached out with both hands and touched the money lightly, fingers dancing like a concert pianist's.

The telephone rang in the kitchen. Jack muted the morning news with the TV remote, then checked the caller ID display on the portable phone. It was another out-of-area call, and by this stage of the game, Jack knew what that meant. He hit the Speaker button so that Theo could hear the conversation, but he answered through the handheld receiver so that the caller couldn't tell that he was on speaker.

"So much for our little secret, Swyteck." The voice was disguised, like before, but this time the anger was more evident. "We had a deal to keep the cops out of this. Ten minutes after you dug up the bag of bones, the nursery was crawling with FBI agents."

"What do you expect me to do when a body turns up? I was afraid it was Mia's."

"Mia's?" he said with a condescending chuckle. "Apparently you aren't as smart as I thought you were."

"Whose is it?"

"Why don't you let the FBI tell you? Now that they're in on our little secret."

Jack couldn't explain away the FBI. He simply had to shift the focus to Mia, no matter how abrupt the transition. "I have your money. I want a simultaneous exchange."

"Dream on."

"That's the way it has to be. No cops. Just you and me."

"How much are you paying?"

Jack hesitated, but somehow he couldn't say a quarter million with a straight face. "Two million."

There was silence on the line. Finally, he said, "You got my interest."

"No Mia, no money. Simple as that. It's simultaneous, or it doesn't happen."

"I pick the spot, I pick the time."

"Fine. Where do you want to do it?"

"You already know: the Devil's Ear."

The very words made Jack's heart sink.

"Go to wilderness campsite number twenty-seven at two a.m.," he said. "And this time, leave the FBI at home."

"You got it."

"I mean it, Swyteck. This is the real deal. No cops. Or your girl-friend ends up exactly like Ashley Thornton. And then I'll find you."

There was something different about his tone—a chilling finality. The response caught in Jack's throat, and the call ended before he could say another word.

"You okay?" asked Theo. He walked to the refrigerator and opened it, as if watching Jack negotiate with a kidnapper had worked up an appetite.

"I think so."

"You done good, Jack." Theo found a leftover slice of pepperoni pizza behind the jar of mayonnaise, sniffed it, then put it back. "Real good."

Jack took one last look at the suitcase filled with hundred-dollar bills. He knew it wasn't enough—that it wasn't anywhere near what Mia was worth. But what on earth had possessed him to offer two million dollars? "Am I crazy? Or is this the right thing to do?"

Theo dunked a pickle spear into a jar of mustard. "Close your eyes."

"What?"

"Just close them."

Jack complied. Theo said, "Now open them."

It seemed like a silly game, but Jack did it.

"What do you see?" asked Theo.

"You."

"Exactly." He popped the mustard-coated pickle into his mouth, yellow goop all over his lips. "Now, is this what you want to be lookin' at the rest of your life? Or do you want to see Mia again?"

It struck Jack as funny at first, but Theo wasn't laughing. The big guy put down the pickle jar and looked Jack in the eye. "Do you remember how happy you were the day you introduced me to Mia? Do you?"

"Yeah," he said quietly. "I do."

"How many fuckheads are lucky enough to find someone who makes them that happy? Seriously, dude. Do you think *I'm* ever gonna find a woman like that?"

Theo's delivery was never the smoothest, but whenever their backs were up against the wall, it seemed that Jack couldn't argue with a word he was saying.

Jack closed up the suitcase full of cash. "Okay. Let's do what we have to do."

57

Andie Henning was in a holding pattern. The medical examiner's office was making no promises. They might identify the remains in the plastic bag by lunchtime, or they might never make an identification. The final answer depended on test results and, like any successful investigation, a healthy mix of good judgment and good luck.

Having been up all night, Andie wanted nothing more than to shower and catch a quick nap. First, however, she had to find her way out of the busy medical campus. The ME's office was in the Joseph H. Davis Center for Forensic Pathology, a three-building complex on the perimeter of the University of Miami Medical Center campus and Jackson Memorial Hospital. It had been dark and relatively quiet when Andie arrived, but at 10 a.m. the campus was bustling with activity, people headed to the spine institute, the eye institute, and other world-class specialists.

Andie stopped at the traffic light near the Sylvester Comprehensive Cancer Center. A patient in a wheelchair crossed with the green WALK signal, a bit of sad irony. At first, Andie surmised that the handsome young man pushing the chair was the woman's son or grandson. As they passed before Andie's vehicle, however, it became apparent that she was actually quite young, disease having robbed her of her youth. Andie tried not to stare, but she was unable to look away. She wondered if the woman had just received good news or bad, if she was still hoping for recovery or clinging to what little life she had left. Andie herself knew those feelings all too well. Fear and hopelessness had driven her to utter desperation—and, ultimately, to the state penitentiary in Walla Walla, Washington, where she visited the man who had murdered her mother. It wasn't something she'd wanted to do. It wasn't mere idle curiosity about her genealogical roots. That pathetic excuse for a human being was the only living person who could tell her who her biological father was. In her entire life, Andie had never even considered searching him out. Suddenly, however, finding him became a matter of life and death, as the oncologist had made so clear on that cloudy gray morning in Seattle.

"How bad is it?" Andie asked. She'd been waiting for hours to speak with her sister's treating physician at the University of Washington Medical Center, and she ambushed him as soon as he stepped out of the elevator.

"It's an uphill battle," he said.

"What does that mean exactly?"

His deep sigh almost made an answer unnecessary. "Your sister is a fighter, but we can't give her the level of chemotherapy she needs without a successful bone marrow transplant."

Andie tried to keep her composure, but after all the sleepless nights and unanswered prayers, fear and frustration were taking control. "I don't understand. We're twins. Why didn't her body accept my bone marrow?"

"Because you're not *identical* twins. That puts you in the same category as any other sibling, which means that this was an allogeneic transplant, not syngeneic. The chances of an HLA match between siblings is only about thirty to forty percent."

"Okay, so I'm not a match. What about unrelated donors? Can we try that route?"

"I'm afraid the chances of a match would be small. Siblings or parents are our best alternative. Do you have any other brothers or sisters?"

"No. I mean, like I told you before, none that I know of. Both my sister and I were raised by adoptive families. And our biological mother is dead."

"What about your father?"

Andie looked away, embarrassed. She'd anticipated the question, but that didn't make it any easier. "I don't know. I would have to find him."

"How long would that take?"

"How much time do I have?"

Again, the heavy sigh. "Leukemia is curable, but like any cancer, the sooner the better. I wouldn't want to wait more than eight weeks to resume treatment. Ten weeks, tops. And remember, even after a successful transplant, the engraftment process takes anywhere from ten to twenty-eight days. So you have just a few weeks to find him and get him in here for the harvest."

Andie had no reason for optimism, and it made her skin crawl just to think about the perverse terms Mr. Wicasa had spelled out for information about her biological father. But with her sister's life hanging in the balance, only one response came to mind. "Don't worry. I'll find him. Whatever it takes, I'll find him."

A symphony of car horns blasted impatiently from behind her. Andie looked up to see that the traffic light outside the University of Miami cancer center had turned green. Her cell phone rang at the same instant. She shook off her memories of Seattle, drove through the intersection, and answered the phone. "Henning here."

It was Agent Crenshaw. "I can't locate him."

"What do you mean?"

"He's not answering any of his phones. I drove to his house, he doesn't answer the intercom. I checked two of his job sites. Nothing."

"Was his car in the driveway?"

"No, but he has a five-car garage, and I couldn't get close enough to see inside."

"So he could just be avoiding us."

"Yeah," said Crenshaw. "Or my instincts could be right: That *was* Ernesto Salazar in the bag Swyteck dug up."

$\cdot$

Mia woke from a deep sleep, deeper than any before in her captivity. She felt languid and confused, like a patient shaking off the effects of general anesthesia. The throbbing pain on the side of her left thigh was a poignant reminder of what had happened. The needle went in, and she blacked out. It had been that quick.

She had no memory of moving from one location to another, but her surroundings were surely different. This new room was even smaller than the last one, perhaps eight by ten. It was dimly lit by a single low-wattage ceiling fixture. The floor was bare concrete. There were no windows and no air-conditioning, and the smell of mildew lingered in the air. The room temperature was in the high eighties, she figured, perhaps ninety. Her skin glistened with a thin layer of sweat. Just sitting on the floor, no physical exertion whatever, she could feel her clothing cling to her body. She probably would have slept even longer but for the smothering effects of the hot, heavy air.

She quieted her breathing and listened. Nothing. Her new prison was as silent as the old one. She tried to change position, but it was difficult. Her wrists were cuffed in front of her body so that she could feed herself. Her ankles were chained to an exposed wall stud. He had actually cut a hole in the Sheetrock and drilled a hole through the wooden stud so that he could fasten her securely. She wasn't going anywhere unless she planned to take the entire building with her. She slid closer to the wall and inspected the opening. It was just large enough to snake the chain through one end and out the other. Not exactly a yawning invitation to the great escape—unless you were a millipede. She noticed one inching across the concrete floor. It was black and wiggly, no longer than her little finger. She spotted another one on the floor, then another on the wall, then a half dozen more climbing toward the ceiling. They had come through the hole in the drywall, which gave her pause. Millipedes had once infested her flower garden in Palm Beach, and the pest control company told her it was because of all the decaying wet leaves in the neighbor's yard. A few had crawled inside her house, but as a rule they didn't go far from their food source. It was a little thing, but at this stage of the game, even tidbits of information seemed important. If the millipedes were on this side of the wall, food was on the other side. That meant leaves or vegetation of some kind. The outdoors. Freedom.

She gave the chain a tug, and the metal cuff pinched her ankle, no give whatsoever. The millipedes were showing her the way, but it was no more useful than birds showing her how to fly. Irrational as it was, she pulled even harder, as if determined to yank the chain from the stud or even the stud from the frame. The four-foot length of chain stretched like a steel rod, taut and tense with her considerable leg strength. The force only savaged the point of least resistance, the tender skin around her anklebone. She stopped pulling. The chain went limp and rattled onto the floor. The edge of the metal ankle cuff was sharper than it appeared. There was a small cut above her anklebone, and it was beginning to bleed. She reached to blot it dry, then stopped short. She withdrew her hand and sat perfectly still, watching the slow trickle of blood from the fresh wound. Just the sight of it triggered memories of her own blood oozing down her thigh in long, narrow stripes, like veins without casings. A plastic surgeon could have fixed that old scar years ago, much the same way she had changed her nose and chin to disguise her true identity. She'd left the scar alone, however. Part of her wanted never to forget why she was running.

And why she had to keep running.

There were footsteps outside the door. Instinctively, she sat up straight and assumed a state of readiness, though she never knew what to expect. She heard a key enter the lock, the tumblers turning. Her gaze was fixed on the doorknob. It squeaked as it turned, and the door opened. The sudden burst of brightness told her that it was daytime, but it lasted only an instant. He entered quickly and closed the door, dropping a bulky duffel bag on the floor. He was dressed in black, his body a shadow in the dim lighting. Mia didn't look at his face. She was focused more on the duffel bag at his feet. She feared another film in the making, but he would never have dropped sensitive camera equipment on the concrete floor so carelessly.

"How do you feel?" he asked.

Mia wasn't sure how to respond. He'd never asked before. "Okay, I guess."

"Good." He got down on one knee, unzipped the bag, and rummaged through it. He removed something and came toward her, stopping just a foot away. "Kneel for me."

It was the position she hated most, him towering over her while she knelt before him. She hesitated, but only for a second, fearing his reprimand.

"Look up at me," he said.

Her head rolled back slowly. She was gazing upward, focusing on nothing, really—just this dark torso somewhere above his belt buckle. Sometimes, bad lighting was a blessing. She tried not to cringe as he brushed her hair aside, clearing her face.

"Try this on," he said.

A ring of cold latex suddenly surrounded her face, and instinctively she withdrew.

"Hold still!" he shouted.

She stiffened, and he pressed harder. It was a mask, she realized. A diving mask.

"Close your mouth, breathe in through your nose," he said.

Her compliance brought suction around her face, the mask clinging to her skin. It popped when he pulled it off, breaking the watertight seal.

"Excellent." He turned and walked back to the duffel bag, then dropped the mask inside. "You ever dived before?"

"You mean scuba dive?"

"Yeah. You ever done it?"

Again, she wasn't sure how to answer. "Once. In Cozumel."

"Cozumel, huh? Good cave diving there."

"We didn't do caves."

He snorted, or perhaps it was a chuckle. "First time for everything, honey."

Mia said nothing, though she understood completely. By *first* he meant *last*.

The door opened and closed quickly. He was gone, but he'd left the duffel bag behind. He would return soon, she was sure of it. And they weren't just going for a swim.

Mia could feel her spirits sagging, but then she remembered a little surprise of her own. Whatever drug he'd used to knock her out had almost washed her memory clean, but clearer thoughts brought renewed hopes. She raised her pant leg just above the ankle and checked to make sure her ace was still there. She wasn't disappointed. Tucked inside the hem was a long shard of glass from the broken lightbulb. She was careful not to break it—and not to cut herself. It wasn't the biggest piece, but it was big enough, maybe two inches long. She'd managed to squirrel it away after the last videotaping, when he'd ordered her to clean up her wounds. She felt good about herself now, the way she'd managed to get her hands on a weapon of sorts. It was crude but effective, and she wasn't afraid to use it.

The only question was when.

59

Jack had been to quieter places, but they were usually dotted with gravestones. At two o'clock in the morning, the Ginnie Springs campground was two hundred wooded acres of black silence. Visitors were allowed entry twenty-four hours a day, so Jack and Theo had no trouble getting in. Finding their way around in the dark was another matter.

"Says here that Hernando de Soto explored these parts in 1539." Theo was seated in the passenger seat, flashlight aimed at his souvenir map. "You think he stopped at the Hardee's on his way through High Springs?"

"Could you cut the jokes and just navigate, please?"

"Just trying to loosen you up, dude. That's all."

Jack checked his grip on the steering wheel. Any tighter and he would have snapped it in half. He was wound too tightly, but there was a fine line between relaxing and letting your guard down. "Sorry, man. The psychos I'm used to dealing with are judges, not kidnappers."

The first turn after the entrance gate took them past the combination dive center–country store, which was closed. Directly across the road, clearly marked on the map, were fifty-three campsites with electrical hookups. About half of them were occupied, roughly an equal number of tents, RVs, and trailers. The lone sign of life was a drunk old man peeing behind his pickup truck. Jack's headlights hit him squarely in the privates, lighting him up like a casting call for *The Full Monty*. Busted at 2 a.m. He had to feel like the unluckiest guy on earth—though, considering what lay ahead, Jack would have gladly traded places with him.

"You want campsite number twenty-seven, right?" said Theo.

"Yeah, but it's definitely not one of these."

"How do you know?"

"Because he said *wilderness* campsite twenty-seven. You don't get electrical hookups with a wilderness campsite."

Theo layered on the street talk and said, "I'd like to argue with you, but there be certain things they jis don't teach us boys in duh hood."

It didn't seem possible, but the winding road got even darker and quieter as they continued away from the dive center and main campground. Jack spotted a small wooden sign just beyond the point where the pavement gave way to gravel. He stopped the car and flipped on the high beams. WILDERNESS CAMPSITES 12 TO 31, it read. An arrow pointed to a footpath just off the road.

"Looks like you hoof it from here, boss," said Theo.

Jack checked his watch. Twenty minutes before his two o'clock deadline. Jack got out of the car and went to the trunk. Everything was bathed in the orange-red glow of the taillights, though he saw more red than orange, which reminded him of blood. He wasn't sure if it symbolized his blood or Mia's, but it didn't matter. He had to shake off such morbid thoughts or he'd never get through the night. He inserted the key into the trunk and popped the lid. For a moment, he didn't move, his gaze fixed on the precious cargo.

A footstep startled him, but it was Theo. "You sure you don't want me to go with you?"

"Just give me a hand here and stay with the car."

The Kevlar jacket from the FBI was in the trunk. It seemed to have replaced the blue blazer as the staple in Jack's wardrobe. Theo helped him on with it and adjusted the straps, making it good and snug. At two o'clock in the afternoon, the heat would have been unbearable, but at 2 a.m. it was passable. Jack reached for the backpack, but Theo stopped him.

"One other thing," he said as he pressed a 9 mm Glock pistol into Jack's hand.

"Henning said no weapons."

"Henning isn't toting a suitcase full of cash."

Jack had used one before, but there was still something about holding a gun that gave him a rush. He unzipped the backpack and dropped the gun inside, among the bundles of hundred-dollar bills. "All I need now is the musical theme from *The Godfather*."

Theo started humming.

"That's *Love Story*, you moron."

"Sorry. At least I was in the right decade."

Jack slammed the trunk lid closed. Theo was trying to play it cool, but Jack could see the concern in his eyes. "It's gonna be fine," said Jack.

"*It* ain't what I'm worried about. Just let me follow behind you, like twenty yards or so, in case something goes wrong."

Jack shook his head. "If he spots you, he'll think you're FBI. And that's bad news for Mia."

"You could say the same thing about the FBI."

"At some point we have to trust Henning when she says the FBI can cover me without being detected. Besides, if they see you stalking me, they might unload on you."

"So, you just want me to sit here?"

"Keep your cell phone on. If I get a bad feeling about this, I have you on speed dial."

"At what point should I just come lookin' for you?"

"You hear something that sounds like a badger with its tongue caught in a bear trap, I'd say that's a good time to come running."

They exchanged little smiles. Then Theo wished him luck, and Jack headed into the forest. The footpath was narrow, and without a flashlight he would have been lost immediately. Splashes of moonlight broke through the occasional opening in the leafy canopy, lighting up the Spanish moss that clung to the tree limbs like tattered old fishing nets. The ground was soggy in spots, and if Jack listened carefully, he could hear the gentle sounds of moving water not too far off, the Santa

Fe River. Wildlife chimed in, the croak of bullfrogs, the screech of a bird in the darkness, perhaps a heron or an osprey. After several minutes of hiking through the brush, over fallen logs, and around ant mounds, Jack came to a clearing and read the sign. Wilderness campsites were filled on a first-come, first-served basis, no reservations. Nice and convenient for last-minute planners and kidnappers alike. Jack continued down that path, passing several tents in the darkness. Maybe it was because he was literally on a rescue mission, but these little pockets of shelter seemed unusually flimsy and vulnerable. They were just nylon on sticks, modest protection from wind and rain but not much else. Anywhere along this isolated trail, it seemed so easy for a man with a knife and no conscience to get away with murder.

Finally, just before the footpath began a long curve around a cluster of cypress trees, Jack's journey came to an end. The beam of his flashlight bathed the marker to campsite 27.

Jack was supposed to be there at 2 a.m., and he was right on time. He had no instructions on what to do upon arrival, but he was practicing his lines in his head. *Simultaneous exchange. Nonnegotiable.*

His flashlight swept the site, coming to rest on his first surprise. A red nylon tent was perched on the highest ground, which in Florida meant an elevation of perhaps six inches. Somehow, Jack had built up an expectation of a vacant site. He wondered if some camper had simply decided to pitch his tent there, unwittingly jeopardizing Mia's release. Or had the kidnapper himself pitched the tent there to stake his claim to the site? Perhaps the tent itself would play some part in the plan.

He switched off his flashlight, allowing his pupils to adust to the moonlit sky. The minutes slowly ticked away, and as his night vision improved, his speculation kicked in. Was it possible that the kidnapper himself was inside the tent? *No way, couldn't be.* But the tent had to be there for a reason. Jack checked his cell phone. He had service, so if the kidnapper wanted to reach him, the call would come through. Jack tried to recount their last phone conversation word for word. *Be there at two a.m.* was what he remembered. And of course, there was the warning not to bring in the FBI, which Jack had ignored. He looked around, and if the FBI was out there, they were certainly doing a bang-up job of making it look as if they weren't. Maybe they were in some of the tents he'd passed along the way.

Jack took two steps toward the red tent and stopped. He picked up a stone, tossed it toward the tent, and waited to see if anything stirred inside. Nothing. He pitched a handful of pebbles, enough noise to waken even the soundest sleeper, but there was no response. Either no one was inside, or someone was in there lying in wait. Unless, of course, the someone was Mia. She could have been tied up, unable to respond. Or dead. The scene at the Whitmore Nursery flashed through Jack's mind—the dirt flying, his heart racing as he unearthed the bag of human remains. He wondered if that had been a prelude to this evening, a sick trial run before Jack raced inside the tent and unzipped the sleeping bag only to find . . .

He stopped, refusing to let that image form. On impulse, he hurried across the campsite and went straight to the tent entrance. He unzipped the flap and switched on the flashlight. The tent was empty, except for a note on the ground, instructions of some sort.

He crawled inside, grabbed it, and started reading. Before he got through the first sentence, his cell phone vibrated in his pocket. It startled him, but it was also a relief. Another note or videotape from the kidnapper offered no opportunity to negotiate. Jack needed to talk to him. He reached for his vibrating phone and did a gut check, preparing himself for the negotiation of a lifetime. He was about to answer, then stopped.

It was a text message, but it wasn't from the kidnapper.

MONTALVO IS DEAD, it read.

The words hit like ice water. He hit Talk and returned Andie Henning's call by speed dial.

60

·

At 2:45 a.m. Jack was deep into the forest, following the footpath through the dense undergrowth. He couldn't see the river, but he could smell the swamp in the air, the sulfurlike odor of standing water and rotting flora just off the banks. Jack carried a flashlight in his right hand, the kidnapper's note in his left. In the dead of night, it would be easy to get lost in these woods, which explained why the kidnapper had gone to the trouble of drawing a map and leaving it inside the tent. The directions were quite clear—unlike everything else at the moment.

Jack's conversation with Andie had been nothing short of head-splitting. Montalvo was dead, they were sure of it. He'd been dead for years, not weeks or months, a bullet hole just above the left eye orbit. Confusing, yes. But Jack barely had time to think before the cell phone was vibrating again. It was an out-of-area call. He knew it wasn't Andie; they'd agreed not to talk again until after he made the drop. That left only one alternative. He flipped open the phone, the words coming like a reflex.

"Did you kill Montalvo?"

There was a pause on the other end of the line, but the gravelly tone told Jack that he'd guessed right as to the caller's identity. "That's the first intelligent question you've asked in a long time, Swyteck. I guess you finally figured out whose body that was at the Whitmore Nursery. Or do your friends at the FBI deserve all the credit?"

"All I want to know is who killed him."

"Curiosity can be a very dangerous thing."

"Was it you?"

"No. Wasn't me."

"Then how did you know where his body was buried?"

The silence on the other end of the line seemed insufferable. "Because your girlfriend told me," he said, his voice taking on a decided edge. "I finally forced it out of her. Would you like to know how?"

"I don't believe you."

"Why else would you have found the ground freshly dug if the bones were seven years old? I had to dig it up, see for myself that Mia was telling the truth before I sent you there."

Jack stopped at a fork in the footpath. He was about to speak, but the caller beat him to it. "Did you bring me what she's worth?"

"I have your money, don't worry. Where's Mia?"

"Where's the FBI hiding this time?"

Jack mustered up his poker voice. "They're not here. It's just you and me, like you said. Now where's Mia?"

"We'll get to that."

"No. I told you before, it's a simultaneous exchange or nothing. It's nonnegotiable."

"I'll decide what's nonnegotiable, you fuck. Here's the deal. And listen up, because I'm not gonna say this twice."

61

The divers were lying low, but they were itching to go.

FBI Agent Peter Crenshaw didn't feel like second in command. There was no denying that Andie Henning was in charge of the Wrong Number Kidnapper task force, but Crenshaw still had twenty more years of experience. A decorated Vietnam veteran and former Navy SEAL, he knew more about scuba diving than anyone else on the team, including the two local search-and-rescue guys who claimed to be cave-diving experts. Granted, he'd never dived the Devil's Ear, and he wasn't so brazen as to say that "diving was diving." He knew that caving was different, but he'd done plenty of wrecks with narrow openings and tight spaces, some more than two hundred feet deep, where noon resembled midnight. He'd scoured rivers with churning water so murky that the only option was to feel your way through it. So when Henning gave the standing order that no one was to enter the Devil's Ear without her say-so, he wasn't going to look for reasons to disobey her. But if one came his way, he was determined to use his own better judgment.

"There's a light in the Ear," said one of the search-and-rescue divers. His name was Danfield, a lean triathlete with a military-style buzz cut and biceps that showed through his wet suit. Crenshaw had asked him to do a little scouting. He returned in just a few minutes, wet with river water, and he lay flat on his belly beside Crenshaw and the other S&R

diver. Dressed in black wet suits and hidden amid the bushes, they were invisible in the night, speaking barely above a whisper.

"Are you sure?" asked Crenshaw.

"I know what I saw," said Danfield. "There's a light in there, deep. Somebody's diving."

"Couldn't it just be some recreational divers?"

"You don't lose track of time when you're cave diving. It's after three a.m. Park closes at midnight. You get caught down there after-hours, you lose your cave-diving privileges. That's a death sentence to a caveman."

Crenshaw reached for the encrypted telephone in his bag, but Danfield grabbed his arm and stopped him. "Don't."

Crenshaw said, "Henning gave an order not to dive till she said so."

"She gave the same order last time. Mrs. Thornton ended up dead."

Crenshaw considered it, his gaze drifting toward the flat black water that marked the opening to the cave system. In the soft moonlight, the surface rippled with little rings from the strong undercurrents.

"Well?" said Danfield.

"I'm thinking about it," said Crenshaw.

"Don't think too long. I was on the team that pulled Mrs. Thornton's body out of the Ear. That's a performance I don't care to repeat. Every minute up here is a waste of precious time. If our kidnapper is dragging another victim down there to her death, do you want to be the one to tell the family why we sat on our asses and waited?"

Again, Crenshaw's gaze carried toward the spring entrance. Perhaps it was a just a fleck of undulating moonlight on the surface, but for an instant he could have sworn that he did see a sweeping flash of light beneath the surface—a diver in the Devil's Ear.

He grasped the telephone.

"You're actually going to call her?" said Danfield, groaning.

Crenshaw shot him a steely look. "Command center needs to know our position at all times, but that doesn't mean I'm requesting permission. We're going in, boys. Whether Henning likes it or not."

62

.

A fine mist began to fall. It gathered on the canopy above, hissing
like static in Jack's ears. After several minutes, enough moisture
had collected on the higher leaves to create little droplets that fell to
the palmetto scrub and wild grape vines below. Soon, the entire forest
glistened in the sweep of Jack's flashlight.

Montalvo is dead. Three little words that Jack couldn't shake from his
head. All this time, he'd operated on the assumption that he was dealing
with Montalvo. It turned out that he knew nothing about the man on
the other end of the phone line. Well, almost nothing. According to the
kidnapper, it was Mia who had told him where to find Montalvo's body.
It was Mia who had killed Montalvo. Jack wasn't ready to accept either
of those assertions as true, at least not without some convincing corrob-
oration. But one thing was certain. Whoever he was, the kidnapper believed that Mia was somehow connected to Montalvo's death, or at least
to the disposal of his body. Working against that mind-set, Jack had to
wonder: Was there really any chance that he would release Mia alive?

The mist stopped, but it had cooled the night air, causing an eerie
fog to rise from the surrounding swampland. Jack checked his map
one more time, taking care not to smear the ink with his wet hands. The
directions took him another hundred yards north around a cluster of
wild magnolias. He stopped quickly. One more step would have landed
him in the pond. At least it looked like a pond. On closer inspection,

however, he could see the water rising to the surface. It was a spring—a small opening to the vast underworld of Florida's aquifer.

Following the kidnapper's instructions, Jack went to the bushes and found the metal capsule. It was about two feet long and shaped like a torpedo. He opened it. As expected, it was empty. He removed his backpack and unzipped it. The cash was in neat bundles.

It was decision time.

Jack didn't have anywhere near the two million dollars he'd promised the kidnapper. Yesterday morning, rather than fill the bag with counterfeit bills, Jack had made the executive decision to bluff his way through the negotiations with a quarter million dollars. Now that it was time to pay, however, Jack couldn't bring himself to put his friend's money at risk. He stuffed his share of it, fifty grand, into the watertight capsule. Theo's money went back in his backpack. Then he jotted down a note on a piece of paper.

> Here's $50,000 more than your mere promise to release Mia is worth. You get the rest—you get what she's worth—when I get Mia. Simultaneous exchange. Nonnegotiable. Call me.

He read it twice, making sure it said everything that needed to be said. Satisfied, he tucked the note in with the stack of bills, sealed the capsule shut, and carried it to the water's edge. Fastened to a log was a thick nylon rope. It had a loop at the end, and an indeterminable length of rope descended into the water, disappearing somewhere inside the cave below. Jack tied the capsule to the end of the rope, then lifted the capsule with both hands. He knew what he was supposed to do, but it gave him pause.

Fifty thousand dollars. It didn't sound like much in this world of nine-figure Lotto, until it was your money, and it was literally going down into a hole in the ground. The kidnapper was at the other end of this line, he knew, somewhere deep in the bowels of the underwater cave system—a system that honeycombed beneath the surface for hundreds of miles, through millions of tons of sand and solid limestone.

Much of it was unmapped—a tactical advantage that the kidnapper was poised to exploit, Jack was sure of it. Eventually, he would emerge somewhere in the swamp, perhaps popping up through a recently formed sinkhole that no one else knew about. Until then, he would wind his way through tunnels and caves, perhaps a hundred or more feet underground. It might seem like an awful lot of trouble, but he had surely anticipated that Jack would plant a GPS tracking system inside the capsule along with the money. So long as he was underground, the GPS chip was worthless. The guy was no dummy, that was for sure. But he had to come up somewhere, at which time the GPS chip would reactivate. Then the FBI would know exactly where he was.

That was the plan, at least.

He pitched the capsule into the pool. It landed with a splash, and then it bobbed on the surface in a way that reminded Jack of fishing with his dad as a kid, a little perch or sunfish on the end of his cane pole. Then he waited. A breeze kicked up, and the light patches of fog began to disperse as quickly as they had arrived. Rising water from the spring continued to break gently at the surface, causing the capsule to turn gently in a clockwise direction.

Finally, the capsule jerked at one end. Jack couldn't see anything below the surface, but someone was down there, and he was tugging on the line. A little voice inside told him to dive in and see who it was, but that was just foolishness. He had to stick to the plan, wait for the kidnapper's call, tie him up in negotiations for a simultaneous exchange while the FBI closed in around the GPS coordinates.

The capsule jerked one more time, and then it began to sink, slowly and steadily. It was like watching the *Titanic*—the bow first, then the stern rising up above the surface as the metal tube began its long descent into darkness.

Fifty thousand dollars down the hole, just like that.

And there was still no sign of Mia.

Phase One of Jack's plan was complete. Now all he could do was hope that fifty thousand dollars was enough bait to make the kidnapper call back—to lure him into Phase Two.

63

.

A gent Crenshaw slipped into the black water without a splash, without a sound, almost without a ripple. For a moment he was a young Navy SEAL back in Vietnam, but the cold water quickly shattered that image. Seventy-two degrees didn't sound that cold until you were in up to your eyeballs in the dead of night. Slowly, the heat from his body warmed the thin layer of water beneath the tight-fitting rubber of his wet suit, gloves, and booties.

"You know you don't have to do this," said Danfield. The divers were three heads bobbing just above the surface, their regulators not yet in place.

"I'm no damn good to anyone standing around up here," said Crenshaw.

Danfield nodded, then gave a thumbs-up and switched on his diving light. Crenshaw and the other diver did likewise. It was startling, the way a flip of a switch could transform the impenetrable blackness into a pool so bright and crystal clear. The divers tucked their regulators into their mouths. Danfield went first, followed by the other search-and-rescue diver. As they submerged, their air bubbles quickly rose to the surface, and the lights refracted against their glistening trail like a hydrogen lamp on a cache of diamonds. Crenshaw watched with a combined sense of excitement and apprehension as he sucked a quick breath of dry air and then followed the fins of the lead divers.

The pace was quick, of course, with Mia's life potentially hanging in the balance. Crenshaw was not nearly as fit as he had once been, and he found himself sucking more air than he would have liked. At a depth of fifty feet they reached the opening to the Devil System. It was larger than he had expected, and the combined lamp-power of their three dive lights made it almost inviting. Danfield stopped and signaled the others to do likewise. As they hovered a few feet above the floor, the sweep of their fins kicked up a hurricane of white sand. They were just outside the "gallery," as cavers called it, the cave system's first section, which was like a large foyer. *So far, so good,* thought Crenshaw. He'd dived much tighter spaces before at much greater depths.

Danfield's mask flashed with the reflection of the dive light. Crenshaw couldn't see his face, but he did see the signal. One slashing gesture with his hand, left to right, straight across the throat, which meant "cut." The divers simultaneously switched off their lights.

The depths went black.

It lasted only a few seconds, but even in that short time, Crenshaw could feel his pulse quicken and hear himself exhausting far too much of his precious air. A less experienced diver might have warmed his wet suit on the spot, but Crenshaw kept control. He was so focused on not freaking out, however, that he almost forgot the purpose of the blackout. He peered into the gallery, toward the ever-narrowing restrictions beyond—and he saw it. Or at least he thought he saw it. A trace of light from somewhere deep within the cave.

Someone was in there.

Danfield switched his light back on, as did the others. On the leader's signal, the team entered the Devil's Ear.

Jack was headed toward the river, exactly as the kidnapper had instructed him: "Drop the money and follow the path north to the riverbank." It was clear that the kidnapper would be underwater—under*ground*— for the next few minutes, at least. Jack used this opportunity to touch base again with Andie Henning.

"He took the money," Jack said into his cell phone, walking as he spoke. He explained exactly what had happened, ending with the capsule's disappearance into the spring.

"Crenshaw was right," said Andie. "He *is* down there."

"What?"

"Crenshaw and his dive team saw a light in the Devil's Ear. They're down there now in pursuit."

Jack stopped in his tracks. "No one is supposed to be down there. Not until he calls me back to negotiate the simultaneous exchange."

"We changed our plan. The divers spotted a light inside the cave and went in."

"Did it occur to them that the kidnapper might see *their* lights? In which case he'll know that I called in the FBI. That'll give him the green light to kill Mia. I only gave him fifty thousand, so he's going to be pissed off as it is."

"Jack, after what happened to Ashley Thornton, we have to be aggressive. This is our best shot. If he's down there, we can only hope that Mia isn't down there with him. If our divers can find him, corner him, and capture him, we might get Mia back alive."

"What do you want me to do?" said Jack.

"Keep following the kidnapper's instructions. Let him think that things are going according to his plan. We'll take it from there."

"What if he finds his way out of the aquifer before your divers can catch him?"

"Did you put the GPS tracker inside the capsule?"

"Yes."

"Good. He has to surface sometime. As soon as he opens that capsule and starts counting his money, the tracker will tell us where he is. In the meantime, you should just continue to follow his instructions. I have several teams in the field. We're watching you at all times. If you're in danger, I'll tell you."

It wasn't Jack's plan to go quietly out of harm's way, but if things were coming to a head underwater, there was little else he could do. "Okay, I'm headed for the river. Just one thing more. And I want an honest answer."

"Shoot."

"Do you think Mia's still alive?"

The pause on the line wasn't very reassuring. "I'd pull you out of here in a heartbeat if I didn't think there was a chance."

Not the most encouraging response, but it was honest enough. "Thanks. I needed to hear that." He switched off the phone and started toward the river.

64

At a depth of fifty feet in chilly water, Agent Crenshaw focused on his breathing as the search-and-rescue diver fastened the guide-line to a protruding rock at the cave's entrance. Rigged like an oversize fishing reel, the long yellow rope would follow them into, and guide them out of, the Devil's Ear. Without it, they'd be lost, left to their own devices to find their way out of an underwater labyrinth that played for keeps, entombing its victims in watery limestone catacombs until someone happened upon them.

The lead diver let out the line and darted through the gaping cave entrance. Crenshaw followed the shiny fins ahead of him, careful not to fall behind as the bubbles roared in his ears. Their dive lights probed and scanned the cave, peeling away the darkness to reveal strange knobs and hollows of rock. They kept moving forward, and Crenshaw was increasingly aware of the rock formations overhead. *Overhead.* It was a benign enough word, but it had rather disturbing implications for possible escape routes. In an overhead environment there was no going up—no ditching the weight belt, popping your buoyancy, and heading for the surface when equipment failed or nerves cracked. The way in was the way out. Period. Crenshaw checked his equipment, then breathed a little sigh of relief to find that both of his backup dive lights were still with him.

They were swimming faster, and the blue-silver cone of light stretched out before him to reveal the first narrowing in the cave. It wasn't a welcome sight. Crenshaw was just getting things under control, getting comfortable with the notion of cave diving. Now he was supposed to follow the leader into a so-called opening that was, at best, like crawling into the gaping mouth of a hungry prehistoric shark. He checked his gauges. Still at fifty feet, but the ceiling was so much lower. How was that possible? It could only mean one thing: There was less water and more earth above him, more tons of solid limestone between him and the outside world. Wasn't it the ancient Greeks who entombed their dead in limestone—the perfect casket, turning the body to dust in just forty days? He shook off that thought and caught his breath.

The silence was remarkable, almost unnerving.

A flash of light crossed his path, and Danfield was suddenly right in front of him. He was looking straight into Crenshaw's eyes, and he was giving him the okay signal. After a moment, Crenshaw regained his focus and realized that he had zoned out for a second. He blinked hard and took control of his breathing. He returned the okay signal, then followed the flash of Danfield's fins through the first restriction.

Beyond that tight opening, deep within this underground honeycomb, Crenshaw had hoped to find another sprawling gallery, something on the order of Poseidon's ballroom. But the narrowing continued, and the farther he swam, the tighter it seemed to get. If he stretched his arms out wide he could simultaneously touch the walls on both sides of the cave. It would have been impossible to stand upright. In fact, there wasn't even enough head clearance to sit upright. He was barely able to advance in the prone position. He heard his tank scrape on the rocks above him. His fins brushed against the sandy floor below. He was churning up dust, as were the divers ahead of him, and a flick of his light caught only a rolling cloud of darkness in his path. The air hissed through his regulator. What if the airflow stopped? he wondered. Could he possibly turn around and get back at this stage? He patted his chest, searching for the spare regulator, the octopus. It wasn't there. Yes, yes, there it was. But what if *that* failed, too?

He kept finning forward, fighting the almost uncontrollable impulse to turn back. The ceiling continued to drop, which didn't seem possible. They were diving deeper, surrounded, walled in, going places where life itself depended on valves, hoses, diaphragms, lights, and countless other man-made gadgets that could malfunction at any moment. A little mustard-colored eel nipped at his wrist. *You've got the edge down here, buddy.*

Finally, the tunnel widened. There was room to maneuver—not much, but enough to be thankful for. Crenshaw checked his air supply. He'd blown way too much. He flashed his light at Danfield, who was giving the signal again—that slashing gesture across his throat. It was time to cut off the lights. Crenshaw shook his head. Danfield swam toward him, the anger on his face apparent even through the mask. Both S&R divers had switched off their lights. Only Crenshaw's was beaming. Danfield gave the signal once more. Crenshaw bit down so hard on his mouthpiece that his teeth ached. His fingers felt numb, but he flipped the switch.

He felt swallowed by the darkness.

Another roar of bubbles swept past his ears—too much air, way too fast. His mask felt askew, or maybe his mind was just playing tricks in the darkness. He adjusted it anyway, cleared it with another quick burst of air. He felt a burning sensation, then cold, as if the sudden and total darkness had thrown off his body's thermostat. His breathing was becoming erratic. He knew it wasn't possible, but his head felt as though it had swelled to twice its normal size. He was a split second away from the breaking point when, suddenly, he spotted a faint grayish glow from beyond. It was barely noticeable at first, but as his eyes adjusted to the blackness, the ball of light in the distance grew brighter. A light switched on, then another. Danfield and the other S&R diver finned quickly ahead. Crenshaw turned his light back on and followed.

Fear was replaced by adrenaline, and Crenshaw was swimming with a determination equal to that of his teammates. They passed a jagged cluster of blackened rocks, then turned a tight corner. Even with their own lights on, the light ahead was visible. They were closing in, and Crenshaw was like a new man, spurred on by the excitement of the chase. He swam past the second diver and was about to overtake Danfield, but they both stopped short. The light from beyond was moving away from them, but they could go no farther.

They had reached the iron bars.

Suddenly, Crenshaw recalled the video feed from the recovery of Ashley Thornton. Her body had been chained to iron safety bars that the park had installed years earlier to prevent divers from exploring the most dangerous reaches of the Devil's Ear. Crenshaw grasped the bars and shook them like a man falsely imprisoned. They didn't budge. The light on the other side was fading. He and Danfield exchanged looks of exasperation, unable to speak, but they were clearly sharing the same thought. Mia's kidnapper had found another way into the Devil's Ear. He knew these caves better than they did.

And he was getting away.

•

65

The footpath proved to be the long route, taking Jack past several cottages and campsites before he finally reached the Santa Fe River. His own sense of direction could have gotten him there much faster, but according to Agent Henning, it was more important for him to make the kidnapper think that he was following the kidnapper's plan. It was a tough job to swallow, since he had been set on negotiating a simultaneous exchange. The FBI had taken over and sent in its divers before Jack could actualize the second half of his plan. Jack wasn't happy about that, but it hardly seemed in Mia's interest to fight the FBI now.

The trip took almost twenty minutes, around patches of ground too swampy for passage, over sand dunes, and through hardwood hammocks. Finally, the map led him to the aluminum fishing boat described in the kidnapper's note.

The river was about seventy-five feet wide in these parts, with willow-swept banks that sloped to depths of ten to fifteen feet. The current was gentle, moving just fast enough to indicate that he had been walking upriver, away from the great Suwanee. Theo's rendition of "Old Folks at Home" suddenly popped into Jack's mind, carrying him back to a carefree day when he'd lost that hearing over the statue of David and then introduced his best friend to Mia. That all seemed like years, not weeks, earlier. Jack could only imagine how long ago it must seem to Mia.

The fishing boat was tied to a piling, no lock. Jack gave it a quick sweep with the flashlight. There were a few dead crickets on the bow seat, presumably bait left behind by a panfish angler. A pair of oars stretched almost the entire length of the boat, but fortunately Jack would not be rowing. The boat had a small outboard engine and, if the kidnapper was true to his promise, a full tank of gas. Jack untied the boat, then climbed inside as he shoved off from the bank. He stuffed the backpack with Theo's cash securely beneath the seat at the bow. The current was stronger once he got away from the shoreline, and he felt himself drifting downriver. He pulled once, then again, on the engine's starter cord. On the third attempt the outboard whined, gurgled, and spit river water before it finally hummed with confidence at idle speed. Jack's directions were to head upriver at no-wake pace.

He turned the boat around and began the journey, wondering if the winding river was carrying him closer to, or farther from, Mia.

The FBI's on-site command center was stone silent, but the tension was high. Andie Henning and her team of technical and field specialists were in the main cottage at the Ginnie Springs campground, a small wood-frame building that was situated perfectly for on-site coordination of law enforcement activities. The only drawback was the heat. The air conditioner was broken, and the windows had to remain shut with shades drawn, lest an outsider detect the FBI's presence.

A tech team in the kitchen was ready to intercept cellular telephone communications. Another tech agent in the bedroom stood ready to track any signal from the GPS transmitter that Jack had placed in the capsule filled with ransom money. In the living room, Andie studied a detailed map on the wall. It was the most up-to-date charting of the spring systems of the Suwannee River basin. Standing at her side was Agent Crenshaw, his wet suit still dripping river water onto the hardwood floor. Behind him was Bruce Gelhorn, director of the Suwannee River Water Management District. He was a lean man with the classic raccoon suntan—a sunbaked face with white ovals around his eyes that matched the shape of his sunglasses. Gelhorn wasn't just the cartographer; he'd personally dived most of the many springs below the confluence of the Santa Fe and Suwannee rivers.

Andie heard a bit of radio squeal in her headset, followed by an update from the leader of the field team that was posted at July Spring, across the river from the Devil's Ear. "Swyteck is headed upriver at about three knots per hour," the field agent reported.

"Copy," said Andie.

She turned her attention back to her map. "Why would he send Swyteck upriver?"

Gelhorn went to the map, pointing as he spoke. "I suppose the only way to answer that is to look at what you've got up there. It's basically a series of springs with a sprawling underground network of caves. Some of it is mapped, some is unmapped."

Crenshaw said, "But my dive team saw the light in the Devil's Ear. I saw it, too, with my own eyes. That means he has to be in this area."

"It's a limestone honeycomb down there," said Gelhorn. "You could spend your whole life looking for someone and come up empty-handed."

"He can't get too far away before he has to come up for air," said Andie.

"Don't be so sure," said Gelhorn. "He's obviously an experienced cave diver. We know that much from what Agent Crenshaw and his dive team just witnessed. Not many people could find a backdoor entrance into the Devil's Ear, on the other side of those iron bars."

"I agree with you," said Crenshaw. "But like Agent Henning just said, unless he's got gills, he has to come up for air."

"Eventually, yes. But surely he planned ahead and figured that the FBI might be covering Ginnie Springs and the Devil System like a wet blanket. In which case, I doubt he'll be popping up anywhere in this area."

"What are you saying?" said Andie. "He's using spare tanks?"

"That would be my bet."

"Spare tanks from where?" said Crenshaw. "Carrying one active and a spare is hard enough down there."

"Again, I'm assuming that this guy's a planner who knows the caves in these parts extremely well. He might have figured out that the FBI would force him to stay down longer than he would like. To cover that scenario, maybe he stashed tanks throughout the system in advance. It's easy to hide stuff in crevices or behind knobs of rocks. He could swim to it, change tanks, continue on his way, change tanks again, swim some more. He could do this several times while working through the system. The aquifer is all interconnected. Now, he can't stay down forever, but he could push it for several hours this way. That's long enough for him to swim well out of the area covered by your field agents before he has to surface and make a run for it on dry land."

Andie fell silent. Gelhorn had just laid out a scenario that her team wasn't prepared to cover. "So if that's the case, it's all going to come down to how quickly we can respond to the GPS tracker once he surfaces. Which brings me back to my original question. Why send Swyteck upriver?"

"Because the kidnapper is headed downriver?" said Crenshaw.

"Or because he wants us to *think* he's headed downriver," said Andie.

"I could suggest another possibility," said Gelhorn. "There is a point upriver where the Santa Fe runs underground."

"The entire river?"

"Yeah. A three-mile stretch ending here," he said, indicating, "at O'Leno State Park. The siphons between here and there can be kind of dangerous."

"Siphons?"

"They're the opposite of a spring. Most of Florida's major siphons are on the Sante Fe, draining over three hundred thirty million gallons of water every day directly into the aquifer. We've even named some of them, like Big Awesome Suck and Little Awesome Suck. There are others, too. Sometimes it's a gentle whirlpool. Other times it's like a giant flushing toilet a good fifteen feet across. Big and powerful enough that it could easily suck down anything that floats along, like a log or even a kayak or canoe."

"Or a person," said Andie.

"Yeah. Or a person."

Andie picked up her phone.

"Who you calling?" asked Crenshaw.

"Swyteck," she said. "Something tells me that we just figured out why he's traveling upriver."

66

.

He ditched his first pair of spent air tanks about a quarter mile northeast of the Devil's Ear. Cold numbed his lips as his groping glove reached for the fresh tank and unclipped the regulator. His teeth bit down on the mouthpiece, and his lungs were eagerly sucking air the instant he blew it clear. In all, he had six replacement tanks stashed away in the darkest reaches of the cave system, enough to get him beyond any reasonable police perimeter. The dive lights on the other side of the iron bars, however, had definitely reshaped his notion of a *reasonable* perimeter. He hadn't expected the FBI to put Mia's life in jeopardy by coming down to search for him. Perhaps the law enforcement coverage was broader, more aggressive than anticipated. Maybe additional divers were up ahead. He couldn't take the risk.

It was time to implement Plan B.

His dive light found the next marker. In addition to stashing air tanks, he'd spent weeks fastening metal tags to the walls of his predetermined escape route. By following his markers, he could navigate through the caves without a lifeline. He finned forward, soaring through water clear as mountain air, his body sliding just inches above a floor of rippled silt. The tunnel narrowed, then curved left. Smaller, circular tunnels branched off like capillaries from an artery. They were too narrow for human passage. They were perfect, however, for storage of the ransom money.

He grabbed a knob of rock and held himself steady, the current flowing past him. It wasn't too powerful—further confirmation that this was indeed a suitable place to hide the money. Squirreling away the capsule hadn't been part of his original plan, but it seemed necessary now that Swyteck had called in the FBI. Surely they had persuaded him to drop a GPS tracking chip into the ransom capsule, which raised an obvious question: What kind of amateur did they think they were dealing with? It was no skin off his back to hide the capsule down in the caves and return for it in a week, a month, six months. Then, even if the cops did catch him pulling the capsule full of money out of the aquifer, he could simply claim to be a lucky recreational diver who had happened upon the loot.

With one good shove, he wedged the capsule deep into a long, narrow opening. He tugged it once, then tried to jerk it from side to side. It didn't budge. This baby wasn't going anywhere until he came back to get it. He turned around—not an easy feat in such tight quarters—and finned down the narrow tunnel toward the next marker.

The current was getting stronger, not yet of the first magnitude, but close. He was making good time, but he had to slow himself down. Too much speed and he might miss his marker altogether. The marker was, in effect, his lifeline. Every move he made was in relation to the series of markers. At each junction, he could continue swimming to the next replacement tank, or he could bail out and surface.

Plan B was the bail out.

He was coasting now, just enough air in his "wings" (as cavers called them) to hover between the floor and ceiling and ride the current. Flashes of blue and violet glinted at the outer reaches of his dive light, nothing but darkness beyond. It was easy to see how divers became disoriented down here, the way the ceiling, walls, and floor converged into shades of gray, dark shadows, and then a black door to the abyss. He cut his speed and braced himself against a rock cluster, coming to a complete halt. He turned and shone the light back into the tunnel he'd just exited. It didn't look at all familiar—not a good thing for a cave diver. Had he been less experienced, he might have freaked. He knew better, however. Nothing ever looked familiar when viewing it from the back side. He flashed the light forward, down the tunnel ahead of him. The silver-blue cone swept across gray and black hollows of limestone until, finally, the little sparkle in the distance gave him all the reassurance he needed. He finned with confidence toward the square chrome marker that pointed the way out.

Mia lay perfectly still, her ear pressed against the wall.

She'd tried the same tactic before, in the other little rooms in which he'd held her captive over the past . . . what was it? Two weeks. Longer? In both of those other places, she'd been able to pick up noises from the outside world. Nothing discernible—just noises. Here, however, she heard only her own breathing. Maybe it was the extra insulation. Perhaps it was the isolation. Either way, the complete absence of external sound was uncanny.

Had he left her there to die? Would anyone ever happen by and find her? Would wild animals pick up her scent and feast on her remains, or would the millipedes have her to themselves?

She tugged hard at the chain that bound her ankles to the exposed wall stud. She'd been working at it for hours—left foot, right foot, left, right, using the long chain like a band saw to cut through the wooden stud. It was slow work, but she was making progress. She had to pace herself, however. It wouldn't do her any good to exhaust all her energy. She had to maintain a state of readiness. She harbored no illusions as to his intentions. The chances of being released were close to nil. She knew better than anyone that this kidnapping was about revenge, not ransom. Her only hope was to make her move when he came back—if he came back. Both her timing and her execution would have to be perfect.

She closed her eyes and waited, watching the plan unfold in her mind's eye. Then she started pulling on the chain again, left foot then right foot, slowly gnawing her way to freedom.

67

The limestone chimney carried him straight up, and he broke the surface in a low-lying area. The spring-fed waters were too clear and cold to call it a swamp, but thin reeds, cypress trees, and wild brush provided ample concealment. No diver liked to enter or exit the spring system in the middle of a marsh, so this little opening to the watery underworld was perhaps his best-kept secret.

He removed his diving equipment and stashed it in the bushes. He had no plans to come back and get it. The million-dollar ransom from Mr. Thornton had certainly made it expendable—not to mention whatever additional cash Swyteck had put inside the capsule. The black wet suit was good camouflage by night, so he left it on, including the hood and booties. He kept the diving gloves on, too. It would cost him a little dexterity, but there would be no fingerprints.

He had to assume that law enforcement was scouring the area, probably equipped with night vision. Walking or running to the cottage was out of the question. On his belly, he slithered like a water snake through the flooded fields of waist-high sawgrass. It took only a few minutes for the river to come into sight. Flashes of moonlight undulated against the gently flowing waters. Like a patient alligator stalking its prey, he slid down the bank and entered the river in complete silence. As the current carried him downriver, he couldn't help but feel some frustration. He was giving up the very ground that he had worked so hard to gain in the tunnels below. But the FBI had forced him to reevaluate everything. No matter how well he knew these caves, swimming to his escape was no longer his best option. The sight of those dive lights in the Devil's Ear had made him feel cornered, and he had to adjust accordingly.

The surest way out was with a hostage—an *expendable* hostage.

Much of the wooded land along this stretch of the river was privately owned, and every so often a cottage appeared on the shoreline. He was more familiar with the passages below the river, but as the big bend approached, he recognized the boat launch up ahead. This was his exit. He drew a breath and swam the remaining fifty feet underwater. He surfaced beneath a wooden pier that jutted out into the river. Fastened to the pilings at the end of the pier was an aluminum fishing boat with a small outboard, much like the one he'd told Swyteck to take upriver. Beside it was a larger fiberglass flats boat with a Johnson 115 outboard. Neck deep in river water, he followed the pier to the shoreline and quickly climbed the banks.

The cottage was about a quarter mile inland, just a two-minute sprint even in dive boots. Still, he couldn't run up the gravel road without some risk of detection. He opted for a slower route through the forest, moving tree to tree, crawling from one cluster of hardwoods to the next. It took almost ten minutes, but when he finally reached the cottage, he felt confident that he'd gone under the FBI's radar.

Even if they'd spotted him, at least now a hostage was within his grasp.

The garage behind the cottage was padlocked. He found the key exactly where he'd hidden it, beneath a rock at the end of the driveway. He quickly unlocked the door, ducked inside, and closed up behind him. Inside the garage was the heavily insulated shed he'd constructed—a box within a box, so to speak. Teresa could have kicked and screamed at the top of her lungs. No one would have heard a thing, even with the small air vent. Perhaps it was *too* small. It had to be like an oven inside there. He wondered if his hostage—his ticket out of there—was already dead.

The key to the locked inner shed was hanging on a hook near the light switch. He fumbled for it in the dark, too cautious to turn on the garage light. He found it, then struggled again in darkness to find the keyhole. On the third try, success. He turned the key, listened for the click, then gently pushed open the door. A blast of hot, stale air pelted his face, even worse than expected. Again he wondered if the stifling conditions had proved too much for her. He closed the door and switched on the light.

Teresa was a motionless heap in the corner. He watched from across the shed, then clapped his hands. She didn't move. Not even her breathing was evident. "Teresa," he said.

She didn't flinch.

As he crossed the room, a strange odor assaulted his nostrils. It was either the heat working on human waste, or possibly decay and decomposition. She was balled in the fetal position, eyes closed, her back against the wall. He nudged her shoulder blade with his foot. She still didn't move. He knelt down to take her pulse—and she suddenly sprang to life, coming at him with the blinding speed of a hungry lion.

It was a total blur, and before he could react, a shard of glass—the broken lightbulb—found its mark. His head snapped back. His scream nearly rattled the walls as blood oozed from his punctured eyeball. He stammered and rolled to the ground, and he could hear the chain of the handcuffs rattling as Teresa whisked past him. One door slammed, then another. The eye was ruined, he knew it. But he stood to lose far more—*everything*—if he didn't regain control.

He stumbled out of the shed, found a rag on the tool bench, and pressed it to his eye. It was immediately soaked with blood, but he was undeterred.

For Gerard, he reminded himself. This was for Gerard.

He grabbed the pistol from the toolbox and ran after her.

68

.

L ow-hanging branches slashed at her face in the darkness. Mia ran as fast as she could, but her toe still hadn't healed from the making of that first sadistic videotape, and it was slowing her down. Her hand was bleeding badly. The sharp piece of glass had done almost as much damage to her hand as to his eye. She screamed once for help, then thought better of it. She was somewhere in the wilderness, and the only person who could possibly hear her was him. Making any noise would only give away her position.

Running wasn't easy with her hands cuffed in front of her body and a four-foot chain joining her ankles. But she'd been abducted while jogging, and at least she was still wearing her running shoes. This was certainly no time to pamper an injured toe. She kept going, slicing through the brush until she came to a dirt road. It was decision time: Turn left or right? She had no idea. A set of footprints in the soft, spongy earth caught her attention. They were leading to the right— toward a low-hanging moon. Was it a moon rising in the east or setting in the west? No way to tell; she was clueless as to the time of day and equally uninformed as to her surroundings. If there were footprints headed in that direction, however, there had to be *something* down there. She started down the road at a fast-paced walk. With each stride, she grew more accustomed to the ankle chain, and soon she was nearly at an all-out sprint.

The narrow road was lined by tall, ghostly cypress trees that stood like sentries on either side. Much farther ahead, however, the road glistened in the moonlight. Then she heard the staticlike hiss in the air, and she realized it wasn't a road at all. The moon was bouncing off moving water. A river! Her legs were aching, her toe was throbbing, her whole body felt stiff from captivity. She pushed beyond the pain, then reached inside and found another gear that rocketed her toward the river. She was breathless when she reached the riverbank, her heart pounding. She glanced nervously over her shoulder. She didn't see him, but her own footprints were like a road map in the dirt. Even a man with one eye could follow that trail. She debated whether to swim for it, but that wasn't an option with her hands bound together. Just then she spotted the boats tied up at the pier just fifty yards downriver. Without a moment's hesitation, she became a blur on the riverbank, gobbling up that fifty yards with the determination of an Olympic champion.

She hopped onto the larger boat first, the fiberglass flats boat with the big outboard engine. Just orienting herself was a challenge, the struggle to catch her breath competing with her powers of concentration. The ignition had no key in it. She rifled through the side drawers, the captain's cubby, every little compartment that might hold the key, literally, to her escape. She found nothing but fishing tackle, a flashlight, and an orange-and-blue bottle opener that cried "Go Gators" when she grabbed it. She threw it aside in frustration, then froze.

He was coming down the road, almost to the riverbank.

She hopped from the flats boat into the smaller aluminum fishing boat. This one required no key. She untied the boat from the pier and pulled the engine's starter cord. It was an awkward movement with her hands bound, and the first pull nearly sent her tumbling overboard. She took another look back. He was fifty yards away. She changed her stance and pulled again. This time the engine grumbled, then purred happily, piercing the silence of the slow-moving river. The sound, the vibration, the churning of the water—they all added up to freedom for Mia, and it almost made her giddy. She pushed off from the pier, took a seat at the stern, and cranked the throttle. The front of the boat rose slightly, but not much. The boat was barely moving. She turned the throttle harder. The engine struggled, but the boat was at a crawl.

The anchor! It had never occurred to her that someone would anchor a boat that was tied to a pier—maybe it was to deter teens on joyrides—but she was definitely dragging the anchor.

She threw it into reverse, and the boat lunged back toward the pier. She hurried to the bow and grabbed the anchor line. Again she glanced toward the riverbank. He was just twenty-five yards away. She pulled furiously on the line, reeling it in as fast as possible. Finally, the anchor broke the surface and landed in the boat with a dull thud—which was followed by the deafening crack of gunfire and the cold pop of a bullet piercing the starboard side at the waterline. He was firing his pistol from the shoreline, and the boat was about as much protection as aluminum foil. Mia dived toward the engine, grabbed the throttle, and cranked it to the max. She heard another shot, but it missed the boat and hit the water like a stone that couldn't skip. The damage to his eye had apparently thrown off his aim. She twisted the throttle until her wrist hurt, until it wouldn't move any farther. The little boat was a speedster now, racing up the river with all the power its engine, and Mia's prayers, could deliver. She was keeping low, her head just high enough to see out over the bow. She braced herself for the sound of more gunfire, but it was the lionlike roar that jerked her head back for one final look at the pier.

The flats boat was rumbling. He was coming to get her.

69

•

For the third time, Agent Henning tried to ring Jack on his cell phone.

Before he'd set out to deliver the ransom, she'd practically begged him to tie into the FBI's radio network. He'd flatly refused to wear anything that might signal—literally—to the kidnapper that he'd called in the FBI: no radio, no GPS tracking chip on his person, no detectable gadgets, period. Wearing a flak jacket and dropping a tracking chip in with the ransom had been part of Jack's plan all along, and that was as far as Jack was willing to go. A little more cooperation would have made Andie's life easier, but she couldn't blame him for maintaining some modicum of distance between himself and law enforcement. Not after the way the Thornton case had turned out.

"Come on, Swyteck. Answer already." Andie was pacing furiously across the living room. Her telephone was pressed to her right ear; a radio headset, which linked her to the field agents, was feeding into her left. Andie was still assimilating the latest update from team one, positioned north of July Spring, when Jack finally answered his telephone.

"Are you okay?" she said. "I called three times and you didn't answer."

"Didn't hear it. Motor's too noisy, I guess."

She could hear the engine whining in the background. "My field agents tell me that two boats are racing upriver, north of July Spring."

"It's not me. I'm puttering along at less than five knots. Don't know exactly where, but it's way upriver from July Spring, I'm sure of that."

"I know it's not you. What I'm trying to tell you is that they're coming up behind you. Fast. Ditch the boat on the riverbank and take cover in the woods."

"Who is *they?*"

"That's not important."

"Is Mia on one of those boats?"

"Please, just listen to me. Head for the woods and take cover. We'll handle it from here."

There was a pause, a silence that was just long enough to tie her stomach in knots.

"I think I'm losing you," said Jack. "Bad connection here."

"Jack, don't—" She stopped, realizing that she was talking to dead air. "Damn him," she said as she put the phone away.

"What's wrong?" asked Crenshaw.

"He's going to get in the middle of this, I know it," said Andie.

"Did you warn him about the siphons in those parts?" asked Gelhorn.

Andie was about to dial him back, but she knew he wouldn't answer. "No," she said in a voice that halted. "I didn't."

70

J ack cranked the throttle and pulled a sharp U-turn. The cold spray of river water coated his face like a fine London mist. The small engine struggled, but finally his boat gained enough momentum to plane off and cut through the black water, throwing a V-shaped wake that glistened in the moonlight. Startled by the sudden noise, a flock of egrets took flight from the shoreline, a fluttering blast of white in the night sky.

Andie's words were still playing in his mind: two boats racing toward him at high speed. One of them had to be Mia; the other, the kidnapper. It was the only scenario that made sense. Why else would Andie refuse to tell him who was in the boats and insist that he take cover in the woods? This was no time to hide, however. Theo's advice rang in his ears: *Do you want to be lookin' at me or Mia the rest of your life?* Suddenly, racing down the Santa Fe, the answer to that question was as clear as the springs that fed this river. Jack had laid too much on the line to stand on the sidelines and hope for the best from the FBI, whose record in dealing with the Wrong Number Kidnapper was less than impressive. He remembered his visit to the FBI's Miami field office. Mr. Thornton was in the reception area, on the other side of the bulletproof glass, seated with his elbows on his knees and his head in his hands as he waited to see Agent Henning. The look on that widower's face was unforgettable— the hollow expression of a man who would have done more, who would have done it differently, if he'd had it to do all over again. Jack didn't want it to end that way. Not if he could help it.

He reached inside his jacket and checked the gun that Theo had given him—just in case.

"Come on, come on," Mia muttered over the engine's whine. She would have done anything to make her boat faster. The engine was sputtering, incapable of a sustained full-throttle performance. The bullet hole in the hull was just at the waterline, and the boat was taking on about a gallon a minute. Her escape was steadily losing momentum. She checked over her shoulder and saw the flats boat closing in on her, just over a hundred yards behind her. The fix was in on this horse race. No way could this little fishing boat outrun the more powerful engine. She had to get ashore, disappear into the woods, find a place to hide or maybe grab the attention of someone who could help her.

She spotted an eddy just ahead, behind a massive tangle of tree roots that reached into the river like prehistoric fingers. It looked like a good place to ditch the boat. She angled toward shore and prepared to make a run for it.

The rising engine noise told Jack that he was drawing closer. At first it seemed as though his own outboard was straining louder. Then he realized that it was a motorized concert, the combined rumble of his engine and those of the oncoming boats. He couldn't see them, but he knew the gap was shrinking between him and Mia—between him and her kidnapper. As he approached the river bend, however, the noise lessened. Had the boats stopped? Had the chase ended badly for Mia? Jack cursed at the engine, as if that might speed his way around the bend. He took a wide turn, steering more toward the middle of the river as he came around a hammock of cypress trees that extended out over the banks. A small aluminum fishing boat, like his, was drifting toward shore. The engine was tilted forward in the retired position, its idle propeller up above the waterline. A man—no, a woman—was paddling furiously with a single loose oar.

"Mia!" he shouted.

She stopped and looked. It wasn't clear that she recognized him. She might have heard only his engine, not his voice. But she seemed ecstatic to see him—*anyone*—nonetheless. She started waving the oar back and forth, signaling for help.

She couldn't possibly see the flats boat coming upriver, full speed, straight toward her.

The windshield shattered on the flats boat, another burst of glass that nearly took out his good eye. He'd heard the bullet whistle past his ear, so he knew the shot had been fired from behind him. Sniper, he realized. The FBI had called in a sharpshooter, and that was his warning shot, the proverbial blow across the bow. The next one would shatter his skull unless he cut his engine and threw up his hands in surrender.

Not in this lifetime. They already had him for the murder of Ashley Thornton, and kidnapping Teresa was another life sentence.

He hit the deck but kept one hand on the steering wheel. He jerked it from left to right, slamming the boat into an erratic path, side to side, making himself a moving target—an errant missile skimming down the waterway. He had an extra set of tanks and diving equipment onboard, but suiting up was out of the question with a sniper on the riverbank. A hostage was the only ticket out of this mess, but he didn't need two.

It was time to deal with the only living person who could identify him as the Wrong Number Kidnapper.

71

Jack took a hard turn to starboard and gunned his boat toward Mia. Even in the moonlight, she didn't seem to recognize him until that last moment. Her boat was drifting with the current, the engine off. The flats boat was closing fast but moving in a bizarre serpentine path. Jack cut quickly in front of Mia, his boat curling around the bow before he took it down to idle speed and rafted up, side by side.

"Jump in!" he shouted.

"Jack? What are—"

"Get in!"

The flats boat was barreling down on them. Suddenly, two quick gunshots roared above the engine noise and pierced the aluminum hull. Jack quickly returned the fire, shooting blindly at the flats boat, no driver in sight. The motorboat continued its erratic path at ramming speed. Jack knew his boat didn't have nearly enough power to maneuver out of the way.

Out of the corner of his eye, Jack spotted the backpack at the bow. It still held two hundred thousand dollars of Theo's money. But it was out of reach.

"Jump!" he shouted as he sailed through the air and across Mia's boat. He grabbed her by the shoulder on his way down, taking her with him, losing his gun in the confusion. They splashed into the cold river just an instant before the much larger motorboat flattened the aluminum fishing boats like big empty beer cans.

Jack was somewhere below the surface, the water fizzing and churning in the aftermath of the crash. The water was black and cold, and his only thought was to find Mia. She was a good swimmer, but he had seen the chains that bound her wrists and ankles—impediment enough for any swimmer. He dived deeper and deeper until his hands hit the bottom. It was too dark to see anything, but at this depth he could feel a current so strong that it could only mean an opening to the aquifer somewhere in the riverbed. For a spring, it seemed strange that the water wasn't pushing him up to the surface. It was sucking him down, like a whirlpool.

Jack fought the current, swimming upward, groping in the darkness for Mia. After a minute, he couldn't fight his need for air any longer. He popped to the surface and drew several deep breaths while looking in every direction—upriver, downriver, and then toward the sloping bank. The current was strengthening and taking him downriver. Ahead of him, in the moonlight, he spotted the flats boat drifting aimlessly, the motor dead silent and no one aboard. Had he fallen off his boat in the crash?

The distant hum of another engine cut through the night, a speedboat coming upriver. *The FBI?* Jack wondered.

Jack heard a scream, then a splash. "Mia!" he called. His head was just barely above water, but he could see her struggling to stay afloat, clinging to some wreckage. He started swimming toward her, but something broke in the water between them. Suddenly, he was staring at a pistol, visible even in the darkness. A hand covered in black rubber diving gloves squeezed off a shot just an instant too late. Jack was already underwater, and the muted crack of gunfire sounded like distant thunder. Apparently, Mia's kidnapper had decided that Jack was one hostage too many.

Surfacing at this point would mean certain death. Jack forced himself to stay hidden in the black water as long as possible, long enough to convince the shooter that he'd been hit and swallowed by the river. The current continued to carry him downriver, and the strange downward pull was getting even stronger. Jack had to come up for air soon. One option was to swim as far away as possible and hope that his head would pop up somewhere beyond the gunman's range. But that would leave Mia to fend for herself, handcuffed. Without another moment of thought, he chose his only real alternative.

Jack dived down ten or more feet, a depth that put him in total darkness from the vantage point of anyone looking down from the surface. Looking up, however, there was just barely enough moonlight for him to see shadows above him—the vague outline of a man treading water. Jack noticed no tanks or fins. He may have been wearing a wet suit, but he had no diving equipment. Ten feet downriver was a more slender shadow on the surface, that of Mia, her legs fighting with the chains and kicking furiously in escape mode.

Jack was hovering just above the riverbed, which he used as a springboard to propel himself up like a rocket. He hit the diver square in the midsection.

The ensuing moments were a complete blur, but Jack felt as if he were wrestling an alligator. Jack tried desperately to grab his opponent, but the wet suit made him difficult to control. Jack was already at a disadvantage, needing air. It was as if the diver had instinctively exploited that weakness. He grabbed Jack by the hair and pulled him under. Jack wasn't about to challenge a trained scuba diver to a game of "who can hold his breath longer." He slashed and kicked, using all his strength to bring their battle to the surface.

Jack finally broke free, but he was still going down. It wasn't the diver who was keeping him under. The current was pulling them both down. And he was no longer moving downriver. He was caught in a counterclockwise swirl. He'd never been in a whirlpool before, but he knew rip currents from Florida's beaches. He swam with all his strength, not directly against the current, but perpendicular to it. It seemed as though he was getting nowhere, but the pull was lessening. His head finally broke above the surface, long enough for him to steal a breath of air and catch a glimpse of the shoreline straight ahead. He kept swimming, slowly winning the battle against nature. He wasn't completely out of the siphon, but he made it to a fallen cypress tree that jutted out into the river. He grabbed on and held tightly, exhausted.

Before he could catch his breath, a gloved hand emerged from the other side of the log and grabbed him by the hair. Jack managed to work his arm up around the diver's head. It was covered with a rubber diving hood, but Jack's fingers inched over the crown until he could feel the bare skin of his forehead. Jack twisted and turned, and for a split second he was staring straight into the diver's face, into that ruined eye.

It was the face of Theo's friend Richie, the bouncer from Club Vertigo II—the same bouncer who'd handed Teresa the Got the Look business card in Montalvo's Atlanta club.

With a quick jerk, Jack went for his wounded eye. It wasn't a solid hit, but Richie recoiled immediately, as if Jack had hit an exposed nerve, and lost his grip on the fallen log. The siphon immediately took hold of him. Jack watched him swirl in the moonlight, arms and legs desperately reaching for the surface. This time, he was too tired to win the fight. He went around and around for almost a minute, caught in nature's drain. Then he was gone, sucked into the aquifer with no tanks, no light. And no chance of survival.

Just as Jack caught his breath, he spotted the backpack full of cash floating toward the siphon's spiral. "No!" he shouted.

Theo's money followed Richie to a watery grave.

72

·

Together, Jack and Mia watched the moon set from the front porch of Ginnie Cottage, the FBI's makeshift command center. The FBI had a doctor on-site to tend to Mia's immediate needs, but fortunately the wounds to her toe and inner thigh were not serious. There was a psychologist there as well, but Mia just wanted to talk to Jack.

The occasional squawk of a police radio rose above the hum of cicadas in the field. A dozen agents came and went, some with actual work to do, others simply enjoying the afterglow of a job well done. Jack and Mia weren't exactly alone, but it was the closest they'd come in a long time to a private moment, the two of them seated side by side on the slatted wood swing. Jack could have asked her a thousand questions, but it was too soon. Her body was still cool from the river. Her hair was still damp against his shoulder. She laced her fingers with his and stroked the back of his hand, the way she used to after making love. Tonight, however, she was squeezing much harder. It felt as though she would never let go. Jack was fine with that.

The FBI had plucked Mia from the river first. They found Jack clinging to the fallen tree about two hundred yards farther upriver. Jack immediately told them about Richie, but he sensed that Andie had known it was him for some time. As usual, she'd kept it to herself. Divers were still searching for the body, and they were confident about finding it, eventually. They weren't nearly so sure about recovering the capsule that held Jack's fifty thousand dollars in ransom money, and they were even less optimistic about the backpack and Theo's two hundred thousand dollars. Jack could live without his own money, but Theo's was another matter.

The screen door squeaked open and then slammed shut on its spring. The footsteps crossing the porch had a certain deliberateness about them, as if bad news was on the way. Jack looked up to see Andie Henning standing in the dim glow of the yellow porch light.

"Everything okay?" said Jack.

"Yeah, fine," she said. "The media are already starting to gather at the park entrance, so I'll have to deal with that soon enough." She angled toward the empty chair facing the swing. "Mind if I sit down for a sec?"

"Please," said Jack.

She sat on the edge, as if not looking to make herself too comfortable. "Mia, I know this might be something you'd rather not talk about, but I'd like to take a statement from you about the kidnapping."

Jack said, "Do we really have to do this tonight?"

"It's okay," said Mia. "Let's get it over with."

"Good," said Andie. "But . . . um."

"But what?" said Jack.

Andie seemed to be having trouble forming her words. "First, I need to tell you that you have the right to remain silent. Anything you say can and will be used against you in a court of—"

"Wait a second," said Jack. "You're giving her Miranda? What for?"

Again she paused, but this time her voice was a little firmer. "Murder."

"It wasn't murder," said Jack. "This guy Richie got what he deserved."

"I agree. And maybe Gerard Montalvo did, too. But a woman has a right to kill the man who raped her only in self-defense. Not out of vengeance."

Mia started to speak, but Jack stopped her. He gave Andie a serious look. "All right, cut the games. Level with me, Henning. What's this all about?"

Andie struggled, then said, "Jack, I can't—"

"Can't tell me. I know, I know. It's like the mantra for this case. For once, surprise me, would you? Just to keep the conversation lively."

"It's not that simple."

"Nothing's ever simple with you. From day one, every time I asked you for information, all I ever got was the same old excuse that you're not authorized to discuss the investigation with me."

"That's not true."

"Even after you finally promised to try and get me a higher level of clearance, I never heard another word about it."

"I'm sorry, but in case you haven't noticed, you can't spell bureaucracy without the bureau."

"I'm sure you have your share of administrative hassles. Bottom line is that the flow of information in this case has been pretty much a one-way street, and I'm tired of it. So if you think you can just walk out here onto the porch before the sun is even up and, out of the blue, start reading Miranda to my client—"

"Your *client?*" said Mia.

Jack paused. As usual, Andie was making him crazy. "Just for once, Henning. Throw me a bone."

Andie studied his expression, but she didn't argue. She drew a breath and said, "I want you both to know that it doesn't make me happy to have to do this. Believe me, no one is more sympathetic to victims than I am. I suppose the only thing worse than being raped is to be courageous enough to come forward and press charges, only to have no one believe you."

She looked at Mia and said, "Failing that polygraph examination was the beginning of your frustration, I'm sure. Polygraphs aren't one-hundred-percent reliable. Jack and I both have seen liars pass and honest people fail. If you ask me, the prosecutors put far more faith in the polygraph than they should have. But that didn't give Mia the right to take matters into her own hands."

"That's your theory," said Jack. "I don't hear any evidence."

Andie hesitated, as if debating whether to say more. "Why don't you ask Mia what the Atlanta DA decided to do with the case after she failed her polygraph."

Jack glanced at Mia. He wasn't about to ask her anything in front of an FBI agent, but from the look on her face, he could almost guess the answer.

Andie said, "They decided to plea-bargain. Adjudication withheld. Montalvo wasn't going to jail. He wasn't even going to have a conviction on his record. From a legal standpoint, it was as if the rape had never happened."

"That's not much of a motive for murder if you can't prove that Mia knew what kind of sweetheart deal was being offered."

"She was the *only* person who knew. The DA spoke to Mia first. Montalvo disappeared before the DA could even call his lawyer to make the offer. And now we know what happened to him."

"It was Richie who led me to Montalvo's body," said Jack.

"With information provided by Mia. That's what Richie told you, Jack. He was able to lead you to Montalvo's body because Mia told him where the body was buried. The grave was freshly dug because he had to dig it up to make sure she was telling him the truth."

"That's hearsay."

"Spoken like a true defense lawyer, Jack."

Mia made a noise. "This is not—"

"Not now," Jack said.

"Jack's right," said Andie. "Now is not the time. I'm out of my jurisdiction here. You'll have plenty of time to present your side of the story to the district attorney in Atlanta. I speak with all sincerity when I say that I hope the DA will try to do justice here and not go for the headlines."

It might have sounded snide in another setting, but Jack could sense from her tone, from the look on Andie's face, that she was not speaking with coplike bravado. She was telling them all this for their genuine benefit, to do with as Jack and Mia saw fit.

"I can take your statement now," Andie told Mia. "Or like I said, you have the right to remain silent."

"I think Jack and I should talk," Mia said.

"Good choice." Andie rose and started toward the door.

Jack got down from the swing and followed after her, leaving Mia behind. "Andie," he said as she reached the door.

She turned to face him.

"How long do you think we've got before the DA comes knocking?"

"Two days. Three, maybe."

"Do you have a murder weapon?"

"They found a thirty-eight-caliber slug with Montalvo's remains. You may want to ask your client about the handgun she bought and registered in her own name three days before Montalvo was shot."

"I'm sure it was for protection."

"Maybe."

"Her lawyer, Henry Talbridge, will tell you how Montalvo was harassing and threatening her throughout the preliminary hearing."

She shared a solemn expression that told him without words that there truly was nothing more she could say, then changed the subject—slightly. "By the way, what you did in that river was pretty amazing, Swyteck."

"I don't know. Maybe it'll hit me later."

"Not if you're lucky."

He could see the weariness in her eyes, the weight of so many cases that seemed to keep on hitting her long after they were over. "Yeah, I think I take your meaning."

She reached for the door, but Jack stopped her. "Thanks," he said. "You know, for the heads-up."

"Don't say I never gave you anything."

Jack nodded, a silent thank-you, knowing that this one was huge. They exchanged a little smile as Andie opened the screen door and disappeared inside. Jack slowly went back to Mia on the swing.

73

.

Andie treated her team leaders to an early breakfast at the Great Outdoors Trading Company and Cafe in High Springs, a bit of Florida history that has been in the same brick building on Main Street since 1895. Fortunately for Andie's wallet, the menu featured no fewer than twenty-four items priced from $4.95. Andie kept telling herself that she wasn't that hungry, but she kept pace even with the scuba divers in polishing off the famous Swedish oatmeal pancakes with real maple syrup. The guys appreciated her gesture, and even Agent Crenshaw managed to pat her on the back and say, "Nice job."

A midmorning flight took her from Jacksonville to Miami, where she and Paul Martinez prepared for an afternoon press conference. Typical of a special agent in charge, Martinez was big on the team concept. In front of the cameras he would undoubtedly stress the coordinated efforts and joint contributions of every agent involved in the hunt for the Wrong Number Kidnapper. Andie had no problem with that approach, but she enjoyed having a few minutes alone with him before the press conference, where Martinez spared no adjectives in conveying his praise for the job Andie, in particular, had done. Then it was time to prepare him for the more difficult questions the media might throw at him.

"I want to keep this relatively simple," said Martinez. "I understand our position that this Richie character was out to get Mia Salazar because she killed his friend Gerard Montalvo."

"Right," said Andie.

"I'll defer to the DA's office to say as much or as little as they see fit about Montalvo's murder. But I'm sure I'll be asked why Richie kidnapped and murdered Ashley Thornton."

"I guess we'll never know for sure, now that he and Mrs. Thornton are both dead."

"True, and I suppose my answer could simply be that I don't care to speculate on the matter. But between you and me . . . what's the connection?"

"No connection. That's what made her a good target."

"How so?"

"Had Richie kidnapped no one but Mia Salazar, we would have figured out much sooner that someone was avenging the death of Gerard Montalvo. Kidnapping that auto mechanic's wife up in Georgia and then Mrs. Thornton in Ocala put a whole different spin on things. He had everyone from the divers in the Devil's Ear to the profilers up in Quantico thinking that we were looking for the Wrong Number Kidnapper."

"Your theory would be a lot easier to swallow if he hadn't killed Mrs. Thornton."

"We're dealing with an ex-con, total scumbag by all accounts. He made a million dollars on that kidnapping. People have killed for a lot less."

"Granted. But he still didn't have to kill her if his only goal was to make us think we were dealing with a serial kidnapper."

"Maybe he had every intention to let her live, but she saw his face and was able to identify him. Then he had to kill her."

Martinez considered it. "Like you said. Speculation. Good fodder for the talking heads on CNN."

"That's right," she said with a thin smile. "If we answered every question, all those retired FBI agents would have nothing to do but play golf."

They finished the prep session by one o'clock, a full hour before the scheduled news conference. The sleeping bunk downstairs was tempting, even with its lumpy mattress, but Andie's mind was too engaged for a nap. She went to her office and closed the door, taking a few minutes to herself before facing the media.

She was perfectly still, seated behind her desk. Andie had enough unfinished paperwork to keep her busy for a week, but it was the last thing on earth she felt like tackling. There was plenty to do, but nothing terribly urgent—nothing to keep her mind occupied, nothing to prevent her from thinking about why she was even here in Miami, why she had left Seattle, why she would never go back.

These times alone, with her demons, were truly her most dangerous moments.

74

Jack, Mia, and Theo were back in Miami by noontime. They blew right through Palm Beach County on the turnpike, as Mia wasn't ready to deal with her husband. Her sister, however, was still in town from Atlanta. Jack knew it would be an emotional reunion, so he gave them some private time in Cassandra's hotel room while he waited alone in the coffee shop. He was on his second cup of coffee when Cassandra finally came down, alone.

"She's out cold," she said as she slipped into the booth. Her dark brown hair was pulled back with a broad white headband, which sent Jack into a double take. Many times he'd seen Mia the same way, usually with her long, dark hair wet from a shower or swimming. It was not a look that flattered every woman's face, but these two sisters pulled it off beautifully.

"I figured she'd hit the wall soon," said Jack. "I bet she sleeps for two days."

"At least."

The waitress approached with a pot of coffee and an empty mug for Cassandra. She poured and served, then hurried to the next booth. Jack watched the white stream of sugar flow from the dispenser and dissolve into Cassandra's coffee as he spoke. "So, I guess you two had a lot of catching up to do."

"That's an understatement. She told me what Agent Henning did to her, how they're probably coming after her for the murder of Gerard Montalvo. Bastards."

"Sounds like you two covered a lot of ground in a hurry."

"There's so much we wanted to tell each other."

"Like the truth?"

A puzzled look came over her face. "What do you mean by that?"

"There's something I need to get to the bottom of, Cassandra."

"Whoa. That had an ominous ring to it."

He looked up from his steaming coffee. "I think you've been lying to me."

An awkward smile drained from her face. "What?"

"I don't believe you when you say that for seven years you thought your sister was dead. Agent Henning doesn't either."

"It's true."

"No, it's a lie."

She seemed on the verge of another denial, ready to dig in her heels. Something in Jack's demeanor, however, told her not to bother. She looked away nervously, toward the cashier, toward the slowly revolving display rack of dessert pies. Anywhere but at Jack. "How long have you felt this way?"

"Honestly, I was getting bad vibes right from our first conversation. I asked if your sister had a cut on her thigh, and you said you didn't remember anything about that from the preliminary hearing. Turns out, it did come out at the hearing, and the whole thing was public record. That's the problem with lying. Sometimes you pretend to know way too little."

"That doesn't mean I knew she was alive all this time."

"No. But Henning figured that out when she asked you why you didn't push the prosecutor in Atlanta to bring murder charges against Montalvo. I have to agree with her. If I thought some scumbag had murdered a member of my immediate family, I'd beat on the prosecutor's door every day, or at least every week. But you never did a thing."

"Do you even want to hear the reason why?"

"Not really. The only explanation that makes any sense at all is that you knew all along. You knew your sister was alive."

She brought her cup to her lips, and Jack noticed her hand was shaking. She swallowed and said, "Let's say I did know, just hypothetically speaking. Would it make a difference to you? Would you stop trying to help her?"

"No. You have my word on it. It won't change anything."

She lowered her eyes. For a brief instant Jack thought she would let the moment pass, saying nothing. Then finally the words came in a weak, distant voice. "I knew."

"From day one?"

"No. I'd say it was more like day two."

"You talked to her the day after she went missing?"

"Yes. On the phone."

"What did she tell you?"

She shrugged a little, still uncomfortable. "That she had to leave. Disappear."

"How long?"

"Forever."

"Did she tell you why?"

"For her own safety."

"I presume she was well aware that Montalvo had gone missing the same day."

"Of course. That was why she ran."

"Because she was afraid," Jack suggested.

"Yes, of course. The judge made his ruling right after the hearing. You know, that Montalvo was going to stand trial for rape."

"The rape she lied about."

Cassandra bristled. "Excuse me?"

Jack didn't enjoy being tough on her, but with a DA considering murder charges against Mia, this was no time to pull punches. "She lied about being raped by Gerard Montalvo. That's what the polygraph examination showed."

"Those things aren't always right."

"But it was right this time. I know it. And you've known it for seven years."

Her expression tightened, but there was no denial.

Jack said, "I figure that Mia cut herself before going to the cops in order to make her claim more convincing. There was no semen or other physical evidence of a crime, since she wasn't actually raped. The leg wound made her lie more believable to the authorities."

"My, you certainly seem to have all the answers," said Cassandra.

"But we haven't touched on the biggest question of all: Why did she lie about the rape in the first place?"

"You obviously have an active imagination. I'm sure you have an answer to that, too."

"The results of that lie detector test were really interesting. Mia failed the two rape questions. Then she was asked if Montalvo was responsible for the cut on her leg. The wording of that question is very important. She said yes, and the polygraph examiner couldn't tell if she was lying or telling the truth. That tells me two things. One, she lied about the rape. Two, she felt justified in making the false accusation. Or maybe even compelled to make the accusation. In her own mind, that made Gerard *responsible* for the cut she inflicted on herself."

Cassandra was silent.

"Mia wasn't raped," said Jack. "And Montalvo didn't cut her, either."

"She wasn't after his money," said Cassandra, her voice straining. "Her lawyer made that clear at the hearing when he offered to settle any civil lawsuit for just one stinking dollar. There was no reason for her to lie."

"You're right. Money wasn't driving her. But she had an even better reason to lie."

She shifted from side to side, as if debating whether to get up and leave. "I don't know what you're talking about."

"You answered that question yourself, the last time you and I spoke, when you told me why you didn't attend the preliminary hearing. Do you remember your words? You said your sister made you stay away, because you could be deported."

"That's true. I was an illegal alien. Teresa's visa was still good, but mine was expired. I couldn't go near a courthouse without risk of deportation."

Jack leaned closer, bearing down on her, as if he were cross-examining a squirming witness. "You couldn't prosecute a rape claim."

"That's my whole point. I couldn't be a part of my sister's hearing or even watch it."

"I don't mean your sister's case. I mean your own. Montalvo raped *you*. And you couldn't bring the charges, because you were illegal."

She was struggling not to give him anything, not even through body language, but the force of his words was equal to her seven-year lie. Jack pushed on. "I can understand entirely how that would make you and your sister furious. She was legal, and you weren't. So she stepped into your shoes. She made your story her own, and she took it to the police. That's why it took three days to report the crime to the police. That's why the polygraph showed that she was lying about the rape. That's why the polygraph *didn't show* that she was lying when she said that Montalvo was 'responsible' for the cut on her leg."

Cassandra lowered her head, staring down into her lap. It was almost imperceptible, but Jack was certain that she'd nodded once, a silent confession.

His tone softened. "And that's why Montalvo's buddy Richie had it in for her, even after all these years."

Cassandra finally looked at him. He didn't see much emotion on her face, but there was some pain, maybe even hatred, for what he was doing. Despite it, Jack pushed ahead. "You were raped by Gerard Montalvo. And when your sister failed the polygraph, and the case started to crumble, it was you who killed him."

Jack had hit her with all the cold facts he could muster. She drew a breath, as if trying to recover. "Almost, Jack. You *almost* got it right."

"Tell me where I went wrong."

"I need your assurance that this is confidential. An attorney-client privilege that never leaves this table."

"Fine. It's totally confidential."

She checked over her shoulder, an instinctive move to make sure no one was listening. "The night that Teresa and I went to the bar, the bouncer walked right past me and handed my sister the business card. It was a little game that Montalvo played. Got the Look. Any woman who looked the type to have sex for money, if enough cash was offered, was someone with 'the Look.'"

"I know. That came out at the preliminary hearing. There was no dispute that she got the card and went up to Montalvo's suite."

"But she went only because I encouraged her to go. She came back about twenty minutes later. She practically dragged me out of the club and said we were going home. I could see she was really flustered, but I didn't want to leave."

"Why not?"

She shrugged. "While she was upstairs, another bouncer came by and gave me a card, too. I didn't know what 'Got the Look' meant. My sister didn't tell me it had anything to do with sex for money. She just came down all frazzled and said we were leaving. I told her forget it, I wanted to stay."

"She didn't try to stop you?"

"Of course she did. She told me that this guy Montalvo was a bad actor and that we had to get out of there. I figured that she was blowing it all out of proportion and just wanted to go home, or maybe there were drugs up there—Teresa was very against drugs. Anyway, I lied to her and told her that I'd run into a friend while she was upstairs and that we were going to hit another club. Teresa seemed okay with that, so long as I was leaving Club Vertigo. So she left in the cab without me."

"You didn't tell her that the bouncer had given you a 'Got the Look' card?"

"No. I guess I didn't want her to talk me out of going to the party. I wanted to see for myself."

"So you went upstairs. Then what happened?"

She swallowed hard, and Jack could see the shame all over her face. "You have to understand, I had dreams when I came to this country. I wanted to go to college, have a career. Then my visa expired. Do you know what kind of job opportunities I had? I was a housekeeper making two hundred bucks a week, literally cleaning toilets. All my money was going home to my family in Venezuela. Suddenly, I'm invited up to this suite with some rich boy who puts five thousand dollars, cash, on the table. All I have to do is sleep with him. I said no way. He added another thousand. I still said no. Every time I said no, he pulled out another stack of bills. I mean, this was more money than I'd ever seen in my entire life."

"So you took it."

"No. We struck a deal, and I . . . I got undressed. As soon as we got started, I guess I came to my senses. I couldn't believe what I was doing, and told him to stop. He wouldn't. I tried to push him off me, but he just kept going and saying, 'You know what you are, bitch, you know what you are.' I couldn't get him off me. When he was done, he called in his muscleman, Richie. They both laughed in my face as he kicked me out the door half undressed. I didn't take the money, but I told Montalvo that he'd pay, all right."

"So, at that time, you were determined to bring rape charges?"

"I think so. Actually, I didn't know what I was going to do. By the time I got home it was almost five o'clock in the morning. My sister was worried sick, and when I got undressed she saw that I wasn't wearing any underwear. Like I said, Richie threw me out of the suite half naked. I was lucky even to grab my dress and shoes. Teresa knew I wasn't the kind of girl to come home with no panties, and she kept pushing to know what happened. I didn't know what to say. I wasn't even sure I had been raped, legally. I told Montalvo yes, then I said no. It was confusing to me."

"It's rape," said Jack. "Saying yes doesn't mean you can't change your mind."

"That's what Teresa said. But she was also smart enough to know that I couldn't go to the police. I was illegal in this country and would have been deported. I didn't ask her to do anything, but she was my older sister. She has always looked out for me."

"Lying to the police was Mia's idea?"

"Yes, but she was doing it only to make sure that Montalvo got what he deserved. Can't you see that? Her little sister was raped, and that bastard was going to get away with it simply because I was illegal and powerless to protect myself."

"So she told the DA that she was Montalvo's victim."

"Yes."

"And the cut on her leg? Self-inflicted?"

"She tried, but she couldn't bring herself to do it. So . . ."

"You did it?"

She nodded. "I didn't want to, but Mia was convinced that her rape claim wouldn't fly without some physical evidence of an assault. She said that Montalvo tried to make her watch some pornographic movie about a woman cutting herself. Her hope was that the cops would search his suite and find the video, which would show his fascination with that sort of thing and support her claim that he cut her in that exact same spot."

"All right, I'm with you so far. But how did you end up killing Montalvo?"

Her eyes began to well. Jack didn't like the way she was looking at him. "Cassandra, are you saying . . ."

"She was just looking out for her little sister," she said, sniffling back tears. "When she failed that lie detector test and the DA told her that they were going to plea-bargain, Montalvo and his goon kept on threatening her. She wouldn't back down. Then the judge made his ruling, and Montalvo turned up the heat."

"Turned it up how?"

"That night, we went out to dinner. When we were driving home, we noticed this car that was following us. Teresa kept driving, but the car kept tailing us. Then we stopped at a red light, and we could see that it was Montalvo."

"What did you do?"

"Teresa kept driving, and he kept tailing us. She finally pulled into a parking lot. She'd had enough of his threats. All she wanted to do was to tell him that he'd better back off or she'd call the police. But he'd scared her so much over the course of the preliminary hearing that she'd started carrying a gun in her purse. He threatened her again that night in the parking lot. Things got out of hand. He came at her, like he was gonna hit her, and she, she . . ."

"She shot him?"

"Yes. And *that* is the real reason his friend Richie was out to get her, not me, after all these years. It didn't matter to him that it was self-defense."

"It matters to the law," said Jack. "But why did she run if it was self-defense?"

"We had to make a decision. Montalvo's body was in the trunk of her car. She'd just flunked a polygraph examination and the prosecutor was going to drop the case. It was probably only a matter of time before the DA could prove that the wound on her leg was self-inflicted. Who was going to believe she shot Montalvo in self-defense?"

"You were a witness. You could tell the police what happened."

"Yes, but that was the problem that got us into this mess in the first place. If I was her witness, I'd be deported."

Jack felt numb, as if every bit of air had suddenly been sucked from the room.

"We just kept driving all night and didn't stop until we got to Miami." Her voice was cracking, and she was no longer looking at him. "We buried the body in that nursery, right where you found it. Teresa hired a fishing boat to take her to the Bahamas. I took care of shipping her car off to South America on a freighter full of stolen vehicles."

"That makes you an accomplice after the fact."

"I don't care what it makes me. I just hope it doesn't make you think badly about Teresa. She's the bravest person I've ever known." She paused, as if she wanted to say more, but she grabbed her purse and rose. "I'd better get back upstairs and check on her."

As she walked toward the exit, Jack looked beyond her, through the

big plate-glass window in the front. Outside the coffee shop, a Grey-
hound bus stopped at the traffic light. A little voice inside his head told
him to run out, hop that coach, and ride it to wherever it was going—
just get away from Miami and everyone in it. He should have known
that it was a fairy tale, his thinking that Cassandra would be the one to
stand trial for murder and that he and Mia would live happily ever after.

He ordered another cup of coffee and waited, alone, wondering
what he would say to Mia when she woke.

75

Mia Salazar was weighing on Andie's mind. She didn't like being deceitful, even when interrogating a suspect. But that was exactly what she'd been with Jack and Mia at Ginnie Cottage.

Andie didn't put blind trust in polygraph examinations, but she had grossly understated her level of confidence in the one Mia—Teresa—had failed. The only physical evidence of a sexual assault was a cut on the inside of Mia's thigh, which she was able to replicate on videotape with a broken lightbulb. Sure, the lack of semen, pubic hair, or other physical evidence could have been explained by the fact that Mia had gone home, showered, washed her clothes, and waited over seventy-two hours before reporting the rape to police. That explanation rang hollow, however, in the face of a failed polygraph.

Andie swiveled her desk chair around to face the window. She wasn't at all interested in the cars in the parking lot or the traffic backed up on I-95. She was seeking a distraction of any kind. Her mind's eye could see where this train of thought was leading her, and she didn't want to go there. The little voice inside her head, however, didn't seem to care what she wanted.

She turned back to the papers on her desk, her gaze coming to rest on the bold black letters running across the top of the page: **"Grand jury to be empaneled in seven-year-old Montalvo murder case."** That information wasn't public yet. The DA's office had drafted a press release, which it planned to issue sometime after the FBI's upcoming news conference. As a courtesy, the DA's office had asked for Andie's comments on the draft. Not many details were disclosed, but the major weakness in the prosecution's case was obvious: If Montalvo didn't rape her, why did Mia kill him?

Andie had her own theory. It was viable but personally troubling. It made her ask herself the tough questions all over again, the ones that had caused her so many sleepless nights. The answer, ultimately, had forced her to leave Seattle. It was about families and living with the choices we make in truly life-or-death situations: When two sisters loved each other the way only sisters can, was there *anything* one wouldn't do to protect the other?

Andie was staring at the phone, thinking. It was hard to say what had motivated Mia—whether she was protecting her little sister, whether Montalvo had threatened her and her sister, whether she was acting at least partly out of guilt, knowing that if she had looked out for her little sister and taken her home that night, the rape never would have happened. In the end, Andie might not have made the same choice Mia had made, but she could at least begin to understand it.

She wondered if Mia could understand the choice she had made.

She picked up the telephone and dialed the number. It was midmorning in Seattle. Her brother-in-law answered.

"Steve, hi. It's Andie."

"Hey, how are you?"

"Good, thanks. I'm pretty good."

"You sure? You sound kind of down."

"I'm fine, really, just a little tired. Listen, there's something I've been meaning to tell you."

He paused, as if the slight quake in her voice made him wary. "Is something wrong?"

Andie swallowed the lump in her throat. She wasn't sure where to begin, so she skipped to the bottom line. "I'm sorry," she said, her voice just above a whisper.

"Sorry for what?"

"I'm sorry that . . . I couldn't do more for Susan."

"I think we all feel that way, Andie. The truth is, we did everything we could. It just wasn't enough."

She could have argued the point. Steve had been the last one to give up hope, thinking somehow a donor would come through. Andie could have told him about that devil of a man imprisoned in Walla Walla, how he could have led Andie to her biological father and a possible bone marrow transplant that might have saved her sister's life. She could have told him exactly what she *didn't* do, but she was speechless. No one could fault her for the choice she'd made—no one but herself. Because she knew in her heart that, had she been the one lying on that hospital bed losing the race against time, things would have turned out differently. She would have done it to save her own life. Between sisters—between her and Susan—*that* was the test.

Finding the words, however, was an impossible feat. She'd never told anyone her secret, and she never would. Period. "Thanks, Steve. That's all I wanted to say. How are you doing?"

"Okay. I have my ups and downs, you know. Just take one day at a time."

"Yeah, I think that's all we can do. You take care, all right?"

"I will. Thanks for calling."

"Good-bye," she said, but her voice was barely audible. As she hung up the phone, she could feel her eyes welling, but she quickly pulled herself together. She was in Miami now. The past was behind her.

She gathered her papers and left the office, headed for the press conference.

76

Jack watched the FBI's press conference on television from a king-size bed in a hotel room. Several cable news networks carried it live in its entirety. Paul Martinez did all the talking. Jack didn't see Andie anywhere on-screen, and he wondered if she was staying out of the limelight by choice.

It had been Jack's idea to get a hotel room. He knew his home phone would be ringing off the hook—maybe even a few journalists would be camped outside his front door—just as soon as Martinez's Q&A session ended. The SAC declined to comment on whether Mia Salazar was under investigation for the murder of Gerard Montalvo. Inevitably, the media would promptly follow up to see if Jack had anything to say.

Jack sat up against the headboard and switched off the remote. Finally, Mia emerged from the bathroom.

"How do I look?" she asked, twirling like a runway model.

He smiled sadly. "I'm not the person to ask. I always loved your long brown hair and dark brown eyes."

She jerked her head, a little motion that used to toss her hair from one shoulder to the other. Being a short-haired blonde would take some getting used to, probably even more than the blue contact lenses. "Do you at least like the clothes?"

"The clothes are great," he said. He'd bought them himself at one of the hotel's boutiques while she was dying her hair. Jack climbed off the bed, took a few steps toward her, and stopped. They stood in silence for almost a minute, she looking at him, and Jack looking at a woman he barely recognized.

"I know you don't agree with this," she said.

"You have other options."

"Going to prison for the rest of my life is not an option."

"Self-defense is a complete defense."

"No one will believe me. I lied about the rape. I ran and started a new life as a new person after I shot him. Those are two big strikes against me."

"That doesn't mean a jury will convict you."

"You can't guarantee me that they won't."

"No. There are no guarantees in any trial. But if you run again, the police will come looking for you, and there's no guarantee that they won't find you."

"And if they do, then I'll stand trial. I don't see a downside."

Jack blinked hard, as if she were overlooking a little something, like the guy who had risked his own life and laid out fifty thousand dollars to save her from a psychopath. He wondered if she was running not because she feared a murder conviction, but because she simply preferred a fresh start, a clean slate, a new life.

"I'm sorry, Jack. I love you, and after what you did for me, I know that you love me."

He didn't answer, didn't even confirm the truth of what she was saying about their feelings for one another. He could have launched right into a heart-to-heart discussion about truth and trust, but what was the point? Her mind was made up.

"I'm not running away from you," she said. "Don't ever think that."

"It doesn't have to be this way."

"You're right." A devious smile came across her lips. She took a step closer and said, "Come with me."

"What? I can't do that."

"Why not?"

"Because . . . I can't."

"Because it's crazy?" she said.

"Yes. It's crazy."

"Does that mean you don't love me and don't want to be with me?"

"No, it means that's a crazy idea. That's all."

"Now you understand. To me, staying here and standing trial is crazy. That's all my decision to leave means."

Jack tried hard to think of another counterargument, but he'd done his best. "If you change your mind," he said, "you know where I am."

"If you change yours, I'll be—"

He put his fingertips to her lips, stopping her. "I don't want to know," he said.

She removed his hand, then grabbed him by the back of the neck and pressed her lips against his in one of those long, sad kisses that definitely felt like good-bye. Finally, she pulled herself away.

"Gotta go now. Boat leaves in thirty minutes."

He didn't have any details, just enough to know that someone with a Cigarette boat would drop her in the Bahamas before nightfall. From there, it was off to anywhere in the world. Just like seven years ago.

"Good luck," he said.

She forced a meager smile and kissed him again quickly. Jack could see the tears clouding her eyes—those strange, phony blue eyes—as they took one last look at each other. Then she turned and headed for the door.

Jack didn't watch her go. He just listened as the dead bolt unlocked with the sound of a shotgun shucking. The door creaked as it swung open. There was a pause, and he wondered if she was having second thoughts, or if she had stopped to take another look back at the man she was leaving behind. It didn't really matter which.

The door closed, and Mia was gone.

Jack didn't even know her name anymore.

Epilogue

•

hree weeks passed, and Jack heard nothing from Mia. He tried not
to think about her too much, but he often found himself wondering where she might have gone. Australia, Russia, or maybe somewhere in South America. Anyone who said it was a small world hadn't looked at a globe lately.

When he wasn't thinking about Mia, he tried to focus on his work. Inevitably, however, the thing that weighed most heavily on his mind was Theo's bar and the quarter million dollars that was still missing.

Sparky's Tavern wasn't much to look at, the last eyesore on U.S. 1 before the entrance to the Florida Keys. It was an old gas station when Theo bought it. Most of the money was tied up in the land and liquor license, which is to say that the garage was "converted" into a bar much in the same way that Jack's high school gymnasium had been converted into "Margaritaville" on prom night. The grease pit was gone but the garage doors were still in place. There was a long wooden bar, a TV permanently tuned to ESPN, and a never-ending stack of quarters on the pool table. Beer was served in cans, and the empties were crushed in true Sparky's style at the old tire vise that still sat on the workbench. Some said Theo was too good for his own bar. They were referring to his passion, of course: the saxophone.

Jack watched from a barstool as Theo belted out a solo worthy of the Blue Note. He played an old Buescher 400 that had been passed down from the man who'd taught him how to play. His great-uncle Cyrus was once a nightclub star in old Overtown, and it would have pleased the old master to see Theo blowing the same horn in his own bar.

It was one more reason that Jack couldn't stomach the thought of Theo losing this place to foreclosure.

Theo finished to a round of hearty applause from a crowd that was more drunk than appreciative. He laid the old saxophone in its stand and took the barstool next to Jack. He signaled the bartender, who promptly brought him a club soda and Jack another beer. Theo never drank when he played, one more thing he learned from his great-uncle Cyrus.

Jack reached for his wallet, but Theo stopped him. "Don't worry about it," he said. "This is my toast to your new life."

Their glasses clicked. Jack said, "I'll drink to that."

"Come on. How about a little more enthusiasm, buddy? How long you gonna pine for this Mia?"

"It's not rational, I know it."

"Do you really think you could have trusted her again?"

"I don't know. I guess it's always easier to think you could have solved all your problems and loved someone after she's gone. I'll get over it soon enough."

"Damn straight you will. You're young, you're a hotshot lawyer, you're almost half as good-lookin' as me. You got it made, my man. Made in the shade. The world is your urinal."

"You mean oyster. The world is your oyster."

Theo sipped his club soda, then made a face. "Who the hell pisses on oysters?"

Jack decided to hold that debate for another day. "Theo, we need to talk money."

"Not when I'm playing, man."

"No, really. In another week Ball-Bustin' Bud is going to come calling for his two hundred thousand dollars. All we can tell him is that it's stuck somewhere in the Devil's Ear."

"Don't worry about it. I got it covered."

"What do you mean? We're talking two hundred grand."

"I paid him back already."

Jack coughed on his beer. "Where did you get that kind of money?"

"I told you, don't worry about it."

Jack looked around the bar. Sparky's drew an eclectic crowd, everyone from bikers to businesspeople. Probably a few drug dealers and money launderers, too. "Theo, I hope you didn't do something really stupid."

"Hey, I said don't worry about it."

"Too late. How could I not worry about—"

"Stop right there, dude. You worry too damn much. You know what you need?"

"Uh, two hundred thousand dollars?"

"You need to go hire yourself a high-priced hooker."

"Cut it out, will you?"

"I'm serious. You should do something that is completely *un*-Jack. It'll be good for you. You're always looking for the right girl. Well, if you ask me, relationships are highly overrated. Get yourself a hooker. Think of it. No strings attached, and it's all about you. Maybe it'll put a little adventure back in your life. You know: To go boldly where plenty of men have gone before."

"I'm not hiring a hooker. And it's 'To go boldly where *no man* has gone before.'"

"Trust me, dude. When it comes to sex, ain't nothin' bold about going where no man's gone before." Theo laughed hard enough to rupture Jack's eardrum.

"It wasn't *that* funny," said Jack.

"No, man, it's your face. If you don't do something *un*-Jack in a hurry, you might as well grab your sniper rifle and walk to the nearest bell tower, because you are gonna lose it, buddy."

Theo was still laughing as he started back to his saxophone. Jack took a long pull from his beer, then almost choked on it as he caught a glimpse of the attractive woman who'd taken the barstool next to him. She looked surprisingly hot in her blue jeans.

"Henning? What are you doing here?"

"I'm fine. Thanks for asking. How's Mia?"

Jack smiled a little. "Do you ever give an inch?"

"Only when I see an opportunity to take a mile."

Jack shook his head. She was a paradox, all right, one of those women who managed to annoy and intrigue him at the same time. If he narrowed his eyes just the tiniest bit, he could see a beautiful woman glowing in the soft bar lights. But open them wide, and there was the pit bull ready to tear his leg off.

"Something wrong with your eyes?" she said.

"No, no. I was just—never mind. Seriously, what are you doing here?"

"Tying up some loose ends. I didn't come to bug you, I promise. But I have some good news and some bad news."

"I always hated that game. I hate it even more when I play with the FBI, but okay, I'll bite. What's the good news?"

"Our divers finally found the capsule holding your fifty thousand dollars. They also recovered the backpack with the additional two hundred. It was pinned against those bars blocking off the entrance to the Devil's Ear."

Jack nearly fell off his barstool. "That's not good news. That's *great* news."

"Hold on. I still haven't given you the bad news."

Jack braced himself. "Okay, shoot."

"Turns out, the money in the backpack is counterfeit."

Jack nearly exploded, but he thought better of it in front of an FBI agent. "Counterfeit, you say?"

"Yeah. You have any idea how that might have happened?"

Jack fought the impulse to shoot a deadly glare toward the stage. "I have no earthly idea."

"You sure?"

"Yes. I'm sure."

"You're absolutely sure?"

"Yes."

"You know, you're completely ruining this joke."

"What?"

"Theo was positively convinced that you'd go ballistic right on the spot."

He caught Theo's eye across the room. The big guy was smiling as he gave Jack a mock salute, as if to say, *Gotcha.* "So, the money isn't counterfeit?"

"No. You told me that the two hundred thousand was Theo's money. I called him two hours ago to tell him we found all of it. He kind of put me up to this."

"He did, did he?"

"Yeah, he said if I did it, you'd take me to dinner."

Jack thought she was kidding at first, but the expression on her face said otherwise. He could have come up with a thousand reasons to say no, but maybe Theo had a point. For once in his life, he did need to do something *un*-Jack. "Dinner, huh? Sure. Why not? But there's one condition."

"What's that?"

"Theo's buying. And we pay with a credit card."

"Deal."

"So, where are we going?"

She smiled and said, "Sorry, Swyteck. I can't tell you."

He returned the smile. "Some things never change."

Acknowledgments

•

This is "the Big One-O," novel number ten. To paraphrase Rod Stewart, I can't believe I've been doing this for so long . . . and getting away with it.

This book, like all those before it, would not be publishable without the help and contributions of others. I'm finally convinced that my editor, Carolyn Marino, does indeed know everything. (Can *you*, in the same breath, debate the finer points of bonding out a criminal defendant and then tell me when Prada shoes became generally available in the United States?) My agent, Richard Pine, brought his usual expertise to bear.

As always, thanks to my early readers, Dr. Gloria M. Grippando, Judy Russell, Eleanor Rayner, and Amy Kovner. I'm also grateful to the Suwannee River Water Management District for tons of information on cave diving and Florida's aquifer. Gordon Van Alstyne came up with another fine assist on firearms (yes, a handgun probably will fire after it has been dropped momentarily into a river). Thanks also to David McWilliams, who can recommend everything from a good Chardonnay to a greasy-spoon restaurant in downtown Atlanta (a true Renaissance man).

Through their generous donation to WXEL, south Florida's public television and radio station, Mark and Nancy Gilbert landed a role for their daughter, Dani, in *Got the Look*. It's hardly worthy of Dani's talents, but I hope you enjoy the cameo. I'm glad that we were able to team up to support a good cause.

Finally, I wish to point out that writing a book is not in the least tiny bit like giving birth to a child. Thank you, Tiff, for not punching my lights out when I made the untimely suggestion otherwise. Yes, it's true, men have no idea.